POISONING OF MINDS

POISONING OF MINDS

BOOK TWO OF THE ARMOR SERIES

BY KATARINA KYDE

Flying Squid Leaf Media

This is a work of fiction. Names, characters, businesses, places, events, and incidents are either the products of the author's imagination or used in a fictitious manner. Any resemblance to actual persons, living or dead, or actual events is purely coincidental.

Printed in the United States of America

Second Edition: 2025
Paperback ISBN: 979-8-9918929-3-3
Ebook ISBN: 979-8-9918929-2-6

First Printing: 2015

For Ed—My love, my forever

A NOTE FOR MY READERS:

The Armor Series, at its core, is a contemporary low fantasy about the walls we put up and the armor we all don when we're scared, uncomfortable, or insecure, and moving forward through these times as best we can with self-love and self-acceptance. This central theme is woven into the backdrop of heart-pumping action. Be aware that some scenes within the series are emotionally charged and/or highly action-oriented.

This book specifically, *Poisoning of Minds*, contains scenes depicting child abuse, emotional, verbal, and physical abuse, kidnapping, fear, anxiety, violence, control, blood, death, sexual situations, and profanity.

Prologue

I AM INVINCIBLE

Approximately 4,300 years ago

Mallandian soldier Watrose put down his bat-tle-ax to adjust the ring on his finger. That damn royal Jewelry engineer made Watrose's ring a little too big, and the large carnelian stone kept twisting toward the palm side of his hand, making it difficult to hold his ax. He scowled. Higher ranking warriors had rings that fit. He looked up and turned around after hearing a yell and a thump. He saw an ax firmly planted into the tree he was leaning on. It had narrowly missed his head. The enemy soldier who'd made the embarrassing blunder wore a look of shock and confusion as he desperately pulled on his ax handle, trying to reclaim it from the clutches of the tree.

The amulet Watrose wore glowed as he laughed at his opponent and easily freed the ax from the tree trunk. He raised the ax threateningly. The enemy soldier's eyes grew wide, and he turned and ran. Watrose wasn't much of a runner, but he didn't have to be—not with the strength and endurance granted to him by the chalcedony earrings he wore. He effortlessly bounded after the enemy soldier, who was fleeing for his life and gasping for air. Watrose caught up to his prey and pushed him with as much force as if he were swatting a fly. The enemy soldier was launched forward off his feet and flew forty cubits through the air before landing face first on the ground. As he scrambled to stand up, Watrose raised his ax and decapitated him. Letting out a victory yell, he kicked the soldier's helmet away, held up the head proudly by the hair, and looked around for more enemy soldiers.

The month before in their briefing about the new

armor they'd be getting, Watrose thought his superiors had lost their minds. All the talk about this new protective Jewelry had offended him. Did they think he would actually believe in this magical nonsense? An amulet that protects you from attacks? A ring that can poison the enemy? Earrings that give you the physical ability to fight like five men? And if you wear all three, the powers they grant to the wearer are increased even more? Ridiculous. However, he paid dutiful attention during the briefing and accepted the amulet, ring, and earrings that were issued to him.

The following training sessions left him completely astonished. He came prepared with full armor and all his weapons to the mandatory combat training. However, after receiving the amulet, he was told to lay down his weapons, remove his armor, and stand still while one of his peers was ordered to attack him with a mace. Watrose had run screaming when he realized his peer was going to comply. He was given a reprimand for not following orders along with a promise of a punishment by death much worse than a bludgeoning with a mace if it happened again. Watrose stood still and squeezed his eyes shut as his fellow soldier charged at him, mace raised. A few seconds later, he realized he had soiled himself for nothing. The other soldier had run past and missed hitting him. Watrose opened his eyes and watched with wonder as his fellow soldier continued swinging the mace but kept missing him over and over again. The amulet Watrose wore, made out of an alloy of copper, silver, and gold, and featuring a large black agate stone surrounded by five smaller sardonyx stones, glowed.

Watrose enjoyed the training associated with the earrings immensely. Small boulders weighing about five hundred minas each were waiting for the soldiers to pick them up and throw them at a target about six cubits away. To his surprise, Watrose was able to complete this task with ease. He was also able to run the entire length of the kingdom and back again without running out of breath, even though running a quarter of that distance typically winded him.

One of the largest and strongest soldiers was brought in front of the others to demonstrate the power of the ring. The ring was very poisonous, they were told, and could be used as a last-resort option if there was no other weapon available. The stone on the ring was an orange-red carnelian. Watrose watched with interest as Dagan, the royal Jewelry engineer, twisted the top of the ring ninety degrees to mechanically flip the stone over. The other side of the stone was a mixture of carnelian, cinnabar, and orpiment. The engineer held the stone to the skin of the large and strong soldier for one short moment and then twisted the ring ninety degrees in the opposite direction to flip the stone back to its original position. The soldier looked at the spot on his arm where the ring had touched him and shrugged. A few seconds later, he began sweating and shaking uncontrollably. He blinked his eyes as if he were dizzy and stumbled. A few gasps were heard when the soldier's legs collapsed under him. He became physically sick and then lost control of his bowels. The soldier was carried off by the medical team, and Watrose was relieved to hear that his fellow warrior would continue to experience the effects of the ring for approximately the next twelve hours but that he would make a full recovery. Watrose was grateful that he had not been chosen to participate in the demonstration. He'd already been humiliated enough during the amulet training.

Next, the soldiers were invited to wear all three pieces of Jewelry together, in order to discover that each piece enhanced the power of the others. They were told the ring they each wore was lethal when worn with the amulet and the earrings, so experimentation with it was forbidden. However, they all found themselves to be fully protected against even the most brutal attacks and that they each possessed the strength and stamina of what seemed to be fifty soldiers. Each soldier was commanded to keep the Jewelry that was issued to him and wear it during every battle.

Now that he'd just had a taste of blood on the battlefield, Watrose wanted more. He loved the rush of the pursuit when the enemy soldier had fled, his eyes full of fear. Defeating his opponent with ease made him feel all-powerful and had caused a surge of pride like he'd never felt before. It was immediately addicting for him.

He spotted a group of five enemy soldiers, let out a battle cry, and charged. The soldiers turned to look and charged toward him as well, probably assuming he was absurdly overconfident. They surrounded him and attempted to attack him with their axes and maces, but every single one of them missed. Their bewilderment stunned them for a moment, but they raised their weapons again with the utmost urgency. It was too late, however. Watrose stood in the middle of them and still yelling, spun quickly in a circle holding his ax with his arms straight and forward in front of him. All five soldiers were sliced in two within a second.

Jumping up and down on their blood and bones, Watrose let out a whoop and yelled, "I am invincible! I am a god!"

His comrades-in-arms cheered him on and followed suit as he ran around picking up enemy soldiers, tossing them over the crowns of the pine, oak, and maple trees, and chopping them in half before they hit the ground. The entire battle was short—the sun had barely moved— and not a single enemy soldier was left alive. Watrose had slain the most opposing combatants in the battle— in any battle in Mallandian history for that matter. He knew because he'd counted. He couldn't wait to get back to camp to be commended in front of everyone else.

When all he and his fellow soldiers received was a general, "Good work, men," Watrose felt the rage bubbling through his blood. He held his tongue and fumed throughout the entire briefing and planning meetings for their next attack. However, when he was finally alone with just his peers around their campfire in the evening, he made his feelings known.

"We did the impossible out there today! Defeated an entire army! And I broke a record today for killing the most enemies in one battle! But did we receive any appreciation?"

A few soldiers near him shook their heads no.

"Any praise?"

"No," said a few more.

"Did we get any gratitude at all?"

"No!" He had the attention of his entire unit now.

"Why don't we get any respect? They could've given us a demonstration of the amulet first before putting us in a simulated battle situation without knowing what to expect. They didn't have to make our fellow warrior sick in order to warn us about the ring," he exclaimed, pointing at the man who'd had the misfortune of being used to demonstrate the poison of the ring the month before. "I want better treatment! I'm not a lowly peasant—I'm a soldier! Even with this Jewelry, I have no desire to work tirelessly for nothing in return! Who here is receiving enough land and grain allotments to work hard all day, go through humiliating training, perform better than anyone in history, AND be underappreciated?"

Everyone shook their heads and cheered Watrose on.

"What the hell are we doing this for anyway? So the king can rule over more land? Personally, I'd rather be at home with my wife and family."

Shouts of agreement echoed throughout the camp.

"I've got a mind to leave and go home! The king and the generals aren't going to like it, but what are they going to do? They can't hurt us—we have the Jewelry! They may have it too, but there're more of us than there are of them! Together we can take them down, put an end to this war, and go home! Who's with me?"

Roars of approval filled Watrose's ears.

THERE WAS ANOTHER SET OF EARS ringing with this change of events. Yarim, an assistant to the king, had been walking by the soldiers' camp unnoticed and heard everything the troublemaker Watrose had said. He immediately got into his horse-drawn cart and made the day's journey back to the king's palace.

"Your Majesty," Yarim began, "I fear we have a mutiny on our hands."

Part 1

THE STRONG DO WHAT NEEDS TO BE DONE

Chapter 1

Present day

Thursday, September 3, 2015

The morning sun made 27-year-old Anise Viston squint when she looked in the mirror above her dresser to brush her hair. Her stomach clenched when a sudden blur of movement in the reflection looked like someone walking in the hallway near her bedroom door. Anise quickly took in a breath. She'd thought she was alone. Heart pounding, she tiptoed over to the door and carefully looked out. She jumped when she came face-to-face with someone from her past.

"Surprised to see me?" asked an old woman with wild brown eyes. The woman tugged at her unkempt white hair.

"Grace?" gasped Anise. "What are you doing here? You're supposed to be in prison!" Her heart pounded harder.

"You really thought prison walls could hold *me*?" laughed Grace. "Give me the amulet." Solidifying her demand, she held a knife to Anise's throat.

"No! You can't hurt me as long as I'm wearing it." Anise put a hand to her chest to feel the amulet but found only the softness of her pajama shirt. "Oh god, where is it?!"

"So I *can* hurt you," replied Grace with an evil smirk. She raised the knife and took a jab at Anise.

Anise ducked and then gave Grace a swift kick to the knee, causing the older woman to fall. Jumping over Grace as she started to rise, Anise dashed to the front door of her apartment. She could hear Grace's pounding footsteps behind her. Anise swung open the front door and planned to run down the hall and out of the building to find help, but someone was standing in her way. "Nate?" she said to the dark-haired man standing outside her door. "You're supposed to be in prison, too."

He took her into his arms. "Did you miss me, honey?" he asked, giving her the mischievous sideways smile that Anise always wanted to bite into.

"Yes," she admitted to him, getting lost in his cobalt blue eyes. She closed her eyes as he leaned in to kiss her.

"There you are," Anise heard Grace snarl. "You can't escape me!"

With a jolt, Anise's eyes flew open, and she found herself lying in her bed looking into a pair of light green eyes. She touched her chest and let out a sigh of relief when her hand closed around the amulet.

"Are you okay?" Jonathan asked her. "You were tossing and turning. That must've been one hell of a dream you were having."

Anise let her body relax, thankful to be awake. "I'm okay. I was just dreaming about Grace chasing me with a knife."

Jonathan put his arms around Anise and pulled her close to him. She rested her forehead on his bare chest and wrapped her arms around him, too, melting into his warm, comforting embrace. The sun's first rays were filtered through gray clouds as they dimly shined through the white lace curtains and onto her yellow paisley sheets.

The nightmares about Grace trying to kill her happened every now and then, but dreams about Nate happened more often. His appearances in her sleep usually ended with a kiss or sometimes even more. Anise felt Jonathan squeeze her tighter, bringing her back into the reality of the moment. *I will not feel guilty about my dreams*, Anise promised herself. *They're only dreams.*

"Grace Brevain has been locked up for three years now. She's in a maximum security prison in another state serving a life sentence," Jonathan reminded her. "There's no way in hell she could ever get out. You're safe."

"I know," she mumbled into his chest. "I just can't seem to shake these dreams." She squeezed him tightly. "I'm glad you're here," she added.

He stroked her long and wavy brown hair. "Me too. And I don't just mean right now. These last four months have been the best time of my life."

She snuggled in closer. "That's the sweetest thing anyone's ever said to me."

"I'd love to hold you all day," he said to her, "among other things." His lips kissed her cheek then her ear and traveled down to her neck.

"Mmm," she replied with a smile. She felt his excitement grow and press against her abdomen. "It's too bad we both have to get up and go to work."

He ignored her comment, and she felt a hand slowly traveling up her inner thigh.

"On the other hand, we have a *little* time before we have to get up." Her legs parted when his fingers reached the top of her thigh.

He kissed her mouth as his fingers softly teased her. When her moisture saturated his fingertips, she straddled him. He lovingly ran his hands and eyes over her slender body starting at her knees, moving forward to her hips, and up until they reached her breasts. They roamed over every part of her he could reach but avoided the amulet that hung heavy on her neck. With her back arched, she closed her eyes and let the pleasurable sensations make her not care that they were running late.

Anise rode him until she couldn't help but climax. She kept going just a few moments more until he climaxed as well. Sweaty, and breathing heavily, she put her head on his chest for a couple minutes as he held her tightly.

"I love you," he whispered.

"Love you, too," she said. Taking a peak at the clock, she groaned. "But now I really need to get up."

"Yeah, me too," he replied, looking at the clock as well. "I'm having dinner tonight with my friends Candace, Will, and Matt. They've been wanting to meet you. Can you make it?"

She shook her head. "No, sorry. I promised Vanessa I'd look at some bridal magazines with her. I could meet you after at your place. Or you could come over here again."

"Sure, we might be late though. Matt wants to check out a band that's playing at a bar downtown. Or you could meet us there."

"I think I'll just stay in. We've been out late the last few nights, and I've got some sketches I've been wanting to work on."

"Okay, but you're coming tomorrow night, right?"

"Of course! I'd never miss a chance to see Even Fury. I love watching my boyfriend rock out on stage," she purred at him, rubbing her hand on his chest.

His eyes looked at the floor as he gave her a shy grin.

"And I'm free to join you Saturday at the hospital, too," she added.

"Good. You're gonna love it. The kids are great!"

"I meant to ask you—any new exhibitions coming in soon, Dr. Casley?" she added with a teasing smile as she got out of bed. Jonathan, a museum curator, had recently earned his PhD, and Anise was so proud of him.

"Oh, yeah!" His face lit up as he ran a hand through his slightly-too-long-to-look-professional light brown hair. "I can't believe I forgot to tell you—the Mallandia exhibition is finally coming to our museum. Dr. S. is so stoked!" Jonathan was referring to his supervisor and mentor.

"No way!" Anise said, her eyes wide. "The one we saw in Springfield? With the earrings?"

"That's the one." He grabbed his dark-rimmed glasses from the bedside table and put them on.

"Wow. Definitely let me know when it opens. It'll be nice to enjoy it without having to worry about how to protect the earrings from Grace." She closed her eyes and her body shuddered involuntarily at the memory. She was also still unsettled from her nightmare.

"Dr. S. and I are going to start setting it up tomorrow, but it won't be ready for several more days. Let's plan on going to see it next weekend," he replied. "Maybe he'll be there. He's been asking to see you."

"It's a date," she said, kissing him before laying out a skirt suit and going to take a shower.

After they both showered and dressed, Jonathan grabbed a granola bar and took a bite. "Dr. S. keeps telling me that he thinks the Armor Jewelry can be used for peace instead of war."

"Yeah, you've said," Anise sighed, trying not to roll her eyes. "Could we not talk about Dr. Smithton's weird utopia plan anymore? It feels like you turn into someone completely different every time we discuss it."

"I know I've been mentioning it a lot," Jonathan admitted. "But it's not really so far-fetched if you think about it. The amulet, ring, and earrings were used as armor by the Mallandians to win battles. What if the Jewelry was given to law enforcement or the military in today's world? How much easier would it be to defeat terrorists?"

"It would," she agreed with another sigh. "But not everyone is honorable. There's always someone who would misuse it, and that person could cause a lot of trouble." She petted Max, Jonathan's Siberian husky, who was begging for a piece of her bagel.

"Of course. So we'd have to be really careful who we gave the Jewelry to."

"Yeah, but who's going to decide that?" Anise asked. "That would have to be someone who's in control of the military or law enforcement. The president?" She frowned as she noticed Jonathan's eyes getting a glazed-over look as they did every time he brought up the utopia ideas.

"No, we're talking about a worldwide peace-on-earth movement."

"Well," she continued, hoping the subject would change soon, "it's not really worth talking about anyway. We couldn't give a set to each military or law enforcement member since only one Jewelry set is still in existence."

"Right," he agreed. "So the one person in charge would hold the Jewelry and have to be responsible for keeping the peace in the world."

"That's a big job for one person," Anise said. "And who would that be? If they're in charge of the order of the entire world, that sounds like a dictatorship to me. If the leader isn't always fair and just, it won't be a utopia at all."

"It wouldn't be a dictatorship," argued Jonathan. "Everyone could do as they pleased as long as it didn't hurt anyone else."

"Okay," she said. "But there's always going to be someone who thinks something isn't fair. That someone else has more than he does. And *that* person will create problems. I don't think peace on Earth is possible. What do your co-workers think about this?"

"I don't know. I haven't discussed this with any of them. More of them are moving to Florida."

"Again? Isn't that like half the people who work at the museum?"

"Yeah. Strange, right?"

"Yes. And it's for that project Dr. Smithton mentioned to you years ago?"

"I think so. It seems like anyone who retires from the museum is being picked up for that project. Some of the younger people are being recruited for it too."

"What is the project anyway?"

"I don't know that either. I tried asking Dr. S. about it, but he didn't give me too many details. Some archaeological digs."

"And it's in Florida somewhere?"

"Yeah. The exact location has moved a few times. I think everyone's in northern Florida now."

"Maybe they're on the verge of a new discovery." She looked at the clock. "And now I really need to get to work."

"Would you considered donating blood?" Jonathan asked her.

She gave him a confused look. "That's random. Is there a blood drive at the museum?"

"No." Jonathan paused. "I'm not sure why I just said that."

"See, this is what I mean. Every time we discuss Dr. Smithton's utopia you say something strange, and that's not like you. And it's been happening more and more lately. Are you sure you're okay?"

"I'm fine," he insisted. "Are *you* okay? I know you can hold on to those nightmares sometimes."

"I *am* a little shaken up still," she admitted, as she slipped into her heels and put her favorite pencil behind her ear.

"Don't worry," he smirked. "Grace is so small. I'm sure she's somebody's bitch."

The image made Anise laugh. His glazed look was gone, and he wasn't saying anything odd anymore. He grabbed her hand, and they stepped up to her front door.

"Maybe next weekend you could try going to the museum without wearing the amulet. Put it in that safe I bought you," he said, making it sound like a mere suggestion, as if he hadn't already said it a million times before. "You'll be protected—there are guards all over the museum, and I'll be right by your side."

Her entire body felt heavy from his pressure. Would he ever let this go? "Please don't start with that again. I told you, I'll take it off when I'm ready."

"I know, but it would be better to keep the amulet in a safe. It's too precious to be worn out."

"You keep saying that, but how I feel is important, too," she retorted, trying not to bark at him.

"Of course! I didn't mean to imply that it's not. But I'm worried about you. Needing to wear the amulet all the time to feel safe isn't right." His loving eyes were full of concern. She hated every second of it.

"Jonathan, I don't like having to wear it to leave the apartment either. It certainly isn't a cure for my anxiety, and because it's so heavy and bulky, it feels more like a hindrance than a help at times. But I'm not ready to take it off either. The idea is scary and can bring on a panic attack all on its own."

"I know, and that's not right. You need to do something about it."

"I'm doing the best I can right now. When you talk like that, it makes me feel...broken."

"You're not broken, Anise." He tried to wrap his arms around her, but she pulled away, not wanting his touch at that moment. He sighed. "Look, I'm sorry. It's just that the panic attacks you get are scary."

"For who—me, or you?" she snapped at him.

"For both of us. I don't want you to have to go through that."

"I don't want to talk about it anymore."

"Maybe you should try medication instead. Or therapy. Preferably both. I'm happy to do some research on therapists for you."

"Jonathan, I'm not ready. Please drop it." She gave him a look that said she had enough.

"I'm sorry. Consider it dropped. You're right; you should do whatever works for you. And on your own time."

Anise frowned. That was better, but she knew him. He'd bring it up again.

He gave her a kiss. "I'll call you before I go out tonight," he told her as he pulled a denim jacket on over his t-shirt. Opening her coat closet door, he pulled out her long vinyl jacket. "It's drizzling," he said, handing it to her. "And you always park as far from the door as possible."

"I know. I love walking in the rain!"

"But you get cold."

"It's just for a few minutes! And I love it—the sound of the rain on my umbrella, the smell of the wet concrete, the fresh air on my face, the tingling feeling of the wet drops on my arms..."

"But then you shiver."

"I'll drink something warm at the office."

"But you drive to different offices all day long," he protested. "And you park far away at each one. Wear it. You'll be more comfortable," he said with a knowing smile as she gave in and put it on.

"I know. You're right. It just won't be as fun."

"If you can wait until tomorrow night, we'll have fun then, I promise." He took her into his arms and kissed her again.

"And just what are you promising, Jonathan?" she asked him in a coquettish voice, biting her lower lip.

"Whatever you want," he replied in a soft voice, his cheeks turning red.

✳✳✳

GRACE BREVAIN AND SEVERAL OF HER fellow inmates stood over the body of a newly murdered inmate. The corpse was lying unnaturally on the concrete floor, and the blood she was losing pooled around her.

"This is what happens to people who think it's okay to try to push around old ladies!" Grace said sternly, pulling on her hair. "Don't think this won't happen to you if you don't start treating me with the respect I deserve!" She looked around at the shocked and intimidated looks on the faces of the other women. She knew what they'd originally thought about her—she was elderly, small, and a little frail, therefore making it easy to take advantage of her or bully her. This was the best way to show them that she was the toughest of all of them. "Got it?"

The wide-eyed heads of her fellow inmates bobbed up and down. "Yes, Grace."

"Good," said Grace. "Now get back to your cells. There'll be a count soon."

Back inside her cell, Grace lay on her mattress and stared at the ceiling. Three years in this hell hole. This was no life for an old woman. No freedom and nothing but disrespectful guards and fellow inmates who were all candy-asses. She hated people. She shouldn't even be here. If her son Dan had only stuck with the story she'd fed him, neither one of them would be locked away right now. But Dan was weak; she'd always known that. He didn't have what it takes to do what needed to be done. Had he killed the museum guard like she told him to, there wouldn't have been a witness. She should've known better than to trust him, too. When the police questioned them, he'd felt it more important to protect his son than his mother. She'd never felt so betrayed in all her life... well, that was debatable. But still, after all she'd done for him, this is what he does to her? The ungrateful brat.

"Grace BREE-vin?" said the new guard taking the count.

"It's pronounced "Breh-VAIN!" snapped Grace as

she jumped up. "Emphasis on the 'vain!'"

The guard rolled her eyes. "Vain. That sounds about right."

Grace lay on her bed again and sighed loudly in annoyance. Almost screaming at the sight of the bees charging at her and the ants circling her, she took a deep breath instead.

No, I will not let these hallucinations scare me any-more. They seem so real, but they're not.

She pulled on her hair, ignored the iridescent bee-tles crawling up her wall that weren't actually there, and wished her life had been different. Her eyes closed in defeat. Now she was just old, misunderstood, and locked away like an animal.

Her eyes flew open. *NO!* She wasn't going to give up. As long as she was alive, there was still hope for a good life. And if anyone would be able to turn their life around given the same situation, it would be her. A plan began to form in her mind. Dan's son Nate, her grand-son, was different than his father. He was weak, too, but far smarter than Dan. Nate had turned in the stash of artifacts that she'd stolen in return for a minimum, four-year sentence. He should be getting out in less than a year now, sooner if they released him early for good behavior. As soon as possible, she'd need to ask for a pen and paper to write him a letter and ask him to visit. She'd have to think of something to say that would make him actually show up instead of toss her letter in the trash. The wheels in Grace's mind started to turn. "I will see you again, Thomas. Very soon."

Chapter 2

Seventy years ago

Tuesday, April 3, 1945

Gently and carefully, Grace bathed her baby brother in a large basin. She dressed him warmly, placed him in a stroller for newborns, and wheeled him through the woods that surrounded their rural family home. Shortly after Grace's tenth birthday, Danny had been born, and now he looked up at her as she sang sweetly to him.

When they got to a small clearing, Grace spread a blanket on the ground and sat with Danny in the shade of a large oak tree. A few early wildflowers dotted the grassy area, and the birds whistled and chirped in the afternoon sun. "It's so peaceful here," she told her brother. "I wish we could stay here instead of living at home." She read to him from her favorite book about ancient civilizations.

By now, her mother would be cooking dinner, her older sisters, the twins, would be helping with prepping the food and setting the table, and her father would be on his way home from work. Soon, she'd be back in that small house of horrors.

Her mother did the best she could, but with housekeeping, shopping, laundry, cleaning, cooking, and four children, she had little time for the nurturing Grace longed for. The twins were very close with each other but ignored their younger siblings. Her father was incapable of love for anything besides alcohol. "You love me, don't you Danny?" Grace asked the sleeping baby in her arms.

"Grace!" she heard her sisters calling in unison. "Come home right now!"

She rolled her eyes. "It's Tweedledum and Tweedledee," she whispered to her brother. She gave him a kiss on the tuft of red hair on top of his head. "Time to go back down the rabbit hole." Her stomach ached with fear as she wheeled Danny back toward their house. "Maybe it'll be a quiet night," she reassured herself. "Maybe nothing will happen."

"Here," her mother said, handing Grace a bottle as soon as she stepped in the door. "Please feed your brother." Annie Polk wiped the sweat from her brow with her apron, pushed the red hair out of her face, and continued putting the finishing touches on dinner.

"Annie, what the hell is this?" Joseph Polk roared after walking through the front door. His words were slurred. "I worked all day, and I'm hungry! Where's the rest of the food?" He scratched his head under his mud-brown hair and glared at his wife.

Grace turned her head away from him, disgusted by his stench of sweat and alcohol.

Annie and the twins were setting the table. "That's all we have," she replied, her head down.

"You went to the market; why didn't you get more?!" he snarled in her face.

"I spent all the money we have," she said firmly, looking him in the eye this time. Grace's sisters continued preparing the food and tried to stay out of their father's way as they went about the small kitchen. The twins' matching red pigtails swung back and forth as they hurriedly set the wooden table for dinner. Grace looked down at Danny, who was sleeping in her arms, and hummed softly to him.

"There's not enough food, and now we're out of money, too?" Joseph yelled. "I don't get paid for another three days, Annie. What the hell did you think we were going to do?"

"I don't know," she mumbled.

"Oh, well that's perfect!" He threw his hands in the air in exasperation. "I told you what to do in a situation like this!"

"I will not steal!" Annie said to his face. "That's a sin!"

"So you'd rather starve to death?" Joseph asked her.

"Yes, I would."

"And what about your children? You'd rather let them starve to death than steal food for them to eat?"

"The food I made tonight is for you and the children. I won't be eating."

"Damn right you won't," Joseph agreed.

Grace hated when her father came home from work. There was always something that upset him. If her mother had been able to get enough food for them tonight, he would've found something else to scream at her about. Almost every night, he threatened her mother's life. He'd point his gun at her, try to run her over with the car while the children were made to watch as she ran, or he'd simply pound her with his fists until she could barely move. Grace wondered if she'd get another beating tonight—or worse. Her mother was trembling with anger and fear, which caused her to drop the main course on the floor.

Joseph jumped out of his chair, grabbed Annie by the arm, and smacked her across the face. Grace's sisters screamed as Annie fell to the floor. Grace breathed heavily, trying not to cry and focusing all her attention on calming Danny, who had started to wail. Annie grabbed the cast iron pan from the floor, got up, and raised it against Joseph.

Her husband laughed at her as he grabbed her arm. "You could never kill me!" he roared. "Killing is a sin," he added in a mocking tone.

She burst into tears which angered him.

"You're weak! You're worthless! And I've had more of you than I can take!" he shouted, ripping the pan from her hand and raising it above his head.

"Joseph, no," Annie said, backing away. "The children..."

The twins screamed and begged their father to put the pan down. Grace focused all her attention on her brother. She rocked him and made soft, soothing shushing noises.

"The children need to learn by your example," Joseph explained to his wife before he struck her over the head with the pan. Annie fell on her hands and knees with a loud cry. She screamed and tried to crawl away as he hit her head again and again until she stopped moving. Laughing, he exclaimed, "Finally she's not talking back! It's about goddamn time, Annie!" he shouted at his wife's corpse as he kicked her in the face. He took a swig from his flask. "I should've done this years ago!" He grabbed her by the hair and dragged her behind him. Grace could hear her mother's body being thrown down the stairs and a shovel being driven into the basement's dirt floor.

Annie's blood had splattered on the cabinets and sunny yellow walls. It left a trail to the basement door where she'd been dragged. Grace tried to calm her older sisters who were still screaming. "Stop crying," she told them in a desperate tone. "You know that makes him mad! Please stop!"

The brutal murder of their beloved mother was apparently too much for them to handle, and they couldn't help but moan and wail with grief. When Joseph returned from burying Annie in the basement, he turned toward his loud daughters. "Shut up!" he warned them. "You're being weak!"

The twins couldn't stop, and Joseph seemed to be losing his mind with rage. He pointed a finger at the twins. "Listen up! There's a lesson you need to learn here. Weakness was something that was beat out of me, and everyone should be held to the same high standards that I was. I was taught that to be somebody in this life, you have to be strong. Weak people like your mother are worthless and deserve to die. Now, I've tried to be a little more lenient with my children than my wife, but you two girls are now young teenagers—almost grown ladies. This kind of behavior is no longer acceptable."

The twins sobbed loudly. Joseph put his hands over his ears for a moment, but the crying continued. He grabbed his gun and pointed it at them. "You know I hate loud noises! Shut up!" he warned. "Now!"

The two girls grasped each other's hands and started screaming even louder. They bumped into each other as they tried to run in different directions. Grace watched, not knowing what to do, as her sisters managed to run toward the kitchen door in hysterics. Pulling frantically on the handle, the door swung open only to be closed again by Joseph who was standing behind them. The twins turned around and let out one last scream before their father shot one and then the other. They slumped to the ground, heads resting on one another.

Grace had let out a short, involuntary scream at the sound of the gunshots. She covered her mouth with her hand as her father grabbed her sisters by their hair and threw them down the basement steps. "I'll be right back," he told Grace.

She wasn't sure what to do. If she ran, she'd have to take Danny with her, and her father could easily run after and find a small girl with a screaming infant. Plus, he would see running as being weak and would most assuredly kill her. Then what would happen to Danny?

Her father reemerged into their kitchen where Grace was sitting. She looked up at him and although she wasn't making a sound, she realized there were two tears running down her face. She quickly wiped them away and asked Joseph in a shaky voice, "Are you going to kill me, too?"

Joseph wiped the dirt from his hands on his pants. "No, Gracie. You're still a child, and you're still learning. Besides, you've always been my favorite. You're smart for a young girl, and you have a naturally strong character and a dominant personality. I admire that. So, never be weak, Gracie. Weak people are the bane of society. They leech off the strong and want to be taken care of instead of taking care of themselves and contributing to the community. They use up resources that should rightfully go to the strong. Everyone should always be strong enough to do what needs to be done. I've made it my personal mission to rid the earth of as many weak people as possible. I'm a savior of the world, my girl, and that's what's going to get me into heaven. I won't make an exception for anyone, not even my own flesh and blood. In fact, let me give you a piece of advice, Gracie. If you ever do anything weak when you get older, you better kill me before I kill you. I've never told anyone that before, Gracie. That's how much I love you. Do you understand?"

No. She didn't understand. How could someone who worked hard be weak? How could someone who tried to be nice be worthless? They were good people with lots of value to offer. They should still be alive. Grace looked at her father. "I understand," she said, glaring at him.

Sixty-six years ago

Monday, March 7, 1949

JOSEPH POLK HAD JUST GOTTEN HOME from his graveyard shift, and he sat at the kitchen table, polishing off the last of Grace's birthday cake she'd baked for herself the day before. Grace was begging him to let her stay home from school. "Please, Father? Danny is so sick; he needs me to take care of him."

"No, Gracie. You're going to school. Now get! If I hear that you were late, you'll get the beating of your life," Joseph said sternly, swigging some strong-smelling alcohol from a flask.

Grace frowned. "I'm sorry, Danny. I have to go. I'll see you after school. I love you." She hugged her little brother, quickly ran a comb through her long, red locks, and ran out the door.

Seeing Grace leave made Danny scream with all the power of his lungs while his face burned with fever.

"Quiet, son," Joseph warned, the noise triggering his rage.

Danny kept screaming. "Grace! I want Grace!" Giant tears rolled down his cheeks.

"Quiet!" yelled Joseph, grabbing Danny by the shoulders and shaking him. The motion, his illness, and being so upset made Danny vomit on his father before he continued screaming. With a look of utter disgust, Joseph threw Danny toward the ground with all his might. Danny's head smacked the edge of the table hard on his way to the floor, and his crying stopped instantly. Joseph looked down and saw that the force had broken his son's neck. He cursed under his breath. "Lord, forgive me. I know you blessed me with anger to rid the world of the societal leeches, but my son was an innocent child. Forgive me for misusing my gift. Please welcome my son into your eternal kingdom. Amen." Picking up his son's body, he carried him downstairs to bury him in the basement with the rest of the family.

"Where's Danny?" Grace asked when she returned from school.

"Sit down, Gracie," her father said.

Grace felt a knot in her stomach and stayed standing.

"I said 'sit down'!" Joseph commanded her.

"I said 'where's Danny'?" Grace shot back. She then thought better of her actions and sat. She knew that Joseph respected the fact that she didn't submissively comply with his order for her to sit immediately but at the same time was angered by the lack of control he had over her.

"Danny was very sick, Gracie. He didn't make it."

"What? He's dead?" she shrieked.

"Now, don't be too upset," her father said. "Children die of the flu all the time. They just don't have the immune systems that we do."

The blow of the bad news silenced Grace for a few moments. Danny was a very healthy little boy, besides getting the occasional cold or flu. He'd only been sick for a day. The flu doesn't kill that quickly, right? Grace spun around and faced her father.

"You're lying!" she screamed at him, tears running down her face. "He cried too much, and you killed him, didn't you? You're a monster!" She ran down to the basement and saw a mound of dirt that she knew must be her brother's newly dug grave. The basement had always been a terrifying place for her, even before her father had turned it into the family cemetery. It was dark, and there were always so many insects everywhere—spiders in the corners, ants on the ground, and bees near the ceiling. Iridescent beetles that would've been beautiful under any other circumstance munched on the leaves of the flowers her father must've laid on Danny's grave. She dropped to her knees and dug in the mound with her hands until she uncovered his face. His skin had turned an unnatural shade, and rigor mortis held his mouth and eyes wide open. The ants had found him and were in every facial orifice. Grace screamed at the top of her lungs in horror, over and over again. She felt small parts of the ceiling fall and land on her head as her father stamped on the floor upstairs in an attempt to stop her screaming. Why did she leave this morning? She knew better. Guilt overwhelmed her as she ran back up the stairs in hysterical sobs.

"You better shut the hell up, girl!" her father told her.

She shoved her way past him and ran into his bedroom. Diving under his bed, she grabbed the gun he kept there in a box. Head held high and gun behind her back, she walked confidently into the kitchen, although she couldn't stop sobbing.

"Look at you, Gracie. You look pathetic. I'm so ashamed of you right now. You're being weak!"

"No!" she shouted at him in between crying hiccups. "*You* are! *You're* the one who's pathetic! My love for Danny is what got me through living with you the last four years! It gave me strength! To love is *not* weak! And to show it isn't either!"

"You're getting on my last nerve, girl! Stop crying and carrying on! Losing control of your emotions like you are is shameful!"

"You lost control of your emotions when you killed Danny! *And* when you killed my mother and sisters! You're a hypocrite!" she shouted at him. She tightened her grip on the gun.

"How dare you!" he said, his eyes narrowing. "I was doing what had to be done! They were worthless and deserved to die! I was ridding the world of leeches! And speaking of leeches..." He disappeared into his bedroom. "Where the hell is my gun?" He came back into the kitchen.

"Now it's my turn to do what has to be done," Grace told him, pointing the gun at him from across the room.

"Oh!" Joseph said in mock horror. He laughed. "Now who's the hypocrite? You're going to kill me because you think I'm weak?" He laughed again. "You don't have what it takes. Put the gun down, Gracie. I know how much you loved your brother. I'll cut you a break just this once. That's how much I love you."

"Do you think I'm stupid?" Grace yelled. "As soon as I put this gun down, you'll kill me. I didn't forget your warning!"

Joseph laughed again. "It looks like you take after me, Gracie. But you're wrong; I could never kill you. You've always been my favorite."

"You're lying!" she screamed at him. "And just so you know, I don't take after you. The only reason I'd kill anyone is if they leave me no choice! And right now, that person is you."

Before her father could respond, she pulled the trigger. The bullet hit him in the chest, and he grabbed at his heart while looking at Grace with wide eyes and his mouth hanging open. She didn't want to hear any last words. She pulled the trigger again and again before using all her might to push his body down the stairs. She didn't bother to bury him; he didn't deserve a burial. Let the insects eat him. After saying a prayer for her baby brother, mother, and sisters, she took the gun, all the cash she could find, some food, and a few belongings and started walking away from their rural home that she never wanted to see again.

She walked for days until she arrived in the nearest city—Springfield. Her father may have been a monster, to say the least, but Grace felt he was right about one thing. The strong will do what needs to be done in order to survive. She lived off the streets, stealing what she needed, and checking into shelters when it got too cold. She forged signatures on the necessary paperwork so she could still attend school. She stayed in the school's library every night until it closed, got straight A's, and did things she wished she could forget to earn money.

Grace told none of her classmates about her living situation because how could they possibly understand what she was going through? Their problems were so petty in comparison to hers, and it was hard to respect them when they'd whine about something that seemed so miniscule to her. She tried not to view them as worthless, as her father would have done, but she couldn't help it. Although she was lonely, she made no friends, except one.

Friday, October 28, 1949

ON A PARTICULARLY COLD NIGHT, WHEN the shelters were full, Grace had been on her way toward the homeless camp under the largest bridge in town with hopes to share someone's trash can fire. She never saw her attackers coming, and she screamed as they beat her, removed her coat, and ran. Her consciousness faded in and out as she lay in the gutter, bleeding. She awoke to someone pulling her into a sitting position. A weathered, old face covered by a scraggly, gray beard looked at her and twitched awkwardly. Grace recognized the man as the one the others had called crazy and dangerous. She gasped, remembering the warnings she'd been given to stay away from him.

"What are you doing out here, little girl?" he demanded. "Don't you have a family?"

Grace shook her head no.

"Oh." The man scratched under his beard. "Well, I don't either." He sat next to her, and his face twitched again. "I'm Jim."

"I'm Grace," she said, still scared.

"Looks like they got you good," he said, eyeing her bruises. "You can't let them do that to you."

"What was I supposed to do?" Grace asked him. "I had a gun, but that was stolen from me a couple months ago."

"You have to fight," he told her.

"I'm a small person," Grace argued. "And I'm not very strong."

"I'll show you something," Jim said, pressing his fingers into her shoulder.

"Ow!" Grace screamed as she grabbed her shoulder. She looked at Jim with horror and was about to get up and run when he offered her his shoulder.

"Now you try."

Grace pressed her fingers into Jim's shoulder.

"No, it's more like this," he said, moving her fingers a little closer to his neck.

She pressed her fingers again, and when he let out a yelp, she stopped.

"Good," he said. "See? You don't have to be big and strong."

"Where did you learn that?" Grace asked him.

"I've had extensive training in Kyusho Jitsu," was all Jim would say.

"Can you teach me more?"

Jim looked at her as she shivered. "Yes," he said, "but first, come to the camp and share my fire."

As they walked, Grace noticed Jim's twitching happened not only in his face, but in his arms and legs too. "Why has everyone told me that you're crazy and dangerous?"

"Because that's what I make them believe."

"Why?"

"Because when people think you're crazy, they don't mess with you," Jim said with a laugh.

"So you're not dangerous?" Grace was still afraid of

this virtual stranger.

"You have to develop your instincts if you're going to survive here," he said. "What do your instincts say? Do *you* think I'm dangerous?"

Grace still wasn't sure, but she felt grateful to him as she stood by his fire warming her hands. "Thank you."

"You have a lot of other things to learn too," Jim informed her. "These streets are brutal, as you know."

"Will you teach me?" she asked, having a glimmer of hope for her survival. "I'm scared...all the time."

He gave her a warm smile. "Stick with me. Someday soon, you won't have anything to be afraid of. I promise."

Sixty-two years ago

Tuesday, September 8, 1953

THE CAMPUS OF SPRINGFIELD UNIVERSITY WAS large and a little intimidating, but Grace was grateful to be there. She looked at her map and headed up the stairs of a large building on the quad. Upon graduating high school, she'd earned a full college scholarship, including room and board, and she'd excitedly signed up for ancient history classes—something that had always fascinated her. Now, on the first day of classes her freshman year, she promised herself to take every opportunity the university offered her. She was determined to make something of herself. It's what Jim would've wanted.

Walking through the crowded hallway, she saw and heard nothing but her memories of him. He'd introduced her to the kind restaurant owners who let them have the unsold food at the end of the day and had shown her where to go to find donated clothes and school supplies.

He'd helped her panhandle to earn the money for her college application. Her plan had been to sneak Jim into her dorm room and bring him food from the cafeteria so he could be warm and start to fight off the illness he'd had for the last several months. It was the least she could do after everything he'd done for her. But she'd found him dead one July morning in his tent next to hers under the bridge. The authorities had taken him away and that was it. She'd never felt more alone.

The lecture hall was enormous, and almost every seat was already taken. Her advisor had told her she was smart to register for this class early, as Professor Dromly's classes filled up quickly. She finally found a vacant spot next to a pleasant-looking young man with gray eyes and short, wavy blond hair. He smiled at her, and she gave him a slight nod.

She looked around at the other students as they chattered to each other. A twinge of jealousy surged through her body. The university's campus was large and overwhelming. It would be nice to have someone to talk to. A friend. Her mind turned to Jim again as she thought about how she missed him. She reached into her bag and pulled out her textbook, notebook, and a pen. As she took off her jacket, her textbook slipped off her lap and landed with a thud.

WHEN HER TEXTBOOK FELL TO THE floor as she situated herself in her seat, he picked it up and handed it back to her, mesmerized by the beauty of the redheaded woman who'd sat down next to him a moment before in the university's largest lecture hall.

"Thank you," she said, taking the book.

"You're welcome," he replied. He discreetly ran a comb through his wavy, blond hair and tried to think of something else to say, but nothing was coming to mind. He heard the woman snicker as they watched their professor walk onto the stage.

"Why is he wearing a cape?" she asked.

"Perhaps he fancies himself a superhero," he replied.

Her laughter was like a song, and he beamed at her.

"I hear Professor Dromly is one of the best," he continued. He motioned to the crowded lecture hall. "As you can tell, his classes are very popular."

"That's good to know," she said. "I want to make ancient history my major, so I'm glad to hear I'll be getting worthwhile instruction."

"Ancient history is *my* major, too!" he said excitedly, grateful to have something in common with her. She appeared to radiate an ethereal glow like she was too good for this world. A perfect angel on earth.

"I'm Grace Polk," she said, offering him her hand.

He shook it. "Morty Smithton."

Chapter 3

Present day

Friday, September 4, 2015

Morty Smithton couldn't remember the last time he'd been so excited. A one-year wait had turned into two, then three. But now, the Mallandian exhibition was finally in his museum, and he and Jonathan were starting to set it up for the official opening next week.

"Where should we put the earrings, Dr. S?" Jonathan Casley asked him. He held the sky blue chalcedony earrings the Mallandian warriors had used as armor in battle.

Morty took the earrings carefully from Jonathan's hand. "I have the perfect place for them," he replied, smiling. He placed them in the display. "But we'll just put them here for now," he added to himself, under his breath.

"I'm really glad we were finally able to afford the new display cases and security measures," Jonathan said as he worked. "Not that we have to worry about Grace try-ing to steal something anymore."

"No, we certainly don't," Morty agreed. "Grace is in maximum security prison without any hope of rejoin-ing the outside world." He almost felt sorry for her. She could've been right by his side. Instead, she betrayed him and made a series of unethical decisions that still angered him to this day.

Thinking about her made his memory travel back even further in time. As a child, Morty had been short, skinny, and an introverted bookworm. The other boys in his neighborhood bullied him mercilessly, and he came home from school every day for ten years with broken pencils, torn books, black eyes, homework fished out of the toilet, or an empty stomach due to stolen lunch money. After his growth spurt at age 15, he grew to be a head taller than anyone else in his class and was left alone. However, the hurt feelings and insecurity remained to this day. The world was a cruel place, and instead of continuing to be a victim, right after his 16th birthday he made it his life's mission to try to do something about it. He began reading every book he could find on the philo-sophical ideas of creating a utopia on Earth and thought about how it could possibly come to fruition. Absolutely nothing seemed plausible, however, until he came across the amazing powers of the Mallandian Armor Jewelry while a student in college. Every society needed rules and laws, even a utopia. The amulet, ring, and earrings gave him a way to enforce the laws a utopia would need. He smiled as he remembered his youthful enthusiasm regarding the subject. Touching the cuff bracelet in his pocket, he thought about the potential it held to help him make things right in the world that had gone horribly wrong.

"Jonathan, could you come over here for a moment?"

Jonathan looked up from across the room and headed over to his mentor. "What's up?"

"I wanted to talk to you about Anise," Morty said. "How has she been? I haven't seen her in a while."

"We're planning to come to see the exhibition when it opens next weekend. It'll be Saturday, but you can see her then if you're going to be here."

"I'm sure I will be. I typically do a little work on Saturday afternoons."

"Great! I know she'd like to see you, too."

"Does she still have the amulet in a safe location?"

Jonathan shrugged. "If you consider her neck to be a safe location. She never takes it off, not even to shower or sleep. I once tried to get her to leave her apartment without it, and she had a panic attack and ran back inside. She's never stopped having nightmares about Grace chasing her. And when her parents were killed in that accident a couple years ago, her anxiety got even worse. I think the trauma from those experiences is what caused her agoraphobia."

Morty frowned. His stomach clenched like it did every time he thought about how Anise's parents died. "Agoraphobia. I don't know much about that. Isn't it the fear of wide open spaces?"

Jonathan shook his head. "Not necessarily. I've been doing some reading about it. Some people might be afraid to be in wide open spaces like an empty field, but others are more afraid of enclosed, crowded areas like a mall or movie theater. A better way to describe it would be fear of having panic attacks in places or situations outside of your comfort zone. Some people don't leave their home at all, while others do but with anxiety. Some people feel less anxious if they bring someone with them, but for others that doesn't help."

Morty nodded his understanding. "And how do Anise's symptoms manifest?"

"She can leave her apartment and feel okay as long as she's wearing the amulet and it's fully charged. But without it, she won't step outside the door. I keep trying to get her to leave the amulet at home because I'll be there with her, but that doesn't work for her. I wish she'd try though. Having the weight of the amulet around her neck all the time is causing her some shoulder and neck pain."

"I'm very sorry to hear that."

Jonathan ran a hand through his hair and sighed. "I don't know what to do, especially when she gets a panic attack. Seeing her like that kills me. It makes me almost as scared as it does her. I feel useless. I'm trying to get her to go to a doctor and get some medication, but she refuses."

"Perhaps if we reassure her that Grace is never getting out of prison, she may feel better."

"I've said that, but I don't think I was much comfort to her," Jonathan replied, looking at the ground.

"I'd be happy to talk to her about it when I see her next week," Morty offered. "Feeling like she has to wear the amulet to be safe is no way to live."

"I couldn't agree more," Jonathan replied.

"Besides," added Morty, "the amulet is very precious and shouldn't be worn at all. It should be locked away in a safe."

"That's what I keep telling her."

"I do hope she'll reconsider allowing me to hold on to it for her. I have several impenetrable safes where it would never fall into the wrong hands. Why don't you gently warm her up to the idea? She's more likely to listen to you than to me."

Jonathan rubbed the back of his head, looking uncomfortable. "I'll try again, but I don't know how much good it's going to do. She's already annoyed with me for bringing it up too much. And like I said, she won't leave the apartment without it, so I doubt she'd ever let it out of her sight."

With his hand in his pocket, Morty slipped the cuff on his wrist and hid it with the sleeve of his sports coat.

"Have you mentioned how we believe the Jewelry can be used for peace?" He watched Jonathan's eyes start to relax and glaze over. The time it took for them to do that was getting faster. Morty was pleased.

"I have," Jonathan confirmed. "But she's not buying it."

"Not to worry," Morty said, putting a hand on Jonathan's shoulder. "She'll come around and realize this is the right thing to do. Would she be willing to donate blood?"

Jonathan's brow furrowed. "I brought it up, but she thought it was strange I'd ask when there's no blood drive. Then the topic got changed somehow."

"No matter. Another time. But please make sure you bring her to visit me more often."

Jonathan nodded. "I'm trying."

Morty slipped the cuff off his wrist and put it back into his pocket without Jonathan noticing. He watched as Jonathan's eyes began to focus as normal. "I think we've done enough work for today. Why don't you head out? I wouldn't want to keep a young person from his Friday night."

Chapter 4

Fifty-nine years ago

Wednesday, September 12, 1956

M y pencil just broke *again*," Grace complained loudly as she threw it to the floor in exasperation.

"Shhhh!" came a disapproving hush from a stranger. "This is a library!"

"Oh, shut up!" Grace snapped.

"I'll sharpen it for you," Morty offered. He picked up her pencil and hurried off. He watched her fluff her shoulder-length red curls as he turned the crank on the pencil sharpener. Smiling, he thought about how close they'd gotten over the last three years. With Grace, the emotional connection was unlike anything he'd ever felt before. It had taken her a long time to trust him, but once she did, she'd poured her heart out to him, and he'd done the same. She'd told him about her abusive father and what she had to go through in order to survive after he died and get where she was today. For some reason, she never wanted to talk about what had caused his demise. She was angry and snapped at others often, including him, but knowing what she'd been through, Morty couldn't judge her too harshly. Overall, he admired her strength and drive to not let anyone stand in her way or treat her with less respect than she deserved, and he was proud of her for opening up to him when he could tell it was difficult for her to do so.

He'd told her about the bullying he'd endured and how it had inspired him to work hard to always do the right thing. He'd confessed his ideas about creating a utopia on Earth so no one else would have to go through what he had endured. She'd listened politely, even though he got the impression she was not fully sold on the idea.

"What'd you put for question five?" she asked him when he returned, grabbing her pencil out of his hand.

"Nothing yet. I'm not sure I understand it. I was hoping you did."

"I don't. Let's plan on going to see Professor Dromly before class tomorrow and ask him about it."

"Good idea," agreed Morty. "But let's try one more time to figure it out ourselves first."

After an hour, they wrote down an answer to what must assuredly be a trick question.

"I don't want to study anymore," Grace told him. "Let's go get something to eat."

"Sure."

They got up to leave and started walking toward the door. As they passed the man who had shushed Grace earlier, she grabbed the pencil he was writing with and broke it in two before throwing it back on his table.

"Hey!" he complained and got up to confront them.

Morty hurried her out of the library. "Grace, why do you have to do things like that?"

"He deserved it," she replied. "He's lucky that's all that happened to him."

Morty looked at her in wonder. Grace was such a tiny

woman, especially compared to him. At 6'4" he was over a foot taller than her. Where she found the confidence to stick up for herself—whether or not she really needed to—was beyond him. This beautiful, pint-sized bully fascinated him to no end.

GRACE LOOKED BACK AT MORTY AND frowned at him. Why did he run away from the situation? There was no need to usher her out of the library so quickly. He was so much bigger than the candy-ass who had shushed her and could've easily won in a fight against him, if it had even come to that. Why was he so afraid when all she wanted was for him to be on her side and stick up for her?

They walked along the streets of downtown Springfield. "Hamburgers?" he asked her.

"No. Pizza."

He held the door for her at their favorite pizzeria, and they were seated by a window. "Can you believe we have only one school year left before graduation?" he asked her. "What do you plan to do next?"

"I want to get my PhD," she told him. "I applied for a grant award that'll pay for school, books, and room and board to the candidate that has the best presentation on whatever topic they come up with for this year. They're supposed to announce the topic in the next couple of days."

"Oh..." Morty replied. He looked out the window.

"What is it?" Grace demanded.

"Well, it's just that..."

"Spit it out!"

"I applied for the same grant," he said.

"I see," she replied. "Well, may the best person win."

"You're not upset?" he said, looking relieved.

She shrugged. "My grades are better than yours. I'm

not too worried."

He looked hurt. "Grace, I plan on working hard on this presentation. I'm not going to hold back at all. To win this grant would be a great honor."

Her eyes narrowed. "Are you saying the only chance I have at winning would be if you held back and purposely didn't do your best work?"

"No, of course not. I just don't want this to come between us. You're my best friend, and I don't want anything to ruin that."

"You're my best friend, too. This won't come between us," Grace assured him. *Because you have absolutely no chance of beating me*, she thought.

"I'm so glad to hear you say that." Morty paused for a moment and then reached across the table to take her hand. "Go to dinner with me."

She laughed. "We're already having dinner," she told him, as their pie was placed on the table between them.

He laughed, too. "No, I mean go on a date with me. I want to take you to a fancy, expensive restaurant and hold your hand as we walk around town."

She took her hand back and grabbed a slice of pizza. "No, Morty."

His smile fell. "Why not?"

"Because we're friends, nothing more."

"But we're so good together. I can't imagine my life without you. I love you, Grace." He took her hand again.

She squeezed his hand and looked him straight in the eye. "I care for you, too, Morty. But only as a friend. I'm sorry." She took her hand away.

He took a deep breath and hung his head. They sat in awkward silence for the rest of the meal. She noticed his gaze went everywhere except to her. She loved him dearly, and she often thought he'd make a great husband. But as hard as she tried to have romantic feelings for him, she just couldn't. He was kind to her and good-looking, but he was meek, easily intimidated by many people, and in confrontational situations he was worthless. He was someone her father would have called weak. Not that she wanted to let the memory of her father's crazy opinions influence her, but it was difficult to not hear Joseph in her head every time she came across someone who wasn't as strong as she was. If she listened to her heart, she wanted a man who would be confident and strong, someone who would stick up for her in any given situation. Someone who was her equal, someone she could discuss things with, not someone who always looked to her to be the leader. As wonderful as Morty was, he simply wasn't that man.

Thursday, September 13, 1956

THE NEXT DAY, THEY WAITED FOR Professor Frederick Dromly in his office before class. Morty looked at the framed pictures that decorated the walls and bookshelves as Grace drummed her fingers impatiently on the desk.

"Look at these!" Morty exclaimed, becoming more impressed with every photograph he saw. "Dromly must've been in the army before he became a professor. Here he is receiving a medal of some kind from Truman!"

"Uh huh."

"He's been all around the world. Europe, Asia, the Middle East...and look, this is him on a summit."

"Uh huh."

"Wow! What mountain do you suppose this is?"

Grace barely glanced at the photo and shrugged.

"Grace, you're not even looking. These are really interesting."

"Fine." She got up and grabbed a frame from a bookshelf. "Why does he have a picture of himself crawling out of a dumpster?"

Morty gave her a look of bewilderment. "What?" He gawked at the photograph in her hand and was horrified to discover she wasn't joking.

The door opened with a loud creeeeeeak. "Morty and Grace!" Professor Dromly greeted them. "What can I do for you?"

"We're having some trouble with question five on the homework," Morty answered. He and Grace sat in the chairs across from the young professor's desk.

Professor Dromly's brown eyes sparkled. "Ah, yes. The notorious question five. Evilly crafted to make students rip their hair out in frustration. If I have to begin balding early, so does everyone else." He laughed at his own joke. "It's a trick question, and I plan to go over it fully in class today." He took a glance at the answers they'd put down and then looked at the two of them in disbelief. "How long did it take for the two of you to come up with this?"

Grace shrugged. "About an hour?"

"This is the correct answer!" Professor Dromly cried. "None of my students have ever gotten this right. *I* didn't get this right when my professor challenged me with it in my school days. I'm shocked and impressed! I'm surrounded by brilliance!"

Morty and Grace smiled at each other, proud of themselves.

Professor Dromly continued, "While I've got you two here, let me ask you something. How did you feel about the lecture on Mallandian culture the other day?"

"I loved it," Grace answered. "They were a fascinating people."

"I was enthralled as well," Morty chimed in. "I was hoping you might be able to recommend some further reading."

"I'm so glad to hear that!" Professor Dromly exclaimed. "Have I ever told you about the time I went running with the bulls in Pamplona? It's amazing what losing a simple bet can compel you to do."

Morty knew Grace must be thinking the same thing he was. Were they about to hear another of their professor's unbelievable but fascinating stories Morty had dubbed Dromlyisms? "No," they replied simultaneously. Morty opened his mouth to ask one of the many questions forming in his mind when Dromly continued speaking.

"I admit I'm not much of a runner. Never understood why someone would voluntarily jog on a track. But I guarantee that if you try to tell a bull that, he won't care. Anyway, my point is that with the right motivation, you can go further and faster than you ever thought possible. I believe that motivating you and encouraging your brilliance is my duty as your professor. So here's my question to you. I have an acquaintance who knows someone...anyway, that person's neighbor's son has a piece of jewelry that was passed down to him from his parents. From its description, it sounds like it originated in Mallandia during ancient times. My wife and I are planning a trip up to Canada in a few days to visit him and take a look at it. The university is allowing me to take some students along as a learning experience. A few graduate students of mine will be joining me. I normally don't take undergrads on my excursions, but you two are exceptional students. Would you like to accompany me?"

Morty and Grace exchanged excited looks.

"Yes!" cried Grace.

"Absolutely!" exclaimed Morty.

"Excellent!" Dromly punctuated his delight with the tap of his fist on his desk.

"What kind of jewelry is it?" Grace asked, wide-eyed.

"It's a ring with a carnelian stone. It was said to have been Armor Jewelry used by the Mallandian warriors. There's an incredible legend that accompanies this ring as well as a pair of earrings and an amulet that belong to the same set. I'll tell you all about it when we're on our way to Canada. Make sure you bring your trip journals!"

said Professor Dromly.

Grace rolled her eyes so only Morty could see, and he suppressed a laugh. Dromly and his trip journals. They were his prized possessions.

"But for now, let's get into the lecture hall. It's almost time for class to start," added Dromly, draping his black cape around his shoulders. He glanced in a small, round mirror that hung on the wall next to his office door and ran a hand through his curly brown hair. "Balding isn't the right word," he said to no one in particular. "It's only a receding hairline, and only the very beginning of this misfortune, but at age twenty-nine, it's devastating enough. But I digress. Onward!" he said, shooing his students out the door.

Morty followed Grace into the lecture hall where they sat in the front row. Professor Dromly was their favorite instructor and being chosen to go on one of his field trips was a big honor. They excitedly whispered to each other about how amazing their trip would be and tried to imagine just what "Armor Jewelry" might mean.

After class, Professor Dromly motioned for Morty to approach him.

"I'll catch up with you in a minute," Morty said to Grace. She leaned against the wall and waited for him in the hallway.

"Yes, Professor Dromly?" Morty asked, stepping onto the stage.

"Morty, I know it was a while ago when you first asked, but are you still interested in working for me this year? My department finally got some extra funding. I was really impressed with the way you handled that question on the homework and could use your help in a cryptology project I'm working on. I think you'd make a valuable addition to my team."

"I'd be honored!" Morty replied. "Will you be asking Grace, too? She put in as much work as I did on the homework."

"I unfortunately only have funding for one more assistant," Dromly told him, "and I need you to keep the nature of your work with me just between us and my other assistant. It's a confidential project—I wouldn't want another archaeologist beating me to the punch on this."

Morty was intrigued. "You got it!"

Dromly gave him a nod. "Good man."

"WHAT DID HE WANT?" GRACE ASKED Morty when he joined her outside the lecture hall.

"He just wanted to offer me an administrative position in his office," Morty said, not looking her in the eye for some reason.

"Wait for me," Grace said. "I want to tell him I'd like to work for him, too."

Grace approached Dromly with her request, and he told her that he didn't have any further funding for a second new assistant.

"However, there is something you can help me with, if you're interested," he said. "I can't pay you, but it could serve as your research project for the semester."

"What is it?" she asked, intrigued.

He pulled a three-inch rounded black stone out of his briefcase. Its sides were wrapped in an alloy metal of gold, silver, and copper, and it was at the end of a five-inch long handle made out of the same metal. It almost looked like a magic wand.

"I found this on a recent excavation trip to Europe," he told her.

"It's beautiful!" she exclaimed. "Whatever it is." The black stone was so shiny and smooth she could almost see her reflection.

"The stone is obsidian," he said. "I found a legend that

calls this a seer's jewel. First, you're supposed to make a connection with it." He handed it to her. "Hold it in both of your hands, press the stone to your heart, then to your forehead for at least three seconds each."

She followed his directions.

"Now look in the stone and tell me what psychic visions it's showing to you."

She laughed as she looked at the stone. "You know, I actually thought I saw a flash of a red light for a second there, but that must be my eyes playing tricks on me because now I don't see anything except my reflection. Sorry, Professor Dromly."

"Oh, that's a shame," he replied with a grin as he took it back from her. "Regardless, I'd like you to do as much research as you can on the cave I found it in and the surrounding area. It was said to be a very spiritual place, so I'd like you to include in your report who used the cave, why, and any other interesting historical facts you might be able to find."

"Thank you so much for this fascinating topic!" Grace said, grateful. "I was struggling with ideas!"

"I know you'll do a great job!" Dromly said.

Grace raced off to tell Morty about her new project.

***

THOMAS WHIPPED UP THE STAIRS TO the stage. Even though he'd been looking for Dromly, he scowled when he caught sight of him just the same. Thomas had a bone to pick with the professor. Again.

Dromly gathered his papers and headed off stage, either pretending not to see Thomas or too lost in his own mind to acknowledge anyone else's presence.

"Hello, Professor," Thomas called out.

"Thomas! Hello," Dromly said, looking up in surprise. "How are you? And your Miss Bertram?"

"I'm very well, thank you. Betty, too." A big smile spread across his face. How could it not when the topic of conversation was Betty? "The wedding's next month."

"You're a lucky man," Dromly said, smiling back. "What can I do for you?"

"Who was that?" Thomas asked, his eyes lingering where a young, redheaded woman had just dashed off the stage. He grew suspicious. She had red hair. Dromly should've said something about her before doing what Thomas suspected he already did. They were supposed to be a team, but Dromly forgot that at times that were convenient for him.

"Possibly the most brilliant undergrad I've ever taught. Except for you, of course." Dromly replied with a smirk.

Thomas chuckled. "Of course. But she's a redhead, and you're holding the seer's wand. Did you activate her powers of sight?"

"Nothing happened. We need to find the other part of the legend about this wand or we'll get nowhere. We're missing some vital information."

"Is she the one you wanted to hire to help me with the project? Does she know...?"

Dromly shook his head. "She knows nothing, and she never will. She's brilliant, resourceful...and looks out for herself. We can't trust her. I hired someone else who's almost as brilliant but much easier to..."

Thomas frowned. "Control? Manipulate?"

Dromly frowned back. "Influence. But I'm sure that's not why you sought me out. What can I do for you?"

Thomas cleared his throat nervously. "I'm here because I wanted to discuss what happened at the symposium."

"I'm so glad you were able to attend! Did you hear the applause after I presented, Thomas? Your help with that research was invaluable."

Thomas shifted his bag from one shoulder to the other, then shifted his weight from his right foot to his left, trying anything to feel more comfortable in the moment. "That's what I wanted to discuss. My help *was* invaluable. I couldn't help but notice the printed publications passed out by the other speakers included the names of their graduate research assistants. All but yours."

"I just told you your help was invaluable. You know how much I appreciate you."

"Then why didn't you show it by adding my name to our paper?"

"Thomas, 'our paper' isn't quite accurate."

Anger clenched Thomas's jaw. "If you're insinuating that I didn't write enough of the paper to have my name directly after yours, then—"

"I'm insinuating nothing," Dromly interrupted him. "But we can't have these power struggles if we're going to continue to work together."

"I don't want a power struggle," Thomas insisted. "I just want the recognition I deserve. I did most of the research. I also wrote most of the paper. I should be named on the paper! By all rights, *my* name should've been first."

"And the sources of our department's grant money are far more impressed when *I* write a paper, not an unknown student who hasn't made a name for himself. Those grants are why we're able to do our work in the first place."

"And how am I supposed to make a name for myself when I don't even get credit for my own work?" Thomas felt his face getting hot and angrily ran a hand through his jet black hair. His blue eyes gave the professor a cold stare. "What about the other project we're working on?"

"You mean the Armor Jewelry?"

"Yes."

Dromly raised his eyebrows. "What about it?"

"We started working on it two years ago, and I've done practically all the work so far. I'm the one who uncovered all the legends."

"I'm the one who retrieved the Jewelry. I traveled to Europe, I led the digs, and I brought them home. And not just the Jewelry, but also this wand that I found on my own."

"You wouldn't have known where to start looking if I hadn't done that research as well," Thomas reminded Dromly. "And who's the one who discovered the legends were true?"

"Be fair, Thomas. We discovered that together."

"I'm asking you to be fair as well. I've been working so hard. All I want is to share the professional recognition somewhere."

"You're right." Dromly agreed. "If we write any papers on the Armor Jewelry, your name will be included. Right after mine."

Thomas frowned. "But that was my point. We agreed we wouldn't write papers on the Armor Jewelry. We agreed the world isn't ready for the gifts the Jewelry can give. My career is going to go nowhere if I'm the only grad student who hasn't gotten recognition anywhere. Which is why I wanted to be named on the paper we wrote for the symposium. I worked day and night on that project as well."

"You have been working hard," Dromly agreed. "Have I ever told you about the time I climbed Mount Everest?"

"You?" asked Thomas, looking at the smaller man that stood in front of him. In his opinion, scrawny wouldn't be too harsh of a word.

"Yes! Before taking my group up, my Sherpa guide had led three other expeditions in a row without a break, and due to his exhaustion, he unfortunately twisted an ankle three quarters of the way up. I had to carry him the rest of the way to the summit where I fashioned a sled out of some garbage bags and our backpacks. Luckily, I was able to safely pull him back down to the basecamp while he navigated."

Thomas narrowed his brow in confusion. "You still

went to the summit?"

"My point is that working too hard is never a good idea. I think you should take a break from your research. Concentrate on your classes and have a little fun. Spend more time with Betty. I'm sure she'd appreciate your help with any last minute wedding plans. You need to write your own story, Thomas, and it shouldn't all be about work."

Thomas felt a sinking feeling in his gut. "A break? For how long?"

"Just a week or so."

"But we have the trip to Canada in a couple days to see the Armor ring."

"I won't need your assistance with that."

"But Professor, I found Richard Woods. I discovered that he has the ring. It was my idea to visit him to make sure he has no awareness of the ring's powers, the other Jewelry, or the Plate of Destiny. I really want to be there."

Dromly looked up at Thomas who was several inches taller than he was and wore a stern look that only appeared on rare occasions when he had lost his patience. "I said I won't need your assistance with that." In a hiss, he continued, "And never mention the Plate of Destiny out loud! That artifact is more precious than the Holy Grail! If the wrong ears ever heard we're searching for it, it could be our demise." He brushed past Thomas toward the stairs.

Thomas watched Dromly leave, the stupid cape flapping arrogantly, as if it were mocking him by waving goodbye. He wanted to run after Dromly to tell him he was quitting and wish him good luck in finding the Plate of Destiny without him. But he'd put so much work and time into this project. And direct evidence that gemstones combined with incantations and intention could bring about measurable metaphysical results was the most amazing discovery the world had ever known and would ever know, and *he* was the one who discovered it.

How could he ever give up on finding out more? If only he didn't need the university's resources and Dromly's grant money to do it.

On the other hand, how could he lower himself to working for such an arrogant professor who degraded and used him and punished him when Thomas stood up for himself? Thomas felt his anger fade as he thought of the perfect solution to his predicament. "Who says I have to share my findings with you, Dromly, you rat bastard?" Thomas mumbled aloud. "If you want to know everything I uncover, you can find it yourself."

He thought about the redheaded girl who Dromly had initiated with the wand. If he was going to take Dromly down, the redhead would need to become a key part of the plan forming in his mind. He knew exactly what had to happen, and the very thought made his stomach churn with dread. It wasn't fair that the price to beating Dromly was giving up the one person that had ever made him happy. But he didn't see any other way. As if on cue, he caught a whiff of her perfume and turned around.

"Hello, lover," came a sultry voice as a tender pair of arms wrapped around him.

He looked down and saw brown curls with eyes to match. "Betty." She was so beautiful, smart, kind, and sensual, and he'd never loved anyone like he loved her. But over the last couple of years, his hatred for Dromly had grown larger than his love for her. It was all he thought about anymore. It was an obsession he simply couldn't explain. He absolutely should prioritize Betty and his future life with her. But something in him wouldn't allow that.

"What's wrong?" she asked.

He frowned. She'd always been able to tell when something was bothering him. He'd miss that. "Dromly's being an ass again."

"Again? That's all I hear from you lately. And after all you've done for him? Well, ain't that a bite. You should give him a knuckle sandwich." She kissed him. "Come on, I'll let you buy me some lunch. We'll talk about the wedding. Get your mind off of—"

"No." He took her in his arms. He wanted to hold her one more time. "I love you, Betty. So much. But I can't marry you."

She gave him an indignant look and pushed him away. *"What?"*

"I'm sorry."

"Why?" she demanded. "Is there another girl?"

"No, it's not that."

"So I'm just not good enough for you?"

"No! Of course not."

"Then *what*, Thomas?!"

"I just can't. I can't explain."

"You owe me an explanation!" Her face turned red.

He shook his head. "I'm sorry."

"So...that's it?"

"I'm really very sorry."

Betty's eyes blinked away the growing shock as she stood there with her mouth hanging open, flabbergasted. She slapped him across the face, took off her engagement ring, and threw it at him. "It's your loss!" she informed him.

He watched as she turned on her heel and stormed away. Tears rolled down his cheeks as he watched his love disappear, but he didn't regret his decision. He'd never have peace if he didn't ruin Dromly. He sighed as he thought about what he'd need to do to take Dromly down and make him suffer. It would take a long, long time. But it would be worth the wait. It was all that mattered anymore.

Saturday, September 15, 1956

AFTER THE FLIGHT TO CANADA, MORTY relaxed at the kitchen table of Richard Woods' family home with Grace, Dr. Dromly, and the couple of graduate students that had joined them.

"The Armor ring!" Dromly drooled over the ring on Richard's hand.

"What do you mean by 'Armor ring?'" Grace wanted to know.

"Mallandia was a Bronze age kingdom. According to legend, they discovered a way to make a set of magical Jewelry using an incantation. The ring is said to be poisonous, the amulet is protective, and the earrings give the wearer super strength. They used it as armor during battle."

"The Bronze age? I didn't know my ring was that old," Richard said as he stared at the ring on his finger. "How was it used to poison people?"

"According to the legend," began Professor Dromly, "the gemstone is a mix of carnelian, cinnabar, and orpiment. Carnelian is safe, but the other two have traces of natural poisons in them. Somehow, the poisons were delivered through the skin. Beyond that, I'm not certain."

"So, would their victims die if they touched the ring?" Richard continued.

"Only if the warrior was wearing the other two Jewelry items," answered Professor Dromly. "Wearing multiple pieces made each piece more powerful. On its own, the ring was not said to be deadly. It would, however, make the victim very sick for a while."

"How much is this worth?" asked Richard.

"This is a priceless artifact," began Professor Dromly. "But as a precious family heirloom, it's worth even more. You're not planning on selling it, are you?"

"My father would be very upset if I did," replied Richard. "But someday when he's gone..." Richard saw the disapproving looks from Dromly and stopped talking.

"Richard, this ring has been in your family for generations. Doesn't that mean anything to you?" Dromly asked him.

Richard shrugged. "It's not really a family heirloom. My father said his grandfather bought it from a street vendor when he visited Europe."

"Still," Dromly said. "He must've thought enough of it if it became a family tradition to pass it down from parent to child."

"I guess," Richard agreed. "But I have no idea why. Supposedly, the vendor told my great-grandfather that there's a specific destiny tied to the ring, and it'd find its true owner someday. Something about a specific bloodline. Do you know what that's supposed to mean?"

"Unfortunately, I don't," Dromly replied, his brows narrowing in thought. "But that's very interesting, and it's something of which I wasn't aware. Thanks for bringing that to my attention. I look forward to attempting to find an answer for you." He made a notation of what Richard had told him in his trip journal.

Professor Dromly requested to see the ring and Richard handed it to him. Dromly studied the gemstone. "I'm not an expert on stones by any means," he said to the younger people, "but all I see here is carnelian. I see no traces of cinnabar or orpiment at all." He held the gemstone to the skin on his arm for several seconds, before handing the ring back to Richard. Professor Dromly made a dramatic show of wiping non-existent sweat from his brow. "Looks like we're safe," he teased. He turned his attention to Morty, Grace, and the few other students. "When we get back to Springfield, remind me to show you the old texts about Mallandian legends I was able to get for the university library. Some of them talk about this legend. But for now, I promised my wife a nice dinner out tonight." Dromly rose to leave. "Richard, thank you so much for spending time with us this afternoon."

"It was my pleasure, Dr. Dromly. Thank you for telling me about the legend."

"Richard, would you mind if Grace and I stayed just a few more minutes to get one last look at the ring?" Morty asked him. He had a feeling there was more to the ring than met the eye. Its profile was taller than most rings, and Morty wondered if there was a reason for that.

"Not at all," Richard replied, handing Morty the ring.

Professor Dromly said his good-byes and left along with the other students.

Grace made small talk with Richard as Morty studied the ring. Ignoring their meaningless chatter, Morty ran a finger over the gemstone and felt the sides of it, pondering the possible reasons for the high profile. He supposed it could just be style, but since the purpose of the ring was to act as a weapon during a time of war, he believed that aesthetics would not have been considered as much as function. And large jewelry, especially worn on the hands while wielding a heavy weapon, was not functional. He grabbed the setting and wiggled it. He noticed it seemed loose. He wiggled it again, and this time he felt the entire setting turn. It wasn't loose at all; it was meant to turn!

Morty interrupted the conversation of the other two. "Grace! Look!" She and Richard both turned to see what Morty was doing. He held out the ring so they could get a better view and turned the setting counter-clockwise ninety degrees. Grace let out a quiet gasp as they watched the carnelian stone being mechanically flipped over by the turning of the setting. The other side of the stone appeared different than the orange-red carnelian they were used to seeing. There still were sections of carnelian, however, there were also very prominent bands of yellow and vermilion gems as well.

"That must be the cinnabar and orpiment!" Grace exclaimed, pointing to the new bands of color.

"Let me see that!" Richard exclaimed, grabbing the ring.

"Be careful!" Morty exclaimed. "If we *did* find the

cinnabar and orpiment then you don't want to touch it."

Richard narrowed his brow in disbelief. "You don't actually believe that legend, do you?" he asked, laughing. "You can't be poisoned just by touching a stone."

"No," agreed Morty, "but oftentimes a legend is based upon fact. There might be something about this stone that can affect you negatively. Gemstones can contain harmful minerals."

"That's ridiculous," stated Richard, "and I'll prove it to you." He grabbed Grace's arm.

She let out a loud huff in protest. "Let go!" she demanded.

"Relax," Richard told her. "I'm just trying to prove a point."

"Stop manhandling me you candy-ass!" She pulled away, attempting to free her arm, but Richard wouldn't let go. "Morty!" she cried.

Morty wanted to help her, but he found himself looking at the ground in fear instead.

"You're both going to feel really stupid once I prove to you that this legend is just a fairy tale, and this ring is harmless," Richard said to them, and held the ring above Grace's arm.

"We both know it's not true!" snarled Grace loudly, her eyes shooting daggers at Richard's face.

"I'm not so sure *he* knows," laughed Richard, looking at Morty.

"Even *if* he believes the legend, you have no right to grab me. Now let me go!" She pushed a spot on Richard's hand.

Richard let out a yell of pain and doubled over as he clutched his hand to his abdomen. Morty was amazed at how Grace had been able to protect herself. He wondered where she'd learned that.

After a moment, Richard straightened up, pushed her away from him, and she landed in a seated position on the floor. "Bitch!" he said with a glare as he held his hand. He removed the chain he wore around his neck, threaded it through the ring's band, and hung it around his neck again, tucking it under his shirt. "Leave before I throw you out!" Richard demanded.

Morty wanted to punch Richard in the face but ignored him instead. "Let's go, Grace." He offered his hands to help her up.

"Oh, *now* you want to help me!" she sneered venomously at him. "I don't need your help anymore!"

"Okay. I'm sorry." Morty dropped his hands and let her get up on her own.

"You should be!" she replied angrily.

The two were so involved in their own spat, it took them a few moments to notice that Richard had collapsed and was shaking uncontrollably.

"Is he having a seizure?" Morty asked nervously.

"I don't know!" sneered Grace. "And I don't care! He doesn't deserve our help after being such an ass. Let's go."

"No! We have to do the right thing."

"Fine. Call an ambulance. And leave a message for Professor Dromly so he can contact Richard's parents."

Morty did as Grace told him and then they stood and looked at Richard's shaking body, not knowing what to do.

"What's that smell?" Grace asked, wrinkling her nose.

Morty took a sniff of the air. "I think he shit himself," he whispered to her.

"Disgusting!"

Richard turned his head and began vomiting on the floor.

"Even more disgusting," Grace said, turning away. She let out an annoyed sigh.

✳✳✳

RICHARD'S PARENTS AND YOUNGER SISTER WENT to sit with him in his hospital room. Dromly, Morty, and Grace peered into the room to see Richard. He was unconscious, still, and very pale.

"What happened?" Dromly asked his two students.

"We don't know," replied Grace. "He suddenly collapsed and became sick. He seemed perfectly fine just a few moments before."

Richard's heart monitor began making a series of sounds that frightened Richard's mother. "What's going on? Help!" she yelled to the doctors and nurses who were already running toward Richard's room.

"He's going into cardiac arrest!" said one of the doctors. Richard's parents and sister were escorted out of the room as the doctors and nurses worked dutifully on Richard's heart. Mrs. Woods and her daughter Isabelle sobbed hysterically while Mr. Woods held on to them both tightly, praying.

Several minutes passed, but it felt more like an eternity. When the medical professionals left Richard's room and a doctor began walking over to the family with a somber look, Mrs. Woods began trembling.

"I'm sorry," the doctor began. "We couldn't save him." Mrs. Woods fainted and Mr. Woods, the doctor, and Professor Dromly all attended to her.

Morty pulled Grace aside. "Did Richard have the cinnabar and orpiment side of the ring exposed when he put it under his shirt?" he asked her in a hushed voice.

"Yes, I think so," she whispered back. "Why?"

"Doesn't it seem like he was poisoned? Don't you think it's strange how suddenly his symptoms came on when he had been fine before he touched the ring? And according to the legend Professor Dromly told us, the poisons were delivered through the skin. If Richard had it under his shirt, it would've been touching his skin."

"But Dromly also said the ring wasn't deadly if used on its own," Grace said.

"I know, but think about the different situations," Morty began. "If a solider needed to use the ring in a battle, or if he were captured and needed to use the ring to get away, he wouldn't have time to hold the ring to his enemy's skin for several hours. In order for the ring to work in an effective way, it would need to deliver enough poison to sicken the enemy in a very short amount of time. How soon after Richard put the ring under his shirt did his symptoms appear?"

She paused. "Almost right away," she answered. "He pushed me, and shortly after I got back up, he was on the ground."

"Right, so if he hadn't had any more exposure to the ring, he likely would've been sick, but made a recovery. However, the ring was under his shirt, constantly touching his skin for hours. Perhaps in such a situation, the ring *can* be deadly on its own."

Grace's nose wrinkled in doubt. "But it's just a legend. Besides, Dromly told us the Jewelry loses its charge after a while. Wouldn't he have had to wash it under running water and recharge it in the sun for it to have been able to poison him?"

Morty grabbed his chin while he considered her words. "You're right," he said. Then his eyes opened wide and he looked at her. "He *was* wearing it when we arrived. And he washed his hands before serving us snacks."

"That's right!" said Grace, and Morty could tell she was starting to believe. "And the sun was shining on the table where we were all sitting and looking at it. It got at least a couple hours of direct sunlight!" Then her face fell. "Morty, if Richard's family finds out about how poisonous the ring is, they might accuse us of killing him. It might look suspicious the way we stayed after Professor Dromly left. And no one else was there to see that we didn't do it. We can't tell anyone we found out how the ring works. Not even Professor Dromly. He's seems close with the family; he'd be compelled to tell them for sure."

"But..." Morty thought about Grace's words. Not telling Dromly about the secret of the ring seemed so wrong when the professor was deeply dedicated to learning more about this fascinating and precious artifact and the story that went along with it—especially after including them in his adventures. However, distraught parents looking for answers about their son's death might very well blame the strangers who had stayed behind to further admire a very valuable ancient artifact that belonged to the deceased. "No, you're right," he said. "We'll keep this to ourselves." He was silent for a moment, then added, "I'm a little concerned about others getting poisoned."

"No one but you was able to figure out that the setting turned, and that was only because you were looking for it," Grace assured him. "I doubt anyone else will discover that."

"No, I mean the poisonous part of the ring is still exposed and possibly still under Richard's shirt. When someone discovers it, they could touch it and become ill. It wouldn't be long before they put together the pieces and realize it was the ring that killed Richard. Then they might come looking for us."

They looked over at the door to Richard's hospital room. There was no one near it. The Woods family along with the nearby medical professionals were all attempting to help Mrs. Woods down the hall. Grace whispered to him, "Go in his room now, turn it back the way it was, and put it back under his shirt. Do it now before anyone else goes in there."

"Why me?" He gave her a frightened look.

"You're the only one who knows exactly how to put it back the way it was, and therefore you'll be able to do it faster," Grace said to him. "Otherwise I'd do it. I'll be your lookout and distract anyone who tries to go in there."

While Grace walked over to Richard's family to offer her condolences and ask if she could do anything to help,

Morty slipped unseen into Richard's hospital room. He swiftly and carefully pulled the chain around Richard's neck until the ring came out. Morty grabbed the ring by the band, quickly twisted it clockwise ninety degrees, and watched the stone mechanically flip over to only show the carnelian side. He put it back under Richard's shirt, jogged over to the door, and peeked out. He saw Grace wave at him to signal the coast was clear, and he walked over to her.

"All good?" she asked him in a whisper.

He nodded.

They sat and waited for Professor Dromly so he could drive them back to the hotel. It'd been an exhausting day, and Grace leaned her head against Morty's shoulder. He put his arm around her, grateful for her comforting presence. He'd never seen a dead body before, much less touched one. He shivered.

Grace sat up. "Morty, do you realize that right now, we are the only living people who know how this ring works and that the legend is actually true?"

"You're right," he agreed. "We should find the amulet and earrings and see if they also have powers! If we could collect all of the Jewelry, that power would be a way for us to enforce a utopia on earth!"

Grace rolled her eyes. "You're really serious about that utopia idea?"

Morty ignored her. His newfound hope had him flying.

A glint formed in her eyes. "Regardless, yes. Let's find the amulet and earrings. With that kind of power, we could have everything we want!"

"Let's promise to share any knowledge we find about the Jewelry with each other."

"And to not share the knowledge with anyone else," she added.

He nodded. "I promise."

"I promise, too."

Chapter 5

Saturday, September 12, 2015

Jonathan arrived at Anise's apartment to pick her up for their date at the museum. He sat on her new red couch as she finished getting ready. Her sketchbook lay open on the glass coffee table, and he saw she'd been working on a drawing of her friend Vanessa trying on a wedding dress.

"I just need five more minutes!" she told him.

"No hurry."

She dropped things in her vintage floral tote bag and put on her shoes. He loved looking at her. The curve of her face, the way she moved, the smile she gave him when he told her she was beautiful. He was so happy to be with her, not just in that moment, but always.

Over the last three years, they'd become great friends, and she was practically all he could think about. Several times a week they'd hung out and watched TV, went to the movies, out to eat. He'd even agreed to go to a club a couple times and attempted to dance with her because she'd been so excited about it. He only hoped his awkwardness on the dance floor hadn't embarrassed her because she moved like a goddess. He'd introduced her to his friends in town. He'd invited her to all his family barbecues and events, and his parents had kept asking him when he was going to ask her out already. She and her friends came to watch his band perform most weekends at local bars, and his bandmates had been sick of hearing him pine over her. "Tonight's the night," they'd told him one evening four months prior. "If you don't sing it to her, we will." It was the last song of the night, the one he'd been working on since the day he met her. They'd bought him a shot which he downed on stage before picking up his guitar. He'd looked at her through the whole song and sang everything he'd been feeling that he'd never before said. He'd feared she wanted nothing more than friendship from him for quite a while, and he was never more thrilled to be wrong in his entire life.

With the happy memory in the forefront of his mind, he got up from the couch and kissed her. "We could just stay here instead," he suggested, his hands running through her hair and down her back.

"Hold that thought for later," she told him with a peck on the lips. "We've both been looking forward to the museum, and I'm almost ready."

"Okay," he groaned his agreement as he sat back on the couch. "By the way, I told Dr. S. we'd stop by and see him while we're there. He's been asking how you are and when he can see you."

"Okay, sounds good!"

As she headed to her bathroom, there was a knock at the door.

"Are you expecting anyone?" Jonathan asked her.

"No," she replied, shrugging her shoulders and shaking her head as she headed toward her front door. She looked through the peep-hole. "Aw, did you send flowers?" she asked Jonathan.

He narrowed his eyebrows in confusion. "No..."

"Oh my god!" she exclaimed after swinging the door wide open. "Nate!"

"Hi, honey," Nate said to her, stepping into her apartment, lifting her up, and swinging her in a circle as she wrapped her arms around his neck. He set her back down, and she smiled up at him.

"It's so good to see you! I can't believe you're here!" Anise exclaimed. "Why didn't you tell me you were getting out?"

"I wanted to surprise you," he replied, returning her smile.

"I was wondering why you hadn't called in a while."

What the...? "I thought you were supposed to be in prison for another year," Jonathan said, coming up behind Anise.

Nate took his eyes off Anise for the first time since he'd gotten there. "Hey, Boy Scout." He handed Anise the bouquet he'd brought. "They let me out early for good behavior. I'm a free man now."

"Good for you," Jonathan said flatly as his eyes shot daggers at Nate. *What the hell is he doing here?* The flowers looked expensive.

"They're beautiful, thank you," Anise said to Nate as she put the flowers in water. "And I have something for you." She pulled something large and rectangular out of her front closet and took off the cloth that covered it.

Nate's eyes lit up with delight. "Wow! It's incredible! Thank you. It's perfect!"

"Thanks, I'm glad you like it," she said to Nate, her cheeks turning slightly red.

"It's really good," Jonathan agreed. "*Really* good." Anise thanked him and squeezed his hand with a smile. The oil on canvas painting she'd made was a close up of a motorcycle on top of a skyscraper with city lights and the night sky as a backdrop. The entire bike was black except for the chrome on the tailpipes and wheels, red racing stripes, and a red tire stripe to match. "Is this your bike?" he asked Nate.

"Yeah. Harley-Davidson Night Rod Special. 1250cc V-Twin."

"Nice. So it could get you home pretty quick."

Nate ignored him and turned to Anise. "How much do I owe you?"

She shook her head. "Nothing."

"No," he protested. "You deserve to get paid for your work."

Anise shrugged. "Ok, then whatever you think is fair."

Nate grabbed his phone and digitally sent her a payment. "If that's not enough, just let me know. And I brought you something else, too," he added, grabbing a couple of bags he'd set down in the hallway outside her door. He handed her one and she looked inside.

"No way!" she exclaimed. "Oh my god, this is so awesome!" She pulled out a black leather motorcycle jacket. "Thank you!" She put the jacket on and spun in a circle to show off her new look. Turning to Jonathan, she asked, "What do you think?"

"You look great," he told her.

"I love it!" she said, twisting back and forth in front of the mirror by the door, flirting with her reflection.

"I'm glad," Nate said. He handed her the other bag.

She reached in and took out a motorcycle helmet in her favorite color—purple. Her expression looked happy but also not quite sure of the intent of the gift. She looked to Nate.

"I was hoping I could take you for a ride," he explained.

Jonathan hated that arrogant, crooked grin of Nate's more than anything. Was he asking Anise out right in front of him? "We're on our way out," Jonathan said curtly. "We have a date." He frowned at the smile his girlfriend was giving the psychopath.

"Yeah, now's not a good time, sorry," Anise said to

Nate. "But I don't have any plans for tonight."

"Well, you do now," Nate said with another grin.

Jonathan felt a surge of anger bubbling up and along with it, a splitting headache. He couldn't believe Anise was going to spend time alone with this criminal. Nate couldn't be trusted to keep her safe. Jonathan watched in horror as Nate moved in for another hug, but instead, wrapped his hands around Anise's neck and started strangling her. Anise choked as she clawed at Nate's hands, and her face started turning blue. With all his strength, Jonathan tackled Nate and started punching furiously while screaming obscenities at him. He was surprised when Nate didn't fight back, but instead, just tried to hold Jonathan off. Anise started pulling on Jonathan's arm, begging him to stop. He looked up at her and sat on the floor next to Nate. "Are you okay? How's your neck? Can you breathe?"

"What are you talking about, and what the hell is wrong with you?" she demanded of him, squatting next to him.

He looked at her neck and found it strange there weren't any marks. "He was choking you..." he started to say when he realized Anise was looking at him like he had three heads. "He wasn't?"

"No! Of course not!" she exclaimed, her voice raised. "Why would you think that?" Anise was on the verge of angry tears.

Jonathan knew how much she hated violence and felt bad for upsetting her, but he also felt hazy and confused. His headache was so excruciating at this point that he put his hands on top of his head and pulled on his light brown hair as if he were trying to tear it out. The pulling was the only thing that helped the pain when he got these types of stress headaches. "I watched you turn blue," he mumbled.

"Jonathan, Nate didn't lay a hand on me. He would never do that. What is wrong with you?" Anise demanded again. "You have that weird, glazed look in your eyes again like you did the other day. Are you okay?" she asked in a softer tone, putting her hand on his shoulder.

Jonathan watched as Nate stood up with a stunned look, put his hand on his face, and moved his jaw around.

"I'm okay. I'm sorry," Jonathan said to Anise. He felt his haziness slowly disappearing. "I honestly thought I saw him going for your throat."

"You should be apologizing to *Nate*," Anise said, getting up and walking toward her kitchen.

Jonathan looked at Nate. There was no way he'd apologize until he knew for sure what had happened.

Anise returned with a bag of frozen peas and handed them to Nate. "For your face," she said. "Are you okay?"

Nate shrugged and with a scoff said, "He barely touched me." He extended a hand to Jonathan with an offer to help him up.

What an asshole. Jonathan swatted it away and put his aching head in his hands.

Anise's eyes narrowed. She grabbed Nate's wrist and put the bag of peas in his hand. "Sit!" she commanded, pointing to her couch.

With an amused expression, he complied.

Anise joined Jonathan on the floor. She sat in front of him and looked into his eyes. "Your eyes look clearer now," she informed him. "Are you feeling better?"

"I'm so sorry," he apologized again in a low voice. "I got another one of those bad headaches again out of nowhere, and I think it may be affecting my vision when it happens."

"Promise me you'll go to the doctor."

"I promise."

"On Monday."

"I promise. Now let's get to the museum."

"Are you sure you still want to go?" she asked him.

"Definitely. The headache is going away, and I'm feeling much better."

Nate had put the peas back in Anise's freezer and was staring at Jonathan. "I'm not leaving you alone with him. He has a screw loose."

Jonathan wanted to get up and punch him again, but his head was still hurting, and he didn't want to upset Anise.

Anise walked Nate out into the hallway. Jonathan sat on her couch, closed his eyes, and listened to their conversation.

"Don't worry, I'll be fine," Anise said. "Jonathan's been getting these bad headaches lately, and he thinks they're affecting his vision. He really thought you were going to hurt me, and he was just trying to protect me."

"He does this again, you call me."

"I will, I promise." Her smile could be heard in her voice. "Thank you."

"I'll see you tonight."

"Looking forward to it!" she said, before joining Jonathan back in the apartment.

"I've never seen you behave like that before, Jonathan. I think we should talk about this a little more before we go," she said, closing the door and joining Jonathan on the couch.

"What's to talk about? I promise I'll go to the doctor and get it checked out."

"I'm glad, but it's not just that. I heard the snide comments you made to Nate."

Jonathan's pride crumbled like a cookie. "He has some nerve coming over here and trying to ask you out right in front of me."

"He didn't ask me out. We're just friends."

"You used to date him."

"That was a long time ago. We're only hanging out tonight. It's not a date."

"I'm also worried for your safety if you go riding with him. It wouldn't be the first time he was reckless with your life."

Anise grabbed his hand. "I know you don't like him. And I know you feel that he put me in danger, but I believe everything he did was to protect me from Grace. He knows better than we do how to handle her. He also knows he absolutely could've handled it much better, and he's tried to make amends. Remember, he did let himself get caught so he could erase our tracks at the museum. Otherwise, we'd have been in prison right alongside him. He gave up three years of his life to show us how sorry he is."

"Nate is no hero, Anise," argued Jonathan, a little frustrated. He took his hand back. "He lied to you and pretended to be someone he wasn't to try to trick you into handing over your amulet. How is that protecting you from Grace?"

"He thought if Grace had the amulet, she'd stop trying to kill me. He was trying to save my life."

Jonathan frowned and continued his rant. "And he didn't go to prison to help us; he just wanted to get Grace and Dan locked away to be rid of them. Getting himself caught too was the only way he could do that. He didn't do it for you; he did it for himself. He in *no way* redeemed himself for his mistakes. Your life was in danger more than once because of him. To me, that's unforgiveable. Not to mention, he's a criminal and a psychopath."

"I disagree. *Grace* put my life in danger, not Nate. He admitted that he had lied to me at first, but he apologized and explained everything to me, and I've forgiven him."

"Why?" Jonathan asked with disbelief.

She looked at the ground and her hands began to fidget, twisting her garnet ring around her finger. "Because of how I handled my situation with Brian. I've told you this before. Brian was being abusive and instead of getting help from his sister or my friends or the police in getting him out of my apartment, I lied to him about where I was going and what I was doing. I was scared of what he'd do if I brought other people into the situation.

Nate has been abused by Grace his entire life, and she's incredibly scary. I understand how someone could resort to dishonesty when they're trying to deal with an abusive situation. We each were trying to survive, and we each handled our situations poorly. But if I forgive myself and not him, I'd be a hypocrite."

Jonathan shook his head at her, not knowing what to say.

"Grace would've killed me for the amulet, and everything Nate did was to try to save my life. And he succeeded."

"Is *that* what he told you?" Jonathan scoffed.

"Yes, and I believe him. You would too if you gave him a chance and got to know him."

Jonathan seriously doubted that.

Anise continued, "And since I've forgiven him, we became friends. I like talking to him."

"I know," Jonathan grumbled. "I've never heard you laugh so much as when you're talking to *him*. What's so great about your conversations anyway?"

"Like you, he's a fun, smart, and interesting person."

"How do you know? And how can you call him a friend? You only knew him for a short time three years ago."

"We got to know each other really well over the phone. He'd call me whenever he got a chance."

"Yeah, but prisoners don't get much time to talk."

"Usually that's true," Anise began, "but Nate helped one of the guards with an investment and made him a lot of money. In exchange, the guard smuggled in a cell phone for him. Nate was able to call me almost every day."

"You talked with him every day?!" His heart squeezed in his chest.

"No. But we spoke when I had the time."

Jonathan stared at the floor while his stomach ached. "I don't believe this."

Anise narrowed her brows at him. "You knew we talked often. You witnessed several of our conversations. How is this a surprise?"

Jonathan continued to stare at the floor. "It's a lot more than that. Why is he calling you 'honey?'"

"He's always called me that. It doesn't mean anything."

"And why is he buying you flowers and gifts? If that's what you want, I could've bought them for you."

"You don't have to buy me anything. And neither does he."

"So why did he?"

Anise shrugged. "You'd have to ask *him*."

"I don't like it." Jonathan frowned. He'd never been the jealous type before, and he hated feeling this way but couldn't help himself. "I didn't know you were working on a painting for him."

"He commissioned it."

"How much did he pay you for it?" he asked with curiosity.

Anise grabbed her phone. Her eyes opened wide in shock. "Oh my god. He gave me a thousand dollars."

"What?! That much? He's such an asshole." Jonathan clenched his jaw.

"You don't think my art is worth that much?" she challenged him.

"Of course it is. It's worth more. But you didn't ask for a payment. He only gave you that much because he's trying to impress you."

Anise frowned. "Or he actually thinks it's worth that much and is trying to be supportive of my art."

"Why are you sticking up for him?" Jonathan asked incredulously.

"There's good in him that you haven't seen. I hope the two of you can make peace because I'd like to keep him as a friend," she told him.

Jonathan raised his eyebrows at her. "He doesn't

just want to be your friend. You see that, right?"

"Why, because he's a guy? You have a lot of women friends. We hung out with several of them last night. Ashley, Brittany, Tara, and Emily all came to watch your band play and support *your* art. How is this different?"

"I don't buy my women friends flowers and gifts. He's an arrogant asshole who thinks he can win you back."

Anise took Jonathan's hand again. "Well, he's just going to have to get over it. He knows you and I are together. I've made that perfectly clear."

"He doesn't care!" insisted Jonathan. "I can tell he still wants you!"

"I don't think so. When we talked on the phone, he never said a word about having feelings for me, never asked me out for after his release...the conversations never crossed that line."

Jonathan shook his head at the ground. "That doesn't mean anything."

"Okay. I don't want this to be a point of contention for us," she conceded and grabbed her phone. "I'll text him and cancel."

Jonathan hated that she looked disappointed as her thumbs flew over the keyboard on her phone. "What are you going to say?"

"I think it would be better if we didn't go riding," she read from her screen.

He sighed. "Don't send it."

She raised a doubtful eyebrow at him. "Are you sure?"

Jonathan nodded. "I'm sorry. You should be friends with whomever you want. I trust you," he said, squeezing her hand. "It's *him* I don't trust. He's going to try something, just you watch."

"*If* he tries anything, it's not going to work," Anise reassured Jonathan.

He loved her with everything he had, and there was no doubt in his mind that she loved him, too. But the way she'd looked at Nate, and the way she'd smiled at him made it obvious to Jonathan that she still had some residual feelings for him, whether she would admit it or not. He only hoped that spending some time with Nate would make her see that he's not the guy she thought he was. "Okay," he said. "Are you ready to go see the earrings?"

"Yes!" she chirped. "I've been looking forward to this all day!"

ANISE GRABBED JONATHAN'S HAND AS THEY walked around the museum. He'd been very quiet on the car ride over and had worn a small scowl on his face ever since they left the apartment. Anise knew he was still upset that she'd agreed to go riding with Nate. She'd never seen Jonathan's jealousy act up before, and she hoped it wouldn't happen again. She also hoped Jonathan hadn't been able to tell that she was still attracted to Nate. She hadn't seen him in three years, and ever since she started dating Jonathan four months ago, part of her had hoped that the first time she saw Nate again he'd look haggard from being locked up. But he'd looked better than she remembered, better even than in the dreams she had about him every so often. She'd tried not to look too long at his strong, lean body and handsome face but hadn't been able to help it. The old familiar flush of heat had rushed through her the moment she'd opened her front door and let him back into her life. A pang of guilt twinged in her stomach. *But it doesn't matter,* she assured herself. *It's just a shallow attraction and means nothing. I'll get over it.*

She and Jonathan peered into the display case that held the Mallandian armor earrings. The hoops, each with a pale blue chalcedony stone, brought back a flood of terrifying memories for Anise.

"Beautiful, aren't they?" said a voice right behind her.

Anise had been so lost in her memories that she jumped and gasped as she spun around. "Oh, Dr. Smithton!" she exclaimed, laughing. "You scared me!"

"I'm so sorry, my dear," Dr. Smithton apologized.

She gave him a quick hug. "It's okay! I was just lost in thought about the last time Jonathan and I were in a museum looking at these earrings."

"And I apologize once more for that experience you endured. I know it was quite traumatizing for you."

Anise looked at the ground, her head filled with images of a murderous Grace and Brian's dead body. "It's okay," Anise replied, not wanting to think about it anymore. Her thoughts turned to her brother Les with the mysterious fainting spells no doctor could diagnose—the only reason she cared about the Armor Jewelry at all. "I wanted to ask you...do you remember when you told me that there's a part of the legend that mentions healing abilities when it comes to the Jewelry? I did some experiments with the amulet, and I don't think it has any healing powers. You had said it's probably the earrings that can heal. Have you done any experiments with them to find out?"

"I'd be lying if I said I didn't try them out," Dr. Smithton said, his eyes twinkling. "I was amazingly strong and full of energy when I wore them. But I didn't think about any healing possibilities."

"Could we try something?" Anise asked. "Jonathan has a papercut. I'd love to know if the earrings can help."

"It's just a papercut," Jonathan said. "The Jewelry shouldn't be used at all. It's too precious."

Anise turned back to Dr. Smithton. "Please? I really want to know. Don't you?"

"I have to admit you've stimulated my curiosity, young lady. But I believe they'd need charging first. Why don't you and Jonathan stop by my office before you head out? We can test the earrings then." He took a ring of keys out of his pocket, unlocked the display case, and removed the earrings carefully. "I'll wash them and put them in my office window. They should be ready when you are."

"Thank you, Dr. Smithton!" Anise beamed at him. If the earrings had healing powers, maybe they'd be able to help Les. Of course, there was no way Dr. Smithton or Jonathan would let her take them out of the museum without knowing why. Jonathan didn't know about Les, and she wanted to keep it that way. When she discovered a few years ago that she had a brother, she'd told her friends and Nate only. She'd planned on telling Jonathan, but there was something about his strange behavior lately that made her uncomfortable telling him anything. She'd have to find another way to get the earrings...but maybe Nate could help her with that. Her stomach already ached at the thought of stealing, but she wasn't doing it for greed or any other unsavory reason. Les's doctors couldn't diagnose him, and he was getting worse. The prognosis wasn't hopeful. This could be a life or death situation.

"Why do you want to know if the earrings have healing powers?" Jonathan asked her.

"Don't you?" Anise replied.

"Sure, but out of all the millions of things you could be wondering about them, why that?"

She shrugged. "I just do. I've tried out different things with the amulet over the years, and now I want to know more about the earrings. And the ring."

"Speaking of your amulet, would you consider allowing me to put it in my safe for you? It is a priceless artifact after all, and we wouldn't want it getting lost or damaged in any way."

This wasn't the first time Dr. Smithton had asked to keep the amulet for her. She wondered how many times she'd have to tell him no. "I appreciate the offer," she replied. "But I'm very careful with it, and I'd prefer to hold on to it myself."

"Of course," Dr. Smithton replied. "Would you at least consider lending it to us, just for the length of the Mallandian exhibition?" he asked, his eyes full of hope. "The museum would be forever grateful. It would add so much to the presentation of the display."

Anise put her hand on the amulet which she wore on a chain around her neck under her shirt. This wasn't the first time Dr. Smithton had asked her to lend it to the museum either, and it always gave her a sense of unease. She didn't want to be without it. She felt uncomfortable saying no, and in the past, she probably would've given in. But over the last few years, with the advice of her friend Corinne Kellin, psychologist and older sister of Brian, she was working on being more aware and respectful of her own needs instead of just trying to please others all the time. "I know it would," Anise told Dr. Smithton, "but I feel uncomfortable lending it out. I hope you can understand."

"Very well," said Dr. Smithton with a disappointed sigh. "But I am concerned about you. I hope you realize that even without wearing the amulet, you are safe now. I know how frightening Grace Brevain can be, but she's locked away for life in a maximum security prison. She has no way of coming after you. You'll never see her again."

Anise frowned, a little frustrated that the topic of conversation hadn't yet changed. "Dr. Smithton, I thank you for your concern, but it's not necessary. Really. I know Grace can't hurt me anymore."

"We're going to check out the rest of the exhibition, Dr. S.," Jonathan told his supervisor.

"Wonderful! Enjoy!" said Dr. Smithton. "I'll see you both later."

"He needs to stop asking me for the amulet," Anise grumbled to Jonathan once Dr. Smithton walked away.

"I know you don't like it. That's why I cut our conversation with him short."

"Thank you. But he brings it up every time I see him."

"He based his whole life's work on finding these Jewelry pieces, Anise. He's just excited about it."

She frowned again. "I get that, but he needs to take 'no' for an answer. And I don't like him trying to talk to me about Grace. I don't want to think about her at all."

"Why are you getting upset?" Jonathan asked. "He's concerned about you. I am, too. You shouldn't have to wear the amulet to feel safe. And he's right that the amulet should be protected. It's a precious artifact and shouldn't be worn."

"I've asked you before to stop saying that!" she exclaimed in frustration. "I'll take it off when I'm ready!"

"Okay, I won't say it again," Jonathan assured her. "Do you want to see some cuneiform tablets from Mesopotamia? They're over here."

She nodded and started to relax. She hadn't meant to snap at him. But he'd already promised more than once that he'd stop pressuring her to take off the amulet. She wondered when he'd start making good on that promise.

✳ ✳ ✳

JONATHAN DROPPED ANISE OFF AT HER apartment. "I'm headed to band practice," he told her. "Why don't you come by my place after your...outing tonight."

"Okay. See you then." Anise could tell that he was still upset about her plans to see Nate. After closing her front door behind her, Anise pulled the affirmation card she wanted out of her tote bag and read it out loud. "I trust my ability to make sound decisions." She flopped on her couch and closed her eyes, putting the card over her heart. Silence was exactly what she wanted right now. Even though she and Jonathan had a good time at the museum, she was still a little miffed at how he always sided with Dr. Smithton when it came to what she should do with her amulet. She was done with listening to what other people thought she should be feeling or doing for one day.

She was also heartbroken over the results of the experiments with the Jewelry in Dr. Smithton's office. Once she'd put on the earrings, she tested them by lifting the four-drawer filing cabinet with one hand and the large leather sofa with the other. Excited, she'd then tried to heal Jonathan of his papercut. She'd made the intention to heal him and felt it with everything she had, just like Dr. Smithton advised, but nothing came of it. Whoever had sent Les that letter about the Jewelry must've been mistaken when writing about their healing abilities. Disappointment overtook her as she thought about how she'd never be able to help her brother. Letting out a sigh, she stretched out on the couch and closed her eyes, trying to get the tense muscles in her shoulders to release their death grip.

Relaxing almost turned into sleeping when her cell phone rang. Picking it up and looking at it, she groaned. Corinne was calling. Anise loved Brian's sister, but ever since his death, she felt guilty whenever they spoke. She twisted the garnet ring she wore around her finger. Brian had given it to her on her 23rd birthday, and she still wore it daily. For some reason, she felt guilty when she thought about taking it off. Corinne had no idea the part Anise played in how Brian died. *Let's get this over with,* Anise thought. *If I don't talk to her now, I'll just have to call her later.*

"Hi, Corinne!" she answered as cheerily as possible. She stayed supine on her couch and put her free hand to her forehead.

"Hi, Anise! You've been on my mind. How's everything going?"

"Good! Having a nice weekend so far. Jonathan and I went to the museum to check out the Mallandian exhibition. How are you?"

"I'm okay." Corinne paused. "The reason I called is I wanted to let you know that Nate Brevain got released from prison."

"Yeah, he came by to see me earlier today."

"Really?! Oh my god, are you okay?"

"I'm fine." Anise took a moment to try to make sense of the situation. "How did *you* know he was out?"

"I did something I shouldn't have."

"What do you mean?"

"After Brian died...the grief was overwhelming for me a lot of the time."

"I remember. So what did you do?"

"I called the psychologists at each prison where the members of the Brevain family are locked up. I felt like I wouldn't be able to move on without knowing why my baby brother had to die. The psychologists at the higher security prisons where Grace and Dan are were kind but firm in their refusal to talk to me. And I understand why. Legally, they can't. If I were in their position, I wouldn't either. But the one at Nate's prison took pity on me. She had a family member that had been killed recently too. I flew out to see her and she 'accidentally' left Nate's file on her desk while she left her office for a few minutes. When he got out, she called to let me know, so I wanted to warn you."

"I appreciate you thinking of me, but no warning necessary. He's not the one who killed Brian. That was Grace," Anise said. "All Nate did was try to steal something."

"That's what they say. But he's still a bad guy and shouldn't be anywhere near you. Why did he come to see you anyway?"

"We were friends before everything went down. We kept in touch while he was away, and he just wanted to resume the friendship. He has a motorcycle, and we're going riding tonight."

"What?!" Corinne screeched. "Why would you keep

in touch with him? And how can you hang out with him after what he did?"

Corinne's horrified words were like an explosion in Anise's ear. She grimaced and pulled the phone away. "He did a bad thing, but he's not a bad guy, Corinne. Unless you know something I don't. What did you find in his file? Is he a dangerous psychopath like his grandmother Grace?" *Could Jonathan be right?*

"Well, no. At least not according to the prison psychologist. The file notes describe him as an extremely intelligent and charming person. He was diagnosed with a form of dissociation. She wrote that although he *is* capable of committing crimes and lying without feeling guilt, he's also capable of great devotion and love. The love is only given to people in his 'inner circle,' if you will, meaning only a few friends perhaps and maybe family. With Nate, the only people who are in his inner circle are his two friends that he mentioned, his missing mother, and you. Everyone else he likely sees as objects and not people. It's treatable, and he can make a recovery if he puts in the work."

"He mentioned me?"

"In every session according to the notes. I found that strange at first, but I guess if you knew him before and kept in touch with him, it makes more sense."

"You said he was diagnosed with dissociation. What's that?" Anise asked, sitting up with interest.

"It means he detaches himself emotionally from situations. He grew up in a very abusive household, and it's likely he created this dissociation as a protective mechanism. For a child in that situation, it was a way to not feel the pain and help him survive the verbal, emotional, and possibly physical abuse he experienced on a daily basis."

"Oh my god." Anise's heart broke for Nate. "Poor thing."

"Anise, even though his psychologist believes that he's not a danger to anyone, I would still advise you to stay away from him. He obviously makes bad decisions. Honestly, I don't know how you can even stand to look at him after what happened to Brian. But as your friend, I'll tell you this. If Nate is going to be in your life in any way, you'll need to keep what I said in the back of your mind. Since you are in his inner circle, if he ever acts cold or callous toward you, or if he keeps things from you, it's likely he's just trying to protect himself from getting hurt. Not that you should put up with that behavior or enable him in any way. He's an adult and if he's going to grow emotionally at all, he's going to have to let down his walls, allow people into his heart, and actually feel his emotions instead of pushing them aside. This means feeling the bad emotions as well as finally being able to feel the good ones, too."

"He doesn't feel *anything*?" Anise asked.

"According to the notes, he usually feels only numbness, excitement, or anger, but has no idea what other emotions feel like. He wouldn't even be able to recognize another emotion if he did feel it. In the sessions, they started working on how to feel and recognize emotions, but as you can imagine, something like that takes a long time to work through."

"Wow," said Anise. "That's a lot of information I wasn't expecting. Corinne, I can't thank you enough for this. I feel so much better knowing that Nate isn't like Grace at all. Can I trust him to not lie or try to manipulate me since I'm in his inner circle? I think that's what I'm most concerned about now."

"It seems Nate cares for you, Anise," said Corinne, "and caring about anyone is a huge deal for someone with his diagnosis. His psychologist believes he has every intention to be honorable from this point forward. That being said, everyone has the capacity to lie or manipulate, whether they have a disorder or not."

"That's true," Anise agreed. "Corinne, it's like a weight has been lifted off my shoulders! Thank you so much again. Now I'm really excited about going riding with Nate tonight!"

"If that's really what you want to do," said Corinne, her words drenched in judgment, "just promise me you'll be careful."

"I will," said Anise, already mentally picking out the outfit she wanted to wear.

Anise knew she'd disappointed Corinne and felt terrible. Corinne didn't know the entire story about Nate or Brian, and because she needed to keep the Armor Jewelry a secret, Anise couldn't tell her. She understood why Corinne hated Nate and couldn't blame her. But she was also tired of being told what to do. For the first time in her life, she was making her own decisions without Brian or her parents trying to make them for her or telling her she was doing something wrong, and it felt great. If she was making a mistake by seeing Nate, it was her mistake to make. But something in her told her that she had more wisdom than her parents, Brian, or Corinne gave her credit for.

Chapter 6

Approximately 4300 years ago

How is the anti-mutiny cuff coming along?" Yarim asked the royal Jewelry engineer. "The king wants to know."

"I just completed it," Dagan replied. "I have some very specific instructions to provide to the king on how this cuff works."

"This is a time of war, Dagan! His majesty cannot be bothered with such things right now, when they can be handled by someone else. Give me the instructions, and I will relay them to the king as necessary."

"No!" said the engineer. "It's pertinent that I give the instructions to the king only!"

"Impossible!" replied Yarim. "I am his main assistant. He asked me to collect whatever knowledge is needed and bring it back to him. I will be able to tell him what he needs to know when he has a spare moment. You, however, need to get back to creating more Jewelry sets for the new recruits right away. This comes directly from the mouth of the king."

The engineer frowned, but he was not one to ignore an order from the king. "Very well, Yarim. But listen closely. It is of the utmost importance that my directions are followed exactly."

The engineer brought the cuff over to Yarim, who took in a deep breath when he saw it. "It's magnificent!" Yarim exclaimed.

The cuff was about two inches wide in the middle and was tapered toward both ends with a small gap between them. It boasted three oval-shaped lapis lazuli stones, two rows of five jasper stones that lined the edges, and was made of out the same alloy metal as the other pieces of Armor Jewelry. "This is to be used by the king only. Did you hear me, Yarim?"

Yarim nodded.

"Have him gather all the soldiers together while wearing the cuff. Whatever ideas about obedience he puts in their heads through his words will become their ideas. They will maintain their individuality and warrior spirits, but all talk of mutiny will be gone."

"Excellent! The king will be pleased." Yarim grabbed the cuff and turned to leave when he felt a hand on his shoulder.

"Yarim, my directions need to be followed exactly or there will be consequences," Dagan warned.

"Understood." Yarim took off into the night.

He met with a stressed king. The enemy had many more warriors on their way, and now his own were on the verge of a mutiny. "Is the cuff ready, Yarim?"

"Yes Your Majesty," replied Yarim, handing the cuff to the king.

The king took it and turned it over in his hands. "Excellent. What a beautiful piece. Dagan has given you directions on how to use it?"

"He has. Is Your Majesty ready to hear them?"

Another assistant ran into the room. "Your Majesty, your presence is needed regarding a matter involving your daughter."

The king sighed. "I'll be there momentarily," he told

the other assistant. "Yarim, is it absolutely necessary I hear the directions now?"

"I think not, Your Majesty. Dagan told me *you* must use the cuff, but I believe the task is not so daunting that it can't be handled by one of the commanders," Yarim replied.

"Very well. Take it to the commanders immediately. Relay the instructions to them and have them put it to use right away."

"Yes Your Majesty. I will head to the camp immediately."

NOT HIM AGAIN. COMMANDER ADMAT WATCHED Yarim's short legs run furiously toward him from across the field. He didn't know what it was exactly, but there was something about the king's main assistant Commander Admat didn't like.

"It's about time," he complained to Yarim when he reached the camp. "What took so long? My informant says the soldiers are staying up late every night hatching a plan to take control."

"This, Commander." Yarim handed the cuff to Admat and explained how to use it. Admat called an immediate and mandatory meeting of all the soldiers.

While wearing the cuff, Commander Admat walked up and down the aisles of soldiers, stressing the importance of obedience to authority, loyalty to the king, and staying true to the necessary order of society by maintaining humility. He reminded them that the gods would reward them for staying true to their military duties. He looked at the faces of the soldiers. The unsatisfied expressions they brought in with them had not changed. In fact, he noticed the addition of scowling in response to his speech. Commander Admat looked at the cuff and cursed its worthlessness in his mind. He knew something else had to be done. Something that kept the men busy at night so they couldn't plan their takeover. He ordered them all to return to the meeting area of the camp at sundown before he dismissed them.

"Yarim!" Commander Admat called out once the men were gone.

Yarim came running. "Yes, Commander?"

"This cuff is worthless! Did you see the expressions of the men? They were completely unchanged at the end of the meeting; some of them seemed even angrier. What didn't you tell me about how this is supposed to work?"

"I told you everything, Commander. Perhaps it takes a little more time than just one session?"

Admat frowned. The annoying little man had a point. "Yes, perhaps. Yarim, we will need several tankards of beer, enough to last many weeks. And prostitutes—many of them as well. While we wait for the effects of the cuff to take place, we must make certain the men are busy and satisfied at night."

"Yes, Commander."

Many weeks turned into many months. The soldiers partied every night, battled often, and listened to obedience speeches daily. Commander Admat noticed no positive differences. However, headaches were becoming increasingly more common. Admat figured the overindulgence in libations was to blame. However, the physicians also had to be called in, sometimes several times a day, to attempt to rid the soldiers of evil spirits that were invading their minds. Many if not all of the soldiers were seeing things that weren't there, causing them great distress, fear, and paranoia.

SOLDIER WATROSE HAD BEEN EXPERIENCING STRANGE

events himself. Earlier that day, his superiors had taken away his Armor Jewelry and coerced him to fight in a battle without them. He was terrified and hid in a tree the majority of the time. He held on tightly to the branches while his head felt like it was going to explode. Placing his hand on his head to try to discover the exact location of the pain proved futile. It seemed as if it were in his brain, radiating outward and expanding his skull. He groaned in agony as he tightened his hand into a fist around his hair. Suddenly, he felt some relief. Pulling on his hair helped stop the pain! When the pain subsided, he took his hand out of his hair and noticed the ring was on his finger. Impossible! Commander Admat had taken it from him. He looked down and saw the amulet around his neck. Reaching up, he felt the hoops in his ears. What was happening? And why was he the only person on the battlefield? There was no one else there for as far as he could see from the top of the tree.

Looking around, Watrose got out of the tree and ran back to camp, demanding to see a physician. "I've been possessed!" he wailed.

The head physician came over to him. "Sit down, please," he said. "I'll be right with you." He brought a cup of tea for Watrose. "Drink this. It contains a heavy dose of cassia to relax your muscles and calm your nerves. Now tell me, why do you think you're possessed?" he asked Watrose.

Watrose was embarrassed that everyone was looking at him, so he leaned in and whispered to the physician, "My Armor Jewelry was taken from me right before the battle today. They forced me to fight without it. They're trying to kill me for wanting to go home. I climbed a tree and got the worst headache of my life, but I was able to pull out the pain from my hair. When the pain stopped, I had my Jewelry back. It makes no sense! I'm possessed!"

"There was no battle today, Watrose. You know that, right?" asked the physician in a kind voice.

"What?!" Watrose yelled. Then in a quieter voice he said, "That would explain why no one else was around." He was shaking with fear. "Can you help me?"

"I'll certainly try," replied the physician. "Drink your tea, and I'll be right back."

"Where are you going?" Watrose asked, not wanting to be by himself, just in case there were more evil spirits lurking in wait.

"I have to let the commander know right away when I get another patient. He wants to know when one of his soldiers needs help. You're not the only one who's been experiencing these symptoms, Watrose."

Watrose watched as the physician spoke with the commander. He couldn't hear what they were saying, but the commander looked very displeased. Watrose became nervous again wondering what they were saying about him. Maybe they didn't want to help him because he was the leader of the upcoming revolt against the army. Maybe they found out he was sneaking away from the nightly parties to plan it with others who were also tired of their poor treatment. Maybe they wanted to kill him! He shouldn't have come. Evil spirits or no, he would not trust his life to those who considered him their enemy!

He noticed the physician coming back toward him with something in his hand. What was it? Watrose squinted. *A mace?* He jumped to his feet, ready to fight. Looking down, he noticed the amulet and ring were missing again. He touched his ear—the earrings were gone too. When did that sneaky physician take his Jewelry? And he could smell the cassia, but what else was in this tea? He threw the cup to the ground. His head began to ache again and the pain was overwhelming. "Put down your mace!" he cried, pulling on his hair. The physician started running toward him, mace raised. Watrose let out a battle cry and charged, weaponless. The commanders in the area, who all wore the Jewelry, pounced on Watrose, and knocked him to the ground with such force from the strength of the earrings that everything went black, and he could barely hear the physician and Commander Admat speaking.

"Why couldn't you have just restrained him?" cried the physician in horror.

"He was seeing things that weren't there and thought you had a mace," answered Admat in a confident tone. "He was trying to kill you."

"Don't insult my intelligence," the physician snarled. "You and the other commanders haven't had enough training and practice with the Jewelry and don't know your own strength. It was obvious how you were struggling to control your own movements."

Watrose's eyes flickered open just long enough to see Admat looking at him guiltily before they closed forever.

THE KING WAS LIVID AT HAVING to pull his entire army out of the field. It hadn't just been Watrose's unit that suffered fear, delusions, and intense pain, but every unit that had been exposed to the anti-mutiny cuff. The commanders and king's assistants all stood in front of him. "This is unacceptable!" he boomed. "Bring me Dagan! NOW!"

The royal Jewelry engineer was ushered into the palace by guards. "Dagan," the king began, "the anti-mutiny cuff you created did not work the way you promised. In fact, it created irreversible damage! The soldiers exposed to the cuff have been suffering from extreme pain and terrifying visions, causing them to lash out in violent ways. Some of my soldiers have had to be killed in order to protect others from their violence! My commanders tell me there's still talk of mutiny! This is all due to your incompetence, and justice must be served! Dagan, you caused the brains of the soldiers to malfunction in a very painful way. Therefore, the top of your skull will be chopped off and your brain removed from your head."

Dagan's eyes grew wide and he started sweating profusely. "Your Majesty, I swear there was nothing wrong with the cuff when I gave it to Yarim. There must have been a miscommunication with the instructions. Please, could Your Majesty first tell me how you used the cuff? If the mistake was truly mine, I will accept my punishment. But if I can fix this situation instead, I feel it is my duty to do so."

The king sighed. He liked Dagan and admired his skill. He had also never made a mistake in the past, so perhaps it would be wise to hear him out. "Very well, Dagan. But we'll have to ask Yarim how the cuff was used, as I was not there."

It was Yarim's turn to wipe sweat from his brow.

"What?" said Dagan in disbelief. "Your Majesty, that's the problem right there! I told Yarim that the cuff was to be used by His Majesty only and that if my directions weren't followed exactly, there would be dire consequences!"

"Yarim, is this true?" the king bellowed.

"Yes, Your Majesty," said Yarim, "but it did not seem to be pertinent information. Perhaps if Dagan had shared the reason why only His Majesty can use the cuff, I would've understood the importance."

"The reason is a security measure!" shouted an angry Dagan to Yarim. "If the cuff can be used by just anyone, then whoever possesses the cuff can control the king's entire army!" He turned toward the king. "Your Majesty, the reason I collected the drops of blood from your finger before I finished the cuff is to let the cuff know who it's working for. Only you or your blood relatives—someone with king's blood—can use the cuff to immediately put thoughts, ideas, and wishes into the heads of others by speaking to them in reasonably close proximity. Should anyone else attempt to use the cuff for this purpose, it would take months to years for the deposit of ideas to take place! And in the meantime, the brain of the recipient of the ideas would fight back by creating pain and illusions of what the person fears most. This is what has happened to your soldiers. Eventually, if exposed long enough, the recipients will *turn into* what they fear the most. However, by wearing all four pieces of Jewelry, Your Majesty, and *only* Your Majesty, or his blood relatives, can heal them."

The fuming king turned to Yarim. "You didn't use your ears, Yarim! For that reason, yours will be cut off! In addition, you caused the soldiers damage to their brains. You will also suffer the punishment I was about to wrongly inflict on Dagan!"

Yarim ran. The king's guards caught up to him and dragged him away, screaming.

"Your Majesty," continued Dagan. "There's more I must tell you. May I have a word with you in private, please?"

The king agreed and dismissed everyone else with a wave of his hand.

When they were alone, Dagan knelt before the king and bowed his head. "Your Majesty, first please allow me to offer my most humble apologies. Yarim warned me that you were too busy to hear the details of the cuff. I told him only the least of what I thought he needed to know. I wanted to keep as much information about the cuff as private as possible for the security of His Majesty and the army. I was planning to tell you the details I revealed today as soon as you were able to spare a moment for me."

"Rise, Dagan," said the king, his eyes heavy with stress and regret. Dagan rose. "I should've made time to meet with you for a matter of this importance. What else do I need to know?"

"Your Majesty, I received the instruction on how to make the cuff—and the ring, amulet, and earrings— from the gods. While I was asleep, they came to me in a vision. They gave me an incantation and instructed me to inscribe it on every piece of Jewelry. They told me this Jewelry would give us the ultimate power to rule over whatever land we wished and that they were making this offer in exchange for protection of their most precious possession."

The king opened his eyes wide. "Do you mean the Plate of Destiny?"

"Yes, Your Majesty. As you know, no human eyes shall look upon the Plate of Destiny, as it contains all information about the universe and is for the eyes of the gods only. In my vision, I was told that this task could only be trusted to the royals, for only they are worthy enough to be trusted by the gods. This is another reason for making the cuff's power available to only you. So, should the Plate of Destiny ever be threatened by a human, it is the duty of Your Majesty and all royal resources such as your army to defend it."

The king's chest puffed out. "What an incredible honor to be chosen by the gods!"

"Indeed, Your Majesty. There's one more thing. I was told by the gods that there will come a day when most of the Jewelry will be destroyed. However, there must always be at least one complete Armor Jewelry set in existence at all times, to ensure the protection of the Plate, and that Jewelry set must stay in the bloodline. Your Majesty will need to pass down this information to blood relatives that inherit your cuff, as well as a set of the Armor Jewelry including the amulet, ring, and earrings, and tell them to keep passing down that information, generation after generation, to ensure the Plate's safety."

The king couldn't thank Dagan enough for the information and for his incredible craftsmanship of the Jewelry. "You will be handsomely rewarded," promised the king. "And my descendants shall always be the protectors of the Plate of Destiny!"

Chapter 7

Present day

Saturday, September 12, 2015

Anise finger-combed her wavy brown hair and touched up her lip gloss for the third time. She didn't know why she was so nervous. Needing something to keep herself busy, she added a little more eyeliner, eye shadow, and mascara. She spun around slowly in front of her full length mirror, making sure her outfit looked perfect. Her dark wash skinny jeans hugged her curves and stopped just before they met the tops of her black, high-heeled ankle boots. Her tight, black wool sweater would keep her warm this evening without adding bulk. The amulet was underneath her sweater, and its outline showed, but barely. The black leather jacket Nate had bought her fit perfectly and added an edgy, tough-chick vibe that she loved.

The sound of a motorcycle reached her ears. *Nate.* She looked in the mirror one last time, and the excited butterflies in her stomach grew worse. "You're being silly," Anise scolded her reflection. "There's nothing to be nervous about." She opened the door after his knock and gave him a big smile. He was wearing the black leather motorcycle jacket he looked so good in. "Hi!"

"Hi, honey," he said, stepping inside and opening his arms. "Come here." She happily complied, he put his arms around her for a hug, and she squeezed him back.

"Are you ready to ride?" he asked as he broke the embrace.

"Yeah, just let me grab my helmet and keys."

She shoved her wallet, phone, and keys into the pockets of her jacket and picked up her helmet. Grabbing the brand-new pencil that resided behind her ear, she looked at it and set it on her coffee table. No way would that fit underneath the helmet. She wouldn't need it tonight anyway. "Okay, all set!"

"You let your bangs grow out," he commented as they walked down the hallway and stairwell.

"A year ago Jonathan and I decided we needed a change. So I told him I'd grow out my bangs if he shaved off his goatee. We both really liked our new looks, so we kept them. What do you think?"

They got to his bike, and before putting on their helmets, he reached out and brushed her bang-free hair out of her face. "You look beautiful," he told her, his cobalt eyes giving her their intense gaze that she had dreamt about often over the last three years.

Climbing on his motorcycle after him, she wrapped her arms around his waist and they took off into the dusk.

They rode up to the park at the top of the hill across town, parked, and Anise hopped off, removed her helmet, and shook out her hair. She watched as Nate got off the bike and removed his helmet and jacket, too. "You're wearing short sleeves!" Anise observed. She looked at his arm where there used to be a tattoo he hated covered up poorly by other tattoos he didn't like either. Now she saw nothing but his muscles and the only tattoo he'd kept.

"Yeah," he said, his face lighting up as he looked at his arm. "I can finally wear them again. There was a tattoo removal service that came into the prison once or twice a month. They wanted to help anyone who needed to get rid of ink that no longer represents who they are."

"You got rid of all of them except the motorcycle. No more Satan's helper. Or Satin's helper, I should say," she teased him, referencing his former tattoo's misspelling.

"All gone," he agreed, grinning at her.

"That must've taken forever. Did it hurt?"

Nate nodded. "Yeah. But it was worth it. They did a great job. Barely a trace of anything left; just a few scars."

Anise glanced at his arm again. "It looks great. I'm happy for you."

"Thanks."

"Would you ever get another one?"

He made a doubtful face. "I won't rule it out, but after everything I went through…"

"I get it."

She felt one of the muscular arms wrap around her, and Nate led her to a picnic table under the pines and overlooking the city. They sat on the tabletop with their feet on the bench and enjoyed the view.

"So catch me up, honey. What's new since I last saw you?"

"A lot, but I think I told you most everything over the phone. I told you about my new job, right?" she asked.

"Yeah, but that was a while ago. Tell me again."

"I'm thrilled I don't have to take market research surveys in the mall anymore! I work for the corporate office now across town. I have to travel to all the Bradley Field Services offices in the malls in the city and surrounding cities to brief them on new surveys and clients and to make sure their employees are doing the interviews correctly. I had to buy a car, but I make a lot more money now, so it wasn't a big deal."

"Do you still like it?" he asked.

"I do! I like talking to everyone in the offices, and I like the driving around. I didn't think I would, but it's really nice not to be stuck in one office all day long."

"What else is new? How are your friends?"

"They're doing great! Vanessa got engaged. Erin got a job at a salon that pays her better. And Joy bought a condo."

"And how's your brother?"

She frowned. "He's slowly getting worse. His unconscious spells are getting more frequent and lasting longer, and the doctors still can't figure out what's wrong."

"Sorry. That's rough."

"I told you I got to visit him, right? It was nice to spend time with him."

"What did you do?"

She shrugged. "He couldn't do much. His wife worries and his mother throws a fit when he leaves the house, so we ordered food and talked a lot."

"I'm glad you're getting to know him."

"Me too! He's so interesting. He's a retired Navy Seal and was teaching survival skills for a while until he had to quit because of his condition. He was telling me this story about how one of his classes was dedicated to getting out of constraints. He'd just taught me how to escape if my hands were tied when he had another unconscious spell. Unfortunately, he didn't wake up until a couple days later after I'd flown back home."

"That's too bad."

She nodded. "I'm not giving up hope, and I'm not giving up on the Armor Jewelry either. *If* it can help him, I'll figure out how to do it."

"I have no doubt you will," he agreed. "Did you tell Les about the Jewelry?"

"No," she replied, shaking her head. "I want to, but...I promised Jonathan and Dr. Smithton I wouldn't tell anyone. We've had enough trouble from Grace, we don't need anyone else coming after us for the Jewelry. Not that Les would cause us any trouble, but a promise is a promise."

"Did you ever ask him about the weird letter he got about the Armor Jewelry? The one he mentioned when you first met him?"

"Yeah. He said he talked to our mom on the phone about it. She apparently got the same letter when she turned 18, just like he did. She paid no attention to it. I tried to ask her about it, but she didn't want to talk about it."

"That whole thing is weird."

"I know! It obviously means that either Grace or Dr. Smithton sent that letter, or else someone else knows about the Jewelry and *that* person sent it. But why would they be sending letters to my mom and brother about it? And isn't it the strangest coincidence that *I* ended up with the amulet?"

"It is," Nate agreed. "Did you get to read the letter? Did it give you any clues?"

Anise shook her head. "I was going to ask Les if I could read it, but I didn't get a chance before his unconscious spell."

"I can't figure out why Grace or Smithton would want to involve your family in it. I know Grace doesn't want any competition when it comes to collecting the Armor Jewelry, and I bet Smithton feels the same way."

"Yeah," Anise agreed and began to worry about who else might know about the Armor Jewelry. Would that person come after her and try to kill her like Grace did? She put a hand on her chest to feel the amulet under her sweater. It was comforting and made her feel safe. Not wanting to worry any longer about something that might never happen, she changed the subject. "What about you? You must be so happy to be out."

He looked at her somberly. "Honey, you have no idea."

"I know we talked a lot, but you never told me what it

was like in there."

He shrugged. "Boring. Monotonous. They at least let me take online classes so I could give my mind something to focus on. I read every book in the prison library. And I did whatever grunt work they wanted us to do."

"That reminds me, where the hell is my license plate, slacker?" she teased him.

"Funny." He put an arm around her shoulders and pulled her toward him. She giggled and struggled to sit upright.

"Is that all you did?" she asked.

"Pretty much. That and working out a lot."

"Yeah, I noticed," she said, squeezing his arm. "Nice guns!"

He hopped to the ground and flexed his arms for her in overly exaggerated poses, making ridiculous, dramatic faces while she laughed at him.

"Dork!" she giggled, grabbing his jacket from its place on the table and throwing it over his face.

Nate removed the jacket from his head and draped it over the seat of his bike.

Her gaze moved from his arms to his chest. He'd been in great shape three years ago but looked even fitter now, and his biceps and triceps had the perfect amount of definition. She tried not to wonder what he'd look like without his shirt on.

"Hey!" he said, interrupting her thoughts with a fake serious expression as he pointed at his face. "My eyes are up here!"

Anise laughed and pretended to give him a sheepish look while she bit her lower lip. "Uh, oh. Busted," she said, playing along with his game.

"I know it's hard, honey, but you're going to have to learn to control yourself around me," he scolded with a grin.

She laughed again and pulled her phone out of her bag. "Do you think you could check your ego long enough for us to take a few selfies? I'm looking extra cute tonight in this jacket you got me, and it would be a shame not to have a picture of it."

His eyes flashed as he walked over to her. "At least I own my big ego. What's your excuse, Miss Extra Cute Tonight?"

She hopped off the table with a giggle. "Hey, you picked out this jacket. If my ego is bigger because of my extra cuteness, it's entirely your fault." She raised the phone in front of their faces and snapped a few shots.

She scrolled through the photos she took and started laughing when she noticed Nate had purposely made some ridiculous faces in some of them. Cocking her head at him, she looked up at his laughing eyes. "Really?" Shaking her head, she handed him her phone and took several steps away. "I want a *good* picture of me in my jacket. Maybe we can do that if you're not in it?"

He laughed and aimed the camera. "Hey, be nice, honey."

She struck a pose. "Do you think your ego can handle not being in the photo?"

Nate smirked at the ground and shook his head. "Don't make me come over there."

"Oooooh," she replied with a giggle. "I'm so scared! What are you gonna do?"

"I'm warning you." A devilish look washed over his face.

"Whatever!" she said, taking a step backward when he took a step forward. "You got nothing!" She took several more steps back when he began walking toward her. She turned to run and let out an exuberant shriek when he caught up to her and grabbed her. She felt an arm surround her and fingers wiggling near her waist. Laughing and squirming, she smacked his hand away. "Okay, okay!" she surrendered in between giggles.

He wrapped his arms tightly around her from behind. "Will you be nice if I let you go?"

His breath brushing her ear shocked her out of the moment. *What the hell am I doing?!* The guilt for her inappropriateness started eating her stomach. *We were just joking around. How could I let it cross a line?* It'd all happened so fast, she hadn't seen it coming. Spending time with Nate felt exactly how it used to—the rest of the world disappeared when she was with him. But that couldn't happen anymore! She was with Jonathan now. Anise began talking with the intention of telling Nate that their behavior had to reflect the fact that they were friends only as she took hold of his bare forearms and gently untangled herself from his grip. "Nate, we're friends, and I can't—"

"Holy shit!" He interrupted her and immediately removed his arms from her grasp. "Honey, I'm going to have to warm up your hands before I let you start pawing at me again."

"What? I was *not* pawing at you!" She gave him a playful shove and opened her mouth to continue what she'd tried to tell him but stopped when he took her hands in his and blew some warm breath on them to heat them up.

"Is the rest of you cold, too?" he asked.

"A little," she admitted, silently cursing how good his hands felt on hers. How long would it take to get over her silly attraction to him? Because their innocent playful banter had somehow become flirting, and she hadn't meant for that to happen. She took her hands back and crossed her arms. "It was so warm today I didn't think it would cool down this much."

"Let's go somewhere warmer," Nate suggested. "Are you hungry?"

"Yeah, I could eat!"

They climbed back on his bike, and during the ride, she berated herself for how she'd let their playfulness cross a line. She hoped she hadn't given him the wrong idea. *Maybe he didn't think anything of it,* she reasoned with herself. *Maybe I can try to forgive myself and just not let it happen ever again.*

The bike came to a stop in front of The Blue Pineapple, a downtown bar that had music, dancing, great drinks, and surprisingly good food.

"You remembered this is my favorite bar?" Anise asked with surprise.

"Of course I did," he replied, as his eyes smiled at hers.

"Will you be getting some dessert as your first course?" she asked as they were seated at a table. "I remember you telling me how you like to do that when you go out to eat."

"You know, it's been so long since I ate any dessert at all, I almost forgot about that," Nate replied.

"Well, they have a peach cobbler, new for fall. It's the only dessert with no chocolate, so it's perfect for you. We could split it if you want."

He shook his head. "That habit stemmed from a bad memory I'd rather get past," Nate told her. "Maybe it's time I let that go."

"Okay," she said, happy that he seemed to be in a good place emotionally and was breaking through some of the hold his past traumas had on him. "So, what have you been up to since you got out?" Anise asked Nate when their food was brought to their table. She took a big bite of her burger.

"Got a haircut. Some new clothes. Tuned up the bike. Caught up with my buddies. We've got tickets to the game tomorrow."

"Scott and Peter?" she asked, remembering when she had met his friends years earlier.

He nodded. "Yeah."

She rested her hand on his arm as he wolfed down his meal. "You're eating really fast. You once asked me to remind you not to do that."

He put his burger down, looked at her hand on his arm, and grinned at her. "Thanks for setting me straight."

"You're welcome." She felt her cheeks flushing as

she pulled her hand away. *I shouldn't have touched him. Change the subject.* "So the game sounds fun. Anything else you've been up to?"

"This is going to sound boring, but Scott took care of my condo while I was gone, and I've been going through the mile-high stack of mail he left on my counter."

"I can't even imagine what three years' worth of mail looks like! Get anything good at least?"

"No," he said frowning. "I did get a couple letters I wasn't expecting. Dan and Grace each wrote me."

"Oh. What did they say?" she asked, curious.

"Dan wants me to come visit him. Says he has something very important to tell me."

Nate's face wore a flat expression, and Anise wasn't sure what he was thinking or if she should ask. "Are you going?"

"Of course not. I don't wanna see him. If he really wanted me to know whatever it is, he could've written it in the letter."

"That's true. But he is your father. Maybe he just misses you," said Anise.

He shrugged. "Not my problem."

"What about Grace's letter?"

"I haven't opened it. I'm just gonna toss it."

"Really? I don't think I could do that. I'd go the rest of my life wondering what the hell she wrote!"

Nate shrugged. "You have a point, honey. I'll think about it."

"You're not going to visit *her*, are you?" Her stomach turned at the thought of Grace.

"No way."

"Good. I couldn't hang out with you anymore if I knew you were still in contact with her. Grace tried to kill me, and she's been the source of a recurring nightmare these last three years. I wouldn't feel safe around you if she was still in your life. While we're on this topic, I should let you know that I also can't be your friend if you're ever going to do anything criminal again."

"No more illegal activities, I promise."

Anise's stomachache vanished at his words. She hoped that Jonathan was wrong and that she could trust Nate. "Good."

He nodded at the dance floor. "Do you still think you can dance circles around me?"

She smiled, remembering how she had said that to him the first time they met. "I do," she said. "From what I remember, you're a good dancer, but you've gotta be out of practice. Unless they had inmate dance parties in prison."

His face cringed. "Thank god they did *not*. Unless you count the times I replayed your dance moves in my head." He got up and offered her his hand. She took it, and he led her out to the dance floor in the adjoining room. "Show me what you got," he said with a grin.

"It's so fun to dance with someone who can actually move! Where'd you learn to dance anyway?" she asked as they swayed and bounced to the music.

"I picked it up here and there," was all he would tell her.

They danced to several more songs until Anise told him she needed a break. He bought her a drink, and they stood against the wall watching the other patrons dance.

"Oh my god, it's one in the morning already?" she exclaimed, grabbing Nate's wrist and looking at his watch. "Jonathan was expecting me hours ago!"

"Okay, I'll get you home then," Nate said, turning toward her. He stood in front of her and put one hand on the wall behind her, leaning in close. "Thanks for coming out tonight. It was fun."

"Thank *you*! I had a blast!" she said, looking up into the intensity of his blue stare.

He put his hand gently on the side of her face, leaned over, and kissed her. She felt her abdomen respond with a strong tingle to his kiss. But she pushed him back, moving her face away from his.

"Nate, no. What are you doing? You know I can't do this!" she scolded, narrowing her eyebrows at him. "I'm with Jonathan, and I don't cheat!"

He let out a breath. "Okay," he said as he looked at her inquisitively.

"I'm sorry about how I teased you when we were at the park tonight," she told him, her guilt growing.

"I'm not." His eyes twinkled at her.

"Stop. I feel terrible about it." She looked at the ground, her cheeks burning in shame. "I thought we were just joking around at first. I didn't mean for it to be anything more, but then it crossed a line. Absolutely no more flirting," she demanded, pointing a finger at him. "It led to this misunderstanding, and that needs to not happen again. Ever!" She walked past him and headed toward the door.

He followed her outside. "So you and Boy Scout?" he asked as they headed toward his bike.

"Me and *Jonathan*. Yes," she replied. "You knew that. I mentioned our relationship on the phone. More than once."

"Yeah, but you two were just friends for years."

"We were. But things changed. I need you to respect that or we can't be friends."

"So tell me about him. What makes him so special to you?"

Anise smiled as she thought about Jonathan. "Lots of things. He has a huge heart. Last weekend I went with him to the children's hospital. He goes there every month to sing and play guitar for the sick kids."

Nate stayed quiet, his face not really showing an expression.

Anise continued. "He's so intelligent—just got his doctorate. He's respectful to everyone. Passionate about his work and music. His family has always been so friendly and welcoming to me. And he makes a new friend practically everywhere he goes. I can't even count the number of friends he has. They're all really good people, too. And of course I love watching him perform on the weekends!"

"Perform?"

"Yeah, he fronts Even Fury—that's his band."

Nate shook his head. "Haven't heard of them."

"Yes you have. Remember when we went to the Concert in the Park? They were one of the bands that performed."

Nate shrugged. "I was more focused on you, honey."

"They're really good! You should come with me to hear them play sometime."

"Sure." He nodded unenthusiastically.

"And when my parents were killed a couple years ago, he helped me with absolutely everything." Her eyes grew misty. "There was so much to do and take care of; I wouldn't have been able to do it without him. You know, I almost didn't invite my parents to the dinner that night. If I hadn't... I know I've talked a lot about not having a great childhood, but they're still my parents. I still love and miss them."

"Of course you do," Nate said softly. "And I remember you telling me about the car accident. It wasn't your fault."

"It feels that way." She dabbed her eyes with her sleeve. "Jonathan's been so good to me, such a good friend, and we fell in love." She watched Nate stand there and stare at her, saying nothing. Ashamed of her behavior that night, she wanted only to leave. She'd never acted so inappropriately before; what the hell had come over her?

Am I a terrible person?

She grabbed her helmet off of the rearview mirror of his motorcycle. "I need you to drop me off at Jonathan's. I promised him I'd come over after you and I were done hanging out."

Nate didn't move. "Why are you here with me, Anise?"

The intensity of his eyes made her flustered, and her words came out rushed from her wavering voice. "I... was happy to see you again, and it was so easy to fall into the same way we used to be; I forgot myself for a minute, and I hate myself for it. I'm sorry I gave you the wrong impression. But we're friends, nothing more." She wiped away a few guilty tears that ran down her cheeks.

"Really? And what's that supposed to look like?" he asked. "For the last couple years we've been talking almost every day."

She gave him a half-shrug. "I can't see you every day. I don't see my *other* friends every day."

"My point exactly. You made a lot of time for me when no one else had to know about it."

"Nate..."

"And you're so in love, yet coming out with me tonight was still worth pissing off your boyfriend," he added calmly.

Anise opened her mouth but nothing came out.

Nate put on his helmet and straddled his bike. "Remember that after I deliver you to Boy Scout tonight." He started the engine before she could respond.

JONATHAN CHECKED HIS WATCH WHEN HE heard Nate's motorcycle pull up to his apartment building. Past one in the morning. What did they do for so long? All evening he'd been stressed and worried about Anise. Nate was reckless and couldn't be trusted to keep her safe. Jonathan had tried to keep his mind occupied so he wouldn't get worked up about it. He'd taken his dog Max for a long hike and had dinner and drinks with some friends. But once he got home, the worry caught up to him. He'd had another one of those intense stress-induced migraines for the last several hours. It had not been a good night.

He'd also just listened to a voicemail from Dr. Smithton asking him to try to get Anise to come by the museum. For some reason, his mind had gotten hazy after that.

Anise unlocked Jonathan's front door. "Oh good, you're still up!" she said, her eyes locking with his. She turned to Nate who had walked her to the door. "Good night."

Nate gave her a slight nod in return.

Jonathan glared at him, and Nate looked back with an intensity Jonathan didn't like.

Anise closed the door and locked it. "Sorry I'm so late!" she apologized. "It got too chilly to keep riding, so we went dancing instead and lost track of time."

"You could've used that time to visit Dr. S. instead."

Anise gave Jonathan a bewildered look as she pulled off her boots. "Why would I visit Dr. Smithton on a Saturday night?" She took off her leather jacket and pushed up the sleeves of her sweater.

Jonathan jumped up, walked over to her, and picked up her arms by her wrists. "How did you get these bruises on your arms?" In his horror, his voice raised. "Did Nate hurt you?"

She looked at her arms with a confused expression. "I don't have any bruises," she said. "And your eyes are glazed over again. Do you have another headache?"

"Yeah!" he shouted. "But don't change the subject! Why are you lying for him?"

They heard the door handle rattle. "Anise?" called Nate from outside the door.

She headed to the door, but Jonathan grabbed her arm to stop her. "Don't let him in! He hurt you!"

"Anise?" came Nate's voice as he pounded on the door. "Are you okay?"

"Don't answer it!" Jonathan commanded.

"I'll just let him know everything's fine..."

"No! I don't want him in here. He hurt you!"

They heard a loud kick on the door. Max started

barking.

"No, he didn't! I'm fine, look," she said, holding out her arms.

Another loud kick and the door swung open. Nate headed straight to Jonathan. "Is there a problem in here?"

Max put his front paws on Nate's chest and wagged his tail. Watchdog duties were never something Max took seriously. Nate gave him a quick pet before gently pushing him off.

"Yeah!" Jonathan got in Nate's face. "A big problem! You're bruising my girlfriend!"

"I didn't lay a hand on her!" Nate protested.

"Jonathan, he didn't hurt me," Anise interjected.

Jonathan's headache worsened like electrical shocks running through his brain. "Why are you sticking up for this psychopath?" he demanded. The pain started radiating outward from what felt like the inside of his brain. He let out a cry of agony as he pulled hard on his light brown hair in an attempt to lessen the pounding in his skull.

Nate grabbed Jonathan by the collar of his shirt, spun him around and slammed his back into the wall so hard that Jonathan's glasses fell off. "What the *fuck* was that?" Nate yelled in Jonathan's face.

The pain from his headache was so great, Jonathan couldn't respond. His back hurt now too, and his world was blurry without his glasses. He let out an embarrassing groan instead and pulled on his hair to relieve some of the pain.

"Nate, stop! Let him go!" Anise demanded, pulling on Nate's arms until he dropped them. "Go home, Nate."

"I'm not leaving you alone with him. He's lost his mind."

"No, he hasn't!" she insisted. "He has another migraine that's affecting his vision. He thought he saw bruises on my arms. He needs to relax so he can feel better, but that won't happen as long as you're here."

Nate didn't look convinced.

"Just go, please."

"Fine." Nate walked to the door, looking back at Jonathan. "But it's against my better judgment."

"I'll call you if I need you, I promise," Anise reassured Nate.

Nate motioned to the door jamb where it had bent from him kicking his way into the apartment. "You should get that fixed," he told Jonathan before he left.

"You fucking asshole!" Jonathan started after Nate with clenched fists but felt Anise grabbing his arm to stop him. "No," she told him. "The last thing I want is for you two to start fighting again."

Jonathan sighed and pulled on his hair a little more. Now that Nate was gone, he was starting to feel better. He picked up his glasses. Luckily, they'd sustained no damage.

"Come on," she said to Jonathan. "Let's get you to bed. I'm driving you to your doctor's appointment on Monday."

"You don't have to do that," Jonathan insisted, trying to bend the door jamb back into place.

"Yes, I do. You can't drive as long as your vision is impaired." She closed the door, put him to bed, and crawled in next to him.

He put an arm around her and tried to fall asleep but ended up staring at the ceiling for most of the night.

Part 2

A HUGE COINCIDENCE?

Chapter 8

Friday, February 8, 1957

G race waited for Morty in his room as he finished dressing. "Hurry up," she told him. "I'm starving!" "Hold your horses, woman," Morty called from the bathroom. "I'll be right out!"

Grace sat at his desk and impatiently drummed her fingers. She saw his research project notes for the grant award competition sticking out of a book. She opened the book and pulled out the notes, reading with curiosity as to what her friend's project might entail. As she read, she felt a knot in her stomach. Her project was good, but Morty's was better. A lot better. There was no way her project could beat his, and there was no time to start again as the presentations were the next day.

She put his notes back where she found them and began pacing his room. What was she going to do now? Winning that grant was her only hope of attending grad school. If she didn't win, she couldn't afford to pay for it herself, and graduate school would be a good way to show prospective employers that she was serious about working and having a life-long career. She wasn't someone who only wanted a job until she found a husband. As if she'd ever trust a man to take care of her anyway. She needed her own money, and she needed to ensure she'd be able to find a good job.

"Okay," Morty said, emerging from the bathroom. "Let's go!"

They walked downtown to a favorite hang-out of the local college students and ordered cheeseburgers and cherry sodas.

"You're really quiet tonight," Morty said. "Is everything okay?"

"I'm nervous about the grant presentations tomorrow," Grace replied, glad that the topic had been brought up naturally. She wanted to talk to him about it. Maybe he'd be willing to drop out. There'd be no way she could lose then. The other applicants had IQs of two below grass.

"You're brilliant, Grace. I'm sure you'll win, hands down."

"Why are you entering if you're so sure I'll win?"

"I'm pretty proud of my project," he boasted. "I think I have a slight chance to win, and if I can, it would be a great honor. As you know, the winner gets not only the full scholarship, but also gets their work published and is invited to go on the trip to Europe for the series of lectures and site visits for ancient cultures in the area. It would be my dream come true to meet everyone on that tour. If I didn't at least try to win, I'd never forgive myself."

"Right, that would be incredible," Grace agreed. She looked down at the table, hatching a plan she hoped she wouldn't have to carry out.

He frowned. "It's more than just nerves; I can tell. What is it? You can tell me."

She looked up at him and saw the concern in his gray eyes. "I'm scared, Morty. You know my history. There's no way I can pay for school if I don't get this grant. I've applied for other scholarships, but even if I get them, they don't pay for enough. I'm worried that employers won't take me seriously without a graduate degree. What if they don't want to hire me because they think I'll marry and have a baby soon? And if they won't hire me, how will I be able to find a job that'll pay for living expenses *and* school tuition? I simply cannot afford to lose tomorrow."

"I'll help you pay for school if you don't win."

She looked at him with a flash of hope. "Why would you do that?"

He looked confused. "Because you're my friend, and I love you."

She frowned as she thought about his offer. Morty's family had money—lots of money. But his money came from his parents, not him. "That won't work," she said. "Your parents hate me."

"They don't hate you," Morty argued. "They just wanted me to pay attention to their rich friends' socialite daughters, not..." He paused.

"Not a gutter rat like me," Grace interjected, her eyes narrowed.

"That's not what I was going to say. Don't worry, Grace. If you lose, I'll help you figure something out, I promise."

Grace felt anxiety squeezing her chest. She couldn't count on Morty to give her money. He wouldn't be able to talk his parents into the idea, first of all. Secondly, even if he could get the money, he was only offering because he thought he was in love with her. Once he met another woman, would her funding be cut off? And third, if she accepted his charity, she'd never stop hearing her father in her head saying she was a leech. She felt sick to her stomach about what she was about to do to the only friend she had, but she couldn't see any other options, and she had to do what needed to be done in order to survive.

She took his hand. "Thank you for your kindness," she told him. "I'm feeling a lot better now."

"Of course," he said, a look of surprise washing over his face when she intertwined her fingers with his. "You're welcome."

She grinned at him. "Do you have a dime?"

He gave her one, and she dropped it into the jukebox so she could hear her favorite song of the moment. Walking back to their table, she grabbed Morty's hands and pulled him up. "Dance with me," she commanded.

"What?" he said, laughing, as she dragged him to where other patrons were bopping about. "Since when do we dance?"

"Exactly! We never dance. So let's do it now!"

He gave in to her, and they danced to her song and the next several. They weren't the best dancers in the place, but they certainly had the most fun. When they were exhausted, they walked into the streets of Springfield hand-in-hand.

"You just turned 21. Buy me some whiskey," she demanded, laughing.

He laughed too. "Have you ever had whiskey before?"

"No! So it's high time I tried it!" She grinned at him. "Please?" she said, wrapping her arms around his waist and looking up at him.

"Okay," he agreed, his face full of doubt.

When he was in the liquor store, she slipped into the drugstore next door, quickly made a purchase, and waited for him outside.

"Where do you want to go?" he asked her as he stepped out of the liquor store.

"Let's go drink it in your room!"

They headed back to his place. "What has gotten into you, Grace?"

"I need to let loose a bit," she explained. "And I want

to show you appreciation for your generosity."

He looked confused but didn't question her. When they reached his room, he opened the bottle of whiskey and handed it to her. She took a swig and then spit it out all over his floor.

"Ugh!" she exclaimed. "That's disgusting!"

Morty laughed as he grabbed a towel and mopped up her mess. "I thought you'd feel that way," he said. "So I got you this." He handed her a bottle of white wine.

"You know me so well. Thank you!"

They drank until they were both on the floor laughing at anything and everything.

"We should not be doing this. We have the grant presentations tomorrow!" Morty said, giving Grace a goofy chuckle.

"We definitely should not!" she agreed with a giggle. When he went to the bathroom, she crushed up some sleeping pills she'd bought from the drugstore and put them in his drink.

"I need to get to bed," he told her, when he came back into the room.

"Okay," she agreed. "Just finish this first," she said, handing him his drink.

He waved away the drink. "I've had a lot of fun tonight. But I've also had too many of those. I'll sleep on the floor if you want to stay over. You can take the bed."

She frowned. Her plan couldn't fail now. "Finish this," she commanded again, "and we'll *both* take the bed."

He paused. "What?"

She beckoned him with her finger. "Come down here, giant."

He leaned over with a confused look on his face. She grabbed him by the cheeks and kissed him softly. Stunned, he stood up straight and looked at her, wide-eyed.

"Do I have to say it again?" she asked him, handing him his glass. "Finish this, and then we'll both take the bed."

He grabbed the glass, downed the last of the alcohol in it, and swept her up into a passionate kiss. Morty's lips were tender and firm at the same time, and she enjoyed the kiss far more than she thought she would. He placed her gently on his bed, removed his shirt, and lay next to her, his hand traveling up her blouse. He looked at her face and paused. "We can stop if you don't want to do this."

She'd been thinking about how he may never forgive her for drugging him so he'd miss the grant presentations. If this was the last night she'd have with her best friend, she wanted to feel him as much as possible. Plus, the passion he was displaying for her was unlike anything she'd ever experienced, and it was making her feel something for him as well that extended beyond friendship. "I want to," she answered honestly. "I'm just nervous."

His hand stroked her hair. "You don't have to be nervous. I *love* you, and I always will."

For the first time in her life, she truly did feel loved, and it made her eyes well up. "I love you, too," she said, her voice shaking. She fought the ridiculous tears with everything she had, not wanting them to ruin this beautiful moment.

It was the first time for the both of them, and he made love to her gently until the drugs knocked him out.

Her eyes welled up again, but this time she couldn't stop the tears from falling. It was the first time she'd cried since Danny was killed. Morty would never forgive her for this, and she'd be all alone in the world again. She covered him with a blanket and walked back to her room, drunk and sobbing.

Saturday, February 9, 1957

Sleep didn't come easy, and the early morning hours ticked by quickly. Grace tossed and turned and then got up and went to the grant presentations. She felt nauseated and her head pounded, but when it was her turn, she stood up, smoothed out her dress clothes and hair, and presented her project with the utmost confidence. Looking at the faces of the judges while she was in front of them gave her even more confidence. They were smiling and attentive. Some nodded while others wore a look of concentration. After her presentation was complete, she took her seat with a sense of pride. The good feeling didn't last long, however. Grace felt even sicker than when she had woken up that morning when Morty's name was called and everyone wondered where he was. She could only shrug and say, "I haven't heard from him this morning."

"We unfortunately can't wait for him any longer," one of the judges stated, after everyone else had taken their turn. "Thank you everyone; you all did a wonderful job. We'll now consult on your presentations and post the name of the winner within two hours."

Grace went back to her room to nap until the winner was posted. She took an aspirin and lay on her bed with a cool, wet hand towel folded over her eyes as she thought about her actions the night before. It probably wouldn't do any good to go to Morty and apologize. Even if she explained her reasons, how could he forgive that? She certainly wouldn't forgive anyone who would do that to her. She took away his dream, and he'd be devastated. She couldn't exactly say she was sorry either, because she wasn't. Those dimwits who competed against her didn't stand a chance. That scholarship was hers, hands down.

After two hours, she headed back to the hall where she'd presented. As confident as she was, there were still a few butterflies in her stomach. She looked at the sheet of paper on the bulletin board that revealed the name of the winner, holding her breath. It said, "Please congratulate: Grace Polk!" She let out a sigh of relief.

"Congratulations, Grace," said a familiar voice behind her. She spun around to face him.

"Morty."

"I'm sure your presentation was fantastic." His eyes were slightly narrowed and his tone flat.

"It was. That's why I won," she agreed haughtily, feeling on edge.

"That and the sleeping pills you slipped me last night." He held up the bottle of pills she'd forgotten to hide from him in her drunken stupor. Not that it mattered. He was smart and would've figured it out anyway. "Why?" His eyes now looked more sad than angry.

She opened her mouth to answer him then closed it again. What was the point? She didn't want to hash it out with him for a long, painful good-bye. Best to just end it now and be done with it. "Leave me alone!" she demanded, as she pushed him away and ran.

Monday, March 18, 1957

FIVE WEEKS WENT BY, AND GRACE stepped out of her room to go to class. As she attempted to close the door behind her, she felt it being pushed open. Her arm was grabbed and she was ushered right back into her room. She looked up at the offending party. "Morty, what the hell are you doing?"

"You've been avoiding me for over a month!" he barked at her. "Enough of this. We need to talk."

"I have nothing to say," Grace stated, slightly impressed with his forcefulness.

"You have plenty to say, and neither of us is leaving this room until you do."

She narrowed her eyes at him. "Fine. What do you

want to hear?" she snarled.

"The truth, Grace! Why did you drug me?"

"I already told you," she said in a quieter tone. "I was scared."

"Of *what*?"

"Don't you remember our conversation the night before? I can't afford to pay for school myself. Without a graduate degree, I can't get a job that'll pay me enough to support myself. I was afraid of ending up back on the streets." She looked down at the ground.

"I told you I'd help you," he reminded her.

"How the hell would that have worked?" she demanded. "Like I said, your parents wouldn't have given you the money to help me. Where else would you have gotten it?"

"We both could've worked. I don't know."

"You don't know. Well, there's a brilliant plan!" she said sarcastically.

"I would've found a way."

"Right. Until you found some rich, socialite woman to love, just like your parents wanted. Then I would've been on my own again." She took a deep breath in. All morning she'd felt queasy and this upsetting conversation wasn't helping.

Morty's face showed how offended he was at her last comment. "What kind of a friend do you think I am? I would never let you end up back on the streets, no matter my relationship status. I never wanted those airhead socialites anyway. I always wanted you." He looked at her sadly. "Besides, the last time we spent time together, I thought I *had* found a woman to love. Even if you'd decided you still weren't ready to be with me, I would've waited for you. I'd wait forever for you, Grace. I'd wait a lifetime. I'd wait *two* lifetimes. Please tell me you believe that, because I've never spoken anything more true."

She glared at him. "Such pretty words with such shallow meaning. If you really loved me, you would've dropped out of the competition!"

"I can love you and follow my dreams at the same time!" he replied. "When I said I'd help you, I meant it. Why don't you believe me?"

Grace's queasiness suddenly got the better of her. She ran to her bathroom and became physically ill.

"Grace?" Morty came after her. "Are you okay?"

"Yes," she said, wiping her mouth. "Don't worry about it."

"Are you ill?" he asked in a worried tone.

"No, I'm fine."

"But you never get sick. Are you that upset about what happened?"

"No! Just leave it alone!"

He paused. "Wait, are you pregnant?"

She looked at him and then looked at the ground. "Yes," she whispered, bracing for his upset reaction.

"Really?" he laughed. "That's amazing!"

"You're happy about this?" she asked in disbelief.

His face beamed. "When I was a young teen and being picked on all the time, I was severely beaten one day while walking home from school. Someone found me on the side of the road and took me to the hospital. Due to the damage, I was told it was likely that I'd never be able to have children. This is my one in a million chance to be a father!"

"I didn't know you wanted kids," said Grace, sitting on her bed.

"I've always wanted to have a family of my own! I just thought it could never happen." He sat next to her and took her hand. "I don't want you to feel alone," he told her. "I'll help you, I promise." He gave her a big grin.

She laughed. "Aren't you supposed to be mad at me?"

"I don't want to be mad anymore. And it's not just because of this wonderful news. I didn't realize how scared you were. I know you told me before, but it didn't sink in until you told me again, right now. You were asking for my help, and I didn't do a good enough job making you believe that everything was going to be fine. I'm sorry."

"*You're* apologizing to *me*?" she asked him, bewildered. "I'm sorry for not trusting you. It's really hard for me..."

"I know," he said, putting an arm around her and kissing the top of her head.

They sat in silence as he held her. He looked so happy. She didn't have the heart to tell him she had a meeting the next day with someone her next door neighbor Sue said would do an abortion.

Tuesday, March 19, 1957

THE NEXT MORNING, MORTY STOPPED BY her room again. "How are you?" he inquired.

She shrugged.

"What's wrong? Are you okay?" he asked, concerned.

"I don't want to be a mother, Morty."

"What are you talking about?"

"I'm afraid," she admitted. She took a deep breath to gather her courage to tell him about the abortion. "I don't know how to be a good parent, so I—" Visions of her father passed through her mind.

"You're going to be a great mother. Don't worry!" he interrupted, smiling.

She frowned. He was far too happy to see how unhappy she was. "No, what I'm trying to say is—"

Morty interrupted her again. "Grace, there's something I want to ask you."

"What?"

He got down on one knee and pulled out a platinum, one-and-a-half caret diamond ring. The center stone was a round cut and was flanked by baguettes. "Will you marry me?"

Grace put a hand to her mouth. This was all going way too fast. She looked at Morty smiling lovingly up at her, and she couldn't take it. "Morty, get up!" she commanded him. "Put that thing away," she added, pointing to the ring. "I have somewhere I have to be." She ran out of the room.

THREE BUSES AND TWO HOURS LATER, Grace arrived at an apartment building several towns away. She knocked and was let in by a middle-aged woman. The woman led her to the kitchen table, which was covered with a sheet and had a catheter and wire and some other supplies on top. Everything looked like torture devices.

"That's the doctor over there," the woman said, pointing to the man holding a cigarette on the other side of the room.

His dark eyes seemed to reflect his soul as he looked at Grace. That one look made her feel more judged than she ever had in her life. "It'll be five hundred dollars," he told her, dropping his cigarette in an ashtray.

"Five hundred!?" she exclaimed. "I didn't know it would be that much. I only have *one* hundred. Can we work something out?" she asked, even though she'd been having second thoughts all day. Maybe marrying Morty and having a family with him would be nice. What was she so afraid of, anyway? She wasn't her father. She had done a good job of taking care of Danny. Maybe she *could* be a good mother. She put her hands on her abdomen and felt a wave of love for the little life inside of her. Smiling to herself, she realized there was no way she could go through with this abortion.

Before she could express her change of heart, the doctor walked toward her, looking her up and down. "I believe so," he said. "You're obviously a tramp who enjoys the company of men. Keep company with me before the procedure, and I'll lower the price to one hundred."

Grace slapped him hard across his face and turned to leave.

The doctor grabbed her arm. "Where do you think you're going?" he asked her.

"I no longer want your services!" She glared at him, trying to pull her arm out of his grip.

"That's fine," the doctor said, his grip on her arm tightening. "But first there's the matter of payment for wasting my time. If you won't spread your legs, I'll take that money whether we do the procedure or not."

Grace reached up and pushed a pressure point near his neck until he let out a wail and sunk to his knees. She grabbed her purse and darted for the door.

He caught up to her and slammed her head into the door. Stars danced in front of her eyes as she reached up and held her head, feeling a bump growing under her palm. He grabbed her money out of her purse. "You better make sure I never see you again!" he warned before throwing her and her purse out into the hallway.

Grace couldn't stop her rage. "You better make sure I never see *you* again!" she screamed in his face. "Because if I do, I'll fucking kill you!"

The doctor stepped out into the hallway, grabbed her by the arms, dragged her the three steps to the edge of the stairwell, and gave her a shove. She tumbled down the flight of stairs, receiving merciless assaults from the steps, banister, and wall. Right before she reached the bottom, she blacked out.

She had no idea how much time had passed when she woke. Getting up, she smoothed out her clothes and realized how much pain she was in. Nothing felt broken, but her entire body was turning black and blue. She looked up the stairwell and wondered if the doctor was still up there. If he was, she should leave as soon as possible. She noticed her body start to tremble with fear at the mere thought of how easily that doctor had hurt her. She was lucky to be alive. Gathering her pride and her belongings that had fallen out of her purse, she left the building and hurried to the bus stop. Tears threatened to spill over, but she wouldn't allow herself to cry. *Stop it! You're stronger than this. Don't be weak*, she scolded herself. She took the bus home, counting down the minutes when she could be with Morty and tell him she'd changed her mind.

✳✳✳

MORTY ANSWERED THE KNOCK ON HIS door. "Grace." He looked like he was in great pain. "Go away."

"What? No, Morty, let me in. I need to talk to you." She pulled her long sleeves down until they halfway covered her hands. She didn't feel like explaining her bruises.

"I know where you were," he said. He sat in his desk chair and appeared exhausted.

She stepped inside his room and closed the door. "What do you mean?"

"I mean," he said, standing up, "that when I came back to your room to look for you, your big-mouthed neighbor Sue told me where you were!" He paused, his face turning red and his eyes releasing big, rolling tears. "Abortion? That's illegal and dangerous! And more importantly, how could you kill our baby?"

Grace looked down at the ground. "I already told you I was scared I'd be a bad mother. But when I got to the doctor's apartment and thought about the finality of my decision, I changed my mind. I thought about how I loved taking care of my baby brother. I forgot how good that felt. Having a family with you sounds really wonderful. You'll be a great father." Taking his hand, she looked up at him. "You'll be a great husband, too, if the offer is still on the table."

"You didn't go through with it?" he asked her, his eyes wide open with a look of relief.

"No," she said, putting her hand on her abdomen.

"And you're actually accepting my marriage proposal?" He wiped his eyes with the backs of his hands.

She laughed. "Yes, does that surprise you?"

"Well, yes, to be honest. I wasn't sure you'd ever love me."

"I do love you."

He went to his desk drawer and pulled out the diamond ring. Getting down on one knee in front of her, he slipped the ring on her finger, and she moved her hand back and forth, watching the stone sparkle in the light.

He grabbed her hands and looked at her, misty-eyed. "I'm so happy," he told her as he stood up.

"Me too," she said, smiling up at him.

He kissed her, picked her up, and placed her gently on his bed. "You need your rest," he told her. "What can I bring you? What can I do for you?"

"Just sit here with me. I don't need anything..." She paused, holding her abdomen after feeling a strange twinge.

"Are you okay?" he asked her, worried.

"Yes, fine." Then, she let out a cry of pain. "I'm not okay!" she said, doubling over. "Morty, what's happening?" she asked him, standing up.

"You're bleeding," he said, pointing to the back of her skirt.

She stumbled and almost fainted. He picked her up and ran her to his car. Driving as fast as possible, they arrived at the emergency room in record time. He came around to the passenger's side of the car, picked her up again, and carried her into the hospital. "My fiancé needs help!" he yelled. "She's pregnant and in pain!" Nurses came with a wheelchair as Grace continued to cry out in pain. As they wheeled her away, she looked back to see Morty watching her from the waiting room, nervously wringing his hands.

A while later, Morty poked his head into her room and she looked at him from her bed. "I lost the baby," she told him in a whisper.

He paused for a moment, and then his eyes narrowed. "What?"

"Morty, I lost the baby," she repeated, a little louder.

He sat in the chair next to her bed and put his face in his hands. When he looked up again, he wiped away the single tear that was running down his cheek. "You must think I'm the biggest idiot in the world."

She felt a knot in her stomach. "Of course not! What are you talking about?"

"I know how abortions work," he told her. "You get the procedure done, and a few hours later, you start to bleed and lose the baby."

"Wait, you think I lied to you about not going through with the abortion?" Grace asked him with disgust.

"So you're going to sit there and tell me this is all just a huge coincidence?" he demanded.

"Look, Morty, I didn't want to tell you this, but I guess I have to now. When I was at the doctor's, he was angry that I changed my mind and wasted his time. He told me I'd have to pay anyway and he…" She paused for a moment, not wanting to relive the horrors of the day. She looked down. "He propositioned me," she continued quietly, "and when I refused him, we had a physical fight, he stole my money, and then he threw me out the front door. He told me I better make sure he never sees me again. I was angry and threatened his life. That's when he threw me down the stairs. See, I have all these bruises from the fall. I think that's what made me miscarry." She lifted the arms of the hospital gown to show him her injuries.

Morty didn't bother to look. "Save it, Grace," he snapped. "You just went and did whatever you wanted without talking to me about it first—again! And you lied to me about it—*again!*" He shook his head. "I should've know better than to trust you again after you drugged me. You're right, I *am* the biggest idiot in the world!"

"You're not an idiot! And I'm not lying!" she insisted.

"I wish I could believe you. I really do," he said, getting up from the chair. "But I'm not falling for your lies twice." He headed for the door.

"Morty, where are you going?" she asked him in a desperate tone. "Come back! Please!"

He turned to look at her when he reached the door. She'd never seen him look more in pain than at this moment. "Good-bye, Grace," he managed to choke out before he left her room.

"MORTY!" she yelled. "COME BACK!" But he never returned. She turned on her side so her back was to the door, stared at her beautiful engagement ring, and sobbed. She hated crying and always tried not to, so as not to be weak. However, this was the second worst day of her life and she felt she deserved to be lenient with herself. The only reason she got any sleep that night is because she held on to the hope that Morty might have a change of heart and believe her after all.

Wednesday, March 20, 1957

MORTY WAS FILING PAPERS ALONE IN Professor Dromly's office when he heard a tapping on the door. Grace poked her head in the room. "Morty, can we talk?" she asked him in a soft voice.

He looked up. She stood there looking healthy and just as beautiful as always. He still loved her and wanted more than anything to hold her. But he'd promised himself he wouldn't forgive her this time. He deserved better than someone who lied to him. "Grace. I'm glad you're here."

"You are?" she asked, looking surprised and happy at the same time. She entered the small office and closed the door behind her.

"Yes, I forgot to do this last night." He grabbed her left hand and removed the engagement ring from her finger. "You won't be needing this any longer."

"Morty, please..."

"I realize that next year we'll be in the same graduate program, and we'll have to work together. I would appreciate it if we could be civil to one another in the working environment. But aside from that, I never want to see your lying face again."

Grace's words trembled. "Morty, I—"

"I don't want to hear anything you have to say," he told her. "There's no room for a lying, unethical, manipulative bitch in my life anymore. *Get out.*"

Her sad eyes welled up, and she took his hand. "Morty, I didn't—"

"Shut up!" he told her, pulling his hand out of her grip. "GET OUT!" He opened the door for her and waited for her to go. When she stepped out, he slammed the door shut behind her and locked it. He took out his handkerchief and pressed it to his eyes to stop the tears. He tried to think of something else that might distract him from the heavy, crushing pain in his chest.

He remembered how a little over a month before, Professor Dromly had shown him and Grace the old texts in the library about the Armor Jewelry, and Grace had left early to prepare for the grant presentation competition, which would be the next day, while Morty stayed behind. As Morty searched through them, Professor Dromly left him alone to enjoy them.

Hours went by before Morty put them back on the shelf. Noticing a hole in the wall behind the shelf, he moved several books out of the way, pulled the shelf out as far as he could, and peered into the hole to see if any books had fallen in. He thought he saw something and reached his hand through the wall. What he found was a cardboard box. He had to contort himself into an awkward position, but he managed to pull the box out of the wall and peer inside. To his amazement, the box contained another book about the Armor Jewelry! Fascinated, he flipped through it. On one of the pages, it showed a cuff along with the amulet, ring, and earrings that had been worn by the ancient Mallandian warriors. He read a passage that explained the cuff was used to prevent mutiny in the Mallandian army.

A cuff? A fourth piece of Armor Jewelry?

Someone must've found this text and was keeping it a secret. But why and who? Could this be Dromly's work? Did he know that the powers of the Jewelry were real? Did Dromly perhaps suspect him and Grace of killing Richard Woods with the ring? Wanting to ponder about it more, he tore out the page in the book that featured the bracelet cuff and put the page in his backpack. After starting to walk away, he thought better of it and decided to take the entire book before zipping up his bag and getting ready to go get some dinner with Grace.

Snapping out of his daydream, Morty sat in Dromly's office and pressed the handkerchief to his eyes again. Thinking of something else wasn't working. Grace was in so many of his memories. And she'd betrayed him. He never wanted to see her again. But how could he possibly go on without her?

AFTER MORTY SLAMMED THE DOOR ON her, Grace became overwhelmed with grief. She leaned on the wall next to Dromly's office door and slowly slid down to the ground where she sat with her head in her hands. *Don't be so weak!* she scolded herself, but the tears came anyway.

Morty was the only friend she had, and now he hated her.

"Are you okay?" asked a male voice.

Grace lifted her head high enough to see a nice pair of men's shoes standing in front of her. Embarrassed that someone should see her being so weak, she didn't lift her head higher. "I'm fine!" she snapped.

"You don't look fine," he commented. "Can I do anything to help you?"

She was about to snap at him again when Morty opened the office door. "What the hell are you still doing here?" he demanded of her.

"Leave me alone, Morty!" she exclaimed, discreetly grabbing a tissue from her purse to wipe her eyes.

"Go home, Grace! Or do you have more lies to tell me?" he asked her harshly.

The stranger with the nice shoes stepped up to Morty. "I believe the lady asked you to leave her alone, Smithton."

"What business is this of yours?" Morty demanded.

"When I see a lady being mistreated, I make it my business," the stranger answered.

Grace was impressed by the unknown man. No one had ever stood up for her like that before. In their first meeting, this stranger had protected her like she'd always hoped Morty would but never did. She watched as Morty cowardly ran away from the confrontation by slamming the door. *Typical.*

The stranger offered her his hands. "Let me help you up."

"I don't need help," she replied as she looked away. *I'm strong*, she reminded herself.

"Of course you don't," he answered with a smile that could be heard in his voice. "But I'd appreciate it if you'd allow me to be a gentleman and help you up anyway."

She looked up at the stranger for the first time and couldn't help but notice how handsome he was. His jet black hair looked almost as good as his face, and his cobalt blue eyes sparkled at her. "All right," she agreed and gave him her hands. "Thank you," she said softly, after he pulled her up.

"You're welcome," he replied, looking at her with a gaze that she found mesmerizing.

She felt right away that this was a man she wanted to get to know. "I'm Grace Polk," she said, introducing herself and offering him her hand.

He shook it. "I'm Thomas. Thomas Brevain."

MORTY FUMED INSIDE DROMLY'S OFFICE AS he paced back and forth. *Who the hell does Brevain think he is?* Thomas Brevain was a graduate student and another assistant of Dromly's. Dromly seemed to value his contributions, but Morty felt that there was something off about Brevain even though no one else appeared to agree. His curiosity got the better of him and he peeked out the door to see if Thomas was still talking to Grace. He saw them walking together at the end of the hall. Were they actually laughing together? Grace had just been dumped by her fiancé, and she was *laughing*? In that moment, Morty hated her as much as he had once loved her.

Morty slammed the door again. They deserved each other. What did people see in Thomas that they didn't see in him? Grace seemed to be taking a shine to him. Dromly gave more responsibility to Thomas than to him, and they always had their heads together about something. Their whispering stopped whenever Morty entered the room. *The whole world is against me!*

In a fit of escalating rage, Morty locked the office door, dug through files, and rooted through desk drawers in an attempt to discover whatever secret Brevain and Dromly surely shared. He found a key that didn't fit the desk, filing cabinet, or door. He searched behind the wall art for a safe. When he found nothing, he started pulling up the carpet from a corner he had always noticed was loose. "Ha!" he exclaimed when he found a small trap door. He opened it and pulled out a metal box. Sticking the key in the lock, he turned it, and it opened. He pulled out a piece of paper with Thomas's handwriting on it and read through the notes under his breath. "A redheaded seer is needed to read the wisdom on the Plate of Destiny. Her powers must be initiated by the seer's wand and then activated with the cuff."

He stopped reading for a moment to ponder that. "So the cuff has more uses than just an anti-mutiny tool." And was the seer's wand the same wand that Dromly asked Grace to focus her semester project on? His thoughts then turned to the Plate of Destiny. It supposedly had all the secrets of life and death written on it. He'd learned about it in one of Dromly's books he'd found, and from the notes he'd just read, it seemed Brevain and Dromly were hell-bent on finding it.

He looked back down at the notes Thomas had made. Much of it was written with only key words, short hand, and unintelligible scribbles. There was one part, however, that was all too clear. "Oh, god!" he choked out as he studied Thomas's detailed plan for the Plate of Destiny—*and for Grace*—thinking he might be ill. Grace was to be the redheaded seer, but she wasn't to know about their plan until the time came. They didn't trust her to not find the Plate behind their backs and keep it for herself. And if she wasn't willing to read the wisdom on the Plate for them, they'd force her in a way that sounded like medieval torture. With shaking hands, he put the notes back in the lockbox and the lockbox back under the floor. He covered the floor with the carpet. Reaching into Dromly's cabinet, he grabbed a whiskey bottle and took a swig to calm his nerves.

Now he knew Brevain and Dromly's secrets. Now he understood their plan. There was only one thing left to figure out. What was he going to do with this information?

Chapter 9

Present day

Monday, September 14, 2015

A nise drove home after dropping Jonathan off. She'd driven him to his doctor's appointment in the late afternoon and hadn't been happy with what she'd heard. The doctor had said that migraines can indeed affect vision, but would not cause the kind of hallucinations that Jonathan was suffering. It's possible he could have a brain tumor, lesion, or another kind of brain disease that was causing the pain and disturbing visions. The doctor scheduled him to come in for an MRI, but that wouldn't be for another week. Jonathan told her he didn't want to think about it anymore and appeared grateful when he finally got Anise to agree to drop him off at the museum instead of going home.

She texted Nate from the museum parking lot, asking him to meet her at her apartment because Jonathan wasn't doing well and she needed to talk to him about it. She started her car and pulled out of the parking lot.

Nate needed to be told off for slamming Jonathan against the wall, and she wanted to do it in person to make sure he understood he couldn't treat Jonathan that way. But as she thought about the text she'd just sent, she began to have second thoughts. Jonathan wouldn't like Nate coming over to her place. "But Nate's just a friend," she reassured herself out loud. "There's nothing wrong with me inviting my friend to my apartment."

The rest of the drive home was spent tearfully worrying about Jonathan's health. Was he going to be okay... or was he...?

"You didn't help the situation!" Anise told Nate when she opened her front door for him, her eyes still full of tears.

Nate looked at her with raised eyebrows. She turned and walked away and heard him come in and close the door behind him.

"You didn't have to slam Jonathan against the wall!" she continued. "He thought you were hurting me! He was just trying to protect me!"

"So was I," Nate insisted. "The difference is that my concern was real where his was imagined."

She paused and took a deep breath. "Okay, you have a point," she admitted in a calmer voice. "Still, you didn't have to attack him."

Nate frowned. "I didn't attack him. I was just pissed. He was out of control. The way he was talking to you...I was worried about you."

"He wouldn't hurt me! There was no need for you to go all knight-in-shining-armor and come barging in so dramatically...and passionately...and...." She turned around and looked at the floor so he wouldn't see her smile. *Shit! I shouldn't like that. What the hell is wrong with me?*

"I disagree. If I think you might be in danger, I'm always going to come barging in," he told her. "And that's not the only reason I was pissed. Didn't you notice that stunt he tried to pull?"

"What are you talking about?" she asked him.

"He thinks I'm a psychopath just like Grace is, and he not so subtly tried to remind me that I'm related to her by yelling and pulling on his hair like *she* always does."

Anise mulled that over for a moment. "I didn't think of that. I did notice he did that, but he told me that pulling on his hair is the only thing that helps the intense pain he gets in his head. His migraines start when he gets stressed out, so it makes sense that he'd get pain in a situation where he thinks someone's hurting me." She looked at Nate who seemed deep in thought. "What is it?" she asked him.

"Grace always pulls on her hair when she gets stressed out, too," he said.

"I remember seeing her do that." Anise sat on her couch and patted the cushion next to her, inviting him to join her. "Maybe she and Jonathan have the same thing! She gets hallucinations, too, right? When we were at the museum in Springfield she thought ants were crawling on her and that the ceiling was caving in."

"Yeah, she gets those spells once in a while," Nate answered her as he sat next to her.

"Tell me more about them."

Nate shrugged. "I can't. She never explained what she was feeling or seeing exactly. That's not the kind of thing she'd ever talk about."

"Why not?" Anise asked.

"Having feelings of any kind—physical or emotional—was never allowed. That was something only weak people did—her words."

"Oh. How long has she been pulling on her hair when she's stressed?"

"As long as I can remember."

"And you don't know if she had a growth on her brain or some kind of brain disease?"

He shrugged. "I doubt it. You'd think something like

that would've taken her life years ago."

"That's great! So if they *do* have the same thing, it means Jonathan's not dying!" A sense of relief washed over her, and she leaned back on the couch with a sigh.

"Is that why you're so fiery tonight?" he asked her, putting an arm around her.

She nodded.

"Don't worry," Nate said in a comforting tone. "His symptoms just started, right? I'm sure they'll find what's wrong and be able to fix it since you got him to the doctor early."

She sat up straight and turned to look at him. "Did Grace take any medications?"

"Dan kept shoving pills in her mouth whenever she got hallucinations. I think she was taking some kind of antipsychotic. If she and Boy Scout have the same thing, then *he's* the psychopath, not me," Nate said with a grin.

She smacked his arm. "It's not funny," she told him. She gave him a glare when his expression made it obvious that he whole-heartedly disagreed.

"You know, I'd really appreciate it if the two of you would sit down and talk about this," she continued. "He could tell you exactly what's going on when he gets the pain and hallucinations, and you can tell him if it sounds like what Grace was going through. Together we can figure it out!"

Nate scoffed. "I'm sure Boy Scout would love that as much as I would."

"Oh, Nate, *please*? I'm really worried about him."

"Why don't we wait until we get his test results? Maybe the docs will find something and we can avoid that whole scene."

"All right," she agreed with a frown. "But in the meantime, I want the two of you to call a truce. If you two don't get along, then I don't see how you and I being friends is going to work."

Nate's face grimaced slightly. "A truce. Great. Then

we'll sit around and braid each other's hair."

"I'm serious, Nate. Will you do this or not?"

He groaned. "Yeah, okay."

"Thank you." She stood up and grabbed her car keys while heading to her front door. "Come on."

"Where are we going?" he asked, plodding after her.

"To the museum."

"We have to do this *now*?" said Nate in an unwilling tone.

"Yes. I hate being in the middle of you two. This ends tonight."

NATE FOLLOWED HER SILENTLY AND LET her drive him to the museum. When she'd texted him earlier that evening, he'd dropped everything to come running like a dog even though she'd made it clear she'd chosen Boy Scout the saint. And now he'd agreed to do something he didn't want to do.

What the fuck?

He'd never behaved this way before. Feeling stupid, he wore a scowl as he wondered what it was about this woman he liked so much. If any other woman had tried to put him through this crap, he would've been gone long ago. He looked at her as she drove, and his scowl disappeared. He knew exactly what it was that he liked about her. Pretty face and great ass aside, she was unlike anyone he'd ever known. She chose to see the best in everyone, even someone who had made abundant mistakes like he had. Her incredible kindness and respect wasn't anything he'd seen before, and her loving presence made him want to be a better man, a man worthy of a woman like her.

Looking out the window, he noticed the leaves starting to turn shades of red, gold, and purple. All he'd seen for the last three years had been stark walls and some blue sky when he and the other inmates were let into the courtyard like animals. It had been crowded with almost no opportunity for privacy, barely enough room to even breathe. Cardboard for breakfast, lunch, and dinner. Mind numbing tasks, or worse, nothing to do at all. Not a day went by without some act of violence happening around him. He stayed away from it as much as possible and tried to live each day as a step closer to freedom, if you could call that living.

A week after Anise had visited him, he decided to call her, even though he thought she'd probably hang up. He was thrilled when she accepted the call, asked how he was doing, and told him she was at the hardware store trying to find someone who worked there. She needed to look for supplies to fix the wall where her ex had punched a hole, but she wasn't sure what to get that would do the job well but also fit into her budget. The handyman she'd called had wanted too much for the job. Nate had had just enough allotted speaking time to tell her what she needed to buy and how best to patch the wall before the prison phone cut him off. He'd called again the next week, and she'd thanked him for his help, saying she'd impressed herself and her friends with how good the wall looked. He continued to call weekly and their conversations became more and more relaxed and friendly. One day, he apologized to her again for everything, and she told him she forgave him. A seed of hope sprouted in his chest—maybe she'd be willing to give him another chance—and he'd realized how much he wanted to see her again when he got out.

When he helped a guard with an investment that earned him a windfall, the guard was grateful and offered to do Nate a favor in return. He'd been so excited at the prospect of calling Anise more often. He asked the guard to smuggle in a pre-paid phone as payment for his financial advice, and to ensure privacy, Nate volunteered to mop the cafeteria and the hallways at night. It was just him and the guard while everyone else was in their cell, and even though the guard had headphones on and was half asleep, Nate kept his voice low. For as long as she was able to talk, he got to escape the gray confinement and explore her colorful world, feeling like a real person again. Her soft voice, cute and infectious laugh, and kind words were a respite that kept him going without succumbing to the depression and apathy that threatened him almost constantly.

The guard was happy to keep the phone charged as long as the financial advice kept coming. Nate's calls to Anise increased in frequency gradually until they were speaking almost every day. They talked about everything, and he'd opened up to her like with no one else. She never judged, was always kind, and began opening up more to him as well. Sometimes they'd talk halfway into the night. When he said something flirtatious, he kept it light, and she'd respond positively. They developed inside jokes, and after a while, she could tell what he was thinking by the sound of his voice. He'd never experienced anything like it.

He wanted to ask her on another date for when he got out but couldn't bring himself to do it as long as he was locked up. She deserved better than that, and he'd wait until he was free again. When she told him that she'd started dating Boy Scout, he felt sick. He politely pretended to be happy for her but didn't call again for over a week, letting the blow sink in. When he got over his pride, he called with the intention of wishing her well and letting her go. But before he could get it out, she told him she'd missed talking to him and not to let so much time pass between conversations. Then he knew how he wanted to play it. He felt he still had a shot, and she was worth fighting for.

As they pulled into the museum's parking lot, once more he thought back to how she'd rejected him at the bar on Saturday night. He'd been disappointed but not discouraged. When they were together, it felt like he'd never been away at all, and her behavior that night seemed to agree even if her words didn't. There was definitely something still there. He felt it, and it seemed like so did she, even if she wouldn't admit it.

NATE LEANED AGAINST THE WALL IN the curator's hallway and wondered what he was in for as Anise stuck her head in Smithton's office.

"Hi, Dr. Smithton!" she chirped. "I was hoping to find Jonathan. Do you know where he is?"

"Hello, Anise! Lovely to see you," replied Smithton in his old-man voice. "I believe he's in the library downstairs. If you'd like to wait in here, I'll fetch him for you."

"That'd be great! Thank you!"

Nate followed her into Smithton's office. It smelled of microwaved leftovers and old books, and soft rock was quietly playing from a radio on the corner of his desk. Anise introduced them. "Nice to meet you," Nate said.

Smithton responded only with a suspicious nod. "I'll be right back," he told Anise.

"What's his problem?" Nate asked after Dr. Smithton had left.

"Maybe Jonathan said something about you to him," speculated Anise. "Or maybe it's because you're Grace's grandson. He's definitely not a fan of hers." She shrugged. "But he's usually very nice."

"He's old," Nate commented. "Why didn't he retire decades ago?"

"He loves his job. I don't think he'd be happy if he stopped working. He's spent his life searching for the Armor Jewelry. He's the one who's holding on to the ring for me."

"You're sure you can trust him?" Nate asked, unable to shake the weird feeling he was getting from Smithton.

"Definitely," she assured him. "Dr. Smithton has been Jonathan's mentor for years. They're really close, and Dr. Smithton is the one who helped us with our plan to steal the earrings when you and your family were terrorizing me because of the amulet."

Nate's brow furrowed from her verbal punch. "Honey, you know I'm sorry about that. But I also saved you and served my time. I tried to make up for what I did. You *do* forgive me, right?"

Her demeanor softened. "Yes, I do. I'm sorry my words came out harshly. It still makes me anxious to think about that time. I have nightmares about Grace a lot. And I haven't admitted this to anyone except Jonathan, but since that whole experience, I've been afraid to go anywhere without wearing the amulet. If I try to leave my apartment without it, I get panic attacks. It's been... exhausting."

Nate had never felt worse in his life. What had the prison shrink called this emotion? Empathy? Or maybe guilt? He couldn't remember experiencing either before, and whichever it was, it sucked. He almost wished he'd never let the shrink convince him to start working on recognizing his feelings. "I'm so sorry, honey," he said, giving her a hug. "I feel terrible."

She gave him a quick hug in return. "Anyway," she continued, "yes, the ring is in good hands here. I'm sure it's in his safe right now."

Nate frowned. He didn't trust this Smithton person. "Where's the safe?"

"Right there," she said, pointing. "Behind that painting. Why?"

"There's something off about that guy. I want to make sure he's as honorable as you say." He walked over to the painting, grabbed the corner, and pulled it. It swung away from the wall to reveal Smithton's safe.

"What are you gonna do—break in?" Anise asked with a laugh. "That's not necessary. I trust him."

"I don't," Nate answered. He reached his hand up to the dial.

"You told me you weren't going to do anything illegal anymore," Anise reminded him.

Nate turned back around. "If I think someone's mistreating you, I'm going to do whatever it takes to stop them whether you approve of my methods or not. Protecting you is my priority here."

She must've liked something about that because she looked at the floor and smiled. "So that's how it's going to be, is it? I can live with that." She sat in Smithton's office chair and watched as Nate started spinning the dial. "So are you going to listen for clicks or something?"

He smiled at her. "No time for that method, honey."

"I thought it only took a few moments."

"Only in the movies, not in real life." He continued to spin the dial left and right.

"Then what are you doing?"

"Safe manufacturers typically use the same try-out combinations when they make the safes. The consumer should change the combination after they buy it. But a lot of people don't bother to change it. So I'm trying those right now."

"I think Dr. Smithton is smarter than that," Anise said.

"You're right," Nate agreed. "That didn't work."

"So now what?" she asked, her face wearing a look of fascination.

He took a moment to study the other paintings in the room. *Philosophers? That's strange, considering Smithton's line of work.* He looked up something on the internet with his phone and then tried another combination. It didn't work. He tried another. The safe opened.

"Oh my god!" Anise exclaimed, getting up from the chair. "How'd you do that?"

"Let's look for the ring first," he suggested with a grin.

"Wait, we shouldn't do this. That's his private safe!"

He ignored her and started pulling things out of Smithton's safe and placing them with care on the desk. Opening a box, he showed her the inside of it. "Here's the ring," he said. "I guess you were right about him."

"I told you! So put it back and close it before he gets back!" Her nervous eyes were wide.

"Why don't you be my look-out, honey?" Nate suggested, as he continued to look through the safe.

ANISE WALKED TO THE DOOR AND peered out the small window by the handle. From there, she could see down the hallway. Jonathan and Dr. Smithton would be coming from that direction.

"Holy shit, what's this?" Nate said.

"What is it?" Anise glanced out the door's window again, clutching the amulet before turning around to look at what he'd found.

He opened another small box and showed her a cuff bracelet with three blue stones and several smaller red ones. "I don't know, but it looks like it belongs with the other Armor Jewelry."

"The metal is the same as the metal in my amulet." Something about that felt off. *Could there be another piece of Armor Jewelry?* If so, why didn't Dr. Smithton tell her and Jonathan about it? She gave Nate a worried look. "Take a picture of it."

He opened the camera app on his phone and did as she asked. He took pictures of several other things in the safe as well.

While Nate snapped his photos, Anise grabbed the boxes that contained the ring and the cuff. She opened them and put the Jewelry on. The ring reminded her of being at the museum with Grace and Dan, fighting for her life and Jonathan's. Her chest tightened with anxiety at the traumatizing memory. Her eyes turned to the cuff. It really did look like it matched the other pieces of Armor Jewelry. The exact same metal. Embedded gemstones. She took it off her wrist and flipped it over. "Oh my god!"

"What?!" Nate asked, spinning around. "Are you okay?"

"Yeah—the cuff has the incantation engraved on it. It *is* another piece of Armor Jewelry!"

"I thought so."

"Keep looking," she directed him, pointing to the safe. "I need to know what's going on."

Anise stood by the door, staring at the cuff she'd put back on her wrist. Why was Dr. Smithton keeping it a secret? Her mind turned to Jonathan. Maybe she could get him to ask Dr. Smithton about it...but no. Then she'd have to tell him that Nate broke into Dr. Smithton's safe and that she'd been a willing accessory. Jonathan would get so upset he'd have another stress headache and get hallucinations, pulling on his hair so hard, he might yank some out.

She put her hands in her own hair and tried to imagine how he must feel. Seeing terrifying visions that accompanied excruciating pain must be torturous and scary. He always seemed to see visions of her being injured. She wondered why that was. When Grace had hallucinations, they seemed to be of insects. Anise had a hard time believing that a woman as intimidating as Grace would be afraid of bugs. She wondered if Grace saw anything else in her visions and if Grace was afraid of the insects themselves or if she was afraid of what the insects might represent to her. Anise wondered if the hair pulling was actually a known pain-reliever, and she attempted it with the hopes it would calm her racing heart, but it did nothing to relieve the growing anxiety.

"Honey, you won't believe what's in here," Nate said, placing more of Dr. Smithton's things on the desk.

Anise looked out the window and gasped. "Nate, they're coming!" she cried. She ripped off the Armor Jewelry and returned the pieces to the boxes they'd been in.

✳✳✳

As fast as he could, Nate put everything back where he found it, closed the safe, spun the dial, and swung the painting back toward the wall. They sat down in the guest chairs in front of Smithton's desk seconds before the door opened.

Jonathan looked at Nate and Anise. "What's up?" he asked, giving Nate a what-the-hell-are-you-doing-here look. "Are you okay?" he said to Anise. "You're shaking!"

She opened her mouth to say something but froze.

"She's been upset tonight," Nate told Jonathan. "We need to talk."

"Okay," agreed Jonathan. "Let's go to my office." He and Smithton exchanged a look of concern before Jonathan, Anise, and Nate stepped out into the hallway. "So what is this all about?" Jonathan asked as he closed his office door.

Anise still looked frozen, so Nate spoke up. "Anise is unhappy that we haven't been getting along. She wants both of us in her life and thinks we need to call a truce. I couldn't agree with her more."

Jonathan raised his eyebrows.

"I'd like to pay to fix your door," Nate continued.

"I can pay for my own door."

"I know you can," Nate said. "But you shouldn't have to. I'll send you a payment."

"Fine," Jonathan agreed. "You can pay for my door." Nate offered him his hand and they shook.

"This was upsetting you that much to make you shake?" Jonathan asked Anise.

"Yes," she replied in a weak voice.

"I'm glad you stopped by then," he told her, taking her into his arms and kissing her.

Nate looked away. He hoped what he had done was enough to make Anise happy.

"Me, too," she said, kissing Jonathan back. "Are you ready to leave? I can drive us all back to my place."

"I'm not done working yet," Jonathan told her. "Dr. S. can drive me home."

They said their good-byes, and Anise and Nate walked through the hall toward the stairwell. "I hate lying to Jonathan," she moaned with a defeated look on her face. "I was shaking because I was so scared we'd get caught breaking into the safe."

"But we didn't get caught. All's good." Her face didn't look convinced, so he continued. "Besides, it was only a half lie. It *was* upsetting you that we weren't getting along."

She shrugged. "Yes, that's true."

"Young Brevain," called a voice from down the hall.

They turned around to see Dr. Smithton hurrying after them.

"Oh god, does he know what we did?!" Anise asked Nate in a whisper.

"No. I put everything back exactly as he had it."

"How can you be sure?"

"I put everything in his safe in a certain order on his desk."

"Oh, no!" Anise hissed. "I moved the boxes."

"What do you mean?"

"I opened and moved the boxes that hold the ring and cuff. What if I switched them?"

"It's okay," Nate comforted her. "So what if he knows? He can't prove anything." Nate let the old man catch up to him.

"I have two questions for you," Smithton said. "First, how is your grandmother faring in prison?"

"I wouldn't know," Nate replied. "Nor do I care. Why do you?"

"Morbid curiosity," Smithton said. "That's all."

"What's your second question?" Nate asked, not bothering to hide his annoyance.

Smithton looked at Anise and back to Nate. "I imagine you must know some *unattached* ladies, do you not?"

Nate nodded. "I do." It made him think of the woman barber he'd gone to a week or so ago who'd kept giggling and dropping hints. And on Saturday night at The Blue Pineapple when the bartender slid her number over to him with a wink when Anise went to the bathroom. And one of the women in his Motocross club he'd had a fling with before he was locked away who'd seen him at the practice field yesterday and said they should get together. As tempting as it was—it was over three years since he'd been with a woman—he'd called none of them and had no plans to. "But I think they're all a little young for you."

Smithton snorted in frustration. "That's not what I meant and you know it."

"Dr. Smithton, if you have something to say about my relationship with Jonathan, say it to me," Anise challenged him.

"You are not the problem, my dear," Smithton told her and gave Nate a glare.

"There isn't a problem here at all," she said firmly. "Let's go, Nate." She led the way down the stairwell. "I'm sorry about what Dr. Smithton said to you. He can be ridiculously pushy about things that don't concern him sometimes."

Nate waved it off. "I don't care what that walking corpse thinks of me."

Anise frowned. "Maybe he's not as nice as I thought he was."

Nate was happy to hear her say that. He didn't want

Smithton to sway her opinion of him.

When they got to her car, she turned to him with wide eyes. "Okay," she said, as she pulled out of the parking lot. "You *have* to tell me how you opened the safe! That was so amazing!"

Her admiration made him grin. "I noticed that the three paintings Smithton has on his wall were of Plato, More, and Rousseau, which I thought was interesting because they're all philosophers who put out a work on utopia. I also thought it was strange because Smithton's an historian, not a philosopher. So I looked up when their works were published, and I tried a couple different combinations based on the numbers in the publication years."

"Wow, that's incredibly impressive! I would have never figured that out," she said. "For some reason, Dr. Smithton is really into the idea of utopia. He's never talked to me about it, but he and Jonathan discuss it all the time. Jonathan mentions it a lot—sometimes too much. I think Dr. Smithton actually believes he can make it happen someday."

"I knew something was off about him," Nate said, scowling.

They parked and went back into Anise's apartment.

"I have to show you these pictures, honey," Nate said.

"Oh, right! I almost forgot. Let's see." She sat next to him on her couch.

"This is the bracelet," he said, showing her the first picture he'd taken of Smithton's possessions in the safe. He narrowed his eyes. "I feel like I've seen this somewhere before."

"Really? Where?"

"I don't know." He shrugged it off.

She leaned closer to get a better look, and her upper arm pressed against his. "Dr. Smithton told me and Jonathan all about the amulet, ring, and earrings. Why would he keep the bracelet—I guess it's more of a cuff—a secret from us?"

"I don't know, but check this out," Nate said, showing her the next picture on his phone, and also enjoying how close she was to him. The way she leaned on him felt nice, and every time she moved he caught a faint whiff of a bowl of fresh raspberries mixed with flowers. "This looks like a page torn out of an old book. You can see a hand drawing of the cuff next to your amulet, the ring, and the earrings."

"Oh my god!" Anise exclaimed. "I know what book this page belongs to! Jonathan showed it to me when we first met, and he was telling me about the Legend of the Armor Jewelry. He didn't know why the page was missing." She paused, then turned to Nate with her eyes as wide open as her mouth. "And the first time I met Dr. Smithton, he told me and Jonathan that the page had been missing since the first time he saw the book! He made us believe he knew nothing about it!"

Nate shook his head. Smithton was up to something. He'd have to keep a close eye on him.

Anise leaned back on the couch. "I think you were right about not trusting Dr. Smithton. Why would he lie to us about that? Why would he rip out a page of a book he loves?" She leaned forward again to take another look at the photo. "Does it say anything about an incantation?"

Nate took another look as well. "Not that I see." He showed her the other pictures he took, which were of the ring and the other texts in the safe.

Anise leaned back again, twisting her garnet ring around her finger and then putting her hands on the amulet she wore around her neck. Nate leaned back too and put an arm around her in an attempt to comfort her. She leaned into him, and he could feel her tense muscles relaxing.

"Wait!" she said, her face lighting up with a thought. "I wonder if *this* is the piece of Jewelry that has the healing powers! If we find it, maybe I can finally help Les!

Does the page say anything about it?"

They squinted at the small words in the photo of the torn-out page.

"It says the cuff was used to transfer thoughts and ideas from the wearer to the intended target," he read. "Doesn't say anything about healing powers."

She gave him a look of horror. "Brainwashing?!"

"That's what it sounds like to me."

"So no healing powers." Her eyes welled up. "I still can't help Les."

Nate wished he knew what to say to comfort her.

Anise was quiet for a moment. "Why would Dr. Smithton need to brainwash anyone?"

"Is there anyone you both know that's been acting strangely?" Nate asked.

"The only person we both know is Jonathan. He's definitely been acting strangely with his headaches, hair pulling, and all this talk about a utopia and blood."

"*Blood*?"

"Yeah," she said, taking a deep breath. "The other day he'd mentioned Dr. Smithton's views on utopia again, and then out of nowhere he asked if I'd be willing to donate blood. I asked him if there was a blood drive at the museum, and he said no. He had no idea why he asked me that. It was weird, but I didn't give it any more thought."

"I don't want you to be alone with either one of them until we figure out what the hell is going on," Nate told her as his concern for her safety grew.

"Nate, Jonathan is my boyfriend. I'm going to be alone with him."

He sighed. Protecting her wasn't going to be easy. "If I can't convince you to keep your distance from Boy Scout, at least stay away from Smithton. He's up to something."

"Okay," she promised. "But I don't think he'd hurt me."

"We don't know that for sure," he told her. "This

utopia bullshit sounds like a cult, and your boyfriend is buying into it."

Anise frowned. "Dr. Smithton knows both Jonathan and Grace. I wonder if he's the connection to their headaches." She paused. "Would Grace know anything about the cuff?"

Nate looked at her, surprised. "Do you want me to go ask her about it?"

"No! Definitely not. I was only thinking out loud. I know you don't want to see her, and I don't blame you. You know I don't want you to see her either. I just want to do anything I can to help Jonathan." She sighed. "I definitely don't want you to have any further contact with Grace," she said again. "But would you be willing to come with me to visit Dan? He's the lesser of the two evils, and maybe *he* knows something about the cuff."

"No, honey. I don't wanna see Dan, and I don't think you should see him either."

She turned to him, her lips in a tight line. "Nate, I'm going to see him with or without you. I just thought you might want to come because he said he had something important to tell you. Maybe whatever he has to say is about the cuff."

Nate's brow furrowed at the thought of Anise seeing Dan by herself. Who knows how that would affect her, especially since she was still traumatized by her last encounter with Dan and Grace? "All right," he said, raising his hands in defeat. "We'll go."

Her face beamed at him. "Thank you! Will you contact him, please? Get him to put me on his list of approved visitors?"

"Yeah, okay," he sighed with a frown, still not liking this idea.

"How long do you think it'll take before we can visit? It was a couple of months before they let me schedule a time to come see you."

"My friend the guard has a brother who works at

Dan's prison. He once told me if I ever wanted to visit my dad to let him know, and he'd speed up the process. I'll call him now." While he was on the phone, he felt Anise's eyes watching him with interest and anticipation.

"And?" she asked when he hung up.

"If you can fill out the online application tonight, they'll need twenty-four hours."

"That's it? That's amazing! Thank you, thank you, thank you!" she gushed, wrapping her arms around him. "Let's leave tomorrow after I get off work. I'll take the next day off."

He gave her a hesitant nod and a hug back. She must care about Boy Scout a lot to want to go through all this for him. Nate felt something, but what was it? He ran through the shrink's list of emotions in his head again. Sadness, maybe? Disappointment? Rejection? Confusion? Whichever it was, it felt strange to have an emotion at all in this situation. Usually, if his pursuit of a woman hit a dead end, he'd forget it and look elsewhere. He knew he could have another woman in his bed before the night was over if he wanted to. But with Anise, it was about way more than that, and he couldn't bring himself to give up yet.

She broke their embrace and got up to get them sodas from her refrigerator. Getting her to see that he'd be a better choice as the man in her life than the self-righteous curator would be more difficult than he originally thought. Then again, the hug she just gave him lasted a lot longer than he'd expected. Difficult, but not impossible. Taking her out of town might actually be a good start.

"YOU'RE DOING WHAT?!" JONATHAN EXCLAIMED.

Anise had driven to his apartment after he called to tell her Dr. Smithton had dropped him off at home.

The main living area was lit by only the muted television. She left her shoes and bag by the front door where he'd greeted her with a kiss.

She wanted to let Jonathan know as much of her plan as possible. Nate had made her promise not to tell Jonathan about the cuff, otherwise, she'd have to confess that they broke into Smithton's safe. She intended to keep her promise, as Jonathan would never have approved of her actions, but she hated keeping things from him just the same.

"I'm going with Nate to see Dan tomorrow," she repeated.

"And Nate convinced you to go out of town with him," Jonathan grumbled.

"He didn't convince me of anything," Anise insisted. "I asked to go with him. He's my friend, and I wanted to be there for him."

Jonathan took her hand. "Anise, you have the biggest and kindest heart of anyone I've ever met. I know that you honestly want to help him. But this is the opportunity Nate has been waiting for. He's going to have you alone in a hotel. That's where he's going to try something. I'm surprised he hasn't tried something already."

Anise looked at the floor. Her stomach ached with guilt as she thought about how Nate had kissed her at the bar a couple nights before. "I told you, *if* he tries something, he's not going to get anywhere."

"All right," Jonathan said, wincing and pulling on his hair. "And you'll be back the next day?"

"Yes. Are you getting a stress headache?"

"Yeah. And your face is suddenly all bloody and bruised. But I'm guessing it's really not," he added, squeezing his eyes shut.

"My face is fine," she promised him, putting her hands on his shoulders and leading him to his couch. She sat with him, her arms wrapped around him, until the pain subsided. She knew she had caused his headache this time, and she felt like the worst girlfriend in the world. She reminded herself that she was doing this in an attempt to help him.

Tuesday, September 15, 2015

MORTY SMITHTON SENT AN E-MAIL TO his co-workers and subordinates reminding them of their weekly meeting in the large conference room, due to start in ten minutes. He opened his safe and reached for the cuff.

That's strange.

He always placed the cuff in the back left corner and the ring in the back right corner. Today, they were in opposite corners. He tried to recall the last time he opened the safe. Perhaps he'd confused the boxes. They're exactly the same size, shape, and color after all, and it's not like he hadn't confused them before. But, no, that couldn't be right. The last time he opened the safe was the week before for the weekly staff meeting. He'd put on the cuff for the meeting and had put it back when he was done. He'd only moved the cuff and nothing else. When the meeting had ended, he'd returned it to the back left corner. Of this, he was certain.

He dropped the cuff into the pocket of his sports coat. Nothing was missing from the safe, and everything else was exactly where he'd left it. It looked like nothing else had been touched. His papers were neat as a pin, just how he'd placed them, and the one he kept upside down with a corner folded over to ensure he'd know if someone had rooted through them was exactly the way he kept it. But still. Had someone broken into his safe? Someone must have—there was no other explanation. But who? No one else knew the combination, and it was virtually impossible for someone to guess it. He locked his office door every night. During the day, he was always either in the office or somewhere nearby. Had someone come into his office during the day when he'd been in a meeting or the restroom?

He thought about the visitors he'd had the night before. Would Nate Brevain want to break into his safe? He shouldn't have allowed a relative of Grace's to wait in his office unattended. However, Anise had been there. She certainly wouldn't have allowed...well, perhaps she would have. Jonathan had expressed concern about Nate to him, worried that Nate's recklessness might hurt Anise, or that he may try to make time with her. If she spent her time with such a character, perhaps this sweet girl simply wasn't as innocent as she seemed. It certainly wouldn't have been the first time he'd misjudged a woman. If the young Brevain had managed to open the safe, then Anise would know about the cuff and the missing page. She'd know that he'd lied to her and Jonathan about it. She'd likely tell Jonathan which could possibly ruin all the plans Morty had made. He scowled and mentally reminded himself to have a talk with Jonathan after the meeting.

"Good morning, everyone," he said to Jonathan and approximately forty other co-workers in the conference room. "Please take your seats." Smithton discussed museum business before getting to what the weekly meetings were really for. "The time is near." He put his hand in his pocket and discretely slipped the cuff on his wrist. He looked everyone in their eyes and watched them all glaze over before speaking again. "We are closer now to our utopian goals than ever."

The room buzzed with excitement as each set of eyes glazed over even more.

"I have almost collected everything we need. Soon I will call upon each and every one of you to assist me in a journey. At that time, you will be ready and motivated to help in any way you can. You will listen to and comply with orders without question. You will become more and more loyal to me and my utopian vision every time you hear my voice, every time you think of me, every time you hear my name. Isn't that right?"

"Yes, Dr. Smithton," answered the monotone voices in unison.

Chapter 10

Fifty-three years ago

Monday, January 8, 1962

"I'm sorry, I can't make that deal without board approval," Grace told the potential buyer who'd breezed into her office without an appointment. "If you'll wait about a week..."

"Impossible!" scoffed the buyer. He leaned back in his chair on the other side of her desk. "My gallery needs these pieces for the opening day of the new exhibition. I have no interest in adding them a week late! You're a board member. Certainly you can approve this. It's either now, or we have no deal, Dr. Brevain." The investors that had accompanied him nodded as they stood against the wall in her small office. The buyer looked at Grace expectantly, his beady little eyes boring a hole through her head.

Grace pursed her lips in frustration. The Springfield Museum where she worked as a curator with Morty and several other members of their former graduate research team was running out of funds. The chief curator had introduced several exhibitions that were expensive, and unfortunately, poorly attended. Several of the senior curators had already been let go, due to their higher salaries, and the salaries of all other staff members had been decreased. The deaccession of a few small items had been attempted, but failed to bring in the amount needed to satisfy the debt. The museum was set to close in less than a month if enough money couldn't be raised in a timely manner.

"Perhaps you could move the opening day," Grace suggested.

The gallery owner laughed. "Sweetheart, that's out of the question. Now, will you sell, or won't you?"

Shit.

Ignoring her desire to punch him in the throat, Grace quickly weighed her options. These men wanted to purchase three of the museum's most valuable pieces and were offering thirty-six million dollars for them all—which was quite generous. That would more than pay for the museum's debts and allow them to stay open. Plus, then she wouldn't lose her job. The only thing that could go wrong was if her approval of this sale actually caused her to be fired instead. Deaccessions required a majority vote of the board. Grace was just one board member and was not in a position to authorize a deaccession on her own. However, these buyers made it clear they weren't going to wait, and Grace knew that some of the board members were out of town and wouldn't return for several days. For the last year, ever since she started her career as a curator, she'd been trying to find buyers to save the museum. She'd gotten several discreet offers from black market buyers, but she refused them all. She wanted to do this correctly.

Grace tried not to glare at him. "You should at least talk to our new museum director. He'll be back in a couple of hours."

"I am talking to *you*," the gallery owner said, with an air of finality. "This is the last time I'm asking. Do we have a deal or not?"

Grace took a deep breath. "Yes, we have a deal. I'll prepare the paperwork."

Tuesday, January 9, 1962

TO GRACE'S GREAT RELIEF, HER BREAKING of the rules was rewarded with the gratitude and appreciation of her peers, fellow board members, and her superiors. She was commended with a bonus from the museum director and a small office party thrown by her colleagues.

She was cutting herself a piece of congratulatory cake when she heard a voice behind her.

"I suppose congratulations are in order."

She turned around in surprise. "Morty!" He hadn't spoken to her in the last five years unless it had been absolutely necessary, which at times, it was. They'd been on the same research team as graduate students and both ended up employed at the Springfield Museum. Somehow, they'd found a way to work together. "Thank you."

"I have to say, I'm quite impressed," he continued. "I don't know that I would've taken the risk of losing my job in order to make that deal without board approval."

Why does that not surprise me? Grace thought. His expression was flat and he looked uncomfortable, but she was happy he was speaking to her. Could he finally be ready to forgive her? "I just wanted to save the museum."

"You're really someone who gets things done, Grace. You always have been."

"Well, again, thank you, Morty."

"Do you remember all our talks about creating a

world peace movement?"

She raised an eyebrow at him. "Well, they were mainly *your* talks about finding a way to make utopia a reality, but yes. Why?"

"I believe that if we collect all the Armor Jewelry, we can do it!"

"Oh, Morty, are you still obsessed with that? We talked about this. You'd have to find a way to change people's thoughts so everyone agrees all the time; otherwise, not everyone will be happy. It's impossible."

"What if I *have* found a way?" he said with a knowing smirk.

She gave him a quizzical look. "What are you talking about?"

"There's a new way to use the Jewelry," he began, then stopped talking.

"Really? How?!"

"That's not the point. I'm putting together a group to help me find the rest of the Armor Jewelry. I want you to be in it."

She shook her head at him, disappointed. His voice sounded so formal. Not at all the friendly, caring way he used to speak to her. "I thought we were going to find that Jewelry together, just the two of us. Isn't that what we promised each other?"

"And I thought we'd be married with a child. Isn't that what we promised each other?" he snarled, narrowing his eyebrows.

Grace frowned. He was obviously *not* ready to forgive her. It had been over five years already. Perhaps he'd never be ready to forgive. She pushed aside her hurt feelings. "Fine, do whatever you want. But leave me out of it. I won't have time for that anyway." She stepped closer to him so she could lower her voice. "Thomas and I are having a baby. I just found out I'm expecting."

The repulsed look on Morty's face was so horrifying, Grace had to step back.

"You don't love Thomas anymore," he snarled as his hand twisted strangely inside his coat pocket.

"That's a weird thing to say, Morty! Thomas is the love of my life."

"So you'll have *his* baby, but kill mine?" he hissed, his eyes full of hate.

"I didn't go through with the abortion!" she fired back in a harsh whisper. "And things are different now. I'm older, more secure with my place in life, and I'm married."

"You would've been married and secure with me!" Morty's face turned red.

"I know that! That's why I didn't go through with the abortion!"

"Enough of your lies! Go to hell!" He stormed off. She looked around, grateful that none of their co-workers had heard the conversation. Morty's words about a new way to use the Jewelry swirled around in her mind. She slipped out of her own party undetected and grabbed her purse and keys from her office. She needed to investigate this claim of his.

"WHY, HELLO, GRACE! SO GLAD TO see you!" Professor Dromly greeted her from his desk chair in his office at Springfield University.

"Hello, Professor."

"Grace! Hi!" a third voice piped up.

Grace turned around to see a child with the same sparkling brown eyes as Professor Frederick Dromly, and her heart melted. It was Dromly's young son Kent, who was playing on the floor of his father's office. Kent got up, ran to her, and wrapped his arms around her legs. Kent looked about four or five years old and reminded Grace of her brother Danny. "Hi, Kent!" The boy had the same curls as his father, except Dromly's hair was brown where Kent's was black like his mother's.

"Come play with me," Kent said, grabbing her hand and pulling her toward the toys he'd left on the floor.

"I wish I could," Grace told him. "But I don't have much time. Next time, okay?"

"Okay," Kent groaned and gave her another hug before returning to his toys.

She smiled at him. He was so cute; it made her even more excited for the day she'd get to meet the little one growing inside of her.

"If you're here to visit your husband, you just missed him. He went to lunch," said Professor Dromly.

"Now? It's almost three in the afternoon."

"He's been taking late lunches for years."

Grace narrowed her eyebrows. "That's news to me. But I'm not here to see him anyway."

"Then what brings you by these hallowed halls of academia?"

"I have a question for you."

"I have an answer," replied Dromly.

"It's about the Mallandian Armor Jewelry," Grace said.

His eyes lit up at hearing his favorite subject. "What would you like to know?"

She couldn't ask what Morty meant when he said there was a new way to use the Jewelry. Dromly didn't know she knew the legends were real—or did he? He and Morty were still close. Would Morty have told him? No, impossible. Then Dromly would've known that she and Morty were responsible for the death of Richard Woods, and Morty was too much of a candy-ass to own up to that.

"I was wondering if you'd found out anything new about the legends?" she asked.

The light left his eyes. "Why do you ask, Grace?"

"So you *have*?"

"I haven't." He shook his head more dramatically

than necessary. "What's bringing this on?" he asked, crossing his arms in front of him.

His body language and the demanding way he was asking his questions let her know he was feeling defensive. *He knows something.*

"I'm working on a display at the museum that includes several pieces of Bronze Age Jewelry. It reminded me of the Armor Jewelry and how *fascinating* your lectures were, and I wanted to learn more. If there's anything more to learn, that is." She smiled sweetly, knowing how positively his ego reacted to high praise.

"I see," Dromly said, relaxing his stance and smiling back. "I wish I could help, but unfortunately I have no news on that front."

"That's disappointing." *He may no longer be afraid that I know something, but he's definitely keeping something from me.* "Do you have any books I could borrow about the Jewelry? That way I can at least refresh my memory."

"Not personally," Dromly said. "But you're welcome to check the university library. If you find anything you'd like to borrow, let me know, and I'll check it out for you."

"Thank you! I'll head down there now." *I'm going to figure out your secret.*

THOMAS PARKED HIS CAR OUTSIDE OF the kindergarten. It was almost time for school to end. He heard the dismissal bell ring and saw children racing out of the door onto the blacktop. Then came their teacher. Betty. She was smiling and laughing with her students. He watched as she pulled her coat around her tightly, snowflakes landing on her chestnut brown hair, wishing he was the one keeping her warm. Taking a bite of his burger, he wondered how much longer it would take him to find the

Plate of Destiny. Once he had it, he'd use all four pieces of Armor Jewelry to activate Grace's seer powers. Then she could read the wisdom on the Plate for him using those powers, and he'd have the secrets to living out his best life which he knew—he just *knew*—would include insight on how to take down Dromly. Then, who knows? Maybe Betty would consider taking him back. He unlocked the glove compartment and took out a small box. Opening the lid with cold fingers, he removed Betty's diamond ring he'd had to sell his car to buy. The one she'd thrown in his face.

The ring he'd gotten for Grace was a quarter of the size, but it was more glamorous than anything else she'd ever had in her life, so she was content with it. At least he thought so. He didn't really care. He admired Grace and considered her a friend. She was strong with an impressive intelligence and drive, a force to be reckoned with.

But she wasn't Betty. Confident, sultry, brilliant, funny, kind, clever, sexy Betty. Tears streamed down his face for his lost love, the woman he'd always love. "See you tomorrow, beautiful," he whispered and began the lonely drive back to work.

USING THE CALL NUMBER SHE'D WRITTEN down from her search in the card catalogue, Grace scanned the tall shelves for all the books that contained any information about the Armor Jewelry. Students walked by her, laughing loudly enough to break her concentration. "Shut the hell up!" she growled at them. "This is a library!"

She pulled the books she wanted off the shelves and carefully went through each of them while sitting at a small table in a corner. None of them contained any information about the cuff. She closed the last one in frustration. She felt a tap on her back and spun around in surprise. "Kent! What are you doing here?" she asked, a little annoyed by the interruption.

He handed her a picture he'd drawn. "Aw, is this for me?" she asked, unable to stay mad at him. He nodded. "Well, thank you, it's beautiful..." she began, then looked at it closely. It was a picture of a coppery circle with three large blue circles and some smaller red circles attached to it. She had no idea what it was, but didn't want to ask and ruin his confidence in his art. "Where did you learn to draw this?" she asked instead.

"A book my dad looks at when we're here," he told her. "Wanna see?"

"Yes, show me."

He took her hand and led her to the other side of the library. He stopped in front of a shelf full of dusty old law texts and pointed to the top. She looked up and saw a book similar in color to the law texts but with a different spine.

"I can't reach it," Kent shrugged.

"I can't either!" she laughed. He grinned at her. She found a step stool and brought the book to a table.

He took it and opened it. To her surprise, there was a small, thin key embedded in the pages. Kent removed it and walked over to a smaller shelf in the far corner. Using all his might, his little arms pushed the shelf a few feet forward to reveal a trap door. He opened it and pulled out a metal box. Inserting the key, he looked at Grace and grinned. The box opened and Kent pulled out another book. He flipped to a page near the back and pointed to the hand drawing. She took a sharp breath in. It was a cuff that looked like it belonged with the Armor Jewelry! If what Kent had said was true, Dromly had lied to her.

I knew it!

"This is what you drew!" she exclaimed, and Kent nodded. "Well, you did a great job. But Kent, the drawing is in black and white. How did you know the stones are blue and red?"

"My dad," he replied.

"Your dad told you the stones are blue and red?"

He nodded.

"Did you ever see this cuff in real life?"

His little head bobbed up and down. "He gave it to his friend."

"He gave it to a friend? When?"

"Yesterday."

"I see," Grace said. "What did his friend look like?"

"Big," Kent replied.

"Do you mean tall?"

Kent nodded again.

"Do you know what his friend's name is?"

"Morry Smiffin."

"Interesting." She flipped through the book and inhaled sharply when she reached a section about the incantation that was written on each piece of the Jewelry. This was the only book she'd seen that had the incantation written out. Quickly, she scribbled it on the back of Kent's drawing, both in the curly Mallandian symbols and the English translation. Knowing what the incantation said may or may not be of any use to her in the future, but it was fascinating just the same.

She then read the pages that contained the information about the cuff. "It wasn't part of the original Jewelry set," she mumbled as she read. "It was used by the Mallandian king to brainwash his army for the sole purpose of avoiding mutiny." She stared out the window to let the information absorb. *Brainwashing?*

She looked back down at the book. "The cuff can also have a healing effect on the body if used along with the other three pieces of Jewelry. It all comes down to the intention of the wearer."

On the next page was another piece of the legend of the Armor Jewelry. The directions on how to create the cuff and the rest of the Jewelry had been given to the

Mallandians by their gods in exchange for the protection of an artifact called the Plate of Destiny. The Plate apparently had all the secrets of life and death written on it, and was for the eyes of the gods only. No humans were supposed to see it, however, it was possible for a human to find the Plate and learn the secrets if they somehow were able to possess all four pieces of Jewelry. This is why the gods entrusted the Armor Jewelry to the royals only, who were considered to be like gods themselves. The Mallandian royals vowed to protect the Plate from anyone who wasn't a royal. However, information about the Plate leaked. The Mallandian subjects who heard the story believed that if they could succeed in finding the Plate, they could live in peace and joy forever. Death could even be reversed with the knowledge on the Plate of Destiny.

Grace thought about what Morty, Dromly, and Kent had told her. If Kent was telling the truth, then Dromly knew about the cuff and the Plate of Destiny. Were he and Morty looking for them together? Is this what Morty's "administration job" with Dromly back in college had really been about? Regardless, why would Dromly lie about it to her? She'd been just as good a student as Morty; why didn't they include her? And why did Morty suddenly want *her* to be part of some team to find the Armor Jewelry when it was obvious he still hated her? Did Dromly know anything about this team?

I have to figure this out.

She replaced the book in the metal box, wondering if Morty had any other pieces of Jewelry besides the cuff.

"Don't tell anyone!" Kent warned her. "It's a secret!" He locked the box, replaced it under the trap door, and pushed the small shelf back over it.

"Your secret is safe with me, I promise." Grace put the key back in the pages of the book from the top shelf, replaced it, and put the drawing Kent had given her in her purse.

"Kent," said Grace, looking around for Professor Dromly. "Does your dad know you're down here?"

He laughed and shook his head.

She took his hand. "Come on, let's get you back. I bet he's worried about you."

She saw Dromly frantically looking around the hallway, his cape swirling with every panic-stricken turn. "Look who I found!" she called out.

Dromly placed a hand on his chest and pretended to collapse on the floor while students walking by gave him strange looks. Kent ran to him and laughed when his father grabbed him with a playful roar.

Dromly stood with Kent in his arms and let out a sigh of relief. "Thank you," he told Grace. "He's been running away lately." He looked at his son. "I need to tell you about the time I got lost in the Amazon rainforest."

"Oh, no! Not this story again!" Kent moaned as he squirmed in an attempt to be released from his father's hold.

"Oh, yes. You'll hear it every time until you understand the point of the story."

"But it's so loooooooong!" Kent whined.

"All right, I'll give you the condensed version. But you have to listen. I'd never been to the Amazon before and was excited to go exploring, so I left the group I came with and went out on my own. I wasn't planning on going too far, but I got lost and suffered a broken leg after I tripped over a log while running away from an anaconda. I fell in a small pool and leeches attached themselves to me. For three days I lay on the ground, fighting off poison dart frogs and giant centipedes with a stick. I was very lucky that some kind native people found me and carried me back to their home. They set my leg, pulled off the leeches, and brought me back to the camp of my group I'd been separated from. Now, what's the point of this story?"

Kent sighed with annoyance. "It's bad to run away."

"Yes, and why is it bad?"

"Because I could get lost or hurt."

"That's right. Can you please try to remember that the next time you get the urge to go exploring on your own?"

"Yeeeeesssss," Kent moaned, not bothering to hide his exasperation. "But why did *you* go if it's so dangerous?"

"Because, my precocious young fellow, a life without adventure isn't a life at all. We must live every moment remembering that we're in charge of writing our own life story. But when we go on adventures, getting lost or hurt doesn't make for a very good story. Do you understand?"

Kent pouted and looked at the ground. "I have to go to the bathroom."

Dromly sighed but smiled at Grace. "Did you find a magnificent piece of literature you want to check out?" he asked.

"No," she replied. "I only found information I already knew. But I appreciate your help." *You lying piece of shit.*

"My great pleasure," Dromly told her. "It was nice to see you. Stop by anytime!"

"Thank you!" she said. "See you next time. Good-bye, Kent!"

"Bye," Kent said with a wave.

Grace walked away, truly appreciating for the first time why Thomas wanted to deck Dromly in his smug, candy-ass face. Dromly and Morty must also be keeping all this from Thomas, otherwise, he would've told her about it. She and Thomas had no secrets from each other. *What else are they keeping from us?* She made it her new mission to find out.

Chapter 11

Tuesday, September 15, 2015

Anise heard a knock on her hotel door. She'd just gotten off the phone with Jonathan and had assured him that she and Nate were not sharing a hotel room. After hearing more about how untrustworthy Nate is and that Dr. Smithton doesn't trust him either, Anise had cut their infuriating conversation short, saying she was tired and wanted to go to bed. It hadn't been a lie, it was 10 o'clock and she had stayed up late for the last two nights.

"Hey," she said to Nate when she opened the door. He was wearing a t-shirt and swim trunks.

"Put on your bikini, honey, and let's go to the hot tub."

"I'm kinda tired," she told him. "I think I'm gonna turn in. It's only Tuesday, but this week has been long and stressful, and I need to relax."

"Since when is warm water not relaxing?" Nate asked. "Come on, it'll feel good."

"Yeah, that's true. Okay. Just give me a minute." She pulled her hot pink bikini from her suitcase.

"No hurry." He sat down in the desk chair to wait for her.

When she came out of the bathroom, she felt a bit disheveled. Her bikini was old and sun-faded, and her hair was piled up on top of her head in a loose bun because she'd been too tired to bother to make it look neater. She pushed the insecurities aside. It didn't matter. It wasn't like there was anyone here she wanted to impress.

To her surprise, Nate looked her up and down and gave her a mischievous grin.

"I told you no more flirting," she scolded. *Damn him.* That smile still made her want to sink her teeth into it.

"I didn't say a word!" he protested.

"You were looking at me," she said, throwing on a t-shirt and denim shorts. *It's just an attraction. It means nothing.*

"I'm not allowed to look at you now?"

She grabbed her flip-flops. "Not like that."

"Okay," he said. "How about like this instead?" He looked her up and down, and a horrified expression crossed his face. He turned his head in utter disgust.

Anise rolled her eyes at him but couldn't stop a laugh from escaping her lips as he continued his looks of revulsion. "Stop!" she said with a giggle, grabbing a pillow from the bed and throwing it at him.

With a grin, he caught it and tossed it back on her bed while she grabbed her hotel key. They were almost out the door when her phone rang. "Oh, I have to take this. Go on ahead. I'll be down in a few minutes."

"See you soon," he said.

"Hey," she said into her phone. "What's up?"

"Hey," Jonathan replied. "You know, Dr. Smithton didn't think it was a good idea for you to go out of town with Nate, either."

"Seriously?" She was annoyed immediately. "This is

why you called me again even after I said I wanted to go to bed?"

"Are you in bed?" he asked.

"Not yet."

"Then what's the problem?"

"The problem is that we just talked for half an hour about how you and Dr. Smithton think Nate is untrustworthy. I get it, okay? We really don't need to rehash this."

"Dr. Smithton also questioned *your* trustworthiness. He was wondering what kind of a person would willingly choose to spend time with a convicted criminal. And it's not just once in a while. Since he's been back, you've seen him every night."

"It hasn't been every night, and I don't give a shit what Dr. Smithton thinks!" Anise spat. "And just what are you trying to tell me? Are you saying you don't trust me now? Because before I left, you said you did."

"I trust you."

"Really? Because it doesn't seem that way! And Nate's only been back a few days. I saw him Saturday night when we went riding. I saw him yesterday because I was really upset, and he came over to help. And I'm here in Springfield tonight because I want to help him. These have been unique circumstances, and you *know* that. But by no means do I plan on seeing him every night. You're being really unreasonable."

"He might be after your amulet. You should really let Dr. S. keep it in his safe for you where Nate can't get to it," Jonathan said.

Through her anger, Anise almost laughed. Nate had already gotten into Dr. Smithton's safe. Easily. "Stop it!" she demanded. "We already had this conversation, too. I've told you both I'm keeping my amulet with me!"

"Would you consider donating blood?"

"What the hell does that mean?! Why would I donate blood if there's no blood drive?"

"I'm just asking, Anise. Lower your voice."

Their conversation went on for another fifteen minutes before she couldn't take it anymore and hung up on him. Anise felt her cheeks burning. She wanted to scream but punched a pillow a few times instead. The way Jonathan had spoken to her...it was like she was talking to someone else, not the man she knew and loved. Exhausted, she reached into her tote bag, grabbed the affirmation card she wanted, and flopped in the easy chair, not wanting to move. "I send love and compassion to those who challenge me," she read aloud from the card. There was a light tapping on her door.

"What happened?" Nate asked when she opened it.

She cringed when she realized she'd forgotten about Nate and the hot tub. "Nate, I'm so sorry. Jonathan called again and..." She stopped when the tears started falling.

Wrinkles formed on his forehead. "And what?" he asked.

She wiped away some tears with her fingers. "He kept telling me that Dr. Smithton thinks you're an untrustworthy criminal and that I can't be trusted to make good decisions because I'm choosing to be your friend. My mom and Brian always used to say I don't make good decisions, and he knows how much that hurts me. He kept pressuring me to hand over my amulet to Dr. Smithton so you can't take it from me when I already told him a million times I want to keep it with me. And he asked again if I'd donate blood. He couldn't even answer me when I asked him what he meant."

She dabbed her eyes with her sleeve. "It's like he's a completely different person—like he's possessed or something. He's definitely not himself. Something is very wrong. He obviously needs help, and I hate that I don't know what to do to help him!"

She took in a hiccuping breath. "Also, is he right? Do I make bad decisions? If he and my mom and Brian *all* told me that—"

"No!" Nate boomed. She'd seen his muscles become tense while she'd been telling him what Jonathan said, and he'd frowned with angry eyes when she started doubting herself. "He shouldn't be talking to you like that." Nate's words were gruff. "You're smart, and you make good decisions. I'm going to set him straight when we get back."

"No, please don't talk to him about it," Anise requested, her tears continuing to fall. "He doesn't like you and already hates that I'm here with you right now. It'll make everything worse for me." She looked at him with a sob.

"Come here." Nate pulled her into a tight embrace.

His arms were warm, strong, and comforting. Being so close to him calmed her, and her tears soon stopped soaking his t-shirt. She closed her eyes. The sound of his steady heartbeat was melodically soothing, and she could still smell the last of his woodsy cologne that had almost worn off for the day. His hand rubbed her upper back and made her tight shoulders relax. This felt good. Way too good. Guilt started gnawing at her gut. "I should get some sleep," she announced, forcing herself to step out of his embrace. There would be no more crossing of lines. And she needed some time alone to ponder why her attraction to him that supposedly meant nothing was only getting stronger.

"Okay. Feel better, honey," he said, and kissed her on the forehead before leaving her alone.

She crawled in bed and stared at the ceiling. *Do I still have feelings for Nate?* The guilt squeezed her stomach once more. *No,* she told herself. *I'm just stressed out about Jonathan. Nate was comforting, but that's all it was.*

Satisfied with her explanation of her emotions, she closed her eyes and fell asleep almost immediately.

Wednesday, September 16, 2015

NATE SAT IN SILENCE WHILE WAITING for Dan to come out and pick up the receiver so they could talk through the glass partition. Anise sat beside him. She looked happier and well-rested. He, on the other hand, had barely slept. His angry thoughts about Boy Scout making Anise cry built up so much nervous energy, he'd had to go for a run on the treadmill in the hotel's gym at two in the morning.

He'd eventually managed to relax enough to get into bed, but sleep had still eluded him. His mind had turned to Grace and the letter she'd sent him. He'd decided to read it after all, like Anise had suggested, and he was happy with his decision. He'd spent a good hour reading it and rereading it and wondering what Grace knew. Grace hadn't given him much information in her letter, but it was obvious she wanted him to come by for something. *If you want to protect Anise from Morty Smithton, it would be in your best interest to come visit me,* Grace had written. It had contained just enough information to intrigue him.

Nate's mind was brought back to the present when Dan picked up the receiver on the other side of the glass partition. Nate and Anise picked up their receivers as well.

"Nate, you came! Thank you!" Dan said with a look of relief and joy on his face. "It's so good to see you! How have you been?"

Nate sighed. *Let's get this over with.* "Fine, Dan. You?"

"As good as I can be, I guess. I lost some weight, so there's a silver lining."

Nate said nothing and just stared at his father, waiting for Dan to say something he cared about.

"Hello, Anise. It's nice to see you, too," Dan continued.

"Hi, Dan," Anise replied cautiously.

"This gives me a chance I never thought I'd get to apologize to you," he went on, still addressing his comments to Anise. "I'm sorry for everything that happened at the museum. You didn't deserve any of that, and I'm ashamed I was a part of it. I wasn't brave enough to stand up to Grace. I'm very glad that my son was stronger than I was and that he was able to save you from going to..." He looked behind his shoulder at the guards standing by the wall. "Well, you know. You wouldn't have deserved that. You were nothing but strong, brave, and on the side of right. I'm so happy my son has a friend like you on his side."

Anise looked at Dan with wide eyes and then looked at Nate. "Is he for real?" she mouthed to him, shielding her face from Dan.

Nate narrowed his eyes. Dan was either full of shit because he wanted something, or he was talking big now because Grace was locked away, and he didn't have to fear her anymore. Nate didn't care which. "What do you know about a cuff?" Nate demanded.

Dan looked confused and scratched his head under his red hair. "What's a cuff?"

"Great," Nate said, annoyed. "We came here for nothing."

Anise grabbed his hand. "We have reason to believe there may be a fourth piece of Armor Jewelry in the form of a thick bracelet called a cuff," Anise explained to Dan. "We were wondering if Grace had mentioned anything to you about it."

Dan shook his head. "No, I'm sorry, I don't know anything about it."

Anise frowned and looked at the ground.

Nate had enough. "Great, thanks for nothing," he said to Dan as he pushed back his chair and stood up.

"Son, *please*, wait. There's something very important I need to tell you," Dan begged.

Nate stood motionless and glared at Dan while still holding the receiver to his ear. Anise grabbed his hand again and pulled him back down into his chair. "We're here," she reasoned. "We might as well hear him out."

Silently, Nate sat and stared at Dan.

"It's about your mother," Dan told Nate.

"What did you do to her?" Nate demanded, leaning in closer to the glass that separated them.

Dan looked down at his lap, and his face burned as red as his hair. He took a deep breath. "Lorelei got on Grace's bad side. Grace was furious with her and felt threatened by what Lorelei found out about her. Grace ordered me to..." He looked back at the guards again. "I'm sure you know what I'm trying to say."

Nate sat frozen for a moment. He knew very well. Grace had ordered Dan to kill Lorelei. He saw Anise's eyes fill with tears and felt his mind trying to take him somewhere else to escape how he was feeling. *Focus.* He didn't need to run through his list of emotions. This one was pure hatred. "You fucking bastard..." Nate said through gritted teeth.

"I didn't! I didn't!" Dan insisted. "I couldn't. Nate, I know you won't believe this, but I loved her."

"So then what the fuck happened to her?" Nate demanded.

Big, rolling tears started streaming down Dan's face. He continued quietly with his hand over his mouth so the guards wouldn't hear. "She's okay. I'm sure she hates me for what I did, but I had to." Once more he looked back at the guards. "My lawyer is waiting outside for you. He'll hand you a letter from me explaining everything."

Nate felt numb. It was like he was outside of himself watching everything go down.

Dan gasped a hiccupping sob. "Now that Grace is going to be in prison for the rest of her life, Lorelei is safe. I want you to go get her and bring her home." Dan wiped his eyes with his sleeve. "Nate, say something."

"You sick fuck!" Nate began. He chewed Dan out with the most horrendous language he could think of. Dan sobbed uncontrollably. When Nate was out of words, he slammed down the receiver. "Let's go," he mumbled to Anise and started toward the door.

He heard Anise scolding Dan into the receiver. "What you did was heinous! If Nate decides to alert the authorities..."

"Let's go," Nate said again, and made his way toward the exit. For a moment, everything was still, and he felt nothing. It was like he was walking around in a dream—a time and a place that didn't really exist. He was startled when he heard Anise's voice.

"Wait up!" she called out.

Nate's mind was still hazy. "I didn't realize you weren't right behind me," Nate commented as they exited the prison. "I didn't mean to walk off without you."

"It's okay," she said, brushing it off. "Your dad is a piece of work."

"What did he say to you?" He hoped Dan hadn't upset her.

"I asked him—" Anise was interrupted by Dan's lawyer greeting them in the parking lot and handing Nate an envelope.

Without a word, Nate snatched the envelope from the man's hand and continued his long, quick strides to the car. He opened the passenger side door for Anise and then got in the driver's side and ripped open the envelope. His eyes scanned the letter. "He hid her. For the past 26 years, he's been paying some associates in some remote place in Nevada to hold my mother captive and take care of her. He told Grace that he killed her so she'd be happy."

"Oh my god!" Anise rested her hand on his arm.

"I can't believe she's still alive." He felt hot tears on his cheeks. "All this time."

Anise grabbed a tissue from her tote bag and dabbed

them away. "I'm so sorry."

"Apparently he's been making large payments to them every five years. The five years is almost up, and he's afraid of what they might do to her when the next payment doesn't arrive." Nate clenched his jaw, too livid to say anything more.

He started the car and was mostly silent on the drive to the airport. The feelings were too much. He was grateful that the dissociation was taking over just like it did every time some unbelievable, traumatic shit happened. It made his body relax and his mind go blank.

Anise began filling the silence. "To answer your question about what Dan said to me, after you got up, I asked Dan what Lorelei had on Grace that threatened her so much." Nate listened but wasn't in the state of mind to react. Anise continued, "He said that your mom returned some artifacts that Grace had stolen from the museum. The museum had promised not to press charges—they just wanted their pieces back. I've been thinking—given that information, doesn't the fact that Grace ordered Dan to kill her seem like an overreaction to you?"

"Overreaction is Grace's middle name," Nate said in a flat voice.

"Right, but even for Grace it seems extreme," argued Anise.

"Dan might be full of shit. I don't know if I believe a word of what he said."

"What would be his motivation for telling you a lie like that?"

Nate shrugged.

"I think it's more likely that whatever Lorelei returned to the museum was something that was very important to Grace," Anise continued.

"You think it was the cuff?" Nate asked, feeling his mind begin to clear a bit.

"Yes. Maybe," she replied.

With his mind frozen and numb, he wasn't sure he

would've put that together, but it made perfect sense. At the next red light he looked at her, took her hand, and kissed the back of it to thank her. Not only was this woman beautiful and kind, she was also very smart.

"Do you think we should call the police or the FBI?" she asked. "Who would take this case and bring Lorelei home?"

He shook his head. "This is my *mother*. I don't trust anyone with her welfare except for me. I'll be bringing her home myself."

After a pause, Anise told him, "I want to come with you when you go find your mom."

"No," he denied her firmly. "We don't know what we'll be in for. It might be dangerous."

"You shouldn't have to do this alone. I can help," she insisted.

"You can help me by staying home and staying safe."

"Okay, I admit the thought of traveling to a remote part of the country to find your mother who's been held captive for the last quarter of a century makes me nervous, but I'm trying to not let my fear make my choices for me anymore." She put her hand on the amulet she'd tucked underneath her top. "I'll be safe as long as I'm wearing this. I want to be there for you. Besides, if I'm right, then Lorelei might know something about the cuff. If she can tell me something about it, maybe I can finally help Jonathan."

Nate resisted the urge to roll his eyes. He was sick of hearing about how dedicated she was to Boy Scout—the self-righteous dickhead who makes her cry. He'd love her company, but didn't know what to expect and was concerned for her safety. "I still think you should stay home. I bet Boy Scout would agree with me. If Dan is telling the truth and my mother really *is* still alive, I promise I'll ask her about the cuff and let you know."

"Nice try," Anise scoffed. "I don't want you to go alone. If it *is* dangerous, I want to be there to help you.

And with this," she said, motioning to the amulet, "then I can."

"There's something else you can do with me that would be a lot safer," he countered. "I read Grace's letter. She doesn't say much, but she mentioned that you're not safe from Smithton. I'd bet my life that she knows something about the cuff and what Smithton is doing with it."

"I know you're not suggesting we go see *her*," Anise said in a warning tone.

"I am. She's going to be way more knowledgeable than Dan."

Anise narrowed her eyebrows at him. "I already told you I don't want anything to do with her! And if you go see her I don't want anything to do with you either! She'll worm her way back in your life just like she did three years ago, and once she's there, she'll make another attempt at my life!" She leaned back in her seat with her arms crossed, breathing heavily. She wiped away a few tears.

Her overreaction at his mere suggestion worried Nate. "And I told you I don't want her in my life. I just want to ask her about the cuff. And she can't make another attempt at your life. She's locked away permanently. You have nothing to be afraid of, honey."

"I said no, and I meant it! We're not seeing her, and I'm going with you to get your mom so the amulet can protect us both! I'm not taking 'no' for an answer!" She glared at him with a clenched jaw.

Her unwarranted outburst still concerned him, but he let it go so she could settle down. The more he thought about it, leaving her with Boy Scout might not be safe for her either. Her boyfriend was unstable with his weird headaches and outbursts and the gaslighting he was putting Anise through. But if Nate brought her to Nevada with him, at least he could do everything in his power to protect her. He shrugged in defeat. "Fine."

"Thank you," she said in a softer tone. "When do you want to go?"

Chapter 12

Fifty-three years ago

Monday, March 5, 1962

The museum director called Grace into his office, and she sat in a chair in front of his desk. "We've been getting calls all morning," he grumbled with a frown. "Patrons wanting to cancel their memberships. Sponsors pulling out. Reporters wanting answers. Have you seen this?" he asked, tossing a newspaper over his desk in her direction.

She picked up the paper and started reading the article about the Springfield Museum. An anonymous museum employee had spoken to the media about the deaccession Grace had approved and had called her behavior unethical. "A sale of precious artifacts to a private buyer could easily endanger the integrity of the artifacts, put the future of their care at risk, and prevent the public and future generations from being able to enjoy them," the quote read. "It was an irresponsible act based solely on greed. Artifacts don't exist to protect the future of museums; museums exist to protect the future of artifacts. And that's exactly what didn't happen at the Springfield Museum."

Grace looked up to the museum director's scowl. "I saved the museum," she argued. "We'd have gone out of business if I hadn't. I thought everyone was pleased."

"We were," agreed the director, "until this article put the entire town up in arms. Your actions may have finished us. I have a lot of people to answer to, and they're going to want actions to be taken. I unfortunately have to do some damage control if the museum is to survive. Grace, I'm sorry, but I have to let you go."

Grace stood up. She had plenty of choice words for the director but held her tongue. If she ever wanted to work in the industry again, she'd need an excellent letter of recommendation from him. She turned, marched out of his office, and straight into Morty's. "It was you, wasn't it?" she demanded of him.

"What are you talking about?" Morty asked her, calmly.

"I just got fired!" she snapped at him. "Apparently, *someone* anonymously contacted the press to publicly complain about the deaccession!"

Morty just looked at her and smiled.

"You cost me my job, and now the museum might go under anyway! How could you do this?" She put a hand to her forehead. An awful headache was coming on. She had noticed them increasing in frequency lately, and they usually happened around Morty, especially when he would frustrate her with his constant talks about the group he wanted to start to find and collect the Armor Jewelry. Ever since the party her co-workers gave her a couple months ago, he had stopped by her office daily to discuss it, as if she wanted to hear it.

"I'm sorry to hear you lost your job, Grace. Good luck with finding a new one. You'll need it," he said.

"So you're not even going to own up to what you did?" she demanded. "You're a coward Morty, and you always have been!" She turned to leave but changed her mind. "Why? I just want to know why?"

"Because I can't stand to look at your face every day!" he snarled.

She stormed out of his office and into hers, grabbing an empty box on her way. She threw her belongings into the box and left the museum without saying good-bye to anyone.

Thursday, October 25, 1962

GRACE LAY IN HER HOSPITAL BED, sweaty and exhausted. Thomas stood next to her, and together, they looked lovingly at the screaming infant in Grace's arms. The baby had a healthy set of lungs and a tuft of red hair on top of his head.

"What do you want to call our son?" Thomas asked Grace.

"Danny," Grace replied.

"After your brother."

"Yes. He'll be Daniel Thomas Brevain."

Thomas smiled. "I like it. It suits him." He suddenly saw something move outside the room. He kissed his son's forehead. "I'll be right back," he said. "I left the camera in the car."

He stepped out of the room and ran right into Morty. Grabbing Morty's wrist, he dragged him halfway down the hall so Grace wouldn't hear. "Smithton, what the hell are you doing here?"

"I wanted to congratulate Grace," he said. "How is she? How's the baby?"

Thomas looked up at the taller man, knowing full well he could easily intimidate him. "You're full of shit! Why are you really here? You told her you never want to see her face again, but for months you've been following Grace wherever she goes. Asking her to join some group to find the Armor Jewelry. Telling her she doesn't love me anymore. What the hell, Smithton?" He took another step toward Morty.

Morty swallowed and took a step back, his nervous eyes darting back and forth. "Grace and I are old friends. Why shouldn't I congratulate her today?"

"You're not friends anymore, and you haven't been for years," Thomas said with a snarl. "You're not even co-workers anymore since you got her fired."

"Look at you, playing the dutiful husband," Smithton scoffed. "As if you care about her at all. We both know why you really married her."

"You better stay away from my wife if you know what's good for you!" Thomas warned.

"Grace and I have history," Smithton insisted. "She wants to see me whether you like it or not. Act as possessive as you want, but one kind word from me, and she'll want to resume our friendship. And there's nothing you can do about it."

"I *said* stay away from my wife!" Thomas said as he took a step toward Smithton with clenched fists.

Smithton took a step back and in a reactionary motion, raised his hands to protect his face.

"What the hell is this?" Thomas asked, grabbing Smithton's wrist. When Morty had lifted his arms, Thomas had caught a glimpse of something all too familiar around Morty's wrist.

"None of your business!" Morty replied, trying to pull his arm away.

Thomas held on to Smithton's wrist tightly and pushed back his sleeve to see it better. "This is the cuff from the Armor Jewelry! How the hell did you get this?" Thomas demanded. He grabbed the cuff and pulled, attempting to yank it off of Smithton's wrist.

"Stop!" Morty yelled, and it caught the attention of a

security guard.

"Is there a problem here?" the guard demanded.

"No," Thomas told him, dropping Morty's wrist. "No problem."

"No problem. I'll keep my voice down," Smithton told the guard.

"Did Dromly give this to you?" Thomas demanded. He eyed the guard who walked away but not very far.

"As a matter of fact, yes. Since you quit your position at the university a few months ago to work at the museum, I'm now helping Dromly uncover all the Armor Jewelry secrets that you weren't able to find."

Thomas held back a smirk. Smithton and Dromly couldn't even imagine how much he'd uncovered about the Armor Jewelry and kept to himself. It would take them decades to catch up to him at the rate they were going. Still, he wanted them to never catch up. How much *did* Smithton know? "Are you trying to brainwash my wife with this cuff? Is that why she's been getting so many headaches and hallucinations?" he demanded.

"She's getting headaches and hallucinations?" Smithton asked. "Has she had any other strange experiences?"

Thomas narrowed his eyes. *Shit.* Smithton might know more than he thought. "Like what?" he tested him.

"Like...visions?"

Shit. Shit!

So Morty *did* know about Grace's dormant seer abilities. What was his plan? To try to get her loyalties back to his side so he could get her to read the wisdom on the Plate of Destiny for him and hoard the knowledge for himself and Dromly? Thomas felt a wave of fear wash over him. He needed to get that cuff. Unfortunately, there was nothing he could do in a public place without attracting attention. "Leave her alone! And stop playing with the cuff. You're using it wrong, and you're going to end up hurting someone. You don't know what you're doing!"

"And you do? By all means, enlighten me. Please."

Thomas scowled. There was no way he'd share anything he knew with Morty. Morty would share it with Dromly, and that thought made Thomas fume. He'd made a vow that Dromly would never get anything from him ever again. The piece-of-shit bastard could find it himself. Soon it would be too late for Dromly anyway. Thomas was nearing his goal of finding the Plate of Destiny. He couldn't wait to see the look on Dromly's face when he realized how badly he'd been beaten. "You're leaving, Smithton. *Now!*"

"What do you know that you aren't telling me, Brevain?"

"Start walking!"

Smithton held his hands up in submission. "Very well," he agreed. Thomas followed him out to the parking garage. Grabbing his camera from the car, he watched as Smithton drove away.

"What took you so long?" Grace asked him when Thomas returned to her room. He snapped some photos of her and Daniel Thomas before answering her question.

"Smithton was lurking around outside the door," he said with a frown.

"Morty? What did he want?"

"He said he wanted to congratulate you. But I think he had another motive. I believe I figured out why you mysteriously keep running into him when you're out."

"Why?" Grace asked with deep interest. "Why is he there every time I turn around?"

"He lifted his arms in the hallway when I stepped toward him, and I caught sight of the cuff you told me about."

"What? Did it have three blue stones on it?" she asked, wide-eyed.

"Yes, it did. And several smaller red ones."

"How the hell did he get it?"

"I don't know," said Thomas. "But I think he's been

trying to brainwash you with it, and I'm wondering if your headaches and hallucinations have something to do with that and weren't just pregnancy-related like the doctor thought. What has he been talking to you about lately?"

"He keeps wanting me to join a team he's putting together to find the rest of the Armor Jewelry."

"All that's missing is the amulet, right?"

"Yes. We already know where the ring is," Grace said. "When Richard Woods died, his parents held on to it until his younger sister turned twenty. She's in possession of it now. We also already found the earrings—they belong to a man in Germany. So if Morty already has the cuff, then you're right, it means he's just looking for the amulet. Once he know where they all are, he'll want to collect them and try to start his ridiculous utopia."

"I want you to be very careful, Grace," Thomas told her. "Promise me you'll stay away from him."

"I promise." Grace kissed her son's forehead and then looked back to Thomas. "Are you sure you never heard anything about the Armor Jewelry from Dromly or Morty? Like I told you, I knew they were hiding something from me ever since that day in the library when I found out about the cuff; I just don't know what it is or why on earth Morty would want to brainwash me."

Thomas shook his head. "I never heard anything about the Jewelry from Dromly or Morty," he lied. "Everything I know about it I learned from you."

"Okay," she said. "But if you do hear anything..."

"Of course. I'll come to you right away."

Chapter 13

Fifty-two years ago

Sunday, June 23, 1963

"My god," Morty said when he walked into Dromly's hospital room. The professor had a cast on practically his entire body which lay supine in the stark, white bed. He had one good arm which he used to wave Morty over to his bedside.

"Don't worry," Dromly said. "I'm going to live."

"This must've been some car accident. Are you in pain?"

Dromly nodded. "When I'm silent, I feel nothing but the pain. That's when I attempt to visualize my bones growing back together."

"Does that really help?" Morty asked with a laugh. His smile faded when he saw the serious expression on Dromly's face.

"Absolutely."

"Oh? How so?"

"Morty, as you know, I've been all over the world and

met many different people. Indigenous medicine men and women, shamans, and modern day witches from lands near and far have convinced me that magick is real. Not the abracadabra type of stage magic, of course, but magick in the form of manifestation of desires using the Hermetic laws of the universe." His eyes sparkled. "Wanting desperately and then releasing the desperation, allowing it to turn into a kind of knowing that what you desire will be yours. A knowing that's so sure of itself that wanting it isn't even necessary anymore. In fact, wanting would be detrimental to the manifestation process, as it would indicate some doubt in the mind and heart of the practitioner, and doubt is what negates magickal ability in the first place. Why? Because doubt is the opposite of knowing, and knowing is the seed of manifestation."

Morty cleared his throat. "I see. I'm glad you're okay. Well, that you're going to be okay."

"Thanks for visiting. How have your experiments with the cuff been going?"

"Not bad. Ever since you gave it to me, I've been testing it out on co-workers and other people I know."

"And?" Dromly raised his eyebrows.

"Most of them have responded by accepting some ideas I've place in their minds."

"*Most* of them?"

"Yes," Morty said. "All but one."

"Interesting. What else have you found out?"

"It causes side effects."

"Side effects? I don't recall reading about side effects in any of the legends."

"Yes, headaches and hallucinations. In all of them. Even in the one person who hasn't responded otherwise."

"I see." Dromly shifted and then cried out in pain.

A nurse ran in the room. After assuring her he was okay, he added, "I wonder why Thomas never found out any of this. He had the cuff for quite a while." Dromly narrowed his eyes in thought.

Morty was surprised. He thought about the day he tried to visit Grace in the hospital after she had given birth. Thomas had asked him if he was trying to brainwash Grace because she was having headaches and hallucinations. Thomas knew very well about the side effects. Why would he keep that from Dromly? Thomas had also said Morty was using the cuff incorrectly, so there was more he hadn't shared with their professor. Was there anything else he was keeping a secret?

"I've suspected there are things Brevain is keeping from us," Morty offered.

"As have I," Dromly agreed. "Which is why I took the cuff from him and gave it to you. Speaking of the cuff, I need you to do something for me."

"Certainly. Happy to help if I can."

"I need you to use the cuff to make me an army."

"An army?"

"Yes. Create a troop of people who are ready to do the bidding of whoever is wearing the cuff. I need unquestioned loyalty."

Morty's stomach burned. He didn't like the sound of this request. What would Dromly want them to do? "May I ask why?"

"Someone wants to kill me, Morty. Not only will this army be my bodyguards, but they can help me when I travel to search for the Plate of Destiny."

"Who wants to kill you? Does this have anything to do with the accident? We should call the authorities!"

"He hasn't done anything yet. Well, he has, but nothing that I can prove. They won't arrest him for a potential future crime. That's why I need the army."

"I don't feel comfortable with this, Professor." Morty frowned. "It sounds like the members of this brainwashed army would be in danger of getting hurt or worse."

"I need you to do this for me, Morty. I believe there are others who want the Plate of Destiny. And they'll kill for it if they must."

"Others?! Who? How many?"

"My point is that these people will stop at nothing. Mark my words, this Plate is going to cause a war if I don't find it soon. Many innocent lives will be lost looking for the Plate. It needs to be found by someone like us. Someone who'll use the knowledge of life and death for good. Someone who's smart enough to figure out how to read it and be able to bring back to life all those who passed on unnecessarily. You want to be able to right all the wrongs, don't you, Morty?"

"I suppose, but I don't want to hurt anyone in the process."

"Of course not, but once we find the Plate, we can heal everyone who's been hurt."

"We can?"

"Probably. According to the legends, the cuff is supposed to heal as well as brainwash. Your task is to figure out how to do it. Plus, with the Plate we'll have all the secrets of life and death, remember? We'll be like *gods*, Morty. But the longer this process is dragged out, the more people will get hurt. We need to find the Plate. And the sooner, the better. Making me an army that can both protect me and help me search for it when I get out of here is the fastest way to our goal. Start with your brawniest co-workers."

Morty sat in silence, not knowing what to think. This could greatly impact the amount of time he'd have to attempt to use the cuff on Grace.

"And there's something else I need you to do."

Morty's butterflies returned. "Yes?"

"I need you to go to my office and retrieve the seer's wand."

"The wand with the obsidian on it?"

"Yes. Then you'll need to find every redheaded woman you can and have her form a connection with the wand. These will need to be women that'll be easy for you to keep track of throughout the years. When I find the Plate of Destiny, I'll need a seer with hair of flame to read the wisdom on the Plate." He continued when he saw Morty's doubtful face. "I know it's a big thing to ask Morty, but I need you."

"If I do that, then I'll need to use the cuff on them in order to activate their seer's abilities," Morty said, remembering Thomas's notes from the trapdoor in Dromly's office.

"Yes," Dromly said with a confused look. "But I don't remember telling you that."

"Uh..." Morty cursed himself for saying something he shouldn't have. "Well...well, you did," he lied, not wanting Dromly to know that he ransacked his office. "How else would I have known?"

"Indeed. Perhaps the blow to my head has caused some memory lapses."

"Has Grace made a connection with the wand?" Morty asked, knowing full well that she had.

"Yes. But we can't know which woman will be willing and able to help when the time comes, so having several choices is a smart way to go. Plus, I don't believe we can trust Grace either. Not after what she did to you."

Morty sighed. It was the last thing he wanted to agree to, but if he was going to execute his plan for Grace, he needed access to the Armor Jewelry and therefore had no choice but to stay close to Dromly. "Is there anything else we'd need to do?"

"Plenty," Dromly told him. "Starting with filling in some blanks. I've been finding bits and pieces of the legends about the seer's wand and the Plate of Destiny. But I feel like there are parts missing. I plan on heading back to Europe and Florida as soon as I heal in order to look for them."

Morty grabbed his chin in thought. He wondered if Thomas might know the missing parts of the legends and was keeping them hidden from Dromly.

"Now," asked Dromly. "What have you heard about

my wife and son?"

"Nothing. They haven't visited?"

"No." Dromly sighed and closed his eyes. "But that's a long story best saved for another time."

Monday, October 28, 1963

GRACE SAT ON HER LIVING ROOM floor playing blocks with her son. "Hi!" she chirped at Thomas when he got home from work.

"Hi," he replied, kissing her. "Hi, Dan the Man!" Dan looked at his father with wide brown eyes, stood up, and toddled over to him.

"How was your day?" she asked.

"Excellent! I booked my trip to Florida for next week."

"You're going to Florida? Why?"

"There's a symposium being held. I brought it up to the director and he agreed to fund my travel."

"That's great, but...I was hoping we'd travel places together once Dan got a little older."

"We'll go again, don't worry," he said. "How was your day?"

"Morty came over," Grace told him.

"What?" Thomas snapped. He picked up Dan and gave him a hug.

"He's still trying to brainwash me. It was the same old thing. He wanted me to join his team and said he regretted how we've drifted apart. He just keeps repeating it every time he sees me. And he keeps saying that I don't love you anymore. It's really strange. But it's not working. I love you more than anyone. I have no desire to join his team. And although I used to be sad that we weren't friends anymore, I've accepted it, and I'm okay with it."

"Well, I'm not okay with him coming over here. I told him to stay away from you!" Thomas snarled. "First thing tomorrow I'm going to give him a piece of my mind!"

"Thank you," Grace told him. "But for now, I can tell that someone needs a new diaper." She took Dan from Thomas and went into the nursery.

The phone began to ring. "Hello?" Thomas said into the receiver. After a pause, he peered down the hall to make sure Grace was still in the nursery and then hissed into the phone, "How dare you call me at home again? My wife is here!...I've told you everything about the Armor Jewelry already...Yes, the Plate of Destiny is fabled to bring back the dead. It holds the secrets of life and death... Sure, they come back just how you remember them...You even get to pick how old they are...No, don't worry, you can change your own age too. It'll be like they never left... How did you know I'm going to Florida? Is that why you're calling me now?...Why do you think I'm going to look for the Plate?...I've told you everything you need to know...No, there's nothing I've left out...No, I will not meet your associate at my office or anywhere...I owe you nothing!...Well, I no longer agree to doing you a favor... Go ahead and tell anyone you want that you caught me stealing from Dromly's office! You're in prison now; do you really think they'd believe you over me? Don't call here again!" He slammed the phone down and tried to get his hands to stop shaking. "Idiot!" he said under his breath. "He believes every stupid lie I feed him." Thomas took a deep breath in and let it out slowly. A quiet laugh escaped his lips. *That's not how the Plate works at all.*

"Who was it?" Grace called out.

"Uh...speak of the devil."

"Morty? What did he want?"

"He needs some paperwork and books that I have. I'm going to run them over to the museum."

"Now? No, please don't leave," Grace begged him as she rejoined him in the living room. "Let's have a nice evening together, just the three of us."

"I won't be long," Thomas promised.

"I'm surprised you wanted to start working at the museum," Grace said. "Now you have to see Morty daily and work with him closely. I know he's not your favorite person."

"Better him than Dromly."

"I know you don't like Dromly either, but—"

"Dromly steals my research! He deserves a bullet in his brain!" He went to the bedroom and opened his safe, pulling out a large briefcase and a duffle bag. He couldn't get the phone call out of his mind. Trouble was going to happen, and soon. "How do you feel about moving?" he asked her as he grabbed the handle of the front door. "Would you prefer Europe or Australia? Africa? South America?"

His wife narrowed her eyebrows in confusion. "What are you talking about?"

He shook his head. "I'm sorry. Truly. We have to talk when I get home," he replied, and walked out the door.

Thomas stopped by a mailbox and hurriedly addressed an envelope to his lawyer. He stuffed it with a letter about the Armor Jewelry and the Plate of Destiny addressed to a Mr. Louis Stannell, his young daughter Ms. Deborah Stannell, or the direct descendants of Ms. Deborah Stannell, and the instructions to hand deliver the letter only in the event of his death. If Mr. Stannell was not receptive, a copy of the letter would need to be delivered to Deborah when she became of age. If she was not responsive, then her children would receive a copy.

He also included a letter he'd written to Betty. He didn't mention the Armor Jewelry, but stressed that he got in over his head with something he couldn't talk about. He apologized again for hurting her and professed his undying love for her. He couldn't make her understand, but hopefully he could at least make her feel loved with his words.

Upon arriving at the museum, Thomas parked in the back and pushed the dumpster until it was directly under his office window. He threw the contents of the briefcase and the duffel bag in the dumpster, poured some gasoline over the trash, and tossed in a match. As the dumpster went up in flames, he raced up the stairs to his office and opened his safe and the window. He dropped the items in his safe out of the window and into the flames below. Sighing with relief, he closed the window and his safe. Looking both ways down the hallway outside of his office door, he then headed toward Morty's office. They had something very important to discuss.

Shit!

He just remembered another duffel bag in his office closet full of things he needed to burn. He started heading back to his office.

"Thomas?" Morty said, poking his head out of his office door and seeing him in the hallway.

I'll have to burn them later, Thomas thought. He turned around again to face his colleague. "Morty, we need to talk."

THAT WAS STRANGE, GRACE THOUGHT WHEN her husband left to go back to the museum. What was going on that she didn't know about? Grace had a nagging feeling that something wasn't right. She put Dan in his crib and started gathering his things. She'd have the neighbor baby-sit for a few hours while she found Thomas and made sure he was okay.

After dropping Dan next door and speeding to the museum, Grace hurried inside and headed toward Morty's office. She had seen Thomas's car in the parking lot, so she knew he was already here. For some reason the dumpster was on fire, but she'd call the fire department after she found Thomas and made sure he was okay. She was in the stairwell when the lights went out. "Fantastic," she grumbled, as she felt her way up the stairs in the dark. She got to the floor the curator's offices were on and started feeling her way down the hallway. Where the hell was the emergency lighting? Suddenly, she heard a gunshot. She dropped to the ground, hearing nothing but her pounding heart for a few seconds. Another gunshot made her jump. Quick footsteps scurried and a door slammed. Her first thought was that Thomas would want her to run away too in that situation, but she had to find him. She darted down the hallway as fast as she could go in the dark. "Thomas?" she called out. "Thomas?!"

She saw a beam of light that must be a flashlight. It was coming from Morty's office. She heard Morty let out something in between a yell and a gasp. Hurrying to his office, she poked her head in and what she saw was something she'd never forget as long as she lived.

"THOMAS!" she screamed. He was on the floor, a pool of blood forming underneath him. Breathing heavily, she kneeled down next to his body, unable to take her eyes off the bullet holes in his chest. "NO!" she screamed, touching his chest with her shaking hands and feeling for a heartbeat. She found nothing. No pulse either, and no breath. He was gone. "You!" she screamed at Morty. "How could you?" She got up and beat her fists on his chest. "You killed him!"

"Grace, I..."

"SHUT UP!" she screamed. The lights came back on. *Kill him,* she heard a voice in her head say to her. *He's weak and deserves to die.* She knew what she wanted to do. Morty was as good as dead. "Where's the gun?" she demanded. "How did you get rid of it so quickly?"

"I don't own a gun, Grace."

"LIAR!" She began looking through his desk drawers when the guards came barging in and saw Thomas's body.

"What happened here?" they demanded, guns drawn.

"I was looking for my husband," Grace wailed, her face red with anger and her head pounding. She pulled on her hair so hard that a clump of it came out in her fist. With rage, she threw it on the ground. "The lights were out, and I was in the hallway when I heard the gunshots. He killed my husband!" she said, pointing a finger at Morty.

"I killed no one," Morty insisted. "Thomas and I were talking in my office when the lights suddenly went out. Not long afterward, someone fired two shots into my office from the doorway and then ran away. It was dark, and I couldn't tell who it was."

"Both of you have a seat and don't move," the guards told them. "The police and an ambulance have been called, and they're on their way." The guards stepped out of the office and stood in front of the door.

Grace and Morty sat in his two guest chairs next to his desk. She leaned over to him. "I didn't think you had it in you to kill anyone."

"I don't," he replied.

She looked at him. "I know you. You really don't. You hired someone to do it, didn't you?! I guess I misjudged the depth of your jealousy of Thomas. He's the father of my child, not to mention twice the man you'll ever be, and you know it."

Morty hung his head.

"Look at you trembling, you weak, disgusting candy-ass! You've been planning this for a while, haven't you? You've been hating Thomas for so long, it's been eating you up inside! You baited him to come by so you could claim you were defending yourself! You look like you're about to cry; I bet you're ready to turn that gun on yourself. I think you should do it. You don't deserve to be alive after murdering a good man like Thomas. If I had found any kind of a weapon in here, you'd be dead right now, too." She glared at him.

He nodded and looked worried. "I know."

She leaned toward him and whispered, "I want you to know that I don't plan on killing you anymore."

A wave of relief could be seen on his face. "You don't?"

"No! You killed my husband! Death is too easy for you!" she screamed at him. She sent him hate in her glare and watched him squirm. "I have a better plan instead. You took everything from me, Morty. You took away Thomas, your friendship, my career... so, I'm going to do the same thing to you. I know what you want. You're trying to find all four pieces of the Armor Jewelry. I know how the cuff works and what you're trying to do with it. So, I'm going to find it all first. It'll be mine, and I'll use it to find the Plate of Destiny. And once I do, I can bring Thomas back. I'll have all the secrets of life and death, my husband, and my son, and you'll have nothing but a lonely, sad existence, you weak, pathetic sack of shit. And don't think you won't be rotting in prison for this! I'll see to it that you never see the light of day again!"

Morty's eyes grew wide. "So Thomas told you about the cuff and the Plate."

Grace shot him a dirty look. "No, Thomas never knew until *I* told *him*. I told him after I found out a year or two ago! How did *you* know about them?"

"Dromly told me. And Thomas most certainly knew. He and Dromly have been discussing them for years."

"Thomas knew nothing! Stop trying to mess with my mind! Haven't you done enough?!"

"Thomas wasn't the man you thought he was."

"Shut up!" she yelled at him. "Thomas would've told me anything he knew!"

"You'll never be able to find the Plate of Destiny before I do," Morty told her with a scoff. "The cuff has helped me to get several people on my side. You're all alone now, not that I have to remind you of that," he added, looking at Thomas's body.

Even though she knew he was scared and that his

uncharacteristic bravado proved it, his comments enraged her anyway. She attacked him and had to be held back by the guards.

MORTY NERVOUSLY WRUNG HIS HANDS AND got up to pace his office. Grace needed to know the truth. He wanted to tell her everything—Thomas's plan to use her as a seer once he found the Plate of Destiny, that he married her for that purpose only, and that Thomas had even been keeping things from Dromly. But if he did that, she wouldn't believe him. That's why he had to keep using the cuff on her, so she'd have her seer powers activated and start to have visions of the truth. As angry as Morty was at her, Grace still deserved that much.

And what exactly happened tonight? He looked at his former friend as she sat in his office stewing. Maybe she found out that Thomas had been using her, and *she* was the murderer. Maybe framing him for Thomas's death was a bonus to get back at him for dumping her, getting her fired, and trying to brainwash her with the cuff. He shuddered as he realized how terrified he was of her. Who else would want to kill Thomas but her? Who else might hate Thomas?

Back and forth he continued to pace. As he passed his window, he peered out and saw a figure running across the parking lot. It carried a duffel bag and wore a cape. Involuntarily, he let out a noise somewhere between a yell and a gasp. Of course! *Dromly* hated Thomas for keeping things from him.

"What is it?" asked one of the guards as he came to the window. "Why are you yelling?"

Morty had a realization that if Dromly had killed Thomas, he could be next if Dromly felt betrayed by him in any way. But for now, what was he going to tell this guard? "Uh...there's a fire in the dumpster!" he said, pointing.

WHEN GRACE FINALLY GOT BACK HOME, she held her son, and her tears landed on his soft skin. "I'm so sorry, Dan," she apologized in a shaky, breathless voice. "Your daddy can't come home anymore. Your mommy doesn't have a job or a way to support herself and you. The bad man who killed your father was questioned, but not arrested. He's smart and was able to fool everyone. He didn't fool me, though. I promise you, Dan, I'll take away Morty's dreams and future just like he took ours! I promise I'll do everything I can to make sure you're taken care of." She kissed Dan and held him close. A plan began forming in her mind.

Chapter 14

Present day

Thursday, September 17, 2015

"Hi," Anise said as she stepped into Jonathan's apartment. He was sitting on his couch strumming his guitar. His eyes weren't glazed over, and they lit up when he saw her. This was the Jonathan she knew and loved. The nerves she'd felt on her way over lessened slightly. He seemed completely different than how he'd been over the phone when she was in Springfield. She'd been worried he'd still be angry and say things that didn't make sense. But he seemed happy and calm. He was his old self again. She relaxed a little more, but still wanted to talk to him about the hurtful phone conversations they had had.

The sun brightened the small room which felt warm and cozy. Acoustic and electric guitars hung on the walls next to framed concert posters and one of Anise's landscape paintings of the mountains that could be seen from her apartment balcony. She removed her shoes and stepped onto the light brown carpeting, patting Max on the head when he came to greet her with a wagging tail.

"Hello, beautiful!" Jonathan sang, before getting up to take her into his arms and kiss her. "I missed you."

She kissed him back and thought about what she wanted to say. Looking into Jonathan's eyes, her nerves came back in full force, as she knew he wasn't going to like what she needed to tell him. Plus, the conversation about the phone calls when she was in Springfield wouldn't be fun either. Before she could bring any of it up, he started asking her questions about her trip.

"So how was it?" he asked as they sat on his deep, beige couch.

"Intense," she admitted, putting her tote bag on his wooden coffee table. "I didn't realize how much anger Nate has for his family. I'm glad I was there for him."

"You're a good friend," Jonathan told her. "What did Dan have to say?"

Anise's eyes opened wide. "You'll never believe it!" she said. "Dan told us that Nate's mom, Lorelei, is still alive. That he's been hiding her away in some remote county in Nevada somewhere ever since Nate was little instead of killing her like Grace had ordered him to do!"

"Are you serious?" he asked, his eyebrows raising in disbelief.

She nodded. "Nate was really upset."

"I can imagine," Jonathan replied.

"Dan asked Nate to go get his mother and bring her home. Now that Grace is in prison, Lorelei will be safe."

Jonathan wore a doubtful expression. "Nate should call the authorities, not handle this himself."

"It's his *mother*. He wants to go himself. He doesn't trust anyone else to do it."

"That's stupid. He should leave it to the professionals." Jonathan crossed his arms. "When is he leaving?"

"Tomorrow," said Anise. "And I wanted to talk to you about that..."

Jonathan's eyes narrowed. "Anise, you're not going with him, are you?"

She nodded. "Yes."

"No! It could be dangerous!"

"That's why I don't want Nate to go alone."

"You really think *you* can protect him if something happens?" he demanded.

"I think as long as I'm wearing this, then yes, I have a really good chance at protecting us both," she said, putting a hand over the amulet which was around her neck as always.

"How the hell is he talking you into participating in all his family drama?" Jonathan asked in a raised voice.

"He's not," Anise said calmly. "I offered to go with him. He also told me no at first. But I wanted to go. I insisted."

"Why would you do that?" Jonathan demanded with disbelief. He pulled on his hair and winced in pain.

"Are you getting another stress migraine?"

"Yes." He continued pulling on his hair, his body was trembling, and his face was giving her a look of disgust.

"Are you having hallucinations, too?"

"Yeah." He rubbed his forehead and frowned.

"What are you seeing?"

"Your skin is melting off your body and into a puddle that's saturating my carpet. It's disturbing, but I know it's not real."

"I'm so sorry. What can I do?" she asked. She hated that she was causing him so much stress.

"I just need your skeleton to answer my question. Please."

She took a deep breath and let it out. Jonathan wouldn't like hearing what she was about to say, and Nate wouldn't want her to say it. But she had to. She didn't want to lie to Jonathan. "The reason I want to go is because I think Lorelei might have more information about the Armor Jewelry, and I need to hear what she has to say as soon as possible."

"Anise, if you want more information about the Armor Jewelry, just ask Dr. S. He knows more about it than anyone. Why would you put yourself in a dangerous situation? What could Nate's mother possibly know about it?"

"Dr. Smithton *and* Grace know more about it than anyone," Anise corrected him. "Dr. Smithton said that himself. Dan told us that Grace wanted Lorelei dead because of something she had on Grace. Grace is obsessed with the Jewelry, so whatever Lorelei knows has *got* to be Jewelry related."

"I think you're grasping at straws," Jonathan said, pulling on his hair. "Lorelei could have any of a number of things on Grace. Why is knowing more about the Jewelry so important to you? Or at least why can't it wait until Nate brings her home?"

"Because of you."

"Me? What are you talking about?" He raised an eyebrow at her.

"Jonathan...you've been acting strange lately, and it's scaring the shit out of me."

He narrowed his eyes but listened.

"You've been talking about Dr. Smithton's utopia plan almost obsessively, and it's starting to worry me. It's such an unrealistic idea, but you talk about it like it's something Dr. Smithton actually plans to try." She watched his eyes start to glaze over slightly which made her nervous, but she kept talking. She needed to say this. "You've been asking me about donating my blood when there's no reason for it, and it doesn't make any sense. It really creeps me out, and I wish you would stop. You've also been acting like Grace—you pull on your hair when you get upset, just like she does."

"First of all," he said, his eyes glazing over a little more, "Dr. Smithton's utopia *is* possible. I may not fully understand it, but if he says he can do it, then I believe him. He's never lied to me. The blood thing was just a joke, but if it creeps you out, I'll stop. And I told you, I pull on my hair to stop the stress headaches."

She frowned. The 'blood thing' most definitely had not been a joke, and certainly wouldn't have been consistent with his sense of humor even if it *had* been a joke. Anger bubbled up inside her. She'd been so determined not to keep things from him and here he was lying to her. Her jaw clenched, but she still needed to talk this out. Pushing aside her frustration with him, she continued, "Well, you're wrong about one thing," she said. "Dr. Smithton *has* lied to you. To both of us, really."

Jonathan wore his doubt on his face. "What?"

"Please don't tell Dr. Smithton," she begged him, "but when Nate and I were waiting in his office for you the other day, he broke into Dr. Smithton's safe."

"What?!" Jonathan said again, this time with his mouth agape. He stood up and started pacing while pulling on his hair. "The second he's out of prison he goes right back to his criminal ways, and you didn't tell me until now?"

"I know, I'm sorry," she said. "I kept it to myself because I was worried you'd tell Dr. Smithton. But you won't believe what we found! There's a fourth piece of Armor Jewelry, Jonathan."

He looked at her with raised eyebrows.

"It's a cuff," she explained. "And do you remember the first day we met and you showed me that old text in the museum library with the missing page?"

He nodded.

"Well, the missing page was in Dr. Smithton's safe, too! He lied to us about it, and he didn't tell us about the cuff! I suspect he's known the truth about the powers of the Jewelry way before we ever demonstrated the ability of the amulet to him that day in your office."

Jonathan sat back down, but in a chair next to the couch. "I'm...shocked," he said, shaking his head.

"I know, me too," she agreed, glad that he was settling down. "I wonder why he kept that from us. That's why I want to talk to *someone else* who might know something about the Jewelry."

"No," he said, leaning forward. "I mean I'm shocked that you would be that deceitful." He glared at her.

"Jonathan, I didn't want to—"

"I know you wouldn't have done that on your own," he said. "Nate is a bad influence on you. He's leading you astray, and you need to stay away from him!"

"Well, I'm glad he broke in," she said defiantly. "Now we know that Dr. Smithton is hiding something from us. Don't you think it's strange that you and Grace both have the same weird hair pulling issue, and the only other thing you two have in common is Dr. Smithton, who's been keeping secrets?"

"NO!" Jonathan shouted. "I don't! If Grace and I have the same medical condition, it's purely a coincidence!"

"I disagree!" she said. "I think it's too strange to be a coincidence! Guess what the 'missing page' said was the cuff's power? It's *brainwashing*. And there's definitely something strange going on with your behavior and pain. Maybe if we can find out more information about the cuff, we can reverse your headaches."

Jonathan got up and started pacing again. "You can't possibly believe that Dr. S. is using this cuff to brainwash me and that he's used it to brainwash Grace! I think you're the one who's being brainwashed—by Nate! Dr. S. is the most honorable man I know! Nate is feeding you all this bullshit to turn you against me, and you're believing every word he's saying! I'd bet my life that whatever you two saw was not another piece of Armor Jewelry and the missing page."

"No, it's not like that," she insisted. "Nate's not trying to get me to believe anything. I'm the one who put those pieces together. I saw those things with my own eyes. And I *don't* know if any of my suspicions about the cuff are true or not, but that's why I want to find out. I'm only doing this because I want to help you. I can't stand seeing you in pain. Please, come with us tomorrow."

"There's no way in hell that I'm going!" Jonathan yelled at her. "And neither are you! I'm not going to let you put yourself in a potentially dangerous situation. And I don't think you should be alone with that psychopath again! He's got you breaking into safes—what's next?" Jonathan pulled on his hair before changing the subject. "Did he try anything?" he demanded as his pacing stopped in front of her.

Her stomach clenched, uncomfortable with how Jonathan was looming over her. "No, I told you, we had separate rooms, I talked to you on the phone all evening, and then in the morning we went to see Dan, then came back home."

"So you're telling me that with all the time you've been spending with him, he hasn't tried to come on to you at all?" he asked, with a look of doubt on his face. He sat back down and crossed his arms.

Her eyes bored a hole in the floor as her chest tightened. "The night we went riding he tried to kiss me," she admitted.

Jonathan stood up quickly and opened his mouth to speak, but his anger prevented any words from escaping.

"But I didn't let him!" she continued. "I told him no and that I was with you. He hasn't tried anything since."

"Oh, well, how fucking commendable of him," Jonathan sneered. "I knew this was going to happen. And you didn't tell me until now." He turned to face her. "Is that something you want, Anise? Is that why you keep going off to who knows where with him?"

"No! I told you where I'm going and asked you to come along! I still wish you would come with us."

"So can you look me in the eye and tell me you're not attracted to him at all?"

She opened her mouth to speak and then closed it

again, looking down at the ground.

When she didn't answer his question, Jonathan's lips formed a tight, straight line. "Okay," he said. "We're done."

"Are you breaking up with me?" she asked him, her eyes wide.

"Yes." He got up and opened the door for her. "Go, and take your disgusting skin puddle with you."

She stayed seated on his couch. "There's no skin puddle. It's a hallucination."

"Fine. Whatever. Just get out."

"Jonathan, please, let's talk about this. Yes, Nate has some physically attractive features. So what? Haven't you found some other woman the slightest bit attractive since we've been together? Like maybe that pretty docent who was talking to you last week at the museum?"

He glared at her. "I'm not traveling around the world with the pretty docent."

"You're right. But if I was the one with migraines and she could help you stop them, I'd understand if you were. I've told you again and again that I love you, and I'm completely committed to you. But I really think this trip is my only chance to help you. I'm worried about you, and I don't trust Dr. Smithton."

"Really?" he asked her.

She noticed his eyes completely glazed over for a few seconds each time she mentioned Dr. Smithton which made her believe even stronger that Jonathan's mentor had something to do with Jonathan's condition. This time, however, his eyes stayed completed glazed.

"Do you trust *me*? Would you be willing to donate blood to me?" he continued, as he began slowly walking toward her.

"I-I thought you said you weren't going to make that joke anymore," she stammered, her heart beating fast with anxiety. The amulet started glowing which frightened her even more. It only glowed when someone had the intention of harming her in some way. But *Jonathan* would never harm her, right? She stood up, the adrenaline coursing through her veins. "What are you going to do?" She took a step toward him, hoping a threat might make him back down. "You've seen me kick-box! You know I'm a much better fighter than you are!" When his eyes turned toward her glowing amulet, a look of horror washed over his face, and he pulled his hair as hard as he could. "Just get out," he said as he winced in pain. "And don't come back!"

Anise ran past him and out of his apartment with her tote bag and shoes in her hands. Would Jonathan have tried to hurt her? If so, her kickboxing skills were well-honed, but fighting him was the last thing she wanted to do. In fact, she would bet the only reason he stopped threatening her was because he saw the amulet glowing, and he knew he didn't stand a chance. She was grateful she had the amulet around her neck and felt angry at Jonathan and Dr. Smithton who kept telling her she didn't need it to be safe.

That's obviously not true!

Jumping on her bike, still with bare feet, she hurriedly pedaled to Nate's condo. If something was making Jonathan's brain hurt like Grace's, would it make him violent like Grace, too? Is that why the amulet had been glowing—because he'd had violent intentions toward her? If so, she didn't want to be at home and alone. She had the amulet, but Jonathan had access to the ring and earrings at the museum, and if he wore them, he'd have more power than her and be able to hurt her after all.

She knocked on Nate's door when she arrived at his condo. "Can I stay here tonight?" she asked him, breathless and tearful.

"Of course," he replied, holding the door open for her. "But what's going on?"

She wrapped herself up in his arms and told him the whole story with the exception of Jonathan dumping her.

She didn't want to believe it, and saying it out loud would make it more real. "You were right. I need to stay away from Jonathan until I can figure out how to help him get back to normal. My amulet glowed which means he had the intention to hurt me." Tears began flowing down her cheeks.

"Don't worry," Nate told her, his protective arms clutching her to his chest. "If he tries to hurt you again, I'll be ready for him."

JONATHAN SAT ON HIS COUCH, SHAKING and rocking back and forth. *What the hell just happened?* Anise being hurt was his biggest fear, and he'd had the most disturbing urge to make her bleed. He replayed their conversation in his head. What was the blood thing she had mentioned? He was having trouble remembering. And how could he have broken up with her? He loved her more than anything and only wanted her safety above everything else. And he—*he*—had been the one to threaten that tonight. The shame was overwhelming. She deserved an apology.

Walking over to her apartment felt cathartic—the cool air cleared his mind and sharpened his vision. If this trip was so important to her, he should absolutely go along. Even if she didn't get the answers she was looking for, he'd at least be there for her.

When she didn't answer her door, he figured she was either hiding from him or staying at a friend's place. His calls and text messages of apology to her didn't receive a response.

Jonathan hated that she was ignoring him, but he understood why. He'd frightened her, just like her deceased ex-boyfriend Brian had, according to something her friends had once told him. He couldn't believe he'd acted like a monster. Maybe he should see another doctor, get more tests done. There was obviously something very wrong with his brain.

As he walked back home, his thoughts turned to the unbelievable claims she had made against his mentor. Why would she ever believe a criminal like Nate over a well-respected, kind-hearted scholar like Dr. Smithton? If her claims had any truth to them whatsoever, he wanted to find out, but how? He couldn't exactly ask Dr. S. if he was lying to them; he'd have no good reason to tell the truth simply because Jonathan asked.

He put a hand to his head to pull on his hair. Another migraine was coming on and his vision was getting hazy. He couldn't quite remember why he'd gone walking that evening or why he would ever consider the thought that Dr. S. might have lied to him. It was ridiculous. His thoughts turned to how he could make Anise give him her blood.

Chapter 15

Monday, December 16, 1963

She tried, but Grace wasn't able to find another job as a curator. Her notoriety from the deaccession preceded her everywhere in Springfield. She also wasn't able to get a job as an instructor at the university, even with a recommendation from Professor Dromly. Her options were running out. She took a very low-paying job—the only thing she could get—to pay the bills, but it wasn't enough. She had to pull from the savings account monthly, and within half a year, the funds would run dry.

The plan she'd formed in her mind the night Thomas died popped into her head. She really didn't want to execute it, but she had no choice—it was time for step one. In their hurry to get rid of her, the Springfield Museum hadn't noticed that she didn't return every key she'd been given. From her closet, she pulled a key ring that held keys to every display case in the museum. She had no idea how to break into the museum when it was closed, so she figured it would be best for her to go while the museum was open and hope that no one would catch her. She left Dan with the sitter and headed out.

"Hello, Grace," the security guard at the museum entrance greeted her. "Didn't think I'd see *you* here again."

"Just because I was wrongly let go doesn't mean I've lost my love for ancient artifacts," she snapped at him. "Doesn't the new exhibition open today?"

"Yes, ma'am," the guard replied. "Enjoy. And Happy Holidays."

"Bah humbug," she muttered under her breath.

She paid for her ticket and headed straight for the case that contained gemstone-laden hair accessories that had once belonged to an ancient queen. They were worth a fortune. So as not to arouse suspicion, she wandered around the museum for a half-hour, checking out the new exhibition and then slowly made her way back to the case with the hair accessories. She looked around her. Luckily it was Monday afternoon, so museum visitors were few and far between. The entire room was empty except for her.

Her hands were shaky and her mouth dry. These precious treasures belonged in the museum.

She did not want to do this. *But the strong do what needs to be done in order to survive. It's now or never.*

Taking deep breaths, and with nimble fingers, she used her key to unlock the display case and grabbed the hair accessories, careful not to touch anything else, and stashed them in her purse. She used one of Thomas's old handkerchiefs to wipe where she had touched the display case and locked it.

"Hey!"

Grace jumped and spun around. A guard was headed straight for her. What should she do? Run? Her heart hammered in her chest as her legs froze.

"Grace? I thought that was you," the guard said as he got closer.

"Oh, hello," she replied. She recognized his face but had forgotten his name. Was it Larry? Or Harry? Barry? Something like that.

"It's me, Jack."

"Yes, of course. I know."

"What are you doing here?"

She eyed the display case nervously. "Excuse me?"

"Did you come for the new exhibition?"

She clutched her purse a little closer to her side. Did he know? Was he toying with her, trying to get her to confess out of guilt and fear? Her heart drummed in her ears, and she could barely hear herself speak. "Yes, it looks fantastic. I enjoyed it very much."

"Good...I was sorry to hear about your husband. How are you doing?"

"Taking it one day at a time."

"Yeah, good." He gave her a toothy grin. "I'm glad you came by. You know, I get off at four, if you're interested, maybe we could—"

"It was very nice to see you, Jack. But I really need to get home to my son."

He nodded and looked at the floor. "Oh, sure. It was nice to see you too."

She felt her heart calm down a little. This idiot knew nothing. She said goodbye and hurried out of the museum.

Grace paid the baby-sitter and picked up Dan in one arm and the phone in the other. She looked at a phone number on a slip of paper she'd pulled from an old shoe-box and dialed it. "Hello," she said to the person who answered the phone. "This is Grace Brevain. I'm the one you contacted a year or so ago to make an offer on the items the Springfield Museum had for sale.... No, those items aren't for sale anymore, but I have some others you may be interested in... No, the museum isn't selling them. I am.... Do you really care how I got them?" She laughed at the other person's response. "I didn't think so... Sure, tomorrow would be great."

Wednesday, December 18, 1963

NOW THAT GRACE HAD SOLD THE queen's hair accessories for a small fortune, it was time for step two of her plan. She drove to Springfield University and tiptoed down the dark hallway where the instructors' offices were. She'd spent all day at the public library researching how to pick locks and found a place that sold cheap lock picks. Never had she tried it before, but the lock on Dromly's office door gave in to the tension wrench as Grace raked the tumblers. Proud of herself, Grace stepped inside and closed the door behind her. Dromly was on a trip to Florida, so she could take all the time she needed to find what she was looking for.

She combed through his desk drawers, filing cabinets, and office closet. All she found were class lecture notes, books filled with students' grades, piles upon piles of Dromly's ridiculous trip journals, and other boring things. Sitting in his desk chair, she looked around the room in disappointment. Surely that couldn't be it? What about the Armor Jewelry? She needed to find the entire set before that candy-ass Morty did. Once she had the Jewelry, she'd start searching for the Plate of Destiny and then... She smiled as she thought about Thomas and how good it would feel to be in his arms again.

A memory of a movie she'd once seen played in her mind where the main guy had a wall safe he kept hidden behind a large painting. Her eyes moved to the painting Dromly had commissioned of himself. Getting up from the chair, she looked behind the painting and smirked at the safe he thought he'd so cleverly hidden.

"Ha! I've got you now, Dromly!"

But did she? Picking a lock was one thing. Breaking into a safe was quite another. Besides guessing a random combination of numbers, she had no clue what to do.

Luckily, the combination to his safe was easier to guess than she'd thought. His son's birthday. It opened on her first try. She shook her head at his idiocy as she reached her hand into the safe.

"What?" she cried as she pulled out not one but three amulets. "There were multiple sets of Armor Jewelry?" Dromly had once said in a class lecture that there was only one set left in existence. But when she thought about it, it made sense that there were more. Each Mallandian soldier had been given a set, so it was highly probable that more than one set would have survived. "All I need is one," she told herself as she slipped one into her purse. She put the other two back and rooted through the other contents of the safe. No ring, no earrings, no cuff. "No matter," she said. "I'm still one step closer to the Plate of Destiny. Thomas, my love. I'll see you again."

Hope filled her heart for the first time—ever. It was now time for step three. New year, new life. The house she'd shared with Thomas was all packed up, and she and Dan would move a few states away to start over. It was time to leave all the bad memories behind.

Chapter 16

Present day

Saturday, September 19, 2015

The sun glared in Nate's eyes through the bug-stained windshield as the surreal situation caused him to feel like he was floating somewhere above the car, in the backseat, or just outside the window. He watched himself drive the rental car to a very remote neighborhood in the middle of Nowhere, Nevada per the directions in Dan's letter. He was on his way to pick up his mother. His *mother*. She'd been alive and a couple hours away by plane this entire time. The pulling and wrenching sensations in his gut told him he was feeling an emotion, but what was it? Was he excited? Angry? Nervous? Worried about what she may think of him and his criminal activities?

Anise sat next to him in the passenger's seat, her hands fidgeting and twisting her garnet ring around her finger. They were looking for a small house owned by an older couple. There were several homes dotted throughout the town, but they were spread at least twenty to forty acres apart and each had land that was used to farm, garden, or raise pigs. Nate stopped in front of the boxy green house where his mother was being kept, according to Dan.

"Why don't you stay in the car," Nate said to Anise. "Dan said they're not violent people, but that they might be upset we're here. He's been paying them all these years to keep my mother, and they won't be happy about losing their income. I plan on offering them cash if it comes to that, but if something happens to me, just get the hell out of here and drive back to the airport."

Anise rolled her eyes and got out of the car. "No. I have the amulet, and I'll be fine. If they try to hurt you in any way, I can at least step in between you and them and give us a chance to get away. I came to help, so let me." She gave him a don't-you-dare-argue-with-me look as she clutched the amulet.

Her obstinance was frustrating, but her motives were endearing. He stepped over to her and took both of her hands in his. An overwhelming need to kiss her was growing inside of him, and he felt another emotion too, but couldn't quite place it. Was this...love? He didn't remember ever feeling love before so he couldn't be sure. Maybe with time, he'd know. He didn't want her to reject his advances again—not now—so he just smiled at her instead. "Thank you," he told her. Hand-in-hand, they walked up to the door of the cottage and knocked.

The older couple Dan had mentioned opened the door. They looked at Nate, looked at each other, and back to Nate. The short, rail-thin woman pointed to Nate's face. "You look familiar."

"I'm Nate Brevain, Lorelei's son. Did my father, Dan Brevain, tell you I was coming?"

The couple looked at each other again.

"No," the man said. He coughed and lit up a cigarette. "Why are you here?"

"I want to see her," Nate said.

The couple looked at each other and waved Nate and Anise inside. "Wait here," the man said, and they disappeared into a different room.

The small house was dark with the curtains drawn over the few windows. It smelled like smoke, cat piss, and something else that Nate didn't care to identify. He hated that his mother had been confined here for twenty-six years. Even his prison had smelled better. He took a deep breath and felt Anise squeeze his hand. The couple returned and handed Nate a letter.

"What's this?" he asked. "Where's my mother?"

"She wrote a letter for you," the man explained. He coughed and wheezed and took another puff of his cigarette.

"Where is she?" Nate demanded.

"Two years ago," the man began, "Lorelei was out tending the vegetable garden." He drew back a curtain so Nate and Anise could see outside their window. "Two men shot through a hole in the fence. Killed her."

Nate's eyes grew narrow. He shook his head. "That can't be right. My father just told me that she's alive and living with you!"

"No," the woman told him. "Lorelei's dead. The coroner took her away. Sorry, hon."

"I don't believe you!" Nate shoved his way past them. He stormed through their entire house searching for her. Upstairs, all he found was boxed-up clothing that must have been hers, as they were way too big for the small-framed older woman that lived there. "Was this hers?" he demanded, when the couple and Anise followed him into the room.

"Yes. Take it," they told him.

He looked through the boxes but found nothing but clothes. No Jewelry, no personal items, no journal, nothing of value that he would want to keep. "No," he told them. He supposed they didn't tell Dan of her death so as not to lose the money he'd been sending them. "Who killed her?" he demanded. "What did they look like?"

The woman gave him a shrug. "One was short and fat. The other one really tall."

Nate looked at Anise. "That could be almost anyone." He ran a hand through his hair in frustration. "You said the coroner took her? What happened to her body after that?"

"Don't know," the man said, coughing. "The coroner took her without asking any questions."

Nate looked at Anise again. "This isn't making any sense." He looked back at the couple. "He would've asked how she was shot. He would've called the police."

"He didn't," the woman said, shaking her head. "Said there was no reason to."

"That can't be right." Nate felt something besides the rage that was building up in his chest. Confusion? Devastation, maybe? He didn't care to consider it further. What the hell happened to his mother? "Did he do an autopsy?"

"We ain't never heard more about it," the man told him.

"Who was the coroner? Did he give a name? What did *he* look like?"

The woman shrugged. "Don't remember."

Anise pulled on Nate's arm. "I don't think we're going to find anything else out from them."

Nate glared at the couple. "If I find out that you're keeping something from me..."

Anise tugged at his arm again. "Nate. Let's go."

He wanted to ask them more questions, to make them tell him something that would ease the rage, but his mind was blanking. He let Anise pull him toward the door.

"Wait," the man said. "We took damn good care of your mother for years." He coughed.

"Yeah, thanks for holding her hostage against her will.

I'm sure she lived like a fucking queen," Nate seethed, looking around at the walls that were yellowed from the smoke.

"We're losing our income," the man continued.

"Not my problem," Nate declared, and turned to leave. He sighed at the ceiling and turned back around slowly when he heard a gun being cocked.

"My rifle says it is."

"Fuck you, you're not getting a penny from me," Nate threw at them.

Anise stepped in front of him, her arms slightly raised to block Nate from the gun.

The woman shook her head with a frown. "Sweetie, ain't no man worth getting killed over. And we'll shoot you both if we have to."

"No one's dying today," Anise fired back.

"That's up to you," the woman said.

Nate noticed the amulet glowing from underneath Anise's shirt. And he hated that they were scaring her enough to make her shake. His anger grew. "Yeah, fine," he grumbled. "Just put that thing away." He led them out to the car, opened the trunk, and pulled out a briefcase. "This is all I have." He gave it to the couple who opened it and counted the cash.

"Now get off our property," the man snarled. The couple lowered their gun and disappeared inside their house.

"Fuck!" Nate slammed his hand on the hood of the car.

"Do you want me to drive?" Anise asked him. She was still shaking.

"I'm fine," he said, getting into the driver's seat. Numbness washed over him as all his emotions disappeared. He felt like he was floating above his body again. *Focus. You're driving. And she's still shaking.* "Are you okay?"

"I will be. As soon as we get the hell out of here." She

touched his arm. "I'm so sorry she wasn't there."

Nate noticed how tight his jaw clenched. "Me too." His mother wasn't there. She was dead, again. *Again!* His fingers strangled the steering wheel until his knuckles turned white.

After several minutes of Nate speeding down the deserted highway in silence, Anise turned to him and asked, "Why didn't you put up more of a fight when they asked for money? I counted along with them. A hundred thousand dollars. That was a lot to hand over so easily. Where'd you get that kind of cash anyway?"

Nate's lips turned up as he told his story. "I had this cellmate for a while. He did nothing but brag about how realistic his counterfeit bills are and how smart he was about hiding them. Too bad he wasn't smart about not getting caught. He had several more years to go when I got out, so I helped myself to some of his best work before I came home."

"So none of that money was real?" Anise asked him, wide-eyed.

Nate let out a laugh and shook his head.

"Having counterfeit bills is illegal. You promised you wouldn't do anything illegal anymore. This is the second time you've broken that promise." Her face didn't look upset, but her eyes demanded a response.

"What should I have done instead, honey? Burn the dirty money and hand over my own hard-earned cash? Let those two fuckers take advantage of me like they did my parents?"

She looked at her lap. "I don't know. I guess not."

"No. Sometimes the right thing to do is the choice that's less bad than the other."

She remained silent and stared out the window for a few minutes until her eyes turned back toward him. "What would you have done if you hadn't found the counterfeit money?" she asked.

Great. He was hoping she wouldn't ask. Every time

they spoke about Nate's days as a professional criminal, he felt like she was looking down on him. "I sold a lot of stolen artifacts on the black market when I was a teenager," he told her, wanting to be truthful. "I have a lot of money saved up from those days. Grace showed me what to do with it so it couldn't be found. It's all hidden in off shore accounts."

"Right, you told me that before. So, if you had given them *your* money, would a hundred thousand have been everything you had?" she asked, her untamed curiosity oozing out every pore.

He shook his head as he stared straight ahead, hoping this conversation would end soon. "No."

"Really? How much more do you have?"

He didn't want to answer and tried to think of something to say without giving her an exact number.

The extended silence made her squirm in her seat. "Sorry, I'm asking too many questions. And it's none of my business," she said as she looked down at her hands, her cheeks turning red. She twisted her garnet ring around her finger.

He frowned to himself. The last thing he wanted to do was make her feel bad. He wouldn't have minded telling her the exact number if he didn't feel like she was comparing him unfavorably to Boy Scout. "Don't be sorry. I'm just not used to talking about this with anyone. I have a lot. More than anyone would ever need," he replied, hoping that would satisfy her curiosity.

"Oh. So...can I ask what you've bought with the money you got from the artifacts?"

"Actually, I've only ever bought two things with that money. I bought my first street bike at age sixteen. A couple years later, I bought my watch. Everything else, including the condo, was bought with money I earned legally from my job or my investments."

"Really? So you're just saving it? What do you plan to do with it?"

He shrugged. "Honestly, I don't know. I don't really need it."

"Would you consider giving it back?"

He shrugged again. "I guess could make anonymous donations to the museums I stole from."

She beamed at him. "Really? You'd do that?"

"Yeah," he said, glad that she seemed to be happy with his answers. "Like I said, I don't need it. There's nothing I want that I can't afford to buy with the money I've earned from working. And I've made some *really* good investments," he bragged. Starting to feel a little calmer now, he relaxed his right elbow on the center console and let his left hand drive.

"What did Dan and Grace do with their shares?"

"Dan probably used his to keep Lorelei here. What else he bought, I don't know. Grace didn't work and went on a lot of trips to Europe and Florida, but she never told me why."

"Once all this is over, do you *want* to go back to working in finance?" Anise asked. "I remember you telling me you enjoyed it."

"I would," he said, "but no firm is going to trust a convicted felon with their clients' money."

"Right, that's true. Sometimes I forget how different your life has to be now because of how you helped me escape from the museum." Anise grabbed Nate's right hand and held it on her lap as she stared out the passenger's side window.

Nate glanced at her hand softly gripping his. Was it possible to feel both wretchedly disappointed and content at the same time?

AFTER THE PRIVATE JET NATE HAD hired took off from the tiny airport in rural Nevada, Anise sat back in her seat, enjoying the view from the window. She thought about the night she and Jonathan had tried to steal the earrings at the Springfield Museum. They'd had no idea what they were doing and would've been caught for sure without Nate's help. Nate had given up more than just three years of his freedom so she wouldn't have to go to prison. He also permanently gave up the career he loved, and he'd done all of it so willingly and without the expectation of receiving anything in return. Although she didn't like that Nate felt no remorse about stealing and keeping illegal profits, she couldn't help but admire the selflessness he'd shown toward her.

She knew from what Corinne had told her that his selflessness was only reserved for those in his 'inner circle,' and she wondered what she had done to earn the affection of someone who found it difficult to care about anyone. Anise also wondered if what Jonathan had said about Nate—how he allowed himself to get caught not to save her from going to prison but only to bring Grace and Dan down with him—had any truth to it. Not wanting Jonathan's idea of Nate to have any validity, she pushed it from her mind. But now that she'd thought of Jonathan, a wave of grief hit her.

"So...Jonathan broke up with me." Anise looked over at Nate and saw that he'd been staring at the empty seat where his mother Lorelei would've been had they found her alive.

Shit. Why did I say that?

This wasn't an appropriate time to bring that up. They were here looking for Nate's mother. This trip was about *him*, not Anise and her problems. And seeking sympathy about her break-up with Jonathan from Nate wasn't exactly appropriate either. What kind of response from him had she been hoping for? He took off his jacket, and she watched, picturing his arms wrapping around her in a comforting hug. *Stop it!* These feelings were how she lost Jonathan in the first place. She felt her cheeks flush with embarrassment. Guilt started gnawing at her for how she'd hurt Jonathan.

"What happened?" Nate asked.

She hung her head. "I'm sorry. Now's not the right time to talk about that. Forget I said anything."

"Okay," Nate replied, seemingly unfazed as he unzipped his travel bag and stuffed his jacket inside.

Anise's eyes welled up.

Nate turned to look at her again. "He can't be worth this many tears."

Anise didn't respond. She twisted her garnet ring around her finger. Jonathan had been her best friend for the last few years. Being in a relationship with him had been nice, but it was the friendship she'd miss the most. But if he was being brainwashed by the cuff, and they could figure out how to help him get back to being who he actually was instead of a person she barely recognized, maybe they could at least be friends again. Or maybe more—*if* Jonathan forgave her.

Her eyes turned to Nate as he rearranged the items in his travel bag. She thought about how he'd protected her from Grace. Went to prison for her freedom. Made her laugh. Made her feel safe and happy. Made her want... him. *But how can I have these thoughts about Nate when Jonathan and I just broke up? Jonathan deserves better than that. Plus, Nate is a criminal. He's lied to me in the past. I* should not *want him.* She sunk lower in her seat. Closing her eyes, Anise tried to relax and shut off her mind. She failed miserably. *But Jonathan and I were also criminals when we tried to steal the earrings. We are not morally superior to Nate as Jonathan seems to believe.* This back and forth was exhausting. The guilt hurt so much she put her hands on her stomach to calm it. *Stop spiraling,* she told herself, annoyed by her own behavior. *It's only an attraction. I don't have feelings for Nate. I'm just lonely and missing Jonathan. That's all.*

"I almost forgot about this," Nate said, pulling something out of his bag.

Anise looked up. "Oh, the letter! I almost forgot too! I'll give you some privacy to read it," she said, reaching into her bag and grabbing her headphones. "I'll go sit over there." She pointed to another pair of seats a little further toward the back of the plane.

"No, you don't have to leave. Stay. Relax," he insisted.

"Okay," she agreed, and put her seatbelt back on. She was happy to stay put. The day had been long, and she was tired. Wondering what Lorelei's letter might say made her feel nervous for Nate. She lay back in her seat and closed her eyes. She opened them several minutes later when she felt Nate touching her arm.

"You won't believe what's in this letter, honey." He looked at her, his eyes intense.

"What is it?" she asked, sitting up straight.

"It's dated three years ago," he said and started reading the letter to her.

"Dear Nathan,

As I write this, I realize you may never see it. I'd have to find a way to mail it first of all, and I'm only allowed to go outside to work the land. But, one thing at a time; I'll worry about that after I finish writing it. To begin, I'd like to apologize to you, my little prince. (Even though you turned 27 this past February, you'll always be my little prince.) I don't know what Dan told you about why I wasn't around anymore, but I want you to know I've always wanted to be there with you more than anything. I'm being held here against my will, and it was either that or death. I think about you every day, and I hope you're doing well. Sometimes Dan sends me a short letter with an update on what you've been doing, but it's never enough. From the little I've heard, it sounds like you've grown up to be a very smart and capable young man. I'm so proud of all your accomplishments."

Nate paused and his face grimaced slightly. Anise noticed his discomfort and put a hand on his arm to encourage him to continue.

He read on.

"Knowing Dan and Grace, no one told you anything about me. I don't know if you remember, but you and I returned some stolen artifacts to the museum that Grace had stashed in her basement. I assume they meant a lot more to her than I could ever have imagined because after she found out, she ordered Dan to kill me. Dan, of course, couldn't do it. I have

no doubt he feared that if he didn't hide me away, Grace would've killed me herself. Grace is obsessed with finding a set of ancient jewelry. I'm not sure why, but it means everything to her. I guess she was afraid of what I had seen; I'm not sure."

Nate stopped reading. "She goes on to tell me all about the Armor Jewelry. She talks about the history and what each piece does. She's afraid of what Grace would do with it if she had that much power."

"Did she mention the cuff?" Anise asked.

"Yes. But all she said about it was that it was used to brainwash the Mallandian soldiers into complete submission and that she believes it was one of the pieces she returned to the museum from Grace's basement."

Anise frowned, disappointed there wasn't more information. This wasn't going to help her help Jonathan. She wondered how he was doing and hoped he wasn't having too many headaches and hallucinations. A small part of her also wanted to know if he missed her or if he was glad to be rid of her.

"Here comes the unbelievable part," Nate said, and continued reading.

"Nathan, if you ever do read this, I want you to help me with a couple things. I found the address of where I'm being held on a piece of mail that my captors forgot to hide, and I'll include it at the end of this letter. If you could alert the authorities that

I'm still alive, I'm hopeful they'd find me, and I'd be able to come home and see you again. But before you do that, please take care of the following: I'm fearful as to what might happen if Grace is successful in finding all of the Armor Jewelry. First of all, I know all this is hard to believe, but the Jewelry is as all-powerful as I say. Please, just believe me. Secondly, I need you to find a mother and daughter that live in your town. Their names are Deborah Stannell-Viston and Anise Viston."

Anise's jaw dropped. "What?!" she exclaimed, looking at the letter in Nate's hands to see her name written in Lorelei's handwriting. "How did she know my mother and me? And why did she want you to find us?"

Nate continued reading.

"Ownership of all four pieces of Jewelry is the birthright of these Viston ladies, as all others who had a right to the Jewelry are now deceased. For more history and information about that, the only person I know of that you can talk to is Dr. Kent Dromly. I don't know his contact information, but I'm hoping you'll be able to find

him. When I knew him, he was visiting our town, but I'm not sure where he's from. What you really need to know is that Anise and Deborah are the only people alive who can stop Grace, the reason being is that they're the only ones left with"

"With what?!" Anise cried, dying to find out.

"I don't know," Nate said. "That's where the letter stops."

He showed it to her, and she saw that Lorelei's last words ended in the middle of the sentence and in the middle of the page. "What happened, I wonder?" she lamented.

Nate shrugged.

"Do you know a Dr. Kent Dromly?" she asked.

Nate's brow furrowed in thought. "For some reason, that name seems *really* familiar. But no, I don't think I've ever heard of him." Nate did a quick search online but found no listings anywhere for a Kent Dromly.

"Now what?" Anise frowned. How would she help Jonathan if this Kent Dromly was nowhere?

"Don't worry," Nate told her. "If he's alive, I'll find him."

Part 3

I PROMISE

Chapter 17

Present day

Monday, September 21, 2015

As soon as Anise dropped Nate off at his condo, he jumped on his motorcycle and headed straight back to the airport. Even though Anise would be angry and never trust him again if she found out, he planned to visit Grace and discover what she knew about the cuff and Dr. Smithton. His head was filled with questions that he couldn't ask his grandmother, but maybe the information she gave him could help him find the answers. *Why had she wanted Lorelei dead? Why is Anise the only one who can stop Grace? Does it even matter now that Grace is in prison? Can Anise also stop Smithton? What is Smithton up to anyway?* As he rode, he thought of something he could ask Grace. *Who is Dr. Kent Dromly?*

✳ ✳ ✳

"GRACE." NATE GREETED HIS GRANDMOTHER AS he entered the small room where she sat behind a table.

"What the hell took you so long?" she demanded. She looked at him with an angry face that appeared a decade younger than her eighty years.

"Nice to see you, too," he replied, clenching his jaw.

She frowned at him with what seemed to Nate to be utter hatred. "Why are we in this room?" she wanted to know. "It's cold in here."

"I'm your lawyer."

"You're not a lawyer."

"I am as far as they know," he said, motioning to the door. "We needed privacy."

"Your face has aged," she announced, giving him a frown.

Nate sighed. "I'm here because of your letter. So what do you have to tell me?" he asked her impatiently.

"Plenty. There's a curator at the museum back home who wants all the Armor Jewelry as much as I do."

"Morty Smithton."

"Right," Grace agreed. She leaned back in her chair and crossed her arms.

"Why does he want the Jewelry so much?"

"He wants to brainwash everyone into being happy living in the utopia he plans to create."

Nate sat forward and put his forearms on the table. "He's starting a cult? Can he do that?"

"If he gets all the Jewelry, absolutely. Most of us won't have free will anymore. I imagine he'll execute those of us that he can't brainwash."

"So, he can't brainwash everyone?" Nate asked.

"I don't think so," said Grace, shaking her head.

"What makes you say that?"

"He tried to brainwash me a long time ago. His attempts lasted for years but were never successful. However, he *was* able to brainwash his colleagues."

"*All* of his colleagues?" Nate thought about how Boy

Scout's health issues mirrored Grace's and Anise's suspicion that the cuff may have had something to do with it.

"I imagine so."

"Is he using a cuff to do the brainwashing?"

"Yes. How did you know about the cuff?" she asked, looking both surprised and impressed.

"After I read your letter, I broke into Smithton's safe and found it."

"Did it have three blue stones on it? And ten red ones?" she asked, her brown eyes becoming intense.

"Yes."

"That's definitely it," she said, leaning forward. "Do you have it now?"

"No, I put it back."

Grace sighed and rolled her eyes as she sat back in her chair, exasperated. "That was stupid."

"I didn't know what it was, Grace," he protested, then wondered why he was bothering to explain himself to her. He figured old habits die hard. "So he can use the cuff to brainwash most everyone on earth?" Nate asked.

"No. Not with the cuff. That would take far too long."

"So how does he plan to do it?" Nate inquired. "And how do you know all this?"

"Morty and I go back a long time," Grace said. "And I'll explain everything to you so you can save the day and be the hero," she added. "But first, I want you to do something for me."

Nate frowned. "Of course you do. What is it?"

"There's something I need you to sneak in to me," she began. She lowered her voice and told Nate what she wanted. She explained which guard to bribe to get it to her and how much cash to give him.

"Fine. I'll get it for you." The substance she wanted was dangerous, but he didn't care. It wasn't a lethal dose, so she wouldn't be able to kill anyone with it. He'd get it to her so he could find out what she knew and then bribe a guard to get it back. Even if the information she gave him wasn't as useful as he hoped it would be, it was worth a shot. He stood up to leave and then sat back down to ask her a question that had been rolling around in his head for a long time. "Why did *you* want the Jewelry so much? I'm sure it's not to build a utopia."

"No, it's not," she agreed. "For one thing, I wanted to get better."

"Have you been sick all these years? Is it a brain disorder?" If he could correctly diagnose Boy Scout, that might win him some points with Anise.

Her mouth opened in horror. "No, you little shit!" she sputtered. "There's nothing wrong with my brain!"

"Then what do you mean, 'get better?'"

She pulled on her white hair while her face scrunched up in pain. She reminded him of Boy Scout at that moment. "I haven't always been like this!" she screeched at him.

"Like *what*?"

"Like *this*!" she said with a raised voice. "Like...*this*!" She pulled on her hair again.

"Okay, whatever," said Nate, not understanding what she meant and not caring either. "I'm sorry I asked. I'll be back as soon as I get what you asked for. Be ready to talk then." He got up and left without saying good-bye.

Wednesday, September 23, 2015

THE GUARD GRACE HAD TOLD NATE about stopped by her cell. "I met your grandson last night," he said.

"Oh?" asked Grace.

"Yep." He looked around and then handed her a package. "He wanted you to have this. He seems like a good kid."

"Thank you," she told him. "He is."

Once the guard left, she ripped open the package to verify the contents. Smiling at what she knew would be her only chance for what she wanted, she stashed the packaging under her mattress and the item in her underwear. Nate had come through for her.

She tried not to think about her grandson's face. He was almost the spitting image of Thomas. He looked more like him now than the last time she'd seen him. It had always been difficult for Grace to look at Nate.

Grace had noticed that during their conversation, Nate's eyes were wide as they used to be when he was a child and had asked her questions. She narrowed her brows at a distant memory of how she used to love children in her youth. She had almost forgotten about that. Any feelings of love or tenderness toward anyone or anything had disappeared long ago. She wondered if they would return if she got a hold of all four pieces of the Armor Jewelry and cured herself from the side effects of the brainwashing. Perhaps she would someday find out.

She wondered how different her relationship with her grandson might've been if Morty's brainwashing attempts hadn't caused her the side effects she suffered. She didn't know how to explain that the grandmother Nate knew was not the person she truly was in a way that he would believe. The more she wondered about what might have been if Morty hadn't ruined her life, the more her blood boiled.

Hearing footsteps behind her head, she spun around and saw her father sneaking toward her with a cast iron pan. She screamed as he raised it over his head to strike. A swarm of bees flew at her from the corner of her cell. Her baby brother's dead body rolled off her bed and onto the floor, ants pouring out of his mouth and ears. The bees circled her head and iridescent beetles crawled up her legs. She screamed again and covered her head with her arms as her father took a swing at her.

"Shut up!" a guard called out from down the hall.

"It's just a hallucination," Grace reminded herself. "My father is dead. I killed him."

NATE WAS GLAD THAT HIS VISIT to Grace would be over soon. Then he could leave and never see her again. He entered the small meeting room they'd spoken in last time.

"Thank you," Grace said, "for getting what I asked for so quickly." She sat down at the table.

Nate was surprised at his grandmother's politeness. No, not surprised. Shocked. Something was different. Was she actually in a good mood? "That shit you wanted is toxic. What are you planning to do with it?"

"That's my business," she replied with a smile that made Nate's skin crawl.

Fucking bitch. "Whatever. So what can you tell me about the cuff?"

"Right now, Morty is using the cuff to brainwash his subordinates into believing his utopia is a good idea. He's creating an army out of his co-workers who'll do his bidding when it comes time to venture out and find the item that can tell him how to create the utopia."

"What do you mean? There's a *fifth* item?" Nate asked, floored.

"Not a fifth item of Jewelry," Grace corrected him. "This item is a bronze plate. It's called the Plate of Destiny, and it's supposed to reveal the laws of life and death."

Nate raised his eyebrows. "Meaning?"

Grace continued. "Meaning that whoever reads the messages on the Plate will know their destiny. Or at least how destiny works. They'll know how they're supposed to live their lives in the best way—Morty believes it'll explain how a utopia is possible. They'll know how to bring people who have died back to life."

"Seriously?" Nate wanted to dismiss this unbelievable shit, but after everything he'd seen about the Armor Jewelry...

"According to what we know about ancient Mallandian thought—which isn't much—yes. This is ultimately what Morty wants—to learn this knowledge and use these ancient secrets to create his ridiculous utopia. But according to the legends, in order to find the Plate of Destiny, he first has to be in possession of all four pieces of Armor Jewelry. This is why Anise is in danger. She still owns the amulet, right?" Grace asked.

"Yes."

"And the ring?"

"No. Oh, shit." Nate's face grimaced.

"What?" Grace asked.

"She gave it to Smithton to keep in his safe for her."

"She *what*?! That idiot!" Grace clenched her jaw in a frown.

Nate slammed his hand on the table. "She's *not* an idiot! She didn't know, Grace!"

"So Morty has possession of the cuff and the ring. That means he can overpower her amulet. She could be in danger right now."

"Shit. He has the earrings, too."

"How the hell did he pull that off?" Grace pulled on her hair.

"They're in the traveling Mallandian exhibit. They finally came to the museum back home."

Grace pulled her hair harder. "So he has the other three pieces of Jewelry, and all he needs is the amulet. When did the exhibition start?"

Nate narrowed his eyebrows in thought. "Two weekends ago I think."

"He's had plenty of time to move on this," Grace said to herself, tapping a finger on the table, her eyes looking at something that wasn't there. "I wonder what he's waiting for."

"I want to help Anise," Nate told Grace. "What specifically do I need to do?"

"You and Anise need to possess all four pieces of the Jewelry," she said. "I know Anise is very protective of the amulet. I can guarantee you that Morty wants it more than she does, and he'll do anything to get it. I have no doubt he'd kill her if he gets the chance. Well, he won't do it himself, the candy-ass. Morty won't have a problem getting one of his brainwashed cronies to kill her though."

Nate had no idea why Grace was helping him and Anise—was it just for the tiny amount of the toxic substance? He and Dan had stolen substances for her before; she used them for pain. That's probably all it was for, right? Maybe being locked up with no hope of ever seeing the outside world again was calming her down. He felt something, but what was it? In his mind, he ran through the list of emotions the shrink had given him. Pity, maybe? Or was it confusion? Suspicion? She seemed to be very accepting of her situation, and it wasn't like Grace to give up.

"Do you have any other questions?" she asked.

Nate thought a moment. Grace had wanted Anise's blood in the past. Now Boy Scout kept asking Anise to donate blood. Was there a connection? "Yeah. Why do you want Anise's blood?"

"Next."

"What do you mean, 'next?' Answer the damn question. When we were all at the Springfield Museum three years ago, you handed me plastic bags and wanted Anise's blood in them."

"I mean it's none of your business. Ask me something else or get the hell out."

Nate wanted to crush her under the weight of the heavy table. "Anise said Smithton mentioned something about an incantation. Do you know anything about that?"

"I do. Have you ever noticed the curly symbols on the back of the amulet?"

"Yes."

"Those symbols are on each piece of the Armor Jewelry to include the cuff. They state the incantation, which gives the Jewelry its power."

"Maybe we can use it to try to make another copy of the Jewelry," Nate pondered out loud.

"Your father had the same idea. I watched him try numerous times with no success."

"Just because he couldn't do it doesn't mean I can't."

"Oh, of course," she replied, the sarcasm dripping from her snarled lips. "I forgot how special and smart and how much better you are than everyone else."

Nate sighed in frustration. Whatever pity he may have been feeling for her was gone. "What does the inscription say?"

She narrowed her eyes as she remembered. "Power by one, more by many. Protectors united, destroyers divided."

"The first part makes sense," Nate said. "Each piece of Jewelry has power on its own, but the power is increased when more than one piece is worn."

"That's right," Grace told him.

"What does the second part mean?" he asked.

"As you know, when the Jewelry is united, meaning all pieces are worn by the same person, it's used for protection. The pieces were meant to be used together. But when the Jewelry is divided and the pieces are used against each other, they can cause destruction."

"What do you mean, destruction?" Nate asked his grandmother. "I thought when the pieces were used against each other, they cancelled each other out."

"Yes, at first," Grace explained. "When Morty and I were in grad school, we hadn't yet found out what the incantation says. I found out years later. Morty may or may not have found out on his own; I don't know. But our team was pretending the legends were true—not everyone knew they were actually true—and we were bouncing around ideas with our professor of what might happen if the Jewelry was to be used against each other. The pieces were made to work together, and no one piece is stronger than another. We came up with two possibilities. The first is that the pieces only cancel out each other's powers, which is what we experienced that night we were fighting with Anise at the Springfield Museum. The other possibility is that the opposing energies are so strong that they can't continue on the delicate balance of cancelling each other out indefinitely. The end result would be destruction after an undetermined length of time."

"Destruction of what exactly?"

"Well, that's an excellent question. We don't know. Likely in destruction of the Jewelry at the very least. But given how powerful this Jewelry is, it could be that they destroy whatever or whoever is around them at the time. When I discovered the incantation written out in a book, I gave more credence to the destruction theory we had come up with."

Nate allowed all the new information to settle, trying not to let it overwhelm his mind. He hadn't realized how dangerous all the fighting they'd done with the Jewelry actually was. He hoped to be able to protect Anise from it ever happening again. He looked at his grandmother who actually seemed relaxed and peaceful for once. Nate thought of one more question. "Do you know who Dr. Dromly is?" he asked Grace.

She looked puzzled. "He was the professor I mentioned that I had in college. Why do you ask?"

"Really? Kent Dromly was your professor?"

"Oh, *Kent* Dromly. No. He was the *son* of *Frederick* Dromly, my professor. Why?"

"Do you know where he is now?"

"No. Haven't seen him in years. Again, *why*?"

Nate shrugged. "I just heard the name somewhere. It doesn't matter." He stood up to leave, more than ready to go home. Being back in a prison was bringing back memories he'd rather forget. "Good-bye, Grace."

"Good-bye, Nate." The corners of her lips turned up.

Creepy.

He walked away wondering what was making her smile. She'd never done that before. It was disturbing and made him shiver. At least he'd never have to see her again. As happy as that thought made him, he still had a weird pit in his stomach that felt like it might be guilt. He couldn't stop thinking about the toxic substance, and hoped the plan he'd set in motion would work. Before he left the prison, he sought out the guard that had helped him deliver the package to Grace. "Did you get it back while we were talking like I asked?" Nate wanted to know.

"Sorry, kid. I looked for it, but she must've hidden it somewhere."

Fuck. "In that case, it was nice meeting you," Nate said to the guard and offered a hand.

"Yeah, you too, kid," the guard said, shaking Nate's hand. He looked at Nate inquisitively when he realized the purpose of the handshake was to pass him a wad of cash, and his fingers closed around the hundreds as he put his hand in his pocket. He looked at Nate and waited for the explanation of this unexpected generosity.

"There was a substance in the package," Nate told him in a hushed tone. "I'm holding you personally responsible for making sure she doesn't hurt anyone with it. Can you handle that?"

"Yeah, sure, but like I said, she hid it somewhere. It'll be a big job to find it. I can do it, but until then, we have to make sure she stays in her cell or find someone to escort her even when I'm not here. I can't follow her into the bathroom, you know. I'd have to get a female guard to help."

"Sounds like a transfer would fix that problem. Can you make that happen?"

"Well, yeah, I mean, I can let you know who else you

need to shake hands with. But like I said, it's gonna be a big job." He looked at Nate expectantly.

"Make it happen, and I'll double what I gave you today."

"You'll triple it and we got a deal."

"Deal," confirmed Nate. He followed the guard to the warden's office and felt an emotion coming on. Anger at Grace, anger at the guard, anger at himself for creating a mess to clean up. That was an easy one to recognize.

ANISE GRABBED HER PHONE TO TEXT Nate.

> **Anise: Hey, haven't heard from you. All ok?**

> Nate: Been busy running errands around town. All ok. You?

> **Anise: Yes. I thought we could work on finding Kent Dromly. Come over tonight?**

> Nate: Can't tonight honey. Tomorrow night?

> **Anise: Ok. See you then.**

Anise wondered what Nate was so busy doing. Because he hadn't responded to one of her texts, she wasn't so sure she believed all he was up to was running errands— or was she that forgettable?— but she decided to give him the benefit of the doubt. As much as she didn't want to, she couldn't help but wonder if he'd met someone new. And was he out with this new woman at a restaurant or a concert or... Not wanting to allow him to consume her thoughts anymore, she texted her best friends Vanessa, Erin, and Joy and invited them over for a girl's night with pizza. They arrived just after the pizza was delivered. Anise made sure her amulet was tucked under her sweater before answering the door.

"I brought wine!" announced Joy as she flipped her light blonde hair over her shoulder and held up the bottles.

"Awesome, thanks!" Anise said as she got some wine glasses out of her cupboard. She grabbed some plates and napkins while her friends chatted in her living room.

"Let me see that ring again, girl!" Joy exclaimed, grabbing Vanessa's left hand and fixating her gray-green eyes on the princess cut diamond.

"It's gorgeous," Erin said.

"Blindingly brilliant," Anise chimed in, stepping into the room.

"Let's say what we mean," Joy scolded her friends. "It's fucking huge, and we all hate her." She gave Vanessa a hug. "I'm so happy for you!"

"Thanks!" Vanessa laughed and returned the hug. She looked at Anise. "So what's Jonathan up to tonight?" She took her wool hat off her head, smoothed out her raven hair, and perched on Anise's new red couch. "Band practice?"

"I don't know." Anise hadn't been looking forward to this conversation. She put the plates and napkins on the coffee table that sat in front of the couch. "We kind of broke up."

"Oh, no!" exclaimed Erin. She tucked her bronzy golden highlighted hair behind her ears and looked at Anise sadly with her freckled face. She gave Anise a hug. "What happened?"

Anise sat on her couch next to Vanessa, and her eyes welled up. Her friends didn't know about her adventures with the Armor Jewelry, and she thought it best to keep it that way. If too many people knew about the powers of the Jewelry, that could lead to a bigger problem, especially since Joy couldn't keep a secret to save her life.

She'd thought about what she wanted to tell them and was ready for the line of questioning. "Well, Nate got out of prison and came to see me," she began.

"You've said you were keeping in contact with him, right?" Vanessa asked.

"Yes. We talked often. He called whenever he could," Anise said. "Anyway, I hung out with him a couple times, and Jonathan didn't like it. So, he broke up with me."

"When did all this happen? Has it been that long since we've seen each other?" asked Joy. She made herself comfortable on the floor on the other side of the coffee table.

"Nate got out a couple weeks ago," Anise answered.

"So...this wasn't a date you had with Nate. I know you'd never cheat," Erin said, sitting on the floor next to Joy.

"Of course not. We're just friends." Anise grabbed a slice of pizza.

"So what was the problem? That doesn't seem like Jonathan," Erin added.

"I know!" Anise exclaimed. "That's what's so strange. At first he was a little jealous, but then he said he trusted me, and *then* he completely changed his mind and kicked me out of his apartment." A few tears ran down her cheeks. She didn't like keeping things from her friends, but she also didn't want to tell them how Nate tried to kiss her. That would open up another long line of questioning that she didn't want to have to answer. "But can we change the subject please? I don't wanna talk about him anymore."

"Absolutely," Vanessa agreed.

"Yeah," said Joy, her mouth full of pizza. "I wanna hear more about Nate. What was he in for again?"

Anise frowned. She really didn't want to talk about that either. "He was caught stealing stuff from a museum somewhere," she said, trying to be as vague as possible.

Vanessa narrowed her eyes. "Do you really want to

hang around someone like that?" she asked.

Anise looked at her friend with a serious expression. "You know, I've thought a lot about that and whether or not I can trust him. He has a criminal background, and he lied to me about it at first. Right after he was locked up I was ready to be done with him forever. But I was angry and confused, too. I went to visit him and asked him a lot of questions because I had really liked him a lot, and I needed some closure. He told me all about his messed up, abusive family. He was forced into a life of crime by his dad and grandmother when he was still a kid. Committing theft was a normal day's activity for him, as weird as that sounds. He hadn't done anything illegal since he turned eighteen and left home until three years ago when his grandmother blackmailed him into doing it again. That doesn't make what he did okay, but it makes me understand a little easier why he did it."

"So, I don't understand. I love that you always see the best in everybody, but sometimes you can do it to your own detriment. What makes you think you can trust him now?" asked Vanessa.

"I've asked myself the same thing. I don't know for sure that I can trust him, but he's apologized multiple times, and he seems sincere. He's fine with answering any personal questions about his past that I throw at him. Since he's been back he's been protective and helpful and let me vent to him—everything a good friend would do. He hasn't given me any reason to think he's lying about anything."

"That's all great," Vanessa said. "But he still has a background that's criminal and dishonest. I'm very sorry to hear he was abused, but the trauma of his past could still lead to questionable behavior in the future. People don't change—at least not that quickly."

Anise frowned. "Three years ago I lied to Brian about going on a business trip. He knew I was lying, and it led to him trying to find me and getting shot. I lied because

I was scared he'd destroy my apartment, so it was easier than telling him the truth. That doesn't make me any better than Nate."

"That's not the same thing, Anise!" Vanessa insisted. "You didn't do anything criminal."

Yes, I did. Anise wondered what her friends would think if they knew she and Jonathan had broken into the Springfield Museum to steal the earrings all in the name of what's "right," according to Jonathan, anyway. He'd wanted to protect the artifacts as well as the world from whatever Grace had planned for it. Nate had wanted to stop Grace from hurting anyone else, and he saved Anise's life. They both committed crimes in the process. She could see both wrong and right in each man's actions. They both seemed so sure of themselves. Why couldn't she make up her mind about what she thought about all this? About both of them? Why did she listen to everyone who was judging Nate so harshly when she wouldn't even be alive without him?

"I know what you're saying," Anise assured Vanessa. "And I'm not without some doubt as to Nate's trustworthiness because of his past, but when we're just hanging out and joking around, it's the easiest thing in the world. I'd like to give him the benefit of the doubt. I really like him; I think he's a good person. He's so smart. He makes me laugh. I have an unbelievable amount of fun with him, and I'd hate to lose that." She smiled, thinking about their latest ride on his motorcycle and how much fun they had at The Blue Pineapple.

"But it's costing you Jonathan!" Vanessa exclaimed. "I'm sure he can tell you have a crush on Nate."

Something about Vanessa's statement made Anise feel defensive. *It's just an attraction! Nothing more!* "I don't have a crush on Nate!" she insisted. "I love Jonathan!"

"Of course you love Jonathan," Erin said in a kind voice. "No one's denying that. But you also have a crush on Nate."

Joy's head bobbed up and down in agreement. "You're doing that thing again where you lie to yourself about your feelings when you're into a guy and don't want to be. We talked about this a few years ago."

Anise opened her mouth to protest but closed it again. *Is that what I'm doing?* She blinked and everything became clear. "Well, shit."

Her friends laughed.

"You don't have to hide something like that from us!" said Erin.

"I'm sorry," Anise said, shaking her head at herself. "Joy's right. I do that." She let out an exasperated sigh. "It's so obvious—why don't I see it when it's happening? You know, I often dream about him."

"Oooo, sexy dreams?" Joy wanted to know.

"Yes. And not just dreams while asleep. I've fantasized about him. Often. I kept telling myself it was just an attraction and that it meant nothing, but...I've been having a lot of guilt lately, so deep down I must've known the truth. I just couldn't admit it to myself until right now when you said something."

"It was your defense mechanism," Erin said, her voice full of compassion.

"It was," Anise continued. "I was trying to hide it from *myself* though, not you guys. I just...didn't want it to be true. It makes everything more complicated. I guess I thought as long as I didn't admit it, I didn't have to feel like a terrible person for fantasizing about a man who's done bad things—and even worse, a man who isn't Jonathan since I started dating him a few months ago."

"Don't worry, it's okay!" Joy said, laughing again at Anise's expression. "You can't help how you feel. And it's just a crush. You'll get over it, and if Jonathan's not a complete idiot, he will too. You're the best thing that's ever happened to him!"

"Maybe," Anise acknowledged, but felt conflicted. As

much as she missed Jonathan, she was still afraid of him. Even if he wanted to come back to her, she'd refuse him. She shouldn't get too close to him right now for her own safety. Plus, she realized now it wasn't just a crush that she felt for Nate. Her feelings had been stronger than that since before he even got released, and she felt ridiculous for lying to herself about it.

"He's madly in love with you, so I have no doubt," Joy declared with confidence. "But I can tell there's something else on your mind, too. What is it?"

Anise leaned back on the couch. "I feel guilty about my feelings for Nate. I didn't mean for it to happen. But he's not the only reason Jonathan and I broke up. Even since before we started our relationship, Jonathan's changed. He keeps talking about weird things and pressuring me to visit his boss."

"What weird things?" Erin asked.

"Stuff that's happening at work and blood drives...it's hard to explain. He's saying things that are out of character for him. He makes me feel uncomfortable a lot of the time."

"Wait, this has been happening since *before* you two got together?" Erin said. "No wonder you were hesitant that night at the bar."

"Oh no, and we pushed you to get together with him!" Vanessa said, a crestfallen look washing over her face.

"We couldn't help it!" Joy piped up. "It was such a beautiful spring night, and he looked so cute up on stage singing that song he wrote about his feelings for you."

"I know," Anise said, basking in the memory. "It was the night before his birthday."

"And we pushed you to walk up there, and he jumped off the stage, and you kissed," Joy continued. "The entire bar cheered!" She put her hands on her heart and pretended to faint. "You're so lucky."

"I agree," piped up Erin. "The last guy I dated thought being romantic meant picking his socks up off the floor."

"You didn't push me," Anise assured her friends. "It was my decision."

"Are you sure?" Erin asked.

"Yes. I needed time after Brian's death, and Jonathan's friendship meant the world to me. He was so dependable and predictable, and that felt good to be around. I could tell he wanted more from me than just friendship, and I knew he'd make a great boyfriend, but...I never thought about him in that way because we were such good friends. And if I tried to picture it, I was afraid of us not working out and losing my friend. Then later, he started acting weird, and I started having more reservations, but I thought maybe he was just stressed. So when he made his grand gesture of love up on stage...when a guy does something like that...it feels like it's now or never, right? So even though I had some doubts, I took a chance because I already loved him as a friend. I thought maybe it would be an easy jump to something romantic. I thought maybe we could be really good together. And I do love him, but there's something going on with him, and considering how uncomfortable he can make me now, part of me feels this breakup is a good thing. I just wish I knew how to help him. I don't think it's his fault. He's been having these migraines that are affecting his vision and train of thought."

"How so?" Erin asked with concern in her voice.

"I don't feel like getting into all that," Anise said, thinking about Jonathan's talk of blood, his hallucinations, and his glazed look when he mentioned Dr. Smithton's utopia vision. She also noticed she had some anger toward Jonathan. Grace had been able to fight off the brainwashing—no one told *her* what to do. Why couldn't Jonathan do the same?

"Have you tried talking about it with him?" Erin looked sad for her friend.

"Yes, but it's not helping."

"If his doctors can cure his migraines and his odd

behavior goes away, would you still have reservations about Jonathan?" Vanessa wanted to know.

Anise shrugged and grabbed another slice of pizza from the box. "I'm not sure. My panic attacks seem to be a problem for him. He gets so scared for me when I'm anxious that *I* end up having to comfort *him*, which I honestly don't have the energy for at those times. He knows I don't like it, but I don't think he can help freaking out when he sees me panic. He keeps pushing me to see a doctor or take medication, but I don't feel like I want to do that, at least not now, and it's like he doesn't listen to me when I try to tell him that. I know that no relationship is perfect, and I appreciate that it's just because he cares so much, but..." She shrugged again. "Honestly, I really don't know what, or who, I want right now."

"I once read a study that showed it takes about four months to feel a lot better after a break-up," Vanessa volunteered. "You won't necessarily be completely over it depending on the relationship's duration and level of commitment, but things are supposed to be easier after the four month mark."

Anise leaned back on the couch, feeling a little better. "That's comforting. Four months really isn't that long."

"Time isn't the only thing that can help," Erin chimed in. She opened her purse and pulled out a velvet, drawstring bag. She rooted through it and removed a black stone. Giving it a kiss and handing it to Anise, she said, "Keep this in your pocket. It's a black onyx—to help you get over whichever relationship you choose."

"Thank you," Anise replied, holding the stone to her heart to feel the love Erin put into it. She pushed the stone into a front pocket of her jeans.

There was a short silence filled only by the sound of chewing.

"So, this is incredibly inappropriate timing," Joy said, as she gave Anise a wicked grin. "But I have to ask—do you have any pictures of Nate?"

Anise grinned back with gratitude. Joy could always be counted on to lighten the mood. "I do!" She grabbed her phone and showed her friends the pictures she and Nate had taken of themselves in the park at the top of the hill.

"Oh, *hell* yeah!" exclaimed Joy as she grabbed Anise's phone out of her hands. "Has he gotten hotter? Is that even humanly possible?"

Anise laughed. "I thought the same thing!" she exclaimed. "He worked out a lot in prison."

"I see that," Joy purred with a lustful smirk. "I love that he looks like he's in great shape, but not *too* muscular. You know what I mean? He looks well-defined, but not bulky like he spends every waking moment in the gym. And that jaw line. And that glint in his dark blue eyes that makes him look like he's got something reckless and exciting planned. I mean...I could die."

"Don't drool on her phone, Joy," Erin teased as Anise and Vanessa laughed. "And don't hog it, either. I wanna see!"

"Ok, fine," Joy conceded, handing over the phone. "But I want it back. And seriously, why have we not started drinking this wine yet?"

Anise got up to fetch the bottle opener. Although the hardest conversation was now over, she still needed a break from the dizzying thoughts of both Nate and Jonathan swirling in her head. "Can we promise no more talk about men tonight?"

Joy smirked. "Yes! I want to talk about Yvette," she said, referring to the woman she had recently started dating.

Anise was grateful for her friends' company and her mood lifted as they toasted to a fun night. She hadn't felt this loved and normal in a while. She still didn't know what she was going to do about Nate or Jonathan, but with her friends there, it was easier to push the questions from her mind. At least for now.

Chapter 18

Fifty-one years ago

Sunday, May 3, 1964

Grace heard a light knock-knock-knock and swung open her front door at her new home in her new city. "What the hell are you doing here?" she demanded of her visitor. She squinted up at him in the sunlight.

"What kind of a greeting is that?" asked Morty with a laugh as he stood unwelcomed on her welcome mat.

"How the hell did you find me?" she demanded of his stupid, smiling face.

"It wasn't rocket science," he answered. His hand squirmed around unnaturally in his jacket pocket. Grace assumed he was trying to put the cuff on without her seeing and was about to make another brainwashing attempt. "Grace, you need to join my team to find..."

She tried to slam the door in his face, but he stuck his foot in the doorjamb just in time.

"...to find the Armor Jewelry," he continued. "We

were always so good at working together, and you miss me, don't you? Together we can find it and rule the world!"

"For the millionth time, I am *not* joining your stupid cult!" she screamed at him. "I *will* call the police again!" she threatened. "Maybe in *this* town they'll actually believe me!"

"You didn't renew the restraining order, Grace. It's already expired. And my team is not a cult."

"Why the hell did you follow me here?! First you get me fired, then you stalk and harass me, then you kill my husband! Why won't you leave me alone?!"

"You no longer love Thomas," Morty asserted.

"Is this your sick way of trying to get me back? What the hell is wrong with you? I will *always* love Thomas!"

"Are you going to let me in so we can talk?"

"NO! You wanna talk, you talk from right there!" She pushed the door harder on his foot and pulled on her hair. A headache was coming on.

He gave her a sharp glare. "Fine. I just got a job at the museum on Walker Street downtown. Even if you move away again, Grace, I'll follow you. You *will* be on my team."

"You *moved* here?!"

"Yes," he boasted. "I did. And I brought all of my subordinates with me."

"Your entire staff moved out here too?! Morty, what the hell is wrong with you? Why do you want me to join your cult—"

"My team," he corrected her.

"Whatever. Why do you want me to join so badly?"

"Because together we can find the Armor Jewelry faster than we could separately."

"Bullshit!" she screamed, pulling on her hair, the pain in her head getting worse. "You're afraid I'll find it first!"

"That's ridiculous!" he said with a huff.

"No," she argued, "that's accurate! Well, you can forget it! I'll never join your cult! And I *will* get to the Armor

Jewelry *and* the Plate of Destiny before you!" With that, she hit the heel of her hand into the bridge of his nose. He yelped and jumped backward, giving her the opportunity to close and lock the door.

She screamed when she turned and saw Morty standing in her living room. He looked at her with blood streaming out his eyes and spiders crawling out of his ears. He was gone as suddenly as he had appeared, and Grace realized she'd had another hallucination.

She pulled on her hair as she paced her living room, fuming. Her new carpet was soft on her bare feet, but it did nothing to calm her down. *The nerve of him!* He had no right to move to her new town and keep stalking her. He was obviously threatened by her and probably felt she had a good chance to collect all the Jewelry before him. Perhaps he felt the only choice he had was to keep trying to brainwash her into thinking what he wanted her to think. But why keep trying when it obviously wasn't working? The brainwashing attempts must have been successful on his colleagues, otherwise, why would they *all* have moved three states away simply because he did? But why did he keep thinking it would work on her? And come to think of it, why *wouldn't* it work on her? She was grateful that she seemed to be immune to the effects of the cuff but couldn't help but wonder what made her so different as to have that advantage.

Regardless, this stalking bullshit had to stop. What could she do? She sat on her couch and thought. As far as she knew, the only reason he kept following her was because he wanted to continue the brainwashing attempts. The fact that he had possession of the cuff was what allowed Morty to make those attempts. Therefore, she simply had to take the cuff from him. What she'd learned about breaking into buildings and stealing without being detected would come in handy now.

"Mommy!" she heard a little voice yell. "Mommy, Mommy, Mommy, Mommy!" She sighed and walked through the hallway to the nursery to get Dan who had just woken up from his nap. As she picked him up, and he wrapped his little arms around her, the annoyance she felt was so disturbing, she almost let herself cry. Even just a year ago, his embraces would melt her heart. But now...

She sat in the rocking chair next to Dan's crib, hoping the gentle motion and the soft, mint green color she'd picked for his walls would calm the storm surge inside of her. She was gradually losing the patience she used to have for children. Noise was bothering her a lot when it never used to before. It made her think of her father and how much *he* had hated noise. *It's just stress,* she told herself.

"Everything's going to be ok, Dan," she whispered in her son's ear. "Mommy has a plan."

Monday, May 4, 1964

IT WAS VERY EARLY MORNING, THE waning crescent moon was shining through a hallway window, and Grace had no idea which way to go. She'd successfully broken into the museum in her new city's downtown and was searching for Morty's office. After fifteen minutes, she finally found the door with the nameplate that read "Dr. Morton Smithton." She picked the lock and entered the office. *It's probably not even in here,* she thought, annoyed. She checked the closet and behind the pictures on the walls, but found no safes. Every desk drawer, shelf, and box was checked before she gave up and went home empty-handed. The cuff was not in his office. Her eyes drooped, but she didn't bother to go to sleep as she'd have to be at Morty's in a few hours.

At almost six o'clock, Grace watched the sunrise from

behind the bushes around the side of Morty's house. She watched him drive away about half an hour later, then snuck to his back gate. Keeping low, she went through the gate, closing it behind her. She picked the lock to his back door and searched his entire house. Rooting through kitchen cabinets, the bedroom dresser, the drawers in the bathroom, and every box in every closet proved unfruitful. The cuff was nowhere. Grace swore and pulled on her red hair, but was careful not to pull any out and leave it on Morty's white carpet where it'd point to her like a spotlight.

He must have it with him at all times! she thought. She'd have to take it from him while he was sleeping or in the shower. Grace frowned. Her baby-sitter already told her she couldn't work that evening. She'd have to plan on coming back early the next morning. She wondered what the baby-sitter would think with her being gone at strange hours of the day and what she'd say to the police if Morty accused Grace of breaking into his place. Perhaps the best thing to do would be to take Dan with her. He'd be sound asleep and safe in the car until she got back, hopefully.

As she solidified her plan, she thought about what she'd do with the cuff once she got it, and how she should have already come up with a better plan. *Don't get sloppy,* she told herself. Morty would undoubtedly suspect her and come to her looking for it. Keeping it with her at all times like he did wouldn't be smart. Then he'd always know where it is and would find a way to overpower her and take it.

Back at home, she headed down to her basement to look around for a hiding spot. She shivered. All basements were vile portals to hell, and she'd prefer to never go down there. But there weren't any good places to hide something upstairs, and the strong do what needs to be done.

There must be someplace I can hide it.

As she walked around, she noticed a loose brick near one of the corners. Carefully, she pried it all the way out. Holding the brick in her hand, she peered into the hole it left. She saw nothing but black. With a sigh, she found a flashlight and looked again. There was a decent space behind the bricks. *No wonder it's so cold down here,* she thought. *There's hardly any insulation!* The positive side was that there was enough room to hide the cuff. If she put it in a bag and attached the bag to a stick, she could lower the cuff to the floor inside the wall. She'd include the amulet she took from Dromly's safe, too. Proud of herself, she reinserted the brick in the wall and hung a picture over it.

Tuesday, May 5, 1964

THE NEXT MORNING AT FOUR O'CLOCK, Grace was once again picking Morty's back lock. She'd practiced and practiced on her own doors until she could do it without making a sound. She tip-toed into his bedroom and saw the cuff on his nightstand.

Finally!

Carefully, she stepped over toward the nightstand. When she was almost there, Morty's alarm clock went off. Grace dropped to the ground in horror. Her heart jumped in her chest, and she crawled to hide behind the other side of the bed. She heard Morty hit the button on the clock to turn off the alarm, get up, and walk to the bathroom. When she heard him get in the shower, she stood up and darted for the nightstand. The cuff was gone. *Damn it! He must've taken it into the bathroom.*

She made a beeline for the bathroom and saw that Morty hadn't closed the door all the way. She rolled her eyes when he began singing some cheesy love song. She peered through the crack between the door and the jamb and through the billowing steam saw his shadow behind the shower curtain. Pushing the door open just a bit, she stuck her head in and saw the cuff on the counter by the sink. The water shut off and the curtain was pushed aside. She pulled her head back in the hallway. *Shit!* Having to abort her plan and try again another day would only increase her odds of a neighbor seeing her, Morty catching her, or someone finding Dan alone in her car. Failure wasn't an option. She watched as Morty grabbed his towel and closed his eyes to dry his face.

Now!

In one fluid motion, she opened the door and leaned into the small bathroom, grabbed the cuff, and pulled the door behind her as she stepped back out. She made a mad dash for the back door, closed it behind her, and hunching low, ran to the gate which she was glad she hadn't closed fully. It was still dark outside, and she dove behind his next door neighbor's car to see if he was running after her. She carefully watched through the car window as Morty ran out into his backyard wearing nothing but a towel. He looked around and went back into the house. A few moments later, his front door opened and he looked around again before swearing and going back inside. Grace assumed he was going to call the police so she ran the several blocks back to her car. Looking inside, she saw that Dan was still sleeping peacefully, as she had left him. *Thank god,* she thought. If he had woken up and screamed, that could've ruined everything.

"Thank you, Dan," she told her sleeping son as she drove them back home. She took a deep breath and let it out slowly through pursed lips. "You're a good boy. Maybe someday you'll be able to help me instead of being a hindrance when it comes to doing what has to be done."

✳ ✳ ✳

INSIDE HIS HOUSE, MORTY CURSED GRACE as he got dressed. He hadn't actually seen her, but who else could it have been? He felt violated. How long had she been in his house?

What was even more disturbing now was that Grace had the cuff. He could no longer attempt to brainwash her or continue to brainwash his colleagues. Luckily, they were close to where he wanted them, but for some of them, it would be a bit of time still until they were brainwashed to the point of unquestioned loyalty. And what would Dromly do if he knew the cuff had been stolen? Would he kill him just like he did Thomas? He had to get it back from Grace immediately.

Grabbing his gun, he headed over to her house and banged on her front door. "Grace, open this door!" he ordered.

"Go to hell, Morty!" he heard her yelling.

Frustrated, Morty broke the small glass window next to the door with the grip of the gun, reached in, unlocked it, and let himself in. "Where is it?" he yelled at her.

Dan, who was playing on the light tan carpet, burst into tears.

"Get out of here, Morty! You're scaring my son!" Grace yelled back from her seat on the brown floral couch.

Morty looked at the child and felt like a monster. Dan was looking back at him with tears rolling out of his large brown eyes, his face turning as red as his hair. Grace picked him up and rocked him.

The sight of her comforting a child that wasn't theirs made Morty angry again. He pointed his gun at them. "The cuff, Grace. Where is it?"

She looked at him and laughed. "Put that thing away, Morty. We both know you're not going to use it."

He frowned. She was absolutely right. He hadn't even put any bullets in it. There was no way he could scare her into giving the cuff back to him. If he wanted it, he'd have to find it and take it. He followed the smell of coffee to her kitchen and began rummaging through all her avocado green drawers and cupboards.

"What the hell are you doing?" she demanded of him as she followed him into the kitchen.

He snorted. *As if she didn't know.* "You took my cuff this morning," he told her. "I'm here to get it back."

"I did no such thing!" she protested. "Now get the hell out of my house!"

"I'll leave when I find it!" he told her in a raised voice.

"You'll leave now! Or I'm calling the police!" She picked up the phone as a threat.

Morty grabbed the receiver out of her hands and pulled the cord out of the wall. With all his might, he threw the entire phone to the ground, and it smashed apart, hardware flying across the linoleum floor. "Sit down, shut up, and stay out of my way!" he commanded her.

✳✳✳

"GO TO HELL, MORTY!" GRACE YELLED back.

After watching the phone crash to the ground, Dan screamed at the top of his lungs and buried his face in Grace's breast. All the noise was really getting to Grace. She had an urge to shake him and wondered if that's what her father had done to her little brother Danny. The thought scared her, and nausea squeezed her stomach. Pulling on her hair, she looked at Morty, angry that he was causing her son such agony. *Just let him look,* she told herself. *He'll never find it. And when he's done, he'll leave.* She kissed her son's head. "It's okay, my baby," she whispered to him.

Hours later, Morty gave up. He'd searched every inch of her house and found nothing. "This isn't over Grace. I *will* find that cuff," he snarled at her.

"Fantastic," Grace replied from her seat on the floral

couch, the sarcasm oozing out, as she rocked a much quieter Dan in her lap. "Now, why don't you stay and help me clean up this mess you made? I'll make tea!"

"Fuck you," Morty said, leaning in close to her face.

Dan was sitting on her lap. "Fuck you," he repeated to Morty, which made Grace laugh.

Morty stormed out, slamming the door behind him.

"Dan, you mustn't say that," she scolded. Her son burst into tears like he did every time he thought he'd disappointed her. Grace sighed. Dan was an extremely sensitive child. She wished she had the patience to deal with him in a gentler manner, but for some reason, that was becoming more and more difficult. "Shhh," she said softly as she rocked him, upset by the recurring urge she had to shake him. Trembling with fear and worry about the highly unsettling violent thoughts she had toward her son at that moment, she pushed them away with everything she had and sang to him instead.

Her sweet song put Dan to sleep, and with Morty gone, she leaned back in her chair and relaxed. She hoped that Morty would forget about the cuff, forget about *her* so she and Dan could live in peace. But she knew better than that.

Chapter 19

Present day

Thursday, September 24, 2015

Nate sat with Anise at her kitchen table that was just big enough for two. He'd brought groceries and took over her kitchen. She'd polished off the rigatoni with white wine sauce he'd cooked for her and raved about it. Her brown hair waved perfectly around her flawless, smiling face, and her voice sparkled as she talked to him about her day. He could get used to this.

She got up to put their dishes in the sink. "So...don't be mad."

"Uh oh," he said with a wry smile, doubting that whatever she was about to say would be that bad. "What'd you do, honey?"

As she cleared the table, she told him how she'd confessed to Jonathan that they had broken into Dr. Smithton's safe and had seen the cuff, missing page, and other texts.

He'd been wrong. It was bad. "Why would you do

that?" Nate asked her, his brow furrowed.

"I was trying to explain to Jonathan why I was going with you on your trips because he was so upset about it. I wanted him to know I was going for him—because I'm so worried about him. There was no way to make him believe that without telling him the truth. That, and because I hate lying to him." She sat back down at the table.

"Did he believe you?"

She looked down at her hands in her lap. "No."

"He probably ran right over to Smithton and told him everything," Nate said, shaking his head, his tone sharp.

"No," Anise argued. "I asked him not to."

Nate frowned and clenched his jaw. He didn't believe Boy Scout would keep that to himself for a second. Nate had planned on telling Anise what he learned from Grace about how Smithton was forming a cult with the cuff in order to find the Plate of Destiny to create his utopia, but now he worried that she'd tell Boy Scout, who would then tell Smithton. And if Smithton had any idea how much they knew about his plans, it might prompt him to come after Anise and find a way to shut her up. Grace had said she was surprised he hadn't come after her already. There must be some reason he was waiting.

Nate decided to keep this information to himself. Anise's mouth might get her into more trouble. On the other hand, she needed to know she was in trouble so she'd stay away from Smithton. He needed to tell her something. But if he did, she'd want to know where the information came from. Nate visiting Grace *could not* get back to Smithton. "Just stay away from Smithton," was all he told her.

"I told you I would," she assured him. "But there's something else I wanted to talk to you about too. In your mom's letter, she seemed to know something we didn't and stressed that it was important that I own all four pieces of Jewelry. I think we should do what she asked."

Nate shook his head and one corner of his lips turned slightly upward. "Nope. What you're planning is against the law, and I promised this incredibly beautiful woman that I'd be a good boy from now on," he teased her.

She rolled her eyes at him. "You haven't kept that promise so far. But I'm okay with that because a good boy isn't who I need right now." She gave him a coquettish smirk.

"In that case, I'm your man."

"I already own the amulet," Anise said. "So all we have to do is break into Dr. Smithton's safe again, and we'll have the cuff and ring!"

"And we know exactly where the earrings are," Nate added.

"Right!" agreed Anise. "I want to go with you when you break into the museum to get them."

He laughed and then looked at her seriously. "No."

"Why not?"

"It's not exactly a walk in the park," he told her in an almost scolding manner. "This is serious and illegal work. If something goes wrong, I don't want you to have to suffer the consequences."

"How many times has something gone wrong?" she asked.

"Just once," he admitted. "That night I got arrested at the Springfield Museum. But there were a few close calls on other occasions."

"Just once," she repeated. "And you let yourself get caught on purpose for my sake. That won't happen this time. So what could possibly go wrong? You *are* a professional, right?"

He shrugged. "Yes, I am. But the last time you broke into a museum you got traumatized. You don't feel safe without the amulet anymore. Why would you want to put yourself through that again?" he asked her.

"Because we're in this together, and you're putting yourself at risk to help me. It's only fair that we both go so I can help protect you with the amulet if need be. Besides, I think it would be fascinating to watch you do what you do best," she replied with a smile. "This may be the only chance I get to do that."

"You think being a thief is what I do best?" He felt an emotion from her statement. It was...anger? No. Something like humiliation but not quite that either. It was... hurt that his criminal past seemed to define him in her eyes.

"I'm sorry," she apologized quickly. "That came out wrong. I just meant that we're getting closer, and I want to get to know you better."

"Even that part of me?"

"Yes, even that part. Everyone has a past, and I want you to know I'm not judging you for yours. I'm just honestly interested in learning more about you. You can share anything with me."

The hurt dissipated. "Same, honey."

"Good," she told him. "Then is it okay to admit I'm incredibly curious as to how we're going to break in? Jonathan and I had no idea how to do it when we tried to steal the earrings from the Springfield Museum. We went in during business hours and found a place to hide past closing instead."

He couldn't help but be charmed by her wide-eyed enthusiasm for something he knew she didn't really want to do. "That was a good plan," he told her. "And I have some ideas. I have to go through my old tools and see what's still in working order."

She reached across the table and took his hand. "Thank you for doing this for me. I completely trust your expertise. I know whatever plan you come up with, you'll do it really well."

"I do a lot of things well, honey," he said with a devilish grin.

She grinned back. "I bet you do," she told him in a flirtatious voice.

Just then, they heard a *knock-knock-knock* at the door, and Anise got up to answer it.

Nate sighed. Whoever it was, their timing sucked.

"WHO COULD THAT BE?" ANISE WONDERED out loud as she headed to the door and opened it. "Jonathan!" she said with surprise. Her stomach tightened and her breath quickened with fear upon seeing him until she reminded herself that Nate was with her. She looked down and saw her amulet wasn't glowing. Both of those things made her relax.

"Anise, I owe you a huge apology," Jonathan said, stepping inside her apartment. He looked past her and saw Nate watching them from Anise's kitchen table. "What the hell are *you* doing here?" Jonathan demanded.

"I could ask you the same question," Nate replied, getting up and walking toward them.

Jonathan looked around the room. "What, no flowers this time? No gifts?" The hurt at finding Nate in her apartment was evident in his voice.

"Well, not with that attitude," Nate said, flashing an arrogant grin. "Next time smile and wear something pretty."

"It's time for you to leave," Jonathan told him with a snarl. "I need to talk to Anise."

"I'm not going anywhere," said Nate.

"Guys, I thought we settled this," interjected Anise. She turned to Nate. "You paid him for the door frame you damaged, right?"

"Not yet," answered Nate. He reached into his wallet and grabbed several hundred dollar bills. "Here," he said, as he tossed them in Jonathan's direction. The bills scattered and landed on the floor near Jonathan's feet.

Jonathan gave him a look of pure hatred. He stepped

on the money as he turned to Anise. "I'd like to talk to you, if that's okay. In private."

"No, it's *not* okay!" said Nate, stepping in between Jonathan and Anise.

"I wasn't asking *you*, asshole!" shot back Jonathan as he pulled on his hair.

"*Enough!*" said Anise. "Nate, Jonathan and I do have some things we need to talk about."

"Just a few days ago you were terrified of him!" Nate protested.

"I know, but I do want to talk to him about it," she replied. "Please give us some time."

Nate shook his head. "I'm not leaving you alone with him. You said you were worried he'd hurt you."

"My amulet isn't glowing. I'll be okay. And I'll call you if I need you, I promise. Please, Nate?"

He frowned. After forcing Jonathan to empty the contents of his pockets to make sure he didn't have the ring, earrings, or cuff with him, Nate finally agreed to her request. "Call me as soon as he leaves so I know you're okay."

"I promise."

Nate left, but not without sending a glare in Jonathan's direction first.

"Were you really terrified of me?" Jonathan asked her as soon as Nate closed the door.

"Yes, Jonathan!" she spat at him. "You were talking about my blood, and my amulet was glowing! What the hell was that all about?!"

He took a step toward her and she backed away. He sat down on her couch. "I'm so sorry I scared you," he apologized, looking defeated. "To be honest, I don't know why I keep talking about blood. A lot of things haven't made much sense since I started getting these headaches."

Anise could see that he was sincere both in his apology and his explanation. She felt sorry for him and wanted to go sit next to him, but her stomach was clenching again. She decided to heed her instincts and sat in her kitchen chair instead. "When's your MRI again?" she asked him.

"I had it the other day," he answered, "along with some other tests."

"Why didn't you tell me?"

"We broke up..." Jonathan started to say.

"That doesn't mean I stopped caring about you," she said. "Did you get the results yet?"

"Yeah, good news! No brain tumors, lesions, or diseases of any kind. According to the doctors, my brain is really physically healthy."

"Oh my god, what a relief!" Anise said.

"Yeah, kinda," Jonathan said.

"What do you mean?"

"Well, my doctor referred me to a psychiatrist."

"He thinks it's psychological?" she asked.

"They couldn't find anything physically wrong, so this is the next step."

"When's your appointment?"

"Tomorrow," Jonathan answered her.

"Do you have a co-worker to drive you? You shouldn't drive when you're having visual hallucinations. It's dangerous."

"It's near the museum. I can walk."

"Okay. Well, let me know how it turns out."

"I will." After an awkward pause in the conversation, he apologized again. "I'm so sorry Anise. I can't tell you how much I hate myself for scaring you."

She looked at him and wondered if his issues maybe *were* psychological. Maybe Dr. Smithton wasn't brainwashing him after all. "If it's because there's something wrong with your brain—physically or psychologically— it's not your fault. Just promise me you'll do everything you can to get better. I miss you. The old you."

"I miss you, too," he said, his eyes sad. "I've been wanting to come over for the last couple days, but I've been putting it off because I figured Nate would be here. Looks like I was right."

"Actually, tonight was the first time I've seen him since our trip. I told you I hadn't planned on seeing him all the time, and that's still true."

He dug the toe of his shoe into her carpet. "I'm sorry I let my jealousy get the better of me the other day. I let my pride get in the way. I shouldn't have..." His phone rang. "Excuse me," he told her and took the call. "Hey, Dr. S," he said. After a pause, his eyes started to glaze over. "Yeah, okay. Just give me a few extra minutes. I have to either walk or call a cab...See you soon." He hung up and looked at Anise. "Sorry to cut this short, but I have to go into work for a while. Dr. S. needs help with something. I don't know why it can't wait until tomorrow." He sighed.

She wondered if he'd been about to tell her he shouldn't have broken up with her. She was glad he'd been interrupted. There was no way she'd get back together with him—at least not now. Not while he might still do something to make her amulet glow. Whether it was a psychological disorder or brainwashing by Dr. Smithton, she needed to keep her distance from Jonathan. "Okay, well, thanks for coming by. Keep me updated on your health."

"I will." He got up and walked to her door. He paused and turned back around. "Do you think you could drive me? It's a little far to walk."

"After what happened last time I saw you, I'm not comfortable with that. Can't you take a cab?"

"Yeah," he agreed. He pulled his phone out of his pocket and stared at it.

"What's going on?"

"I'm having a hard time focusing. I feel another headache coming on."

"Okay, I'll get my keys," she said, not wanting him to be alone if he was going to start having hallucinations again.

"Thanks, I really appreciate this."

He didn't seem to be in pain. He wasn't pulling on his hair. His eyes were very glazed over though. Anise's stomach formed a knot, and she regretted her offer. She didn't feel right about taking him to Dr. Smithton now that she knew Dr. Smithton wasn't the kindly older man she had thought he was. However, she knew Jonathan still trusted and looked up to him, and with the amount of glaze in his eyes, there was no way she'd be able to reason with him. Who knows what he'd do if she tried to talk him out of going? At best, they'd argue again. At worst, he might act on an intention to hurt her like last time.

Anise drove him to the museum as quickly as possible without making it obvious that she was trying to speed. She made sure to chatter on about work, her friends, or anything else that popped into her mind to avoid any possible talk about Nate, utopia, or blood. Parking in the garage under the museum, she turned to Jonathan and said, "It was nice to see you tonight."

"You too," he said with a smile.

She saw his eyes were still glazed over, and she was ready to leave as her dizziness and tingling arms told her she was on the verge of a panic attack. "Okay, well, take care. Dr. Smithton can drive you home, right?"

"Yes," replied Jonathan. "But why don't you walk in with me and say hi to Dr. S? He's been asking to see you."

The knot in her stomach tightened. Nate told her to stay away from Dr. Smithton and she knew she should heed his warning. On the other hand, if she saw Dr. Smithton, she might be able to get a feel on whether or not Jonathan spilled the beans about Nate breaking into his safe. It would be great if she could ease Nate's mind as he was so upset about it earlier. She frowned, knowing Nate would tell her not to do this. "Okay, let's go."

The walk from the parking garage to the elevator was short but uncomfortable for Anise, not knowing what to say. Jonathan was usually the one who was good at filling silences, but tonight he stayed quiet. He swiped his badge and typed in his code. They rode the elevator and walked down the hallway in silence and turned into Dr. Smithton's office.

"Thank you for coming so quickly!" Dr. Smithton said to Jonathan. "I'm sorry for interrupting your evening, but it couldn't be helped."

"No problem," Jonathan replied.

"Lovely to see you, Anise," Dr. Smithton said.

"Hi, Dr. Smithton!" she chirped in a voice friendlier than she felt. "Nice to see you too!" She wondered what she could say to him to find out if he knew about Nate's break in.

"I'm sure you wouldn't mind if we all sat and had a little talk." He waved a hand toward a guest chair.

She swallowed and tried to think of what to say. Why did he want to talk? Her stomach clenched again and she regretted not listening to Nate's advice, but she couldn't exactly refuse Smithton's offer. The reason she came up to his office was to talk to him. She hoped he'd unknowingly give her a clue as to whether he was on to her or not. "I don't mind at all," she said, "but I can't stay too long."

"You didn't tell me you had plans," Jonathan said, narrowing his eyes. "Is *Nate* expecting you?"

"Well, *he* can wait," said Dr. Smithton as he put his hand on Anise's lower back and guided her to a chair. "Sit, my dear," he insisted, as he firmly pushed on her shoulders until she was seated.

The click of the office door being locked brought on a dizzying wave of anxiety. Anise wanted to say something in protest of how Dr. Smithton was treating her but held her tongue. As soon as she got a read on him, she'd leave. *And if he tries to hurt me, I'll introduce his knees to my side kick.* She thought about texting Nate to let him know where she was, but decided that wouldn't be necessary. She'd leave very soon, and everything would be fine. She looked over at Jonathan who sat next to her. He stared at

Dr. Smithton without saying a word.

"Anise," Dr. Smithton began, "as you know, Grace Brevain and I were acquaintances when we were about your age. This may be hard to believe, but before I really knew her, she was a very charming and exciting person. I imagine that's how you must feel about her grandson." When Anise didn't react, he continued. "My point is that if Nate is anything like his grandmother—and I suspect he is, based on how he's helped Grace and how he's lied to you in the past—it would be in your best interest to stop your association with him."

Anise held back her anger. *How is this any of his business?* "I appreciate your concern," she told him with a forced smile, "but Jonathan and I have already discussed this." She glanced over at Jonathan, expecting him to agree with her. He said nothing and continued staring at his boss. *That's not like him.*

"I understand," said Dr. Smithton. "Have you considered that Nate may still be after your amulet? That's the only reason you even met him, isn't it?" he asked, obviously trying to put doubt in her mind about Nate.

Anise frowned as she thought back to the day she met Nate. He'd tried to pick her up in a club when she was out with her friends, and she had thought it unusual that a man as good-looking as Nate was more interested in her than in her incredibly beautiful friend Joy, who always got the majority of the male attention. Later, she found out he had targeted her in order to obtain the amulet for his grandmother, Grace. But once Nate had gotten to know her, he developed feelings for her and helped her keep her amulet, turning his back on Grace. She was one hundred percent, completely sure Nate didn't want her amulet. "Yes," was all she said in reply.

"Perhaps you should acknowledge the possibility that Nate is still working with Grace," he went on. "If that's the case, your amulet would be much safer here with me. I'll keep it in my wall safe for you, right next to the ring."

"Like I've said many times before, no, thank you," Anise replied. She looked over at Jonathan again who was sitting as still and silent as a post. His eyes were more glazed over than she had ever seen, and he stared at Dr. Smithton with a wide, eerie gaze. It was as if Dr. Smithton's presence made his eye-glazing issue worse.

Wait a minute. Her heart pounded in her chest and her head spun. There was nothing physically or psychologically wrong with Jonathan's brain. This *was* Dr. Smithton's doing. Jonathan got worse every time he talked to Dr. Smithton on the phone or brought up the utopia vision, and now sitting in front of him, it seemed like Jonathan—the real Jonathan—was barely there at all. She was now sure Dr. Smithton was brainwashing Jonathan with the cuff. Now that she was in his office, would he do the same to her? Make her think that giving him her blood was a good idea? With shaking hands, she rooted for her phone in her tote bag so she could text Nate. She couldn't think of anything he could do to help since the museum was closed and locked down, but knowing Nate, he probably would think of something.

"Has Jonathan told you about our ideas for a utopia on Earth?" Dr. Smithton asked Anise.

"Yeah," she muttered, still trying to find her phone in her bag. "Many times."

"What do you think?" he asked her.

"I don't think it's possible," Anise replied.

Dr. Smithton frowned.

"I told her about how we'd use the Armor Jewelry as a way to enforce the rules and promote peace instead of violence," Jonathan chimed in. "But her argument is that there's always someone who's going to be unhappy with something, and if someone's unhappy or forced to go along with rules they don't agree with, then it's not really a utopia."

"I agree," said Dr. Smithton, to Anise's surprise. "And there may be fighting and even bloodshed at first. But what if there was a way to use the Jewelry to ensure everyone would agree and feel happy?"

Shit! Is he talking about brainwashing them? "Well, then I guess in that hypothetical situation, you'd have a utopia on your hands," Anise replied, gasping a couple times through her tightening lungs. *Where the hell is my phone?* This conversation was getting her nowhere. She still didn't know if Dr. Smithton knew about them breaking into his safe. "But would you really be willing to start a war in the name of peace?" *Finally!* Her shaking hand closed around her phone.

"Don't be rude, Anise," Jonathan said, taking the phone out of her hands.

"Jonathan! Give me my phone back." She stood up and tried to take it back, but he held it out of her reach. Her stomach squeezed and her head spun.

"What if the ends justify the means?" Dr. Smithton asked her, stepping around his desk to loom over her. He pushed her back into her seat.

"Whether they do or not will always be an opinion, never a fact," Anise stated firmly as she pushed his hands off her shoulders. "As long as people have free will to think and feel however they want, there will always be someone who doesn't agree with you. Therefore, you will never be able to create a utopia. It would just be a perpetual war." She turned to Jonathan. "Give me my phone!"

"That reminds me," said Dr. Smithton. "In the event of people wanting to fight back, we'd need to be prepared to help everyone who may get injured in the process. I'd want to have reserves of blood, just in case. It would be helpful if you'd be willing to donate."

Anise sucked in another labored breath and gripped the arms of her chair for support. Is this where Jonathan's blood questions kept coming from? "Well, we'll see if it comes to that," she replied. "I think it's a little premature to be thinking about that. As of now, you're still in the early stages of your idea, right?"

"Jonathan and I are working dutifully on it," Dr. Smithton replied.

"Great, well, if you ever get there, let me know. But I should really get going now." She stood up to leave and looked at Jonathan. "My phone!" she demanded. "NOW!"

"Of course, my dear," Dr. Smithton said, nodding to Jonathan who finally handed her phone back. Dr. Smithton got up and unlocked the door for her.

She darted out of the office, wanting nothing but to get away from the both of them. Running down the hallway, she reached the elevator in record time, but then she thought about Jonathan and what Dr. Smithton had done to him.

I can't leave him there.

She hurried back to Dr. Smithton's office and stopped near his open door. Taking a deep breath for courage, she was about to walk back in when she heard them talking. Anise stood still and listened when she heard her name.

"Thank you for finally bringing Anise by," Dr. Smithton said, "but I need to see her more often. It's going to take a long time to change her mind at this rate. She's getting to be a problem."

"I can't get Anise to listen to me," Jonathan said. "I pretended to need her help so I could get her here tonight, but that's not always going to work."

"No matter," Smithton replied. "I have the other pieces of Jewelry, and I'll be able to take the amulet from her at any time if she decides to continue to be uncooperative. And if she isn't willing to donate blood, there are ways to make her willing."

Anise froze in horror. She should have listened to her instincts—and to Nate—and stayed away from Dr. Smithton. *I am so stupid!* She gathered up her courage again and was about to step inside and drag Jonathan out for his own good when she heard him speak again.

"That's true," said Jonathan. "I'm sure I can think of several ways to force her willingness. We'll make this happen!"

At that, Anise turned and fled down the hall. With adrenaline pumping through her veins, there was no way she could stand still long enough to wait for the elevator, so she ran down the stairs instead. Tears began falling as she pushed through the door at the bottom of the stairs and ran through the garage to her car. How could Jonathan betray her like that? She screamed the second she sat in her car and closed the door behind her. Her fists hit the steering wheel over and over while she cursed his name.

Whether or not it was truly his fault due to the brainwashing, she didn't care. If he hadn't admired Dr. Smithton so completely and without question, he might've realized how creepy this whole utopia thing was and known something was amiss before it was too late for him. She shook violently at the thought of Dr. Smithton. He was making plans to come after her, take her amulet, and force her to give him her blood.

She texted Nate before driving away.

Anise: Meet me at my place.

Almost instantly he texted back.

Nate: On my way.

Chapter 20

Twenty-six years ago

Friday, July 14, 1989

"Nathan, slow down. You're going to make yourself dizzy," Lorelei told her son. In truth, she was the one starting to get dizzy just from watching him.

"I wanna go to the park! I wanna go to the park! I wanna go to the park!" yelled four-year-old Nathan Brevain as he ran circles around the chair his mother sat in.

"Okay," she told him. "The news will be over in five minutes. We'll go then."

"Yay!" he said, crawling up into the soft, brown recliner with her. She held him as they watched the last news segment together. The local museum had several artifacts stolen, and the museum director was asking for them back, with a promise of a reward and to not press charges if only the artifacts were returned safely.

"We should tell Grandma," said Nathan.

"Why?"

"So she can give them back and not get in trouble."

Lorelei crinkled her face in confusion. Nathan certainly had a wild imagination. Grace may be a lot of things—rude, mean, a bitch from hell—but a thief? Lorelei couldn't imagine her mother-in-law breaking into a museum to steal well-protected artifacts, much less getting away with it. Grace didn't want to do anything for herself and ordered Dan around like he was her servant.

Lorelei sighed at her thoughts. If she'd known what a momma's boy Dan would turn out to be, she wouldn't have married him. He was so loving and sweet when they met, and sometimes he still was, but every time there was a disagreement between herself and Grace, he sided with Grace. Lorelei suspected he may even fear his mother, as his desire to please her was unlike anything she'd ever seen.

She should've listened to her friends when they told her not to marry a man she'd only known for three months, especially since she and Dan were so young. Her friends kept telling her to leave him, and she was tempted, but if she took Nathan away from Dan, she could expect a bitter custody battle instigated by her vindictive mother-in-law that Nathan would be in the middle of.

If only she'd left earlier. Six months after they married, they fought almost constantly about Grace, and Lorelei almost left him—but then found out she was pregnant with Nathan.

It had been all right for the most part. When it was just the three of them, Dan was kind and attentive to both her and Nathan. However, when Grace was around—which was way too often for Lorelei's liking—Dan turned into a different person. Grace would insult Lorelei or tell Nathan he was bad, and Dan would agree with her, telling Lorelei she needed to change or Nathan that he wasn't good enough and needed to stop being a bad boy. Lorelei took every opportunity she had to tell her son that she loved him and was proud of him.

"The news is over," Nathan informed her. "Can we

please go now?"

"Yes, let's go."

"And then can we get hamburgers?" he asked.

"Not tonight. We're meeting your dad at your grandmother's for dinner."

"Awww, I don't wanna go there," he whined. "Dad's mean when we're there, and Grandma's always mean."

"I don't want to go either," Lorelei whispered, putting her index finger vertically in front of her mouth to indicate it was a secret. "But we promised. We'll get hamburgers tomorrow night."

At the park, Lorelei watched as her high-energy son ran around the playground, climbing on the equipment and playing with the other children.

"What a handsome little guy," the other mothers told her. "Those eyes!"

Nathan looked a lot like her—the face shape, the almost-black hair, everything looked similar—except for the eyes. He had the bluest eyes she'd ever seen—bluer, brighter, darker, and deeper than even sapphires—and she wondered where they came from. She and everyone on her side of the family had brown eyes. Grace and Dan had brown eyes as well.

When she noticed her son starting to lose energy and slow down a little, she called him over to the sand box. "Let's build a sandcastle, my little prince," she suggested, calling him by the nickname she used often.

"Okay!" he agreed, and sat down next to her in the sand.

"How many towers should we build?" she asked him.

"A hundred," he replied, decidedly.

"That's a lot of towers. Let's just see how many we can build before we have to go."

"Okay," he agreed, pouring a shovel full of sand into a small bucket. "That's a good plan."

When they were finished, they admired their work. "Tell me about it," Nathan asked of her, as he always did when he wanted her to create a story out of whatever they were doing.

"Well," Lorelei began. "This castle is the home of my little prince. He lives here and rules over the entire land," she said, motioning to the rest of the sandbox. She noticed he was looking and listening attentively, so she took this opportunity to build up his self-esteem before he had it torn back down by Grace and Dan that night at dinner. "Nathan," she began.

"Nate," he corrected her, with his preferred version of his name. "Like the baseball player."

"Right. Nate. I keep forgetting." That would be hard to get used to. "I want you to listen to me. You are so smart, and strong, and such a good boy. Some people might tell you that you're not, and if that happens, I want you to promise me that you'll never believe them, okay?"

He gave her a sideways grin. "I promise."

✳ ✳ ✳

Lorelei and Nate arrived at Grace's an hour early. She hoped to offer to help Grace with dinner. They knocked and rang the bell, but no one answered. Lorelei let herself and her son in with her spare key. She figured she might as well start dinner since Grace wasn't home. Maybe she'd win some points with her for that, although that was a long shot. Nothing she did ever seemed to please her mother-in-law.

"Come on!" Nate shouted to her. "I'll show you!" He ran down the steps to the basement.

"Nathan! I mean Nate! Don't go down there!" She ran after him. "Show me what?"

She found him standing on a box in the corner of the room. He removed a picture from the wall.

"Nate, no! Put that back! Your grandmother will be upset!" She started toward him, hopping over the boxes, stacks of books, and other various piles of junk that littered the basement floor.

He ignored her and carefully put the picture on the floor. He then removed a loose brick from the wall.

"Nate!" she exclaimed. "Don't ignore me!"

"I just want to show you," he told her. He reached his hand into the wall, grabbed something, and pulled. Attached to the end of a stick was a plastic bag. Nate pulled it out of the wall and handed it to his mother who had just stepped up beside him.

"What is this?" she asked him.

"The stuff from the museum that was on TV," he explained. "The stuff Grandma should give back."

Lorelei took the bag and looked inside. Sure enough, the contents of the bag matched what she and Nate had seen on the news earlier that day. Except for one item—a cuff with three blue stones on it and many smaller red ones. That hadn't been shown on the news. It looked like something that belonged in a museum though. "How did you find this?"

He shrugged. "I was bored one day," he answered, referencing a time when he had been left at Grace's to be watched while Dan and Lorelei were at dinner. "We should take it back to the museum. I don't want Grandma to get in trouble." He crossed the room and opened the closet door.

Lorelei put the bag and its contents in her purse. "I don't either," she said, as she put the brick back in the wall and hung the picture back over it. Truthfully, she wouldn't have minded too much if Grace got in trouble and went away for a long, long time. However, she wanted to set a good example for her son. "Let's go to the museum."

"I found these, too. In the closet under the floor," Nate told her, holding up a couple more items. His mother held open her large, quilted purse, and he placed them inside, next to the bag of treasures he had pulled out of the wall.

What the hell, Grace?!

Grace could very well get in trouble if anyone knew these items were hidden in her wall and floor. However, if Nate wanted to be an honorable person and do the right thing, Lorelei wouldn't stop him for anything, not even the nagging feeling in her gut telling her that this wasn't going to end well.

TAKING NATE BY THE HAND, LORELEI walked into the museum. She looked around for a member of the museum staff, wondering if she should talk to the security guard about the missing items or ask to speak with the museum director himself.

"Are you looking for someone?" asked a friendly voice.

She turned around to find a man in his 30's waiting for her response. He had gorgeous, loose black curls and warm brown eyes that smiled at her.

"Do you work here?" she asked.

"No," he answered, "but I'm acquainted with most of the staff. Can I help you find someone?"

"I'm not sure," she replied. "Maybe the museum director?"

"He's gone for the day," the man replied. "I could introduce you to the head curator instead."

"All right," she agreed. "Thank you."

"No problem," he told her. "Follow me." They walked down a long corridor and up a flight of stairs toward the museum staff's offices. "Have you seen the latest exhibitions?" the man asked her. "Some amazing artifacts on display."

"No," she answered. "I haven't been here in a while. Are you also a curator?"

"No. I'm a surgeon. My father was a professor of

ancient history and archaeology, and many of the staff members here were his students. They became family friends, and I grew up knowing them. I'm just in town for a conference and thought I'd stop in to visit. " He offered her his hand. "Kent Dromly," he said, introducing himself.

"Lorelei Brevain," she said, shaking his hand. "And this is my son, Nate."

"Nice to meet you, young man," said Kent.

"Nice to meet you," Nate replied, as his mother had taught him.

"Brevain," Kent repeated. "That sounds familiar. Have we met before?"

Lorelei shook her head. "I don't believe so."

Kent stuck his head inside of the office of the head curator.

"You again?" the head curator joked.

"Me again," confirmed Kent. "You have a visitor." He waved Lorelei into the office. "This is Dr. Morty Smithton."

"Hello," said the head curator to Lorelei. "How can I help you?"

"I'm Lorelei Brevain. I wanted to talk to you about some of the museum's missing items my son and I saw on the news today."

Dr. Smithton's eyes were wide when he looked at Nate. "Yes?" his voice cracked. He cleared his throat.

"My son found these," Lorelei said, handing Dr. Smithton the bag that contained the artifacts and wondering why the curator looked like he'd seen a ghost.

Dr. Smithton took the bag, reached in, and grabbed the pieces. He saw two brooches and then pulled out the cuff with the three blue stones and several smaller red ones. He took a sharp breath in and quickly put the pieces back in the bag. "Where did you find these?" Dr. Smithton asked her.

Nate looked at his mother with wide eyes. She stroked

his hair to reassure him. "The news story said the museum wouldn't ask any questions or press any charges if the pieces were returned. I assume I can hold you to that."

"Yes, madam, you absolutely can," he assured her. "I want to thank you both for doing the right thing." He smiled at them. "How about that?" Dr. Smithton said to Kent. "An impressive display of integrity!"

"Very," Kent agreed. "I'm speechless."

"You speak seven languages and you're speechless?" Dr. Smithton joked.

"It has been known to happen," Kent said with a laugh.

Dr. Smithton thanked Lorelei and Nate again and gave them some free passes to the museum. They stepped out into the hallway and Lorelei looked around, trying to remember from which way they had come. These hallways looked like a maze to her.

"I'll walk you down," Kent offered. "I'm on my way out anyway. It was a pleasure as always, Smithton."

"You too, Dromly. Don't wait so long to come by next time," he replied as he closed his office door.

"I could tell from his expression that Morty was thrilled to have those pieces back," Kent told Lorelei as he walked her through the hallways and to the museum's front doors. "It was nice of you to bring them down here."

"I want to set a good example for my son," Lorelei told him.

"It was a pleasure meeting you both," Kent said once they reached the door.

"You too. Thanks for your help," Lorelei replied.

"GRACE!" KENT MUMBLED TO HIMSELF. "THAT'S where I've heard that name before. Brevain is Grace's last name."

Kent hurried toward his car, grateful that he'd brought

his father's trip journals with him. He'd planned on giving them to Smithton who'd been asking to read them for years, but no way would that happen now. He'd seen that cuff before; his father had described it in the journals too, and there was something very special about it. Kent hadn't believed it when his father told him about the metaphysical qualities of the cuff and the other pieces of Armor Jewelry—Frederick Dromly was always telling wild stories. But the expression on Morty's face when he'd pulled it out of the bag...

SITTING DOWN, MORTY TURNED HIS DESK lamp on and took the cuff out of the bag. A laugh escaped his lips as he slipped it onto his wrist. After all these years! It was time to visit his old friend Grace once again.

Kent had seen the cuff when Morty pulled it out of the bag, and he wondered if Kent knew what he'd seen. Had Professor Frederick Dromly shared anything about the cuff with his son? Morty had never told Professor Dromly that Grace had stolen the cuff from him, and now he'd never have to. Dromly was busy searching for the Plate of Destiny in Florida, and he appreciated the fact that Morty would send him another brainwashed co-worker or two every year. Dromly was happy with their performance at being his bodyguards and research assistants, and Morty was relieved that the brainwashing he'd managed to do before Grace stole the cuff from him was enough to please Dromly. In the meantime, he worked at the museum and waited for Dromly to tell him the Plate of Destiny had been found.

Morty walked into the restroom and rinsed the cuff under the running tap. He tried to imagine how Grace's life had turned out and what she'd been doing all this time. Her young son must be grown up. The woman who returned the cuff must be his wife, and the boy, his son. Morty had been knocked speechless for a moment when he'd looked at the lad. The young boy looked like a miniature Thomas Brevain. It had been almost twenty-five years since Morty had been able to try to manipulate Grace's thoughts using the cuff, as he had never been able to find it no matter how many times he forced his way into her house to search for it.

He headed back to his office with the cuff hidden in his pocket. He wondered if the headaches and hallucinations were still something Grace experienced. The co-workers he'd brainwashed with the cuff were still very much on board with his plan. That hadn't changed. However, their side effects of head pain and visions had only gotten worse. Most of them had divorced due to personality changes they had undergone which had just gotten worse over the years. Morty thought it was fascinating how each of them had changed in different ways, and was equally guilt-ridden over having single-handedly ruined their marriages. Perhaps aspects of Grace's personality had changed as well. He was curious to know if she was any closer to finding the Plate and what she'd been doing to search for it.

He placed the cuff on the sill of his office window where the sun was shining in. Sitting down, he stared at it, silently thanking it for finding its way back to him. Finally, he could continue with his plan. He leaned back in his chair and closed his eyes, letting himself wonder if Grace was still beautiful.

"YOU'RE LATE!" GRACE SCOLDED WHEN LORELEI and Nate walked through the door. "We've been waiting half an hour!" She wanted to smack them both. How dare they keep her waiting, especially when she cooked for the ungrateful brats?

"Where were you?" Dan asked her from the dining room table.

"At the park," Lorelei said, joining her husband.

"We saved you from getting in trouble, Grandma," Nate added.

"Nate," said Lorelei, her eyes telling him to stop.

"What are you talking about?" Grace asked her grandson.

"You told me never to lie," Nate reminded his mother. "Grandma, I found that stuff from the museum in your wall. Mommy and I took it back so you wouldn't get in trouble."

Grace looked from Nate to Lorelei and back again. "What?!" she demanded, pulling on her hair. Her head pounded.

"Those pieces were on the news, Grace. Nate found them, and we returned them to the museum. They didn't ask any questions. They were just happy to have them back."

Grace stormed out of the room and made a bee-line for her basement, her feet stomping her anger on every step. She shivered just like every time she entered the basement, but ignored her visceral reaction. She checked all her hiding spots so she could find out exactly what Lorelei had given to the museum.

"Who did you talk to?" Grace yelled at Lorelei as she stormed back into the kitchen. "And who said you could start eating without me?"

Dan dropped his fork. "Sorry, Mother."

"We talked to the head curator," Lorelei responded, twisting her napkin in her hands. "Dr. Smith-something. He was very gracious about it. Why did you have those artifacts anyway? You didn't steal them, did you?"

Dan hung his head and squeezed his eyes tightly shut.

Grace fumed as she sat down, stood up, and then sat back down again. She pulled on her hair and unsuccessfully tried to scream as ants poured out of her daughter-in-law's mouth and eyes. Part of the ceiling started falling on her head. *Do what needs to be done, Gracie,* she heard the voice say. "Of course I didn't steal them! Just who do you think I am?" she snapped.

"Well, how did they get in your basement?"

"How should I know? Maybe they were here before I moved in!"

"No," Lorelei argued. "The news segment said that the two brooches had been stolen very recently."

"Shut up and eat your dinner!" Grace turned to her son. "Dan, a word?"

Dan jumped up. "Yes, Mother." He followed her into the living room.

"She ruined everything!" Grace hissed at her son.

"It's just a few artifacts, Mother. We can easily get more," Dan whispered.

"There were some very important items in my basement that are now at the museum! This is going to set me back years!"

Dan's face crinkled in confusion. "I don't understand, Mother."

"The only thing you need to understand is that I never liked that woman! I put up with her for your sake, but now that she's completely destroyed my plan and knows what we did, she needs to go!"

"What are you saying?" Dan asked, his mouth and eyes hanging open.

"You know exactly what I'm saying. Either you get rid of her, or I will."

Dan began hyperventilating and put a hand over his mouth. Tears started rolling down his cheeks. "Is killing her really necessary?"

"Yes, Dan! Don't be weak!" Grace thought about how Lorelei might find her other stashes of artifacts, possibly leading to her arrest. Then all hope would be lost. "Do it tonight. Get rid of her *and* that little brat of hers."

"Nate?" Dan asked with wide eyes. "No, Mother, please, he's my *son*! I think he'll be a real asset to us when he gets older."

Grace scoffed. "What makes you think that?"

"He's very smart—he's in preschool, and his teacher says he's reading at a fourth grade level and that he helped her fifth grader with his math homework. She says his verbal skills are like a kid twice his age. Lorelei and I had him tested, and his IQ is at 160. The doctors say he's a genius and that we should challenge him at an accelerated school. It's true; I know you can see that."

Grace looked at Dan and considered his request. True, Nate was smart. But he was also headstrong like his mother which wouldn't do. "No."

"Please," Dan begged her. "Please! Spare my son!"

Grace laughed. "You think he's your son?"

Dan narrowed his eyes. "What do you mean?"

"If he's that smart, he certainly didn't inherit that from you or Lorelei. And look at him! He doesn't look like you at all!"

"He looks like his mother." Dan frowned.

"But what about those eyes?" Grace demanded. "Your wife told me no one in her family has blue eyes—they're all brown. You and I both have brown eyes, too. So where did his eyes come from?"

Dan's forehead furrowed and he teared up. "I've already been wondering the same thing ever since Nate was born."

"So you do agree that Nate isn't yours." Since she'd never shown Dan a picture of Thomas, Grace hoped Dan would take the bait. With Lorelei gone, she'd be called on to baby-sit, and she didn't want to waste time doing that.

Dan shrugged. "We'd been doing nothing but arguing at the time Nate was conceived. It's very possible she sought comfort from another man during that time." He angrily wiped the tears from his eyes. "Consider her gone," Dan told Grace. "But Nate stays. He's an innocent child, and I'm the only father he's ever known."

Grace rolled her eyes. "Fine. But keep him out of my way. And don't ever say I never did anything for you."

DAN SAT ON HIS MOTHER'S FLORAL couch and put his head in his hands after his mother had stormed off. *What a big, fucked up mess.*

"What was that all about?" Lorelei asked as she sat next to him. She put her hand on his back.

"I'm sorry about that," he apologized. He shuddered, fighting back a wave of nausea.

I will miss you so much.

In a hushed tone he added, "Mother is really upset and went upstairs to cool off. How about I take you out to dinner tonight instead? Just me and you. Mother already agreed to watch Nate."

Lorelei shook her head. "There's no way in hell I'm leaving my son with that woman ever again. She's not only cruel to me and Nate, but now she's a thief too? How can you not be more upset about this?"

"I don't believe she'd steal anything."

Lorelei scoffed. "The way you always help her and stick up for her is ridiculous! The woman is evil and you enable her! You're going to keep her secret, aren't you? If she needs you to help her cover it up, you'd do it! If she wanted you to start helping her steal things, you'd do that too, wouldn't you? She's the devil and you're nothing but Satan's helper!"

"Don't fight!" begged a little voice from the archway that led to the dining room. Nate stood there watching his parents with large tears rolling down his face.

"We're done fighting, I promise," Lorelei said, sweeping him up in a hug.

"Your mother and I are going out to dinner," Dan told

Nate. "You're going to stay with your grandma."

"No, he's not!" insisted Lorelei.

"You and I need time to talk. We'll ask Bridget to watch him instead. Please."

"Fine," she agreed with a frown.

Dan and Lorelei dropped Nate off with Lorelei's friend Bridget and made a stop at home to change into nicer clothes before going out to dinner. While she refreshed her make-up, Dan made some gut-wrenching but necessary calls.

✳✳✳

AFTER THEY'D ORDERED AND OPENED THE wine, Lorelei saw someone waving at her.

"We meet again," Kent said as he approached the table.

"Kent! What a small world," Lorelei said with a surprised laugh.

Dan narrowed his eyes.

"Dan, this is Kent Dromly. I met him at the museum today when I was...there," Lorelei told her husband.

"Nice to meet you," Kent said, offering Dan his hand.

Dan ignored Kent's friendly gesture and glared.

Kent raised his eyebrows and retracted his hand. "Right, well, Lorelei, I found some interesting information about one of the artifacts you brought in today, and I was hoping to ask you some questions..."

Dan stood up, his sudden motion flipping his chair to the floor with a crash. "She's not interested!" he spat. "And you're interrupting a private dinner!"

"I'm sorry," Kent replied, his hands raised. "Have a nice evening." He turned and left.

Lorelei glared at her husband while her cheeks burned. The entire restaurant was staring at them. "That was rude!"

"And what *he* did wasn't?" Dan picked up his chair

and sat back down.

"I'm sure he was just excited about the artifacts. He was probably hoping I'd tell him where I found them."

"That's none of his business!" Dan exclaimed. "Mother would be really upset!"

"But why?" Lorelei demanded. "Are you going to tell me what the hell is going on with her? What did you two talk about when you left me and Nate alone in the dining room?"

"Don't change the subject!" Dan sputtered. "How many other men do you know that I've never met?"

Lorelei slammed her napkin on the table. "I'm going to the ladies' room," she informed her husband. "When I get back, you'd better be ready to apologize."

She took her time in returning. When she finally sat back down, she first took a sip of her wine. It tasted funny.

"Well?" she demanded of her husband.

"You're right; I'm sorry," Dan apologized. He hung his head but said nothing more.

She took another sip of her wine, still angry with him, and not at all impressed with his apology. "There's something wrong with this wine," she complained and set it back on the table.

Dan took a sip of his. "It tastes fine to me. Let's make a toast...to new beginnings. I promise after tonight, our lives will be very different." He held up his glass.

"I hope you mean that."

They clinked and ate their meals in silence. Lorelei refused to even look at Dan. She sipped on her wine until her glass was empty. It left a strange after-taste, but maybe it was the air or soil quality that affected the vintage.

"I'm going to use the restroom, too," Dan mumbled.

While he was away, Kent made a return. "I just wanted to say I'm sorry if I caused any problems between you and your husband," he apologized.

"Don't worry about it," she said, dismissing the situation with a wave of her hand. "Dan's always been a hothead. Must be the red hair," she joked.

"Okay," he chuckled. "It was nice to have met you."

"You too." She was about to signal for the waiter so she could order a second glass of wine when she started to feel...funny. She put her hand to her forehead when the room began to spin. It was hard to keep her eyes open. She gripped the table hoping the wooziness would pass.

"Dan, I don't feel very well," she told her husband when he returned a few minutes later.

"Let's go home." He put his arm around her, holding her upright as they walked to the parking lot. He placed her in the passenger seat of their car, and everything went black.

Chapter 21

Present day

Thursday, September 24, 2015

I thought I told you to stay away from Smithton," Nate said, frowning after Anise told him what happened at the museum. *She doesn't listen.* Looking after this wayward woman's welfare was going to be a full time job.

"I know," she replied in a tone that told him she was not in the mood to be lectured. "I should've listened. But I thought Jonathan needed my help. Dr. Smithton forced me to sit and listen to his speech about utopia, and he asked me to donate blood in case a war breaks out over it. It was so creepy."

"Why didn't you call or text me?" he demanded as they sat next to each other on her couch. "I would've gotten you out of there."

"Jonathan took my phone out of my hand and wouldn't give it back until Dr. Smithton allowed it."

"Are you *kidding* me?"

"Unfortunately not. But even if I had called, what

could you have done anyway?" she shrugged.

His eyes opened wide with disbelief. "Plenty! The first thing that comes to mind is pulling the fire alarm in the parking garage."

"Oh, yeah, I guess that would've worked." She looked at him sheepishly. "But it would've been awhile before you got there."

"Honey, I was parked outside the museum. I followed you there in case you needed me."

"Okay, fine, I'm sorry," she told him with a big smile on her face.

He couldn't help but laugh. "You don't look sorry."

"I just like how protective you are of me." She gave him a barely-there pout and put her hand on his leg. "Thank you."

He wondered if she was planning to put her hand anywhere else. "You shouldn't have gone. You know that. You're going to get yourself in trouble."

She took her hand back. "Well, I got out of there as soon as I could, and I texted you then. But when I went back to get Jonathan—"

"You went back?!"

"Dr. Smithton is brainwashing him! I didn't want to leave him there."

It took all of Nate's willpower to not roll his eyes. "So where is he?"

She twisted the garnet ring around her finger. "I was going to say that when I went back to get Jonathan, they were talking about how they could take my amulet any time they wanted and make me donate blood." She looked down as she twisted the ring even faster.

"We have to get that Armor Jewelry before Smithton does something to hurt you," Nate told her.

"It has to be tonight," she agreed. "If we wait, Dr. Smithton *will* come after me. Are you up for an adventure?"

"Always," he said with a grin, impressed by her motivation to take action. "But like I said before, you shouldn't go. I'll do this solo."

"You're amazing for being willing to do this for me. But no, I'm coming with you," she insisted. "It's only fair that I help." She moved closer to him and gave him a peck on the cheek. "Thank you," she added. Her eyes looked at his lips and her own parted slightly. When he didn't move, she leaned back on the couch, twisting her ring again.

He fought the urge to kiss her. She was giving him every sign that she wanted him, but now wasn't the time. He had to focus on coming up with a plan to break into the museum. He wished he could talk her into staying home for her own safety, but he knew she'd keep insisting on coming along. "First of all, as hot as you look in those shoes," he said with a lustful smirk, looking at the black, high-heeled boots she wore, "you'll need to put on some sneakers." He got up and offered her a hand.

After she changed, they hopped on Nate's motorcycle and made a stop at his condo. Once they got inside, Anise was still shivering from the chilly evening ride. Nate hung a blanket over her shoulders and briskly rubbed her arms to warm her up. "I'm going to buy a car soon."

She looked confused. "You have a car. I saw it in your garage."

"The hot rod isn't drivable yet. I'm working on it. But in the meantime, I'll buy another one."

"Just so I won't be cold when I ride with you?" she joked with a laugh.

"Yes," he answered sincerely. Her nose and cheeks were rosy from the night air, and he wanted to pull her closer and do a better job of warming her up. But not now. *Focus.*

She watched as he dug through the large safe in his closet, searching for the equipment he'd need that night. He brought out several items and placed them on his kitchen table, making sure that they were still in working order, as they hadn't been used since before he was in prison.

"So what *is* all this stuff?"

"This is my lock pick set," Nate told her, holding it up.

"Is it hard to pick a lock?"

"Depends on the lock," he replied. "Dan's really good at it, and he taught me well."

"What's that?" she inquired, pointing to another item on his table.

"EMI device," he said, and dusted it off. "The museum has a wireless security system. It uses radio waves to send the video the camera picks up to the control panel. This device interferes with the radio waves so all that'll show up on the monitoring screen is snow."

She pointed to the far end of the table. "What are those thin black strip things over there?"

"Magnets. I developed a technique where I can open a door and prevent the alarm from sounding using these. As far as I know, no one else has ever been able to do it." Proud of himself, he flashed her a sideways grin that he could tell turned her on.

"That's amazing," she said, grinning back at him while touching his arm. "And that high-tech item?" she added jokingly.

"Crow bar. To break into the display case for the ear-rings."

"We forgot about gloves!" she exclaimed. "Jonathan bought us some latex gloves that worked pretty well when we went to the Springfield Museum. Should we make a run to the drug store?"

"Boy Scout is an amateur," Nate scoffed. "When you're with a professional like me, you wear gloves made out of the finest leather money can buy." He reached into a nearby drawer and pulled out two pairs of black leather gloves. "Let's see if these fit you. They were Grace's." He stood in front of her as he slipped one of the gloves on her hand.

"It's perfect," she said. "Wow, it's so thin, and the lining is so soft!"

"That's right. If we're going to do this, we're doing it in style."

She took off the glove and put it and its mate in her jacket pocket. "That sounds good to me. Although there's something unsettling about how well Grace's gloves fit me. Like they're trying to tell me that if I wear them, I better live up to her level of...what we're about to do."

"Don't read anything into it," he responded gently. "They're gloves, nothing more."

"You're right." She stepped closer to him. "I'm just nervous," she admitted, and wrapped her arms around him.

He ran a hand through her hair. Nate noticed the coy look she was giving him, but she'd done that before and then pushed him away when he made a move. He didn't want to be rejected now—he needed his ego and confidence to be as strong and high as possible in order to do his best work at the museum. He turned and started putting his equipment in his backpack. "Ready?"

She took a deep breath. "Yes. Let's go."

Friday, September 25, 2015

NOW THAT IT WAS AFTER MIDNIGHT, the air had gotten even colder, and Anise held on to Nate tightly to stay warm during the motorcycle ride to the museum. Once there, they put on ski masks, and she watched with fascination as Nate worked on the side door. He placed the EMI device in the optimal location, picked the lock in three heartbeats, and carefully slipped the magnetic strip between the door and the frame. No alarms sounded as he slowly opened the door.

His expert fingers had gotten them past their first barrier with ease and skill. Imagining what else those fingers might do well made Anise warm, tingly, and grateful for the cool night air. Nate exuded power and confidence, and watching him work excited her more than she cared to admit to herself. What he was doing was wrong and criminal, and she shouldn't like it, but he was so *good* at it, like the rules simply didn't apply to him.

Nate motioned to her to follow him, and they snuck up the dark stairwell to the second floor where the curators' offices were located. Now that they were in the museum, she kept taking deep breaths in an attempt to keep an anxiety attack at bay. She wished she had taken a few sips of a Coke before they left to settle her nervous stomach.

He picked the lock to Smithton's office door and headed straight for the safe. Relieved that Smithton hadn't changed the combination since last time, she let out a breath she hadn't realized she was holding.

"Shit!" Nate mumbled under his breath.

"What's wrong?" she whispered, wringing her gloved hands together.

He rooted through the safe. "The ring and the cuff— they're both gone! So are the books. It's just a stack of papers and...fucking Smithton!"

"What?"

He showed her a piece of paper that had something scribbled on it in Dr. Smithton's handwriting. It read: "Nice try, Brevain."

"Oh god! He *does* know that we know!" Anise grabbed on to the desk to ward off the dizziness. "This is not good!"

"No, it's not," Nate agreed. Carefully, they searched the entirety of Dr. Smithton's office in hopes the ring and cuff would be hidden elsewhere. After several minutes with no luck, they gave up. "Let's at least get the earrings before we get out of here," grumbled Nate. He put the note back where he found it, closed the safe, and they quietly left Dr. Smithton's office.

Anise followed him through the hallway, down the stairwell, and around the corner. The gallery that contained the earrings was to their left.

She was about to take a step forward into the hallway when Nate grabbed her arm and pulled her under the stairs. Her stomach tightened into a knot as he mouthed the word "guard" to her. She covered her mouth and nose with her hands to muffle the sounds of her heavy breaths. Heart pounding, stomach churning, and head spinning, she put her forehead on Nate's shoulder and closed her eyes. It took everything in her to suppress the urge to run away.

He put his arms around her and held her tightly as she hyperventilated into his chest. "Are you okay, honey?" came his barely audible whisper.

"Yes, it's just a panic attack." Immediately, she regretted her words. Now especially, she didn't have the energy to comfort Nate if he freaked out about seeing her panic.

His arms held her tighter. "Everything will be fine. Look at me and concentrate on that," he whispered, his lips touching her ear. "It's just you and me here. Nothing else matters."

She pulled away to stare into his eyes, remembering the first time he'd said that to comfort her and calm her nerves right before they won a dance contest. It amazed her how well it worked to hear those words from his lips. The museum, the stairs, the guard...all melted away.

He took her hands. "You're doing great. The guard is on the other side of the museum now, so it's time to go get the earrings. Once we step into the gallery, the motion detector will go off. But it'll only take us a few seconds to break into the case, grab the earrings, and run out the door we came in—it's right next to the gallery. By the time the guard gets there, we'll be long gone. Are you ready?"

"Yes," came her whispered response. She thought

about one of her favorite affirmation cards. "I can do this."

"Okay," he said, with his mischievous sideways grin and unzipped his backpack. "Let's go."

Hand-in-hand, they hurried silently down the short passage to the gallery. Once inside, they darted to the case that housed the chalcedony earrings. With the crowbar already in his hand, Nate pried open the case with a *craaaaack* and put the earrings in his pocket within a few seconds. They ran toward the door, but as Nate was reaching for his EMI device, an older man stepped out in front of them and pointed his gun at their faces. "Hold it right there," he said.

Anise gasped as she and Nate stopped short. Who the hell was this? He wasn't wearing a guard uniform.

Nate narrowed his eyes as he grabbed Anise's arm and started backing them away from the stranger. The next several minutes felt like a dream to Anise. In her slow-motion vision, Nate stepped in between her and the man, grabbed the man's arm, and wrestled the gun out of his hand. He seemed to grab something from his jacket pocket and punched the man in the face with one solid blow. The man fell to the ground, his nose bleeding in a puddle on the floor. Anise thought it was strange that instead of touching his injured nose, the man's hand grabbed what little hair he had and pulled.

"Hold on to this." Nate handed the man's gun to Anise, and she absent-mindedly took it as they heard the guard running in the hallway. He'd get to the door before they'd be able to. Looking around, there were other doors, but they required a key to be unlocked and Anise knew Nate wouldn't have time to pick them open. Nauseated from fear, she looked up at him to see what he'd do next. He grabbed her hand, and they ran back up the stairs. She followed him up four flights to the top floor and through a door that led to another set of stairs. At the top, they fled out the door and found themselves on the roof. Panting, they ducked behind the large air conditioning unit.

"Stay here," Nate told her, and he ran the perimeter of the roof, looking over the edge of the building. When he came back to her, he put his arms around her and held her tightly as she tried not to let a panic attack start. "We'll be fine," he assured her.

She remained unconvinced. They were on the *roof*. What the hell could they do now?

His eyes intense, he whispered, "Listen, we don't have much time. Here's the plan. The guard should be here any second now. When he arrives, I'm going to create a diversion. I want you to promise me you won't watch me."

"What?! Why?"

"There's no time to explain. Just promise me!" he hissed.

"Okay, I promise," she whispered, confused and dizzy with fear.

"Good," he said. "Instead, I want you to run down the stairs and back out the door we came in. Okay?"

"Okay," she agreed, feeling like she was going to pass out. She really didn't want to be by herself in this situation. "What about you?"

His arms still around her, he whispered, "He just came through the door. Are you ready?"

"Uh huh," she warbled, not feeling ready at all but wanting to be brave.

"You'll be fine," he told her. "As soon as the guard starts chasing me, you run." Nate stepped out from their hiding place and ran across the roof.

Anise wondered what the hell Nate's plan could be. She peeked around the corner to see the guard chasing Nate.

"Freeze!" the guard shouted.

Nate ignored him, and once he got to the edge of the roof, he jumped off.

Anise ducked back behind the air conditioning unit

and covered her mouth with her hand, trying not to be sick. What the *hell* just happened? *Did Nate plunge to his death so I can get away? Oh, shit! I'm supposed to be running!* Dropping the gun that she knew she'd never use, even if she needed it, she dashed for the door, checking over her shoulder. The guard was peering over the side of the building when he turned and saw her.

"Freeze!" he shouted again, running after her.

Like Nate, she also ignored him and bolted down the four flights of stairs, jumping down the last several steps each time she got close to a landing. The guard's steps thundered behind her, and she hoped he wouldn't get a chance to shoot at her. Her amulet would protect her, but what would the guard think when the bullets zipped around her in unnatural ways? If that information got back to Jonathan and Dr. Smithton, they'd know it was her and Nate who took the earrings, and who knows how they'd use that against her? Her legs were jelly, but she managed to zip across the hallway to the door where they'd entered the museum. For a split second, her mind wondered where the old man that Nate had punched out had gone. Pushing through the door, she raced outside, jumped over the scattered pieces of the security camera that somehow had smashed to the ground, and stopped dead in her tracks, unable to believe what she saw. "What?!" she shouted in disbelief.

Nate revved his motorcycle. "Get on!" he demanded. As soon as she climbed on behind him, wrapped her arms around his waist, and pressed herself against his backpack, her stomach dropped as he took off faster than the expansion of the universe. She looked back and saw the guard aiming his gun at the back tire as they fled. Nate wove in a serpentine motion as the guard fired a few shots.

Nate zipped around a corner and kept flying. Anise's heart leaped into her throat when she saw a car pull out and seem to purposely block their path. She was stunned to hear Nate laugh as he sped up.

Holy shit! Holding her breath, she tightened her grip around him as he whipped around the rear of the car as it backed up quickly in an attempt to hit them, narrowly missing a parked pick-up truck on the side of the road. The car's tires screeched as the driver accelerated after them. Anise looked back in time to notice that the driver was the old man Nate had knocked out in the museum. *Who the hell is that?* She heard a few shots being fired from the old man's car, but Nate's snaking path dodged every bullet.

Nate opened up and weaved through six lanes of cross traffic so quickly that the oncoming vehicles didn't even have time to honk. The car followed. Anise turned her head and watched as the car collided with another vehicle, spun into the adjacent lane, and was hit by a second vehicle. Nate kept going at lightning speed until it was clear no one was following them and then slowed down. Soon, he pulled into his private garage under his condo, parking between his hot rod and a couple of dirt bikes. They hopped off, and he put his arms around Anise as the garage door closed. She couldn't control her trembling.

"I'm so sorry," he apologized. "I've broken into museums over a hundred times and nothing like that has ever happened."

His arms were warm and comforting, but she shoved him away and punched him in the arm. "How could you do that to me?" she yelled. "You scared the shit out of me—jumping off the side of the five-story building and leaving me all alone!"

He laughed. *The jackass.*

"I figured you wouldn't like that plan. That's why I made you promise not to watch me. But you did anyway, didn't you?" He grinned at her.

She shoved him again but then allowed him to hold her face in his hands and wipe away her tears of relief with his thumbs.

"It's not funny, Nate! I thought you offed yourself! The guard started chasing me, and I was terrified thinking that he was going to shoot at me and worrying that the old man was waiting for me and what would happen if I couldn't get away!"

He dropped his arms, and a hurt expression emanated from his eyes. "Honey, I would *never* leave you, especially not in a dangerous situation like that. It was the only way out of there for us, and it worked. If it *hadn't* worked, I would've come back in for you. You still don't trust me, do you?" He unscrewed the bolt on the fake license plate he'd used for the evening from the back of his bike and reattached his own.

"I'm trying," she said in a softer voice. "And yes, it did work." After watching him put away his screwdriver, she demanded, "Are you going to tell me how the hell you did it?"

"How I did what?"

"All of it! But mostly how you jumped off the building and lived, Nate! Did you go down a pre-attached zip-line? Have a parachute in your backpack? Fly down like a superhero?"

"The superhero thing," he joked.

"Don't *make* me punch you again," she threatened.

"The fire escape went up to the fifth floor, but not the roof," he explained. "I jumped onto the landing one floor below and got down pretty quickly."

"Why didn't you tell me your plan instead of making me promise not to watch you?" she demanded. "Keeping things from me isn't going to help me trust you."

He put the fake license plate in a hidden compartment in his wall behind a shelf. "The guard was about to walk through the door. I had to save time by not going into every detail, and I'm telling you the plan now. But I'm sorry I scared you." He looked sincere, but it didn't help much in quelling her anger.

Nate held open the door that led to his condo for her and followed her up the stairs. They walked across the hardwood floors to the kitchen, and he filled up glasses of water for the both of them. "It's important to hydrate after a heist. Especially with the amount of running we had to do."

Still miffed, Anise remained silent and looked everywhere but at him. His modern furnishings were mostly black except for the sofa, which was gray. The end tables and small dining table were made out of maple wood and the lamps and kitchen fixtures were all chrome. Looking out the glass door onto his balcony, she saw a string of lights glowing as they twisted around the iron railing, echoing the city lights beyond. She finished her water and put her glass down on the black granite countertop.

"Make yourself at home, honey." He sat on the sofa and motioned for her to join him.

Only now noticing her exhaustion, she was happy to collapse on the comfortable cushions next to him. She noticed the painting of the motorcycle she'd made for him hanging prominently over the back of the sofa. "I'm sorry I punched you."

His face wore a look of confusion.

"In the garage, I punched your arm. And I pushed you. Twice. I'm sorry. I hate violence, and I hate that I did that."

"Oh." It looked like he was trying to suppress a grin. "Forget about it. I did." Nate reached into the pocket of his black leather jacket and handed her the chalcedony earrings.

Taking them, she held them in her palm and stared at them. She'd been so worked up about Nate scaring her by taking a flying leap off the building that she'd almost forgotten the reason they went there in the first place. She felt her frustration with him melt away. "Thank you," she told him. "I know that everything you did tonight was for me. I want you to know how much I appreciate it."

"Why don't you come over here and show me?" he suggested, giving her his mischievous grin and opening his arms to her.

Trying not to blush as she wondered what he meant by that, she scooted over toward him, and put her head on his shoulder.

"Who do you think that old guy is that pointed the gun at us?" she asked, as he put his arms around her. She loved how tightly he held her and let her body relax against his.

"I'm guessing he's one of Smithton's brainwashed followers."

She watched his face in the reflection of the television screen, and she couldn't remember him ever looking so happy before. "You really enjoyed our adventure tonight, didn't you?"

His face broke into the biggest smile. "I loved it. What a rush."

Her curiosity grew. "I think I might've asked you this before, but is it the adrenaline that you love? Or is there something else about it?"

Nate shrugged. "Growing up, it was the only thing that ever made me happy besides riding a motorcycle. Everything else was so boring in comparison, and it was the only time Grace, Dan, and I got along and felt like a real family." He stared off into the distance.

"Then you quit when you turned eighteen?" she asked, remembering the last time they'd talked about this.

"I couldn't wait to get away from them," he confirmed. "I lived a normal, boring life after that. Never broke the law again. Except for the heist that got me locked up. And of course, tonight."

"And you really think your life is boring by being a normal, law-abiding citizen?"

"Not always," he replied, giving her a quick kiss on the top of her head. "Not when I'm with you."

She got a pit in her stomach and sat up straight. "Since it makes you so happy, are you going to go back to your previous life of crime?"

He looked at her with a serious expression. "Of course not. I may have enjoyed the heists, but that was the worst time of my life. I still want nothing to do with Grace and Dan or the life I had with them. I want to be a better man. And most importantly, I want you to be able to trust me. I need to move forward now, not back."

The pit in Anise's stomach disappeared, and a sense of relief washed over her. She took his hand and intertwined her fingers with his. "Good. I'm so happy to hear you say that."

He squeezed her hand and looked at her with his intense stare.

She involuntarily smiled at him, enjoying the pulsing, swelling feelings she got when he looked at her like that. She'd never met anyone that excited her so much. She'd been fighting her immense attraction to him for years, but maybe tonight was the time to give in to it. Putting a hand on his chest, she purred, "You were really amazing tonight. I can't believe you jumped off a building!" She let out a soft laugh as he grinned at her. "And that guy you punched went down so hard and fast. It was like nothing for you."

"I had some help," he admitted, reaching into his jacket pocket and showing her what he pulled out.

"Brass knuckles? How old-school bad-ass of you!"

His aw-shucks shrug gave off an air of humility, but his cocky smirk told her he was obviously enjoying all the admiration she was laying on thickly.

She grabbed the brass knuckles from him and tried them on.

"Don't punch me again," he said as he playfully held a couch pillow in front of himself for protection.

"I would never!" she exclaimed, removing them and setting them on his coffee table. "I can't believe how fearless you are on your motorcycle. I don't know where you learned to ride like that." She gave him a peck on the cheek and kept her face close to his. "And we have the earrings!" she continued in a soft voice. "I can't thank you enough for everything you've done."

"You're very welcome," Nate replied.

She kept her face right next to his and made sure her soft breath danced on his ear. When she put her hand on his knee, he turned his head, and she thought he was going to kiss her. But with a slight sigh instead, he got up and grabbed some blankets and sheets from his linen closet. "It's late. Why don't you stay here tonight and take my bed? I'll crash on the couch."

Anise leaned back on the sofa and wondered if she had done anything wrong. It wasn't like Nate to not flirt back. Maybe he was just trying to be respectful? She *had* demanded that he not try to kiss her anymore. Or maybe he didn't want her after all. Her hands fidgeted and twisted the garnet ring around her finger. She felt him staring at her, and she wondered if she should ask him to take her home instead.

"Honey, I want to be honest with you," he finally said, putting the linens down.

Anise looked at him with nerves twinging in her stomach. She thought about the phone conversations they'd had when he was in prison. How he'd told her he'd never had a serious relationship, never found anyone worth making a commitment to. She knew he was about to tell her he still felt that way, but that since they were friends, he didn't want to hurt her by turning what they had into something physical, then leaving her. "It's okay. You don't have to say anything."

"No, I do. The prison shrink wanted me to work on understanding what I feel because I usually ignore it. I want you to stay over, but I don't want to sleep on the couch. I went through the list of emotions she gave me in my head...I've thought about you for over three years now and..." He hesitated. "This isn't coming out the way I want." He sat next to her on the couch. "Do you remember when you came to visit me in prison, and I told you that we have a strong connection?"

Where is he going with this? Her stomach still twisted. "Yes."

"I still feel it, and it's unlike anything I've ever experienced before. I really like you, and I think you feel the same way. After everything that happened, I know I'm lucky to be here with you right now. I want our first time to be great, and I'm completely blowing it."

Anise was relieved that her feelings for him were mutual and a little surprised that he'd been pulling away from her out of apprehension when he was usually so confident. "I understand. I'm nervous too."

"You are?"

"Of course! I mean, it's *you*. You're absolutely right that we have a strong connection. I also feel it. I've always been so drawn to you, and, yes, I really like you too. I've felt it since the day we met. And I've wanted you so much ever since then." She put her hand on his leg.

"I'm sure this isn't how you imagined it would go down," Nate said.

She let out a soft laugh. "The way I imagined it is ridiculous."

"What do you mean?"

"You'll think it's too girly and romantic."

"Try me."

Anise opened her mouth, and her throat turned as dry as a desert. She laughed at her own shyness. "You give me the best kiss of my life and then sweep me up in your arms and carry me to your bedroom."

He took her hand. "I'm good with that."

Their lips got closer and closer until they were softly touching. Their gentle kisses became more and more passionate. She grabbed the back of his head and pulled, wanting him as close as possible. His hand wandered through her hair and down her back. Breathing heavily, they paused, and Nate held her face in his hands while giving her the intense stare that had filled her waking and sleeping dream worlds while he'd been away. In it, she could see things about him she couldn't explain to herself. She wouldn't have been able to look away even if she wanted to. It was hypnotizing. Without breaking the most profound eye connection she'd ever experienced, he picked her up and carried her to his bedroom.

Nate set her down slowly until her feet touched the cream-colored rug next to his bed. His hand ran through her hair, and his fingers traced the side of her face. He removed her top, and she peeled off her jeans. She stood confidently in her purple lace bra and panties, watching as he dropped his shirt and jeans on the floor. She paused to stand still and take in the sight of him in his black boxer briefs. His gorgeous face, lean and muscular chest and arms...her eyes moved lower. She opened her mouth to express her approval, but closed it again. Raising her gaze to look him in the eye, she tried to speak once more, but nothing came out.

"Is everything okay?" he asked her.

She felt her cheeks stretching from her wide grin. "I've been fantasizing about you since the day we met, and now here we are. I'm so happy and excited out of my mind, I can barely speak, and I can't stop smiling." She looked down, her face burning with embarrassment. "Is that pathetic?"

"Not at all." He wrapped his arms around her and gave her an arrogant but damn charming smirk that increased the tingling desire she was already experiencing. "So how often did you fantasize about me?"

Her head dropped from shyness, and when her eyes raised to look at him, she gave him an embarrassed smile. "Only...a lot."

"Tell me your favorite one."

"I can't," she said, her cheeks burning again.

"You don't have to be embarrassed with me," he told her gently, pushing some of her hair behind her ear.

"Okay," she agreed. "Remember after we went to the Concert in the Park, and you were walking me home and trying to get me to take off my amulet? You wanted to come upstairs to my apartment, but I told you it was too soon. I have a different version in my head."

"I remember. We stopped off in the alley." Nate picked her up and placed her down with her back to the nearest wall.

Suddenly very aware that she was in nothing but her underwear and the amulet, she looked up at him with anticipation.

He put one palm on the wall near her head. "I had you standing against the wall like this."

Anise loved how his eyes traced her. "Yes, and you were looking for my amulet underneath my blouse." She grabbed his hand from the wall and brought it toward her chest. But before it reached her breasts, his hand took hold of her fingers, lifted her arm, and pinned her wrist against the wall over her head. She heard an involuntary, whispered gasp of excitement escape her lips as she looked into his lustful eyes, breathlessly wondering what he'd do next. Fingers of his other hand slowly traced the chain of the amulet over her décolletage and cleavage as her breathing grew quicker. With one swift maneuver of his fingers, her front-closure bra popped open. Anise felt her nipples harden and her moisture flow. Her free hand grabbed Nate by the back of the neck, pulling him in for a kiss.

He kissed her with passion but pulled back to continue her fantasy. "Hold on," he said, letting her wrist free. "I didn't get a good look at the amulet."

Anise removed it from her neck and put it inside the waistband of her panties. She kept the chain looped around her wrist. "If you want to see it, you'll have to search for it again." She let her open bra drop to the ground.

Although at first his eyebrows raised questioningly at the sight of her removing the amulet, his eyes soon flashed wicked intentions at her. "With pleasure."

His hand traveled underneath her purple lace underwear, and she watched him grow as her warm wetness washed over his fingers. He carefully placed the amulet around her neck again, and she knew it was to ensure she'd feel safe. She wanted to tell him she'd never felt safer with a man in her life but was distracted by how his eyes were looking into hers. "You're fucking gorgeous," she informed him, meaning it just as much as she had when she said it three years prior. No, even more so now.

He smirked at her. "Let's go upstairs," he said, just as he had that night.

"No," she said, staring at him with a desire so strong it ached. She pulled his boxer briefs downward until they dropped to the floor. "I want you so *fucking* bad, I can't wait that long. I want you to take me right here, right now."

"Put your hands on the wall," he commanded.

Anise flushed as she complied with his demand. To make his stance not have to be quite as awkward, she brought her legs closer together and stood on her tiptoes. She bent forward slightly and tilted her hips upward, inviting him, and throbbing with anticipation. She felt him slide her panties down her legs, the caressing touch of his fingers exciting every nerve in her body. Looking over her shoulder at him, she watched Nate enter her from behind. "Mmmmm," she moaned with pleasure, a smile forming from finally being able to assuage her years of craving him. Her chin tilted upward, and she arched her back and pushed to feel him deeper inside her, filling her.

He placed his left hand next to hers on the wall, his fingers covering her own. His right hand first grabbed her hip and then migrated forward until his fingers reached the spot that made her moan again.

"I want to see you fucking me," she requested after a few minutes.

Nate stopped so she could turn around to face him. He picked her up, and she wrapped her legs around him. He supported her with one arm and put his other hand behind her head.

Anise felt her back being placed gently against the wall as he entered her and pushed into her over and over. She watched his muscles as he moved and marveled at the strength he had to keep her in that position. "Harder," she begged. His thrusting became more forceful, and his face wore an expression of uncontrollable passion as he looked at her. Her fingers dug into his shoulders as she nuzzled her face against his hair, breathing in the scent of him, and feeling her body get out-of-control excited.

He placed her on the plush mattress of his wood and metal platform bed. "Nate," she said, reaching for him, beckoning, even though he was already joining her on the comforter. She lay on her back, and he got on top, entering her while supporting his weight with his powerful arms.

Their eyes met. His cobalt blue gaze was so strong and unbreakable that she'd never felt more seen or more vulnerable. It was intoxicating. The tension inside her built up with such intensity, she couldn't help but cry out, meeting his thrusts with her hips while her fingers grasped his back, and she climaxed with all-consuming, dizzying waves of pleasure like she'd never experienced before. Watching her movements and hearing her untethered sounds of gratification pushed him over the edge as well. They stayed on the bed, sweating and breathing heavily.

Anise rolled over onto her stomach. "Holy shit, Nate," she said into a pillow cased in dark gray. "You're fucking magical."

He let out a soft laugh and gave her an arrogant

smirk.

"Stop looking at me like that," she said, smacking him with her pillow. "It turns me on every time."

"Really? Every time?" He smirked at her again.

"Well, not *every* time...not that *intensely* every time, I mean...but it's always extremely charming. So stop it!" She rolled onto her back again and put the pillow over her face.

"Why? What's wrong with that?"

"I'm too exhausted to get that excited again!" came her muffled voice.

"Okay," he agreed, removing the pillow from her face with a grin. "I'll show you some mercy."

She smirked back at him and put her head on his chest while he wrapped his arms around her.

"Is that how you imagined the rest of it, honey?" he asked, and held her tighter.

"That far surpassed my feeble imagination," she told him honestly, then felt like she should have been able to come up with something better to say. Something that could make him understand how amazing he had made her feel, how close she felt to him, but there were no words powerful enough.

"So you've been wanting that since the moment we met," he said, his lips forming another cocky smirk.

"Pretty much," Anise admitted. "But you were just after my amulet at that point," she complained, giving him a playful shove. "While I fantasized about you that first night."

"I *was* just after the amulet," he admitted. "But it didn't take me long to start having feelings for you."

"When did that start?" she asked, her curiosity piqued.

"When you were asking me the pasta sauce questions."

She laughed. "Really? During the survey at the mall? Why?"

"I saw that you were really intelligent. Caring and sweet. Beautiful. Innocent."

"I'm not really that innocent." She crawled under his soft, dark gray comforter.

"Yes, you are." He joined her and leaned on his elbow. "I also liked how much fun we had together. Even that first night at the club I had a blast with you. And I liked that you never noticed I was wearing a Rolex."

"You have a Rolex?"

Nate laughed. "Yeah. I've worn it several times since then."

"Oh. Well, I just don't care about stuff like that."

"I know."

"When were you wearing it? Besides the night we met, I mean."

"I wore it when we went riding the other day. You looked right at it to check the time before we left the Blue Pineapple."

"I did?" She laughed.

"I also wore it the day I came to the mall to return your ring I stole."

Her mouth opened in disbelief. "Wait, are you talking about my garnet ring the night we met? You *stole* it?! You told me it accidentally came off in your hand during the dance contest!"

He laughed again. "See? Innocent. I needed a reason to come see you."

She gave him another playful shove.

His expression turned serious. "And even after everything I did, you still had compassion for me. You forgave me, and I don't know what I did to deserve it." His fingers touched her face. "You're so beautiful, Anise, inside and out. How could I not..." He stopped and pressed his lips together as if trying to hold in something he didn't want to say.

"How could you not what?"

"Realize how lucky I am that you're here right now."

"You do deserve forgiveness," Anise insisted. "There's so much good in you, and I wish you could see it. Because the man I see is brilliant, giving, passionate, gentle, caring, confident, powerful...I could go on and on. And when you told me about how you grew up with Grace and Dan, I couldn't help but empathize. Even though yours were much worse, I know what it's like to have shitty parents. I know how it can make you feel like you're not worthy of being treated well in your other relationships. I know how it changes how you think about yourself and what kind of decisions you feel you have to make. We're both working through that, and I feel like you understand that part of me that no one else ever has."

"Same, honey."

"And I want you to know that...maybe it's that indefinable connection we have, but whenever I'm with you, you make me feel more alive than I ever have before. I feel lucky to be here with you, too, Nate."

For hours, Anise and Nate, with limbs intertwined, shared likes, dislikes, thoughts, experiences, stories from their pasts, as well as hopes and dreams for the future. She'd never felt so close to anyone before and wanted the night to last forever. When the dawn came, however, Anise couldn't stop yawning, and they shut their eyes to get some sleep.

"It's so late, and I have to go to work soon," she groaned.

"No you don't," Nate told her. "Call in sick. We'll sleep in."

Anise giggled. When she was that tired, everything became funny. "Okay," she agreed, still laughing.

He laughed along with her and put his arms around her. "Thank you," he whispered.

"For what?"

"For the best night of my life."

Chapter 22

Twenty-six years ago

Sunday, July 16, 1989

Lorelei couldn't remember ever being so tired. Her eyes didn't want to open, and her body felt limp. She stayed perfectly still while she fought the grogginess from her deep sleep. The smell of a cooking meal wafted into her nose; maybe a barbecue? Stretching her neck, she realized that her pillow was much softer than usual. This was not her pillow. The air was so dry. She was not at home. With a jolt of fear, her eyes flew open. *Where the hell am I?!* Something was very, very wrong.

Her heart raced as she threw off the blankets of the unfamiliar four-poster bed and jumped up. Her legs gave out from under her, and she dropped to the hardwood floor in a seated position. Putting a hand to her spinning head, she wondered if she'd been drugged. Pulling herself back onto the bed, she sat on the yellow comforter and looked around the room. The walls were dressed in yellow and pink floral wallpaper, and dancing figurines decorated the tops of the dresser and nightstand. Turning her head, she looked out the window but saw nothing but a vegetable garden full of planter boxes and a very tall fence. She seemed to be in someone's bedroom in a house.

Standing up slowly this time, she carefully walked to the bedroom door and tried the knob. When it didn't open, she rattled it out of frustration. Making her way across the room again, she tried the window, but it was also locked by a mechanism she couldn't open. She heard the door creak, and she gasped as she spun around. "Who are you?" she demanded of the couple that entered the room. "Where am I?"

"Your husband brought you here," said the man. He was middle-aged, and a cigarette hung from his lips.

"Dan? No. Why would he do that? Where is he?" Lorelei asked, trying to look past them and into the hallway outside her room.

The skinny, petite woman wore a look of pity on her face. She stepped forward and handed Lorelei an envelope. "Here, hon. Your husband left this for you," she explained.

Lorelei took the envelope and opened it. The couple left her alone to read it. She removed the letter, sat on the yellow comforter, and held on to one of the posts on the end of the bed.

Dear Lorelei, I hope you'll be comfortable in your new home. Please know I'm doing this for your safety. I don't know what artifacts you returned to the museum, but Mother is very upset. She ordered me to kill you, and as far as she knows, I completed my task. I'm really sticking my neck out for you here, so even though I know you'll be angry, please try to appreciate the fact that I just saved your life. You'll be well taken care of where you are. I promise to send you updates on how Nate is doing every now and then. With love, Dan

Lorelei started hyperventilating and kept holding on to the bed post so she wouldn't faint. *Love?* Disgusting. She crumpled up the letter and threw it across the room with a furious scream. Her pillow soaked up her tears until the woman brought her some of the food she had smelled earlier. Lorelei tried to eat. She'd need her strength if she was going to figure out how to escape. There was no way anyone could keep her from her son.

After she finished her meal, she reached into her large, quilted purse that the couple had left for her on her dresser for some lip balm. It was full to overflowing and she rolled her eyes at how she kept putting items in, but never cleaning it out. First, she pulled out the cardigan that she had worn when she and Dan had been at dinner. Looking at it made her angry at him all over again. Receipts, gum wrappers, a pen, and reminders she'd written to herself on small pieces of paper instead of her calendar came out with it.

She reached her hand back in her bag. "Oh..." she said, pulling out the extra treasures Nate had found under the floorboards in Grace's house. She'd forgotten to return them with the bag of artifacts he'd found in Grace's wall. For the first time, she really looked at them. One item was a book about ancient Mallandian legends that appeared extremely old. Curious. She'd never even heard of Mallandia. Flipping through some pages, she found the book was handwritten and difficult to read, not that she'd have the time anyway. She had to find a way to escape. The other item was some kind of necklace. It was a large, coppery pendant on a chain that had a black center stone and five smaller orange and white stones in a circle surrounding it. She'd never seen anything like it.

She wondered why Dan hadn't kept them to give back to Grace. Probably because her bag was such a mess. Even if he'd rooted around in it, he might not have noticed the book alongside the novel and magazines or the necklace in the side pocket next to her stash of tissues and a smaller bag with a chain strap.

Next, she pulled out a piece of paper that was folded in half and had her name written on it in a handwriting she didn't recognize. Wrinkling her brow in confusion, she unfolded it and began to read.

Dear Lorelei, What I was hoping to tell you tonight when I saw you at the restaurant is that I learned a lot about the cuff you returned today from my father's trip journals—he's an expert on Mallandian Jewelry. I know that someone stole it, and I also know that person wasn't you. There's some information about the cuff that you need to know. I fear you may be in some danger. Please meet me tomorrow for coffee, 10 a.m., at the shop around the corner from the restaurant where you ate tonight. If you can't get away at that time, I'll be waiting there on Sunday morning as well. Yours truly, Kent Dromly

Lorelei folded the note and put it back in her bag. Kent must've slipped the note in her bag at the restaurant when she wasn't looking. He'd been right about the danger. How could doing the right thing turn into such a terrible mess? She couldn't put her finger on it, but there was something about Kent that she liked and trusted. There was also something very special about that Mallandian cuff that Grace and Dan knew, and now Kent knew, too. Wondering what the hell it could be, she regretted not being able to meet with him. Although...she picked up the book about Mallandian legends. Maybe the answers she needed were in this book. If she knew what was so important about this cuff, maybe it would help her know what to do after she escaped. She opened it and tried to read, but she couldn't concentrate. She thought about Nate and wept, hoping that Grace wouldn't punish her little prince too harshly for finding the artifacts in the basement wall.

KENT WAITED AT THE COFFEE SHOP until 11:30 nursing his latte. When Lorelei didn't show up, he wasn't sure what to do. Should he really get involved in all this? It wasn't any of his concern. However, it was possible she may be in some danger. She didn't show up at the coffee shop today or yesterday; what if something had happened to her? He decided to go looking for her at her home.

According to his father's trip journals, besides himself and his father, the only two people still alive who knew about the Armor Jewelry were Morty Smithton and Grace Brevain. Grace must've been in possession of the cuff, and now Morty had it, thanks to Lorelei. Grace had been such a good friend to his mother. He still hadn't gotten over the shock from what he'd read in his father's trip journals about her—how she'd become mean and untrustworthy, evil even. Would she really have hurt Lorelei? One of the journals mentioned that his father had given the cuff to Morty for experimentation, whatever that meant. How then did Grace come to have the cuff? Kent hoped to find out.

He nervously walked up the sidewalk path and tapped

on the front door to a medium-sized home in a nice neighborhood. With any luck, Lorelei would answer, and the red-headed fury she was married to wouldn't be at home. Slowly, the door opened halfway, and Kent saw Lorelei's young son looking up at him. His nose was running, and his eyes were slightly red; he wiped them with his sleeve.

"Hello, Nate. Do you remember me from the other day? I'm Kent Dromly. We met at the museum."

Nate opened the door a little wider. "I remember you."

"Is your mom home? I'd like to speak with her."

The child shook his head. "She's not home."

"Do you know when she'll be back?"

"Dad said that she left, and she doesn't ever want to come back home. He said she doesn't love us anymore and that living with us was making her sad."

Kent's stomach tightened up. *What did they do to her?* "When did she leave?" he asked Nate.

"The same day we met you."

"Did you see her go? Did you hear her say she didn't want to come back?"

"No."

"What happened exactly?"

"We were at my grandma's and then my mom and dad went out to dinner. She didn't come back with my dad."

"Where were you when they were at dinner? Did you stay with your grandma?"

"No, I stayed with my mom's friend."

"All night?"

"No. My dad came to get me and told me I had to sleep over at my grandma's house, even though I didn't want to. He came to get me from my grandma's house this morning."

"Is that when he told you that your mom didn't want to come home?"

The child nodded. "Yeah."

"So, your mom and dad went out for dinner, and it took your dad a day and a half to come take you back home?"

"Yeah."

"Do you stay at your grandma's overnight a lot?"

"No. That was the first time."

Kent peered past Nate into the house. "Is your dad home now?"

"Yeah, but he's sleeping. He said he was really, really tired and that I better not wake him up."

"Yes, let's not wake him," Kent agreed. "You know, I could tell your mom loves you very much and that living with you made her very happy."

"That's what she always told me, too." That realization made Nate look at Kent and narrow his bright blue eyes. "I think my dad is a big liar," he added. "Can I come live with you?"

Kent was incredibly impressed with the way Nate thought and spoke. A child with intelligence far beyond his years. At the same time, Kent's heart broke for Nate. He knew exactly how this child was feeling. When Kent was just a couple years older than Nate, his father had left the country and didn't return for a decade. It had devastated him and his fragile mother who ended up in a mental hospital and died not long after. At least Kent had kind and caring grandparents who did a wonderful job raising him. All Nate had was the ginger whirlwind of rage.

Kent squatted to Nate's level. "I don't think your father would allow that," he told Nate, "but I'll tell you what I'll do. I'll make you a promise. I promise that I'll look for your mom, and I won't stop until I find her and bring her home. How does that sound?"

Nate nodded. "Thank you."

"You're welcome. And here..." Kent scribbled something and handed Nate a business card with his personal phone number written on the back. "If you ever need help, you can call me anytime."

Suddenly, the door swung wide open. "You again! What the hell are you doing here? Why are you talking to my son?"

Kent jumped up to see Dan standing there in his underwear, his sleepy eyes squinting from the daylight under bed-head hair.

"I just wanted to ask Lorelei about the artifacts..." Kent started to say.

Dan stepped outside, grabbed Kent by the collar, and looked him straight in the eye. "Your eyes are brown." Dan shoved Kent off the front porch. "Stay away from my family!"

Dan turned to yell at Nate. "Don't ever answer the door for him again!"

"Hey!" Kent stepped back on the porch. "The boy did nothing wrong. Don't take your anger out on him!"

"Get the fuck out of here!" Dan threatened, his hands turning into fists.

Kent backed away, not wanting Nate to have to see any violence.

"What did he give you?" Dan demanded of his son, looking at the business card in Nate's hand.

"Nothing," Nate replied and tried to hide it behind his back.

Dan ripped the card from his son's hand and glared at it. He tore it into pieces, shoved Nate into the house, and slammed the door.

Kent headed home to call the police.

MORTY STOOD ON HER DOORSTEP. HE hadn't seen her in so long. How would she react when she saw him again? He rang the doorbell. *Be confident. She'll respect noth-*

ing less. The nerves in his stomach twinged as he heard the door being unlocked from the inside.

"Oh, great!" Grace snarled as she cracked open the door and peeked outside. "Go back to hell where you came from, Morty!" She tried to slam it in his face, but Morty pushed the door open.

He stood in the door frame and took in the sight of her. "After all these years, this is how you greet an old friend?"

"Drop dead!" she commanded.

"I heard you lost something, Grace." He raised a hand and ran it through his wavy, blond hair that was starting to turn white. The motion raised his sleeve high enough so she could see the cuff. She grabbed at it, and he laughed as he held his arm up, just out of her reach.

She reached up a hand toward his neck. He'd figured she might try to bring him to his knees with her knowledge of pressure points. Having prepared mentally for this, he caught her by the wrist. She reached with her other hand, and he caught that wrist too. She spit in his face, and he released her by shoving her away. He wiped his face with a handkerchief.

"Yes, I did lose the cuff," she agreed with a sneer. "My four-year-old grandson found what you weren't able to."

"You know, I could still use you on my team to search for the rest of the Armor Jewelry," he said, ignoring her snide remark. "You want to join my team. You no longer love Thomas."

She rolled her eyes and let out an exasperated sigh. "That cuff didn't work on me then, you idiot!" she said. "What makes you think it'll work on me now?"

"It's worth a shot," he shrugged.

"Sure," she agreed. "Because you know you can't do it without me." Her eyes were filled with rage, and he was intimidated by her, but he tried not to let it show.

"Hardly," he said with a scoff. "This is more about keeping my enemies closer."

She glared at him. "So that's it? You brag about getting the cuff back, and you don't even have a new plan?" She narrowed her eyes in confusion. "What about the other artifacts? Aren't you going to brag about them, too?"

Now it was his turn to look confused. "The museum is very happy to get those artifacts back. But why would I waste my breath bragging about that to you?" He wondered why she was smiling so big.

"You're pathetic," she told him. "You have no chance at the Plate of Destiny."

"Neither do you," he informed her, "now that I have this again." He held up the wrist that wore the cuff.

Grace pulled on her hair and started screaming when Morty's mouth opened to speak again. "Bees! Bees!" she shouted. She waved her hands around her head to deter the invisible bees and continued screaming.

Startled, Morty backed away. She was still screaming when he got into his car to drive off. When he looked back as he pulled away, she was writhing on the ground, alternating between flailing her arms and pulling on her hair. He knew she was having a stress-induced migraine and hallucination—a side effect of the mind control attempts with the cuff—and it was all his fault. The same sort of thing happened to his staff at the museum when they got stressed. These side effects seemed to be getting worse in his staff, and in Grace, too, even though he hadn't been in possession of the cuff in decades. The effects of the brainwashing hadn't worn off, either. He felt guilty about inflicting such agony on Grace and the others when all he really wanted was for everyone to be happy and peaceful. However, he allowed himself to be comforted by the fact that he could continue his mind-control efforts and make certain that his staff was as loyal and compliant as possible before sending them to help Dromly find the Plate of Destiny. The more help he sent Dromly, the quicker the Plate would be found, and the faster everyone could be healed. He hoped it was soon. He couldn't take much more of the guilt. Even though he felt awful, he couldn't help but smile as he drove away. She *was* still beautiful.

Monday, July 31, 1989

"I'M NOT BABY-SITTING ANYMORE!" GRACE SCREECHED at her son. "All Nate does is sit there and cry! I can't take the noise!" She wanted to rattle Nate every time he opened his annoying little mouth.

"Well, what do you expect?" Dan snapped back. "He misses his mother. And so do I." He looked down at the ground as his eyes welled up.

"Stop being so weak," Grace told Dan with disgust. "We're better off without that traitorous bitch in our lives."

Dan's face turned red and his eyes shot daggers at her. "I have to go. Nate's crying is *your fault,* so it's only fair you help me deal with it." He turned to leave.

Nate stood with outstretched arms reaching up toward his father with the hope of receiving a hug good-bye.

"How dare you speak to me like that?" Grace spat, laying into Dan for his last comment.

"I can't deal with this right now!" Dan ignored his son and hurried out the door.

"You better get back soon! I have a business trip to go on tonight!" she screamed out the open door to Dan's back as he strode down the walkway.

"Again?! It's the third time in two months."

"So what? I've been going on these trips for years."

"Where do you go? What is this business?" Dan yelled back over his shoulder.

"It's none of yours!" Grace slammed the door. She took in a deep breath and let it out slowly in an attempt to calm herself. When Morty had come by and revealed that

Lorelei had given him the cuff and other various artifacts, he inadvertently let Grace know that he didn't have the amulet. Hope had allowed her to think that maybe her grandson had taken it and kept it somewhere. But she'd asked him, and Nate didn't have the amulet. He'd given it to his mother who intended to return it to the museum but didn't for some reason. So Nate didn't have it, Lorelei was dead, and Morty didn't have it either. Where that amulet had gone, she might never know, but she remembered that Professor Dromly had two more. Dromly had left the university, but she saw him every other month or so whenever she headed to Florida to search for the Plate of Destiny and pretended to assist him on his searches. It was a great way to stay updated on everything Dromly knew about the Plate. She'd just have to work him to find where he'd hidden the other two amulets. That might be difficult. Difficult, but not impossible.

She glanced down at her grandson who was looking back at her with tears streaming out of his big eyes. She frowned. "Don't start crying like a baby again! You're being weak! You know what happens when you're weak."

"I don't wanna do the training!" he wailed.

"Here," Grace said, handing him his teddy bear. "Punch it in the face."

"I don't want to!"

"Stop whining. When you get older, you're going to be in situations where people will want to hurt you. You're going to have to fight back. This is good practice. Now punch it!"

"NO!"

"Do it! Now!"

Nate grabbed the bear and hugged it instead.

Grace ripped the bear from his grasp. "You're a very bad boy!" Grace yelled in his face. "Now punch this god-damn bear!"

Nate glared at her as his little hand balled into a fist and struck Grace in the eye.

She responded by slapping him hard across the cheek. "If you ever hit me again, I'll kill you!" She slapped him again. "Now punch this bear or else!"

Shaking, Nate punched the bear as it looked at him with its sweet face and loving expression. He let out a heartbroken wail.

"Good," Grace told him. "But next time punch harder. Now, try to take my wallet out of my pocket without me feeling it."

Still crying, he did as he was told.

"You're getting better, but you have to be quiet when you do it. Now shut up and try it again."

"I don't want to! I hate you!" he yelled defiantly, his tears soaking the front of his shirt.

"You're weak and worthless!" she told him. This crying had to stop; the noise was making her enraged. She *could* kill him right now. But the aftermath wasn't something she felt like dealing with. The police and Child Protective Services had already been out to the house several times following Lorelei's disappearance. She couldn't take the chance. Suddenly, she had an idea. "Come on, let's go," she said, grabbing her car keys.

"Where are we going?" Nate asked her, wiping his eyes.

"It's a surprise," she told him.

After a short car ride, Nate looked around in wonder as his grandmother marched him into a building he'd never been in before. They walked by the motorcycles, ATVs, and scooters. She stopped when they reached the child-sized dirt bikes.

"Whoa," marveled Nate, his eyes wide.

"Would you like one?" Grace asked him.

His head bobbed up and down, and the tears stopped.

She let him pick the one he wanted. "Since I'm getting this for you, you're not allowed to cry anymore," she told him. "If you cry, I'm taking it away from you. Understand?"

He nodded and wiped the residual moisture from his eyes.

On the way home, she dropped him off in an open field a block from her house and explained to him how to operate the bike as the salesman had explained it to her. She then started the car and sighed with exasperation as she watched him crash within the first five seconds from her rearview mirror. Hoping the experience would either toughen him up or kill him, she drove away.

NATE PULLED HIMSELF OUT FROM UNDER his dirt bike and brushed himself off. Blood was gushing from a cut near his eye, but he chose to ignore it. As much as the fall had hurt his pride, not to mention his body, he had absolutely loved the speed and control he'd gotten a taste of in those few seconds. He was instantly determined to become the best dirt bike rider in the world. It felt good to feel something other than sadness. It was also nice to have somewhere else to be besides his grandmother's house. He'd rather have fallen off his bike all day long than have to hear Grace telling him he was weak one more time. From that day on, his bike offered a much needed escape, and he spent as much time on it as possible.

Once he got the hang of riding, he loved it even more. He'd spend hours building ramps and jumping them, weaving quickly through tall weeds and around trash that had gathered in the empty field, and trying as many daredevil tricks as he could come up with. Grace bought him a new dirt bike once he outgrew the first one.

At sixteen, he used the money he had made selling artifacts on the black market to buy himself his first street bike. Dan forced him to get an after-school job to make it look like he'd worked to save up for it. Nosy questions from acquaintances would have made Grace very angry.

If he wasn't in school, at work, or committing theft with his family, Nate was riding.

And one day he knew he'd leave. He'd ride away and never see Grace again. If she got in his way and tried to stop him...well, she wouldn't be that stupid. And if she was...he'd need to come up with a plan to stop her first.

Part 4

THIS WASN'T PART OF THE PLAN

Chapter 23

Three years ago

Tuesday, May 1, 2012

Lorelei watched herself age as twenty-three years passed. Numerous escape attempts from the couple who held her captive had proven to be futile. Each time, she was caught, and each time, she was punished by being locked in a windowless room in the dark, chilly basement with a single candle as a light source for months. Whether she was in the basement or in the yellow bedroom, to pass the time, she read the book Nate had left in her purse about the Mallandian legends. The handwriting was on the small side, and the English phrasing so different than modern English that it made for a difficult read. She got used to it, however, and eagerly absorbed the tales of warriors, a curse on the royal bloodline, and the Armor Jewelry, especially the parts about the amulet. It was fascinating, and she was grateful she'd forgotten to return it to the museum.

Just for something to do, Lorelei followed the care

instructions she found in the book of legends. She washed the amulet under the running tap in her bathroom and hung it around her neck as she sat in the sun that was shining through her window. She marveled at its beauty, age, and history that she'd read about in the book.

Hearing a conversation outside the bedroom door, she turned her head to listen. It must be one of the couple's neighbors. Although the sound was muffled, Lorelei could tell they were arguing. It was hard to understand most of what was going on. She believed it had something to do with the couple owing the neighbor money. The arguing turned into shouting, and Lorelei sat on her bed, a little frightened and hoping the neighbor would soon leave. She jumped when her door flew open and the neighbor barged in.

"Who is this?" the neighbor demanded. "Is this where all your money is going? To a live-in whore?"

Lorelei stood up quickly, her heart pounding. The couple didn't respond and looked as terrified as Lorelei felt.

"If I can't get the money from you," the neighbor said to the couple, "then maybe I can get it from her." He pulled out a pocket knife and held it to Lorelei's throat. "Where do you keep all the money he gives you?" the neighbor asked her.

Lorelei kept quiet. Her breathing was quick, and her eyes turned downward to look at the knife. She noticed the amulet was glowing, just like the book of legends said it would when the wearer was in danger.

What?!

How could that be? Metal and rock didn't glow, and this amulet certainly couldn't protect her right now. It was just a legend.

"Where is it?" the neighbor yelled at her. "Where is it?"

Lorelei shook her head.

The neighbor moved his arm upward in an attempt

to drive the knife into Lorelei's throat when he suddenly suffered a pain in his hand so intense that he dropped the knife. He snatched it up with his other hand and attempted to stab her in the chest. His first attempt missed her completely and he looked stunned. His second attempt to stab her in the chest brought on another intense pain in his hand, and once again, he dropped the knife.

Lorelei stepped on it as the neighbor bent over to grab it. Her knee hit the underside of his chin with as much force as she had, and his head snapped back, causing him to fall over. "Go!" she shouted at him, picking up the knife and taking a few steps toward him. "And don't come back!"

The neighbor's eyes widened at the sight of the glowing amulet, and he scrambled to his feet and ran, shoving his way past the couple who had been watching from the doorway.

"How did you do that?!" the woman asked her, entering her room.

"I don't know," she responded, quickly tucking the amulet under her shirt, even though it was no longer glowing. "Luck."

"He would've killed us all," said the man with a cough. "We'd like to repay you. Is there anything you want?"

"Yes," Lorelei replied. The book of legends had said something about blood from the Mallandian royal family being important to the cuff. "There's a genealogy website I'd like to look at."

"No internet," the man told her. "We promised your husband you'd have no contact with the outside world."

After pleading, tears, and agreeing to being closely supervised the entire time, they finally granted her wish.

Friday, May 4, 2012

LORELEI PACED HER ROOM. WITH THE powers of the amulet, she'd have a much easier time trying to escape. She could go home and see her son again! Then she'd find the amulet's rightful owner. She finally understood why Grace had been so angry at the loss of the amulet and the cuff. What if Grace had the ring and earrings? If she did and found Lorelei before Lorelei found Anise or Deborah Viston... No. It was too risky. The Viston ladies and Grace lived in the same town—certainly not a coincidence. Grace chose to move to that town many years ago and Lorelei would bet her life that Grace had known exactly what she was doing.

Lorelei hung her head as she realized she couldn't go home again. At least not yet. Grace would kill her. But she could at least get the amulet to the Viston family. Maybe they'd be willing to help her escape and protect her from Grace in return. She'd have to go about it in a much more discreet way than she'd originally planned. She'd have to get the amulet to the Viston's without going home. Perhaps Anise and Deborah already knew about the Armor Jewelry and their legacy. If not, perhaps Nathan could tell them. He'd turned 27 a few months before. A few mournful tears fell as she thought about not having been able to watch him grow up.

She'd have to think of a way to get the amulet to one of the Viston ladies so that she'd accept it. Nathan might be able to help, but if she sent the amulet to him, Grace might see it if she was still in his life. That wouldn't do.

Maybe she could mail it to the Viston's? No...if they received a package in the mail from a person they didn't know, they might not even open it. It would have to be given to them by someone they know and trust. But who did they know and trust? Without being allowed to use the internet, there was no way she'd be able to figure that out.

After coming up with a plan, Lorelei wrapped the amulet and placed it into a padded envelope she found in the couple's desk while they were sleeping. Her long-time friend Bridget most likely still lived in town; hopefully she was still at the same address. She included a letter to Bridget with specific instructions on what to do with the amulet and placed several stamps that she had also taken from the couple's desk on the envelope. Then she sat and started composing a letter to her son.

In the middle of her writing, she saw a young neighborhood child walking down the hill. He'd soon pass behind the fence of the couple's backyard. She stopped writing and begged the couple to let her go outside to garden. They agreed, and she quickly pulled on her sunhat and gardening shoes. Pretending to dig in the back by the fence, she got the child's attention by calling to him.

"Hello!" she said to the child through a crack in the fence.

"Hello," he responded shyly.

"Can you help me?" she asked.

The child stopped walking and turned to look at her.

"Take this and put it in the mailbox down the street," she said, pointing. "Then come back and I'll pay you in candy." She showed him a chocolate bar that the couple had given to her.

The child took the padded envelope that contained the amulet. "What's in it?" he asked out of curiosity.

"A necklace for my friend," she responded.

"What's your friend's name?" he asked.

"Bridget. Please hurry!" She pretended to dig in the dirt and watched as best as she could through cracks in the fence as the child ran to the mailbox and deposited the envelope inside.

The child ran back, and she gave him the chocolate bar, wishing she had finished writing her letter to Nathan so the child could have mailed it at the same time. "Come back tomorrow?" she asked him. "I'll have another letter to put in the mailbox."

"Will you have more chocolate to give me?"

"I'll try," she said. "If no chocolate, then some other candy."

The child waved at her. "See you tomorrow," he said before scampering off.

Monday, July 16, 2012

LORELEI TAPPED HER PEN ON HER desk, trying to think of what she wanted to say. It was just a letter, but she was nervous. She hadn't communicated with her son in any way in 23 years, and she had so much to say it was going to be difficult to condense it into one letter. She'd written draft after draft, but had burned them all in the grill in the backyard. Nothing sounded right, and she didn't want to seem like a lunatic to Nathan after all this time. Today was going to be the day, though. She'd already taken far too long to write this letter. It should've been done weeks ago. Writing furiously to get it completed before the young boy came by on his daily afternoon walk, she didn't look up again until she heard two men talking outside. She put down her pen and begged her captors to allow her to go outside to garden. They granted her request, and she made her way quickly to the fence. "Hello," she said in a loud whisper to the men as they passed by the back of the fence. "Over here!" She threw a few pulled weeds over the fence so they would know where her voice was coming from.

The two men looked toward the weeds and then saw Lorelei through the crack in the fence.

"Hello," answered the tall man.

"Oh, thank god!" she said, having hope for the first time in a very long while. "I've been held captive here for the last 23 years!" She furiously continued picking weeds. "They might be watching me right now. Can you help me? Please? I need to get home!"

"Of course, my dear, don't you worry," assured the tall man. "We're here to help you. But first, there's some information we need to know."

"I'm not sure who they are," Lorelei began, motioning toward her captors' house. "But they're not violent people. If you could just let the authorities know—"

"That's not the kind of information I meant," the tall man said, interrupting her.

She furrowed her brow in confusion. "What do you need to know?"

"My colleague and I are here in search of information about the Armor Jewelry."

Lorelei felt a pit form in her stomach. How did they know about the Armor Jewelry—and that she had a piece of it? Something wasn't right. "I'm not sure I know what you're talking about."

"I think you do, Mrs. Brevain."

"How do you know me? Who are you?" she asked, a sick feeling taking over her stomach.

"Don't fret, I'm here to help you get home. But time is of the essence. I'll be asking the questions right now, Mrs. Brevain. Yours can come later."

She tried to see their faces through the crack in the fence, but their hats and sunglasses prevented her from recognizing them. "What do you want to know?"

"How did you get the amulet?" the tall man asked. "And why did you mail it to your home city?"

She took a deep breath, not certain if she should tell this strange man her secrets. But if she had any chance of escaping by doing so, she had to take that chance. "My son found it in my mother-in-law's basement," she said, "along with some other artifacts. I was going to return it to the museum, but I forgot that it was in my purse when I returned other artifacts. When I woke up, I was here without knowing how I got here. That's when I realized the amulet was still with me. After I learned about it, I sent it to its rightful owner."

"How did you learn about it?"

"Along with the amulet, there was also a book of legends in my purse that talked about it."

"I'd like to see that book," the tall man said. "Now, please."

Lorelei ran back into the house. She retrieved the book, hoping the couple would think she was just going to do some outside reading as she often did. Once back outside, she passed the book through a large crack in the fence.

"Why do you think Anise Viston is the rightful owner?" the man asked her, as he flipped through the book.

Lorelei gasped. "How did you know I wanted her to have it? Did she end up with it?"

"Anise has it, yes. She is an acquaintance of mine."

"Oh, good! Do you happen to know my son as well? Nathan—or rather Nate—Brevain?"

He ignored her. "Why is Anise Viston the rightful owner?" he demanded.

A little intimidated and motivated by hope alone, she responded, "Because she has king's blood. She *and* her mother."

Now it was the tall man's turn to be surprised. "King's blood?"

"Yes, as far as I can tell, those women are the last two alive with king's blood."

"What does that mean?" he asked her.

"They're direct descendants of the king of Mallandia that the cuff was created for," she explained. "Only those with king's blood can use the cuff with immediate results. For anyone else, results with the cuff could take years and cause side effects in people the cuff is used on."

"My, you are knowledgeable," commented the tall man. "I assume that's why Grace wanted to get rid of you."

"You know Grace?" Lorelei asked. "Please, do you know my son? How is he?"

"That hoodlum is in prison where he belongs," the tall man answered, still flipping through the book.

"What?!" Lorelei sank to her knees. "No!"

"Forgive me for giving you a shock, my dear," the tall man said with a sigh. "But your son grew up under Grace's influence. He's just like her."

"That can't be!" insisted Lorelei, tears streaming down her face. "What has he done?"

"I'll explain more once we get you out of here," the tall man told her in a gentler voice. He looked up when he heard shouting.

Lorelei turned and saw her male captor exiting the house, aiming a gun at the two men on the other side of the fence. He fired at them.

"Run!" shouted the tall man's colleague. They ran, got into a car, and took off.

It took Lorelei a few seconds to realize what had happened. She took in a deep, gasping breath as she clutched at her chest before everything went black.

＊

WHEN THE WOMAN JOINED HER HUSBAND in the backyard, he had a grave look on his face. "I didn't mean to. I was aiming at the men. She got in the way," he told his wife and coughed violently. "She's dead."

"Hello?" said a soft voice from outside the fence. "Is the lady with the candy here?"

"What are you talking about?" demanded the man of the child outside his fence.

The child peered through the crack in the fence. "That lady there," he said, pointing to Lorelei's body. "Is she sleeping? Does she have something for me to mail for her today?"

The woman narrowed her eyes at the child. "What did she have you mail for her?"

"She said it was a necklace for her friend."

"What friend?"

"Bridget. I've never heard a name like that. Does she have anything for me to mail?"

"No!" snapped the woman. "Go home!"

The child ran off.

"Shit. Now we have to tell Dan about his wife," the woman complained.

"Hell no. We'll lose our income," the man responded. "But we gotta warn him that she mailed something to this Bridget."

They heard a pounding on the fence's gate, and the woman went to unlock it.

"I was driving by and heard a gunshot. Is everyone okay?" asked a man with curly black hair.

"Who are you?" the man demanded, coming up behind his wife.

The curly-headed man offered a name and explained that he was the new local coroner. He pushed past the couple to the backyard and had them explain what had happened to Lorelei. The man told the coroner that two unknown men had shot Lorelei. He then bribed the coroner to take the body but to not report the death. The coroner agreed, shoving the money in his pocket. He picked up the body, put it in the back of his van, and sped off.

DAN HUNG UP THE PHONE AFTER the man holding Lorelei captive explained what she'd done. He wiped the sweat off his brow. For years, Grace was always livid whenever she returned from one of her so-called business trips. She'd demand to know what happened to the amulet.

He'd always told her he didn't know until one day last year when he got sick of her nagging. He said that Lorelei probably had it in her purse when he killed her, and not knowing that at the time, he had thrown it into a lake in the next town. Grace had forced him to get scuba lessons so he could search for it. Almost every summer day since then, Grace had forced him to dive, but of course, he never found it. The purse was with his wife in another state. Now he had to tell his mother that he had never killed Lorelei, and she had somehow managed to mail the amulet to a friend of hers in town. Or did he?

He picked up the phone again. "Mother," he said when Grace answered. "You'll never believe it. I spotted the amulet on a woman in town, and I followed her home. She must've found it in the lake...No, I don't have it; she was wearing it...Yes, I have the address..."

Chapter 24

Friday, September 25, 2015

Anise woke up early and couldn't get back to sleep, even though she'd only slept a few hours. There was too much on her mind. She rolled over, looked at the gorgeous man sleeping next to her, and couldn't help but feel giddy all over again. It had been an amazing night, to say the least. Nate had made her feel things she'd never experienced with Jonathan or Brian, and the tingling sensations deep inside her body tempted her to wake him for more. He was sleeping so peacefully, however, that she decided to let him rest.

Her thoughts turned to an earlier part of the evening, and a mass of anger lumped in her stomach. Who was that man at the museum that had chased them and tried to kill them? Was he one of Dr. Smithton's brainwashed followers like Nate thought? If so, when did Dr. Smithton decide he wanted her dead? And did Jonathan know that she was on Dr. Smithton's hit list? Was he so far gone that he didn't care if Dr. Smithton offed her? And what exactly did Dr. Smithton want with her blood anyway? She had to find out.

Anise got up and dressed quietly in the jeans and sweater she'd worn the night before so as to let Nate continue sleeping. Worrying that she may have been caught on camera somewhere the night before, she decided that wearing the exact same outfit would be a bad idea. She took off her sweater and grabbed one of Nate's button-down shirts from his closet. She rinsed the chalcedony earrings under the tap in the bathroom and put them on. Slipping into her leather jacket, she grabbed a note card from her tote bag and found her pencil on his nightstand. She left him a note saying she'd be right back, grabbed his spare key, and took the bus to the museum. On her way, she called in sick to work—again. With everything that had been going on lately, she could tell her boss wasn't happy about it, and she hoped her job security wasn't in jeopardy.

She sat on the sunny side of the bus, making sure the earrings and amulet got a few minutes to charge. When she stepped off the bus, she checked to make sure the chalcedony earrings were still in her ears, and she tucked the amulet under Nate's shirt. She removed the pencil from behind her ear and tied a scarf she found in her tote bag around her head to cover up the earrings in a fashionable way that no one would question. She certainly didn't need to be arrested for theft on top of everything.

Anise climbed the stairwell in the museum and tried to focus her racing thoughts. She took a deep breath and knocked on Jonathan's office door. As upset as she was with him, she missed him and her heart leapt with anticipation when the door slowly swung open.

"Anise," he said, surprised. "What are you doing here?"

"Hi, Jonathan," she said, noticing his hair was disheveled like he'd been pulling on it. Anise then looked carefully into his eyes. They appeared to not be glazed over, so she continued. "Can I ask you some questions about Dr. Smithton and his utopia vision?"

"Yeah, I guess," he said, his voice announcing his suspicion of her motives. "But can we do it later? The museum was broken into last night, and the cops are here now asking everyone questions. Someone took the chalcedony earrings."

"Oh, no!" Anise replied, doing her best to look surprised.

"Yeah. My co-worker George was here last night. He saw the people who broke in and went after them. He was almost killed in a car accident."

"I'm sorry to hear that. Is he going to be okay?" She walked into his office, closed his door, and sat down. *So George was the one who came after us.*

He frowned and sat across from her. "Luckily, yes. Unfortunately, he's their number one suspect right now."

"Oh? Because he was here?"

"Partly. The security guard said he chased a man and a woman in ski masks up to the roof, but they both escaped. A gun registered to George was found up there. The security guard said he thought the man was in better shape than George but that he really didn't get a great look. It could've been George; he wasn't sure. They don't have any leads on the woman yet. There's no evidence to place anyone specific here—none of the security cameras captured anything. Seems to me like it was a professional job." He looked straight at Anise and continued. "George said the two escaped on a motorcycle. The security guard said at least one person fled on a motorcycle but that he also saw a car fleeing the scene that matches the description of George's car. That might make George look guilty, but I know him; he'd never steal from the museum. I believe him when he said he was going after the guilty party. The motorcycle and the professionalism of the job made me think of Nate. Who else besides your delinquent boyfriend would go through all that just for those earrings?"

"Nate was with me. *All night*," Anise asserted, growing angry at herself for thinking coming here would be a good idea.

"I don't care," Jonathan said, shaking his head and pulling with annoyance on his tie and his hair. "I just want the earrings returned to the museum." He got up and opened his office door for her. "We're done here."

"We are not!" Anise informed him as she shut the door again. "I came here because I want to know what you and Dr. Smithton are planning. Why didn't Dr. Smithton tell us about the cuff? And what's the real reason he wants my blood?"

"What are you talking about?" he asked in an irritated tone.

She rolled her eyes. "Seriously? You and Dr. Smithton have been asking me to donate blood for a while now. I don't buy his story about saving blood just in case a war breaks out. Who would believe that? I want to know the real story."

"Well, it's for...I mean, I assume it's...you know, I'm not sure. I know he wants it, but he hasn't told me specifically why."

She looked at him and saw his eyes were still not glazed over. He was speaking the truth. "Don't you think it's strange?" she asked him. "Not to mention creepy?"

Jonathan looked down in thought. "It *is* pretty odd," he admitted.

Anise took in a deep breath as she watched his eyes glaze over suddenly. They looked at her as if Jonathan wasn't controlling them at all.

"I take that back. He's already told us it's for his plan to create a utopia on Earth. Whether or not he explains it to us is his business."

"If he wants *my* blood, it's not just *his* business," Anise snapped.

"Why can't you just trust Dr. S.?" Jonathan asked her. "He's the smartest and most honorable person I know. Maybe he has some eccentric ideas, but he always wants what's best for everyone."

"Because I have tangible proof that he's lying! I told you about the page Nate and I found in his safe, remember? He tore it out of the book that has a drawing of the cuff in it! He knew all along about the Jewelry and how it works. He lied to us both! Why won't *you* trust *me* about this?"

Jonathan's face crinkled up in pain as he pulled on his hair. His voice was loud and cold. "Because you make bad decisions. You picked a career that you thought would please your parents, not yourself. You lived with Brian, a monster of a man. And now you're letting an arrogant, piece-of-shit criminal use you for his pleasure. You can't even trust yourself, so why should I? I'd never take your word over Dr. S's."

Anise's mouth opened in shock, but no words came out. Her face burned and her eyes threatened to spill over.

Without knocking, Dr. Smithton opened Jonathan's office door and came in. "It's a little loud in here, Jonathan. I know I don't have to remind you this is a place of business."

"Sorry, Dr. S. I'll keep it down. Anise was just leaving."

"No, I wasn't," she said firmly, annoyed at being pushed out the door. Her heart had started beating faster from anxiety when Dr. Smithton walked in, but even if he had the cuff and ring, she had the amulet and earrings, so she felt safe. "Dr. Smithton, I came here for answers." She couldn't exactly ask him if he was trying to kill her, so she started with something she could ask. "What do you want with my blood?"

"I thought we already discussed this," Dr. Smithton said.

"Like I was telling Jonathan, I don't buy your story of

wanting to keep blood handy in case of war. What's the real reason?"

Dr. Smithton sighed. "You don't have to believe it for it to be true."

Anise narrowed her eyes. She'd watched Dr. Smithton's hand maneuvering in his pocket and suspected him of attempting to slip the cuff on his wrist. Looking at Jonathan, she saw that his eyes were completely glazed over, and he appeared to be staring off into space. Did he even know what was going on? She got up and yanked Dr. Smithton's arm sharply upward to remove it from his pocket.

"Anise, that was rude!" exclaimed Jonathan.

"What has gotten into you?" Dr. Smithton demanded, as he pulled his sleeve over the cuff. It was too late, however.

"You're wearing the cuff!" Anise said to Dr. Smithton as she pointed at his wrist. "I just saw it! I knew it! You've been brainwashing Jonathan!"

"What?" cried Jonathan, standing up. "Is that true, Dr. S?"

"Jonathan, sit down and forget what you hear about the cuff," Dr. Smithton demanded.

"Sure thing, Dr. S." Jonathan sat and stared off into the distance.

"Yes, Anise, I have the cuff," Dr. Smithton admitted to her. "If you'll just listen to me, you'll see it's for the good of all."

"The only reason I'd ever think that what you're doing is good is if you brainwash me. But you won't succeed at that," she told him.

Dr. Smithton chuckled at her as he reached into his other pocket. "I think you're mistaken," he said, as he showed her a pair of light blue chalcedony hoop earrings. "Not so confident now, are you?" he asked, as he pulled off her scarf to expose the chalcedony hoops she wore.

Her jaw dropped as she understood. "You have the

real earrings?" she said in disbelief.

"Not as far as the police are concerned," he said, handing the earrings to Jonathan. "Put them on," he demanded.

"I don't have pierced ears, Dr. S.," Jonathan said, visually upset by the fact that he couldn't comply with the order he was given.

"So fix that!" Dr. Smithton demanded.

"Jonathan, no!" exclaimed Anise as she watched Jonathan shove a pushpin through each of his lobes. He winced in pain as he then pushed the earrings through his new piercings. Blood dripped onto his shoulders.

Dr. Smithton turned his head at the sight of the blood. "Jonathan, tie Anise to her seat." He pushed Anise down in her chair as Jonathan grabbed a thin rope Dr. Smithton handed to him. Anise was surprised to find that Dr. Smithton was much stronger than she thought he'd be. He avoided her kicking legs and sat right on her, holding her arms fast.

She knew she didn't stand a chance. Even though she wore the amulet, Dr. Smithton wore the cuff and Jonathan wore the earrings, which meant that the powers of each of their two pieces would cancel out her amulet when being used against each other. "Jonathan, don't do this!" she begged him as he crouched down to tie her ankles together. "Please!"

He looked up at her, and she watched the glaze in his eyes flicker in and out when he heard her cries. As her tears began to fall, his face crinkled up in pain, and he held a hand to his head as he let out a groan.

"Ignore her, Jonathan!" Dr. Smithton demanded. "You no longer love her."

"What?" Jonathan pulled on his hair and groaned again.

"You no longer love Anise," Dr. Smithton repeated.

Jonathan looked at Dr. Smithton like he didn't recognize him. "You're wrong."

"You don't love Anise. Now, tie her up like I asked you to."

Jonathan let out a cry as he pulled out a fistful of hair. His eyes grew large as he dropped the rope in his hands. Jonathan screamed. "Rattlesnake!"

Dr. Smithton and Anise watched as Jonathan threw the rope to the ground and started stomping on it as hard as he could. Dr. Smithton got up from his seat on Anise's lap, stepped over to him, and grabbed him by the shoulders. "Jonathan! Son, pull yourself together!" He forced Jonathan to look him in the eye.

Anise took that opportunity to run. She could hear Dr. Smithton ordering Jonathan to catch her. A few seconds later, she turned to see Jonathan running after her. With the strength of the earrings, he quickly caught up to her on the landing in the stairwell, and he slammed her against the wall. She saw that his glazed look was back.

"Please," she said, panting. "Don't make me fight you. I don't want to hurt you."

They looked into each other's eyes. Jonathan's glazed look faded, and he dropped his arms to his sides. "I'm so sorry," he said breathlessly, pulling on his hair as he wore an expression of extreme pain. "For everything. I don't know what's happening to me. Go. Now!"

She ran and didn't stop until she was climbing back onto the bus. *Thank god I got away.* A few tears of relief fell onto her jeans after she sat and hung her head. They shortly turned into tears of sadness and anger. How could Dr. Smithton knowingly hurt Jonathan like this? And how could Jonathan be so goddamn blind when it came to Dr. Smithton? If Jonathan had questioned the ridiculous utopia plan right when it was first introduced to him—before the brainwashing had a hold on him—maybe they could've figured out what Dr. Smithton was up to long ago. Her anger made the tears stop, and she no longer felt like crying. She still wanted to help Jonathan, but her feelings of missing him were gone.

Upon reaching Nate's condo, she took a deep breath as she walked into the bedroom where he was awake but still in bed.

"Where'd you go, honey?" he asked her with a yawn, holding up her note.

"Don't be mad," she said.

He groaned as he looked at her. "You went to the museum, didn't you?"

"Yes, and I learned a lot!" She sat on the edge of the bed. "Dr. Smithton has the cuff, ring, and earrings! And he's definitely been brainwashing Jonathan!"

"What do you mean he has the earrings?" he asked with a confused look as he stared at her ears.

"I mean," she replied, as she took the blue chalcedony hoops out of her ears, "these are fake."

"What? Are you sure?" He sat up in bed.

"Yes. Dr. Smithton tried to order Jonathan to keep me captive. They were going to turn me into the police who were there investigating the break-in. Jonathan was able to slam me against the wall when I tried to run. I was wearing the amulet, so the only explanation as to how he was able to do that is that the earrings he wore were the real ones. His earrings canceled out my amulet, and he's stronger than I am."

"So how'd you get away?" Nate asked her with concern.

"Jonathan's eyes look glazed over when he's around Dr. Smithton. But when the glazed look starts fading away, I can tell he's fighting the mind control. The real Jonathan is still in there, and he doesn't want to hurt me."

Nate frowned. "You're lucky you didn't get yourself into more trouble."

Anise continued. "Oh, and Jonathan said the number one suspect right now is his co-worker George. He's the guy that was chasing us in the car last night and the one you punched out. You were right; he's one of Dr. Smithton's brainwashed colleagues. They're suspecting him because they found his gun—the one I left on the roof."

Nate grinned. "That was genius on your part, my beautiful partner in crime," he praised, leaning forward and kissing her.

She kissed him back. "That was pure luck on my part," she admitted.

His expression darkened. "It's also pure luck that you're not being held captive right now by Boy Scout and the walking corpse. God only knows what they'd be doing to you. What's it going to take to get you to stay away from them?" Nate demanded.

"I think I've proven I can handle myself," Anise countered.

"Anise. Please. Do me a favor and stop getting yourself into dangerous situations."

Anise could see the annoyance, concern, and fear radiating from the look he was giving her. She threw her arms around him. "Thank you," she said, "for always looking out for me." She set her head on his shoulder.

He held her too, and the annoyance in his voice was gone. "I always will," he said softly. Gently, his hand stroked her hair as she relaxed into him. "I'm serious though. *Please* stay away from them," he repeated. "But when you don't, then at *least* take me with you."

"I promise," she said, enjoying how warm his body was. "By the way, I borrowed a shirt. I hope you don't mind."

He kissed the top of her head. "My shirt's never looked so good."

Feeling completely safe for the first time in a long while, she removed the amulet and set it on his night stand before resuming their long embrace. It was a relief to get the heavy weight of the amulet off her neck. He leaned back on his headboard as she rested her head on his chest. "You feel so good. Can we stay like this for a little while?"

"As long as you want, honey." After a pause, he asked

her, "Are you okay without the amulet?"

"Right now I am, yes." She closed her eyes and relaxed. "Thank you for never pressuring me to take it off and keep it somewhere safe. And for never pushing me to try to go outside without it. I know I *shouldn't* need it, but I'm just not ready for that yet. I know I will be someday. Hopefully soon. Just not yet."

The muscles in his arms and chest stiffened like they always did when Nate didn't like something. "You don't have to thank me for that. And there's no such thing as 'should' or 'shouldn't;' there's only how things are. If wearing the amulet all the time is something you want to change, let it take as long as it takes," he told her. "You're the only one who'll know when it's time. You don't owe me or anyone else an explanation."

She squeezed him a little tighter. It was the first time she'd taken the amulet off since she and Jonathan had returned from breaking into the Springfield Museum three years prior. Wearing it had always made her feel safer than anything, but now Nate's presence was starting to rival that.

When she was ready to start the rest of the day, Nate got up and grabbed some fresh clothes. "Let's take a shower and then I'll make us some breakfast before we get down to business," he told her. "Do you like omelets?"

"That sounds delicious!" she said. "But what business do you mean?"

"I made a few calls while you were out. I found Kent Dromly. He lives and works in Springfield."

"That's great!"

"Yeah, but right now he's helping out a charity with free surgical procedures in the middle of some remote place I've never heard of. There's no way we can get in touch with him right now."

"When's he coming home?"

"Next Friday."

"So we have a whole week before we can go see him?"

she asked, disappointed. "What are we going to do until then?"

He gave her a mischievous grin. "I have a few ideas."

JONATHAN STAGGERED BACK UP THE STAIRS in extreme pain, gripping the handrail like a lifeline. He leaned against the wall pulling on his hair until he felt a little better.

What the hell is going on?

Everything seemed a little fuzzy and he blinked, hoping his vision would focus. He tried to recall the events after Anise had gotten there in an attempt to clear his mind.

I told her about the break-in and George. She rubbed it in my face that she's sleeping with the psychopath— she was wearing his shirt. She asked why Dr. S. wants her blood and called it creepy.

Now that his head was clearing up, he realized he wanted an answer to that question as well.

Horrified, he began recalling all the times he had asked her to donate blood himself. He remembered the phone conversations they'd had when she'd gone to Springfield with Nate and felt another headache coming on. "I'm making him look safe and sane," he mumbled to himself, almost understanding why Anise had chosen to be with Nate. "I almost tied her up. Shit. I chased her and slammed her against a wall! Why? What is wrong with me?" He pulled on his hair again until the pain subsided enough to walk back to Dr. S's office.

"Where is she?" Dr. S. asked him.

"I let her go," Jonathan snapped, with his eyes narrowed. "What the hell is going on, Dr. S? I said cruel things to her. I was about to tie her up. I chased her. I pushed her against the wall. This is the woman I love! I would never treat her or anyone that way, so why is this happening?"

"Calm yourself, son," Dr. S said gently as he slipped the cuff and ring back on. "Take those earrings out." He handed Jonathan a roll of paper towels and some hydrogen peroxide. "I'm very sorry about your ears. I shouldn't have done that. I should've had you come with me when I had mine pierced. Now, sit down."

Jonathan gladly removed the earrings and dabbed at his bloody lobes with a paper towel. As Dr. S. spoke, Jonathan felt his eyes get that funny, overly-relaxed feeling, the one Anise said made his eyes look glazed over, and he fought it with everything he had. "I don't want to sit down! I want answers! Is Anise right? Are you brainwashing me with that cuff?"

"Jonathan, I—"

Jonathan continued before Dr. S. could answer. "And what about Grace? Did you brainwash her, too? Is that why we both get pain that makes us try to pull our hair out?"

"Sit down!" boomed Dr. S. "Forget all of this!"

"No!" cried Jonathan again as he felt his eyes relaxing more and more. He shook his head and stood by the door. "There are still cops all over the museum. I'm going to find them right now and turn in the earrings. I'll tell them you stole them and that you have the ring, too, and that you stole it from the Woods' residence. You'll go down for the murder of Richard and Marilyn Woods unless you start talking fast."

"Okay," Dr. S. said, taking off the cuff and ring and placing them on his desk. "I'll tell you why I really need Anise's blood and explain what's happening to you. Please, sit down."

Jonathan sat and stared at his mentor, waiting for an explanation.

"The truth is that yes, I have been using the cuff to brainwash not only you, but everyone in the department.

The reason has nothing to do with a utopia. That was a childish notion I entertained in my youth, but I soon came to understand it's not possible."

Jonathan stood up and walked around Dr. S.'s office trying to take in the information he had just been handed. "I can't believe you'd actually brainwash me! And all our colleagues!" he spat. "So, if your ultimate goal isn't to form a utopia, what is it?" He turned to face his mentor and saw that Dr. S. had put on the cuff, ring, and earrings while Jonathan's back had been turned.

"I've told you quite enough," Dr. S. said. "Now forget it all, and go back to work."

Jonathan opened his mouth to protest but felt a wave of calm wash over him as his eyes relaxed even more. The cuff's power was intensified by the earrings and ring, making it too strong for Jonathan to resist. "Okay, Dr. S," he replied, wondering why he had come to his mentor's office in the first place.

Chapter 25

Three years ago

Thursday, July 12, 2012

Morty walked through the door of Doreen's Thrift Shoppe and spotting Anise, waved her over. She gave him a surprised look and a wave back as she stepped over to him.

"Dr. Smithton! Hi!"

"Hello, Anise! Good to see you again. I was hoping you'd stop by the museum so we could discuss your trip to Springfield with Jonathan. He's told me all about it of course, but I'd love to hear it from your perspective as well. It's been over a month now."

"I know, I'm sorry, I've just been so busy spending time with Brian's sister. She really needs a friend right now since Brian...passed. And I've been working a lot too."

"I understand," he told her with a kind smile. "How's your other job going?"

"It's going well, thanks. I started off as a market

research survey taker, but I just received notice that I get to take manager training in a few weeks."

"Wonderful!"

"Yeah, thanks, but it still isn't what I want to do. I keep checking the corporate website to see if there are any other job openings within the company that'll allow me to make better use of my marketing degree."

"You'll find something you enjoy," he encouraged. "Just keep looking."

"I'm surprised to see you here," she commented. "I didn't know you were a vintage shopper."

"Well, this is the place where you found your beautiful amulet, is it not? I thought I'd stop in and see what other treasures it may hold."

"Sure! Welcome!" Anise waved Doreen over. "This is the owner of the shop, Doreen. Doreen, this is my friend Jonathan's boss at the museum, Dr. Smithton."

"A pleasure," said Morty.

"Likewise," replied Doreen. "Anise has told me how much she and Jonathan enjoy hearing about Mallandia from you."

"I'm just grateful that young people want to hear an old man's stories," he replied with a chuckle.

Doreen laughed too. "Now, I know you came in here looking for jewelry. I can show you what we have in our jewelry case," she offered. "But I can guarantee there's nothing as magnificent as Anise's amulet in there."

"Let's take a look," Morty said. He followed her over to the display case on the other side of the store and peered inside. "May I see those cuff links?" She handed them to him, and he inspected them. "Did Anise tell you the history associated with her amulet?" he asked, as he looked over the cuff links.

"Just that it comes from Mallandia about four thousand years ago. I was amazed when I heard that!" Her eyes widened in wonder.

"Indeed. A piece of jewelry that precious is usually

kept within families. It makes one wonder who would donate such an item."

"A woman brought it in a little over a month ago with her other donations," Doreen replied. "She handed it to me and commented about what a unique statement piece it is. She suggested that it would make a great gift for a young woman who'd be confident enough to wear it."

Morty nodded to encourage her to continue.

"Well, I immediately thought of Anise. I needed to find a graduation gift for her, and I knew she'd love it!"

"I haven't known her long, but from what I've seen, she's a remarkable young woman," Morty praised.

"I agree. I'm so proud of her," Doreen beamed, looking over at Anise who was sorting donations on the other side of the store.

"Did the woman who donated the amulet say why she didn't want to keep it?" he asked, bringing the conversation back to the Jewelry.

"No," said Doreen, "and I didn't ask." She lowered her voice. "But she *has* been back in the store a few times since then. She asked if anyone had bought the amulet, and I told her that I had given it to Anise as a graduation gift. She seemed really pleased, but asked that I not tell Anise the amulet was donated by her. It was a little strange if you ask me."

"Yes," Morty agreed. "Did she say anything else?"

"Not really. Since then, she's asked how Anise is enjoying it each time she stops in, which isn't often."

"What an intriguing story! I'm writing an article on Mallandian Jewelry," Morty told her. "I would love to interview this woman and find out how she got the amulet and what she knows about its history. You don't happen to know her name, do you?"

"The last time she was in, she introduced herself as Bridget. And I know she once said that she lives in an apartment just a couple blocks away. Unfortunately, that's all I know."

"Shame," sighed Morty. "I suppose some things will simply have to remain a mystery. Such a nice name though—Bridget. I knew a girl with that name when I was young. She was tall, blonde, and lovely. Wouldn't it be something if that was the same Bridget?"

Doreen smirked. "Sorry to disappoint you, but this Bridget is even shorter than I am and has curly dark hair."

He handed the cuff links to Doreen. "Please wrap them up. The museum will be having fundraising events in the next month or two, and I know Jonathan will get some use out of these."

Chapter 26

Present day

Saturday, October 3, 2015

Anise closed her eyes and leaned back in her seat. She loosened her seat belt a bit to get as comfortable as possible. It was early morning and the white noise of the plane was making her drowsy. She couldn't help but smile to herself as she remembered the events of the past week. Something about Nate's presence made the weekend go by entirely too fast. On the weekdays, she'd count down the dragging hours to when she'd get off work so she could see him again. Every day, they'd done something different together and took turns picking the activity. She'd chosen a night at the theater, karaoke at The Blue Pineapple with her friends, and a painting class in the park. He'd taken her to a baseball game with his friends, an expensive dinner out, and on a motorcycle ride through the mountains to see the leaves changing colors.

She'd watched him practice freestyle tricks on the

Motocross track in a neighboring town and had been equally terrified and impressed with his backflips, mid-air handstands, and when he somehow flew off a ramp, dismounted his bike while flying, spun around, and remounted it, all before making a perfect landing.

"That last one was called the Volt," he told her when he was done practicing. "What did you think?"

She had a million things to say about his incredible talent, skill, showmanship, and confidence but decided to summarize it all as sincerely as possible. "You're *so* hot," she responded, enjoying his appreciative laugh in return and the way he kissed her full of promise of what was to come as soon as they got home.

Last night, they'd stayed in and picked their favorite movies to watch. They'd gone to bed together every night. Her face hurt from smiling so much. Everything had felt delightfully normal—better than normal—and she'd been able to calm her mind, relax, and enjoy their dates as if she didn't have a care in the world.

No matter how hard she tried, sleep always eluded her on planes, and her eyes opened to study the lines of Nate's face, tracing his eyebrows, nose, lips, chin. His eyes were closed and his chest rose and fell softly. Her gaze followed the sleeve of his black leather jacket from his shoulder to wrist. His hands rested on his legs. Anise quietly grabbed her sketchbook from her tote bag and grabbed the pencil from behind her ear.

His hands were what she wanted to immortalize in her drawing. They'd reached for hers every time they went out, held her when they stayed in, cooked for her, rubbed her feet when she'd had a long day at work, protected her, thrown her on his bed when she let him know how much she wanted him. There wasn't an inch on her body that his fingers hadn't touched. They'd intertwined with her own, massaged her back, found her sensitive spots, run through her hair, and had figured out exactly what to do to give her the greatest pleasure. She drew his hand resting gently on hers with the words "Don't ever let go" woven through their fingers.

Her troubles came rushing back to her mind as their plane landed in Springfield. As Nate drove them to the address he'd found, Anise wondered what Kent Dromly could possibly tell them about the Armor Jewelry. At the very least, Anise hoped he'd be able to explain why she was the rightful owner according to Lorelei's letter.

They squeezed each other's hands as they walked up to the front door and rang the bell. A man in his late 50's with curly salt-and-pepper hair opened it.

"We're looking for Dr. Kent Dromly," Nate told him.

"You found him." The man let out a small laugh and shook his head in disbelief. "Nate Brevain. You're just about the last person I expected to be on my doorstep. Please, come in."

Anise and Nate exchanged a look of confusion as they stepped inside.

"I'm sorry, Dr. Dromly, have we met?" Nate asked.

"Oh, so you *don't* remember. Well, you were very young. Yes, we've met. And it's Kent, please." He motioned for them to sit on the couch in his living room, and Nate introduced Anise. "So, since you don't remember me, what brings you by?" Kent asked.

Anise looked around the stark room. She sat next to Nate on a brown couch, and Kent took the matching chair that sat across from them. Besides a small end table next to the chair where Kent sat and a television in the corner, there was no other furniture. No art, family photos, throw rugs, or knick knacks. Nothing that made a house a home. Her eyes wandered to the kitchen. The dining table had books and papers piled on top of it. Fast food bags overflowed the trash can. They declined Kent's offer of a beverage, wanting to get down to business.

"Since you seem to know me, I assume you knew my mother?" Nate asked him.

"I met her once, briefly," answered Kent. "I was at the

museum in your town visiting someone I know. While I was there, you and your mother came by to return some stolen artifacts the two of you had found. I spoke with you both for a few minutes."

"What artifacts were they?" Anise asked, wanting to know what had made Grace so upset that she'd order Dan to kill Lorelei.

"There were a few that I don't remember," Kent admitted. "However, the one that intrigued me was a cuff with three lapis lazuli and ten jasper stones on it."

"Why did that piece intrigue you?" she continued.

"My father was an ancient history and archaeology professor at the University of Springfield," Kent began. "When I saw Lorelei hand over the cuff, I knew I had seen it somewhere before. Then it hit me—my father's trip journals. I've only read a few of them, but he wrote down everything when he was on a mission to see a newly discovered artifact or to learn more about an existing one. Apparently, he had met someone who owned the cuff and wanted to sell it. My father saved up a small fortune with a plan to obtain it and hide it in a secret location."

"Do you have any guesses as to how it ended up in my grandmother's basement?" asked Nate, remembering Lorelei's letter.

"I know that my father gave the cuff to Morty Smithton for... I assume you two already know what it was used for?"

Anise and Nate both answered yes.

"He gave it to Morty for experimentation," Kent continued. "To figure out how it works, I suppose. I don't know how Grace ended up with it. She and Thomas may have stolen it from him."

"Thomas?" asked Nate.

"Thomas Brevain. Grace's husband," explained Kent.

"Grace never mentioned him," said Nate with a confused expression. "I never knew she was married."

"He died long ago, when your father was just a baby,"

Kent explained. "It's possible she and Thomas stole the cuff, and Grace kept it hidden."

"That makes sense," said Anise.

"Why is that?" asked Kent.

"Dr. Smithton and Grace are sworn enemies. According to what Dr. Smithton has told me, they've been fighting over the cuff and other artifacts since their grad school days," Anise explained.

"Yes, I gathered that they were feuding, not to mention somewhat obsessed over certain artifacts, from my father's journals. By 'other artifacts' do you mean the rest of the Armor Jewelry?"

"Yes. How much do you know about the Armor Jewelry?" asked Anise, hoping Kent might be able to tell her how to help Jonathan.

"Not much. It seems that Morty and Grace learned about the Armor Jewelry from my father, and I learned about it from his trip journals. He'd also shown me how they work when I was very small. When I got older, I thought I'd just imagined it, but...then I read a few of the journals..."

Kent then turned to Nate. "After having met your mother, I went back to my hotel where I went through my father's journals. I had brought them with me because I was considering giving them to Morty. He'd always expressed an interest in reading them, but my father had specifically written a letter with the first one he had sent me that said to never let anyone else get their hands on them. Up until that point, I had honored his wishes, but honestly, seeing them stacked in my garage every day just kept making me angry. They reminded me of how we had fallen out when I was a teenager. I haven't seen him in person since then.

"Anyway, I found the one that contained the information I wanted. It seems my father had been extremely angry at someone he called a "traitor." The last entry in the trip journal was a promise of my father's to confront the "traitor," but he never said who it was. It must've been someone close to him who was once on his side. This was all a little unnerving for me, as I had just come from visiting Morty, who by that time had become a treasured family friend. Grace had too. I was concerned for Lorelei's safety—what if Morty was the traitor, thought she might have other pieces of the Armor Jewelry, and decide to come after her? Or what if Grace was the traitor and realized the Jewelry she'd taken from Morty had been given back to him? What would she do about it? I made an effort to talk to Lorelei when I saw her and your father at a restaurant that evening. Your father made it clear that was not acceptable, so I tried to find her at home after a couple days. That's when you answered the door and told me she was gone."

Anise put her hand on Nate's arm after seeing how intense his expression was. She could feel the tightness in his muscles.

"I remember now," said Nate. "You promised me you would keep looking for her." He paused for a moment as he seemed to be reliving a memory. "As a kid, it gave me hope and kept me going. I stared out the window every night for years waiting for you to come by and tell me that you found her."

"I want you to know that I did look for her," Kent assured him.

"I appreciate that," Nate said. "I wish you had found her before I did."

"You found her?" Kent asked, looking confused.

"Well, sort of. My dad's in prison and—"

Kent interrupted Nate. "I know. I've kept up with what's been going on with your family over the years. I wanted to be able to find you if I ever found your mother."

"My dad told me that he'd stashed her with a couple he'd paid off to take care of her in secret in some remote place in Nevada. It was either that or kill her per my grandmother's orders."

Kent shuddered. "I'm really surprised at how Grace has changed."

Nate narrowed his eyebrows. "What do you mean?"

"Like I said, she'd become a close family friend. She took me to visit my mother in the hospital several times after my father disappeared. I was very young the last time I saw her, so I don't remember her well," Kent admitted. "But she was always the nicest person and wonderful around children. I really liked her."

Nate wore an expression of doubt. "You must be thinking of someone else. Anyway, Anise and I went to find my mother, but the couple that was keeping her told me she'd been shot by someone walking by the yard."

Kent hung his head low. "Nate, I need to tell you something," he said softly. "With Grace having turned murderous, and you being in prison for these last three years, please forgive me for not tracking you down to let you know sooner, or at the very least, saying this the second you walked in the door. But your mother is alive, and she's in the next room."

Chapter 27

Three years ago

Thursday, July 12, 2012

After closing his office door, Morty sat at his desk with a cup of hot coffee, unable to contain his excitement. Using internet search sites, he checked the listings for all women named Bridget within a two mile radius of Doreen's Thrift Shoppe. Five appeared in his search results. Writing down each of their last names, he then turned to social media sites in hopes of finding pictures of each of them.

"It's so amazing the wealth of information one can find online," he mumbled to himself as he ruled out the first four women based on the pictures he found that matched their names. "Come on," he said with the spirit of a gambler at the craps table. "Yes!" The last Bridget's profile picture was of a woman in sunglasses with curly, dark hair, just as Doreen had described her. Her name was Bridget Wells and she resided a few blocks from the thrift shop in what seemed to be an apartment or condo, judging by the address.

He guzzled the last of his coffee and put on his suit jacket. There was the possibility that this still may not be the right Bridget. Perhaps the right Bridget had an unlisted phone number or wasn't on social media. However, the one he'd found had the right name, location, and physical description. The possibility that she *was* the right Bridget made his heart beat faster in anticipation. On his way out of the museum, he stuck his head into Jonathan's office. "If anyone is looking for me, please let them know I'll be back after lunch. I have an appointment to get to."

Jonathan gave him a thumbs up. "Sure thing, Dr. S."

Once Morty arrived at the apartment of the dark-haired Bridget, he noticed how fidgety he was. Perhaps excitement and all the caffeine he'd consumed had not been a good mix. He took a deep breath and knocked.

"Yes?" said the middle-aged woman who answered the door.

"Good morning. I'm Dr. Morty Smithton, head curator at the Museum of Ancient History," he said, showing her his work badge that displayed his name and photograph. "I'm looking for Ms. Bridget Wells."

"I'm Bridget Wells." She looked up at him with curiosity.

"Madam, I've dedicated much of my life's work to studying a certain jewelry set from ancient Mallandia, and I'm currently doing some research into the family who's passed it down through the generations. During the course of my investigation, I've come to understand that you recently donated a piece from that set—a necklace—to a local thrift store. I was hoping to speak to you about that."

"Oh, you must've gotten my name from Doreen, the owner of the shop, right?"

"Yes, ma'am."

"Well, you're certainly welcome to come in and ask

me whatever you'd like, but I should let you know that the necklace wasn't passed down through my family." She opened the door and Morty stepped inside the bright, airy apartment.

"Oh, is that so? May I ask how you came to possess it?"

"Sure, I'm happy to tell you what I know, but it isn't much. Please, have a seat."

"Thank you," said Morty as he sat, careful to avoid the several dozing cats that had taken over the couch.

"It was the strangest thing," Bridget began. "Back in May, I received a package from an old friend I haven't heard from in over twenty years. Lorelei and I used to be really close, but we lost contact after a while. I wasn't a big fan of her husband, and so I didn't call her as much after they got married. The postmark on the package was from some city in Nevada I'd never heard of, so I'm guessing that the distance is another reason why we hadn't kept in touch. I didn't even know she'd moved out of the state." Bridget hung her head, a look of sadness washing over her face.

"What was in the package?" Morty asked, eager for her to continue.

"The necklace. Or amulet as Lorelei called it, along with very specific instructions. Lorelei wanted me to make sure that a young woman by the name of Anise received the amulet, but she didn't want Anise to know that it came from her. The instructions said to take the amulet to the thrift shop and somehow give it to Anise in a way she wouldn't question. Lorelei stressed how important that was to her. Strange, right?"

"Strange, indeed," agreed Morty. "Is that when you donated it?"

"Yes," she said. "I've always loved Lorelei, and I missed our friendship, even though it was my fault it fell apart since I hadn't called in so long. See, the last time I talked to her was the night I baby-sat her son. That was decades ago. When they came by to pick him up, Lorelei stayed in the car and her husband Dan didn't even say thank you. I was a little miffed so I waited for her to call me, but it never happened. I couldn't stop wondering if her husband was being controlling and not letting her call me. I don't have a television, and I don't read the news, so it was a couple years before I heard that she had gone missing. I wish I had reached out to her sooner, like maybe I could've done something.

"Since I know now that she seems to be alive and well, maybe she ran away from her husband, which I applaud, but I'm surprised that she didn't take her son with her. He was her pride and joy. I still think I could've done something to help, so in an attempt to ease my guilt, I decided to do everything I could to carry out her instructions to the letter. Since she'd been reported missing, I assume she didn't want anyone to be able to find her, so I didn't call the authorities because the letter told me not to. Honestly, that made me worry more about her. But on Memorial Day weekend, I took the amulet to the thrift shop right before it closed, and I told Doreen, the owner, that I thought it would make a great gift for a young woman. You know, someone confident enough to wear a large statement piece like that. I really tried to put it in her head that a *young* woman should be wearing it. Then I left and hoped she'd take the bait." Bridget laughed.

"Did I miss something?" Morty asked.

"No, I was just thinking of what happened on my way home from the thrift shop that day. This is where the story gets even stranger. This older woman stops me on the street and says she saw me earlier with the amulet and wanted to buy it from me. I told her I had just donated it to the thrift store, and she called me an idiot along with some other choice words I'd rather not repeat. She was pulling on her hair and was extremely upset. Then she tried to ask me where I got it and if I had found it at the bottom of a lake, but I just got away from her as fast as I could! She was getting irate and was scaring me!"

Morty furrowed his brow in worry. How on earth did Grace know Bridget had the amulet? "Interesting...Tell me, did your friend explain to you why she wanted the amulet to go to Anise? Are they related somehow?"

"No, not to my knowledge," answered Bridget. "Lorelei's parents passed away when she was in her late teens, and she didn't have any siblings or any cousins. Her only family I'd ever met or heard of was her husband and their son."

"Was there a return address on the package your friend sent?" asked Morty. "I'd like to write to her to see if she'd be willing to discuss the amulet with me."

"There was no street address," said Bridget, "just a postmark, but I wrote it down." She scribbled the half address on a small piece of paper and handed it to Morty. "I was really hoping I might hear something more from her since the package was so strange. I hope you'll let me know if you're able to find her exact location because I've been trying with no luck so far."

"Thank you," he said, as he took the address and put it in his wallet. "I most certainly will."

"I'm sorry I wasn't more help," Bridget apologized. "I told you I didn't know much."

"You were a *great* help, madam," Morty assured her before he walked out her door.

Is Grace hiding Lorelei? Morty wondered as he walked back to his car. He thought perhaps Lorelei was in hiding against her will per Grace's orders, possibly to keep the amulet safe and far away from him. However, that didn't sound like Grace. Grace would never trust something as precious as the amulet to anyone but herself. So why did Lorelei stay hidden away from even her son for all these years, and why did she suddenly want the amulet to go to Anise of all people? Was there anything else she knew about the Armor Jewelry—or even the Plate of Destiny? Perhaps she did, and she was in hiding *from* Grace instead of *for* Grace. Morty had already made up his mind to find out.

Chapter 28

Present day

Saturday, October 3, 2015

"What?!" Nate cried, standing up. *He has my mother?!*

"I'd be happy to explain everything," sputtered Kent, standing up as well.

Nate ignored him and strode down the hall to a room with a closed door. He tried the knob, but it didn't turn. He banged his fist on the door. "Mom? Lorelei?" When he didn't get a response, he turned to Kent. "Unlock the door," he demanded.

"I will," assured Kent, "but first I need to tell you what to expect."

Ignoring him again, Nate removed a lock pick from his wallet and went to work on the door.

"Nate, please, just listen to me first," pleaded Kent, trying to pull Nate's arm away from the door.

Nate shook him off and had the door open in a few seconds. He barged in, and what he saw made him rapidly inhale a deep breath. Taking careful steps, he felt emotions he couldn't recognize, but he didn't want to try to figure them out at this moment. A woman in her 50's with silver-streaked dark brown hair lay in a hospital bed with tubes coming out of her. She was hooked up to numerous machines, her eyes were closed, and she was motionless. Approaching her bed, he looked at her face. It looked different than the fuzzy bits and pieces he'd remembered, but he noticed her looks bore a striking resemblance to his own. "Mom?" he whispered, touching her arm.

"She can't respond to you, Nate. She's in a coma," Kent explained, coming up behind Nate.

Nate turned toward him, and without warning, he grabbed Kent by the collar and slammed him up against the nearest wall. "Why the *fuck* do you have my mother? And what the hell have you done to her?" he demanded.

Kent's eyes widened and a few nonsensical syllables escaped his lips. His hands fumbled against the wall, as if they were searching for the best way to handle the situation.

Nate felt Anise touch his arm. "This is probably why Kent wanted to talk to you before you came in here," she told him gently. "Let's hear him out now."

Nate let go of Kent's collar and took a step back, glaring at Kent.

Kent cleared his throat as he straightened his collar. Motioning with his hand to the door he said, "Let's talk."

Anise grabbed Nate's hand and led him back to the living room couch.

Kent sat on the chair across from them and started his story. "I was sincere when I made you that promise, Nate. I wanted to find your mother for you, but I had no idea where to start looking. Honestly, I doubted that she was even alive.

"Three years ago, when I heard on the news that you, your father, and Grace had been arrested at the Springfield Museum for attempting to steal the chalcedony earrings, it made me wonder what may have happened to prompt Grace to attempt to get the earrings at that time. I thought maybe Morty Smithton had done something or was planning something to make her react. So I watched him carefully for the next several months. There was nothing suspicious in his behavior until I learned he was planning a trip to a remote town in Nevada—a place he has no ties to. I asked him if this was work related, and he said yes, that he had a lead on something he'd spent years searching for. The only thing I've ever known Smithton to spend years searching for is the complete set of Armor Jewelry.

"When I thought about it, it didn't make sense. He knew which museum the earrings were in. He knew where the ring was—he had kept track of it since he'd met Richard Woods. When Woods died, his parents gave the ring to his sister, Isabelle. She never married, but had a son, named him after her brother, and eventually gave the ring to him. I knew Smithton already had the cuff because Lorelei had given it to him—over two decades ago. And I heard that you had the amulet, Anise. I have a friend on the force who told me the whole story. Apparently, Grace was trying to blame you for why she had broken into the Springfield Museum when you weren't even there?

"Anyway, it all seemed suspicious to me, so I decided to go with my gut and follow Morty. I didn't have a clue where exactly he was going, so I made sure to book a seat on the same flight. He was flying first class, of course, and was with one of his colleagues so he never noticed me back in coach. Once we landed in Las Vegas, I rented a van with tinted windows; I figured it would be easier to stay unnoticed by Morty that way.

"I followed him out into the middle of nowhere and had to stay pretty far behind so he wouldn't notice he had someone trailing him. He and his associate stopped near a remote neighborhood and got out and started walking. When they were far enough ahead, I followed suit, but went around a different way in an attempt to get close enough to hear what they were saying. When I caught sight of them, they were peering through someone's fence, and I could hear them talking to a woman. I could only pick up bits and pieces because they were talking in hushed tones, but I did catch them calling her 'Ms. Brevain.'

"By the time I got close enough to hear them better, it was too late, and I heard a gunshot. They started running, and so did I. They left, but I went to get my van and pulled up to the front of the house. I told her captors that I was the new local coroner, and I took her body and drove off, just far enough away so they'd think I'd left. I couldn't just show up at a hospital with an unconscious woman with bullet wounds and no explanation. Luckily, I always have my medicine bag with me. By some miracle, I was able to stabilize her long enough to get her back home. Here I have the ability and resources to take care of her."

"Has she been in a coma this whole time?" asked Anise.

"Yes," said Kent. "Unfortunately though, there's nothing else I can do for her. The machines are keeping her alive."

Nate saw Anise looking at him with tear-filled eyes. He looked back at her but emotional numbness had taken over. It was hard to think, much less react. She squeezed his hand, and he squeezed back.

"So, there's no hope?" she squeaked out.

"There's always hope," Kent said. "There is one thing that can save her."

"What's that?" asked Nate.

"We'd need to get all four pieces of Armor Jewelry," Kent began. "Although the cuff was mainly used to control the minds of the Mallandian troops to think as one, it was also a powerful healer. But it can only heal when used with the other three pieces, as they increase its power."

"So the *cuff* is the piece that heals!" Anise exclaimed. "I asked Dr. Smithton if any of the pieces had healing powers, and he led me to believe they didn't. He didn't even mention the cuff at all." She frowned but must've put her anger aside because she continued with excitement. "Anyway, we should be able to get all four pieces pretty easily! We have the amulet, and we know that Dr. Smithton has the other three. We just need to think of a way to take them."

"Even if you could, it's not as simple as that," began Kent. "The cuff was made specifically for the king of Mallandia, and drops of his blood were placed underneath the lapis lazuli stones. Only the king or a blood relative of his would be able to use the cuff properly. Its powers are instant if used by someone with king's blood. If not, the effects of the cuff take months to many years to take place, depending on how much the victim trusts the person using the cuff to begin with. Then the victim suffers schizophrenic-like side effects. If the exposure goes on long enough, the victim's deepest fears are brought to the surface and eventually the fears become the victim's new personality. The victim actually turns into what they fear the most."

Nate remembered his grandmother's words—that she hadn't always been "like this." He wondered if she had turned into what she feared the most from Smithton's attempts to brainwash her with the cuff. If she had, then what she feared the most was something extremely scary.

Anise narrowed her brow. "Wait a minute. Kent, Dr. Smithton keeps asking me to donate blood, but hasn't given me an actual reason why. I think I may have a connection to the Jewelry beyond owning the amulet." Anise looked at Nate. "Show him the letter."

Nate pulled out the letter Lorelei had written for him from an inside pocket of his jacket and unfolded it. Handing it to Kent, he explained how he got it. "Both you and Anise are named in the letter," Nate explained, "and she never even met Anise. We were hoping you might be able to tell us why."

Kent took the letter and read it. He looked at Anise. "She says the Armor Jewelry is your birthright."

"Do you think I might have king's blood?" Anise asked Kent.

"It seems that Lorelei thought so," Kent replied, looking thoughtful. "And if Morty wants your blood, it seems he thinks so, too."

"I bet Smithton thinks that if he can get Anise's blood, he'd be able to use the cuff with instantaneous effects," Nate speculated. "So, why hasn't he just killed her and taken it? He's had plenty of opportunity to do so."

"It doesn't work that way," Kent explained. "The cuff was designed so that the king could insert whatever thoughts he wanted inside the heads of others. If there was a thought he didn't want to transfer to them, it wouldn't, because it wasn't his desire. It must be the *will* of the owner of king's blood to transfer ideas. Basically, the blood must be *willing* blood."

"That must be why he keeps wanting me to understand and accept his utopia plan," Anise said. "So I'll *willingly* give him my blood."

"Utopia?" Kent asked.

"Dr. Smithton is obsessed with using the Armor Jewelry to create a utopia," Anise explained.

Wrinkles appeared on Kent's forehead as he thought about that. "It doesn't seem like Morty to believe something like that would be possible, even with the Jewelry. He's very logical and knows full well that the Jewelry has limitations."

"If that's the case, then why would he keep insisting on it?" Anise wondered out loud.

"I think I know," Kent said. "Morty's been experimenting with the cuff, just like my father asked him to. He's been brainwashing people he knows into accepting what he tells them. He must've thought if he can get them to believe something that farfetched, then he's really got them under his control. It's not the idea itself that he had to repeat over and over to brainwash them. He only needed to establish his own leadership with the cuff over them. He could've said any ridiculous thing and it would've worked." Kent shook his head. "It's sad. Grace isn't the only one who's dramatically changed. Morty isn't who he used to be either."

"That's why he kept asking Jonathan to bring me by the museum," Anise realized. "He thought eventually I'd be brainwashed too and willingly donate my blood."

"Why wouldn't he have told you something more believable?" Nate asked her. "If he had said it was for a blood drive or something, you may have done it."

"Maybe," she agreed. "But in that case, I could have felt *obligated* to do it, but I wouldn't necessarily have been *willing*. There's a difference. And like Kent said, Dr. Smithton wanted to be sure. So if I agreed to donate blood for something ridiculous like his utopia, there'd be no question as to my willingness." She smiled at Nate. "But the good news is that if I *do* have king's blood, I can save your mother. I can finally help Jonathan, too."

"If you have king's blood, Anise, according to the legend, you have much more than that to do," said Kent.

"What do you mean?" Anise asked.

"The legend states that a blood relative of the king's must always be alive in order to protect the Plate of Destiny."

"The what?" Anise looked at Kent with wide eyes.

Nate looked down at his lap. He couldn't tell Anise he'd already known about the Plate of Destiny without explaining that he had gone to see Grace, which Anise had specifically asked him not to do.

"The Plate of Destiny supposedly contains information that is supposed to only be known by the Mallandian gods," Kent told them. "It has the secrets of life and death written upon it. The royal family was considered to be closer to being like the gods than anyone else, so they were entrusted with the safekeeping of the Plate and were granted the Armor Jewelry for that reason. Only the one who has possession of all four pieces of Jewelry will be able to find the Plate. They used the Jewelry as armor for their soldiers during war, but its main purpose was for the protection of the Plate. This Plate is what Morty and Grace are ultimately after."

"Up until this point, I would've thought that Dr. Smithton must want the Plate to help him create his utopia. But now I know that can't be right. He must have a different reason," Anise said. "Nate, what do you think *Grace* wants with it?"

He shrugged. "Satan only knows." Remembering Grace's words about not being affected by the cuff, Nate asked, "Are there people who are immune to being brainwashed by the cuff? Or does it work equally well on everyone?"

"According to the trip journals, no one is immune to the cuff," Kent explained. "Some people may be less susceptible to being brainwashed than others, but it would take a very emotionally strong person to be able to sidestep the effects. We're talking extreme strength, will, and determination to resist the cuff. Plus, like I said, the more you trust the person, the faster they can brainwash you."

"Interesting," Nate replied. Emotionally strong would not have been how he'd describe his grandmother, who he'd always thought to be emotionally immature. She was always illogically giving in to her temper, feeling sorry for herself, and blaming everyone around her. However, she wasn't brainwashed, even though Smithton had tried. Maybe she was right—maybe she'd be a completely different person without the side effects from the cuff and whatever it had turned her into. Nate felt he would have developed a new respect for Grace at that moment if he didn't hate her so much. The more he thought about how Grace had wanted his mother dead, the angrier he got.

"Now I feel guilty for being angry with Jonathan for not being able to fight off the brainwashing," Anise muttered.

"Anise," said Kent, "if you do have king's blood, then Lorelei is right—you are the only person who can stop Morty and Grace."

"Grace is in prison. I'm not sure what she'd be able to do from in there. So if we can take the rest of the Jewelry from Dr. Smithton, will the Plate be safe?" Anise asked.

"I doubt Smithton will give up that easily," Nate argued. "And even though Grace is in prison, it's not like her to give up either."

"Nate's right," agreed Kent. "Step one will be to get all the Jewelry. Step two will be to find the Plate of Destiny before Smithton finds a way to take the Jewelry back and find it himself."

"Do we really need to find the Plate?" Nate asked. "What good is that going to do?"

"That's up to the two of you. We don't know what Morty and Grace plan to do with it, and according to the legend, it's the responsibility of Anise and her blood relatives to protect it," Kent reminded him.

Nate glanced at Anise and then turned back to Kent. "What would happen if she didn't? That's a lot to ask of someone who didn't volunteer for this."

During the moment of silence that followed, Kent got up to make coffee.

Anise leaned over and whispered in Nate's ear. "I really don't care about the Plate of Destiny. But I do want the cuff and the rest of the Armor Jewelry. I think I might be able to use it to help my brother Les heal from his fainting issue."

"Why are we whispering?" he whispered back.

"I never told anyone else that I have a brother. You and I are the only ones who know that Les also has king's blood, and I'd like to keep it that way. Given everything that's happened, we have to be careful about who we trust."

"You're right," Nate said.

"I tried healing Les with the amulet and ring, and that didn't work. When I asked Dr. Smithton if it was the earrings that had the healing powers, and he showed me they didn't, I had no choice but to give up because I didn't know about the cuff yet. But now that I know it's the cuff that has the healing powers, maybe I can still heal Les after all! Will you help me?"

"Of course, honey. You don't have to ask."

Kent entered the room with a tray and Anise and Nate accepted the cups of coffee he handed them.

"So what good would finding the Plate of Destiny do for Grace or Smithton?" Nate asked. He wasn't sure that Anise's plan to ignore its existence was a good idea. If Grace wanted it badly enough to kill for it...it must be powerful. And Grace with that much power was a scary thought.

"I'm afraid I don't know. My father's journals say it holds the secrets for life and death. Grace and Morty must know more."

"And where is it?" Nate asked. Maybe he could find it and hide it from Grace so she wouldn't go after Anise for it.

"According to the journals, my father spent significant time in Europe searching for it. He believes it's likely that a cave he found that was very near the location where he discovered Mallandia was the original home to the Plate. He found other artifacts in the cave but not the Plate, so he believes that the Plate had been moved at some point. He speaks of another legend one of his students had written a report about, in which a scientist in the 1800's had found and stolen the Plate but could never figure out how to read it. He thinks the scientist may have brought the Plate to America and hidden it in a cave in the panhandle of Florida."

"And it's never been found?" Anise asked.

"No. My father's been searching for it for decades. If he hasn't found it, then it's still hidden. You have a chance to find it before he does."

"First things first," Nate interjected. "We need to come up with a plan to get the Jewelry from Smithton."

"I'd like to help," Kent offered. "I think I have an idea."

Chapter 29

Approximately 4300 years ago

Y ou sent for me, Your Majesty?" Dagan greeted the king, kneeling. He squinted in the dark room lit only by the setting sun's last rays through the window.

The king struggled to sit up in his bed and cringed while the physician cleaned out a day-old wound under the king's rib cage. "As you know Dagan," the king began, "this is not the first attempt on my life in these last few months. The security measures you put in place to protect my army, my cuff, and the Plate of Destiny did not take into consideration my own personal safety!"

"My most humble apologies, Your Majesty," Dagan replied quickly, his knees beginning to ache from the stone floor.

"In addition, word has been spreading of a commoners' search party to locate the Plate of Destiny! More protection for the Plate is greatly needed!"

"If I may explain?"

The king scowled but granted Dagan his request.

Dagan continued. "The importance of king's blood in using the cuff was not meant to be common knowledge.

Yarim was spouting the secrets of king's blood immediately before he was publicly executed. Unfortunately,
Yarim had not yet revealed that His Majesty's blood must
be *willing* blood for the cuff to work before his brain was
removed. I had immediately begun working on extra
security measures for His Majesty's safety and had a
message sent to you."

The king nodded. "I remember the message, but the
details were entirely too vague. You've been working on
this for months now. What progress have you made?"

"I'm almost done, Your Majesty! If His Majesty will
grant me another week, I'll—"

"The fate of your existence is now the same as mine,"
interrupted the king. "If I live and thrive, so will you. If I
am assassinated, your manner of death will match mine!
You have until dawn!" he boomed.

"Yes, Your Majesty," said Dagan with a bow of his
head. He stood and hurried off on his throbbing knees to
his workshop. It was going to be a long night.

AT DAWN, FRONDOK FOLLOWED HIS FATHER Dagan as
he made his way to the king's chambers. Awake and
propped up with pillows, the king was already waiting.
"Enter, Dagan," he commanded.

Dagan stepped into the room and Frondok nervously
followed. Frondok had not long ago turned of age, was
promoted to his father's assistant Jewelry engineer
instead of apprentice, and had recently taken a wife. He
had never before been to the king's chambers and looked
around in wonder at the fine linens and furniture. Next to
the king were several guards. Many more had been hired
since the assassination attempts. As his eyes roamed the
room, he saw the aging physician mix up a drink for the
king to help with his pain. A healer softly chanted in the

corner to protect the room from evil spirits. Frondok's eyes then landed on the seer. She had long, golden silky hair, and there was a knowing in her eyes that frightened him.

"Speak!" The king's booming voice echoed in Frondok's ears.

"I have done as you commanded, Your Majesty," Dagan began. "I have created additional security measures to ensure neither His Majesty nor the Plate of Destiny will be harmed. Upon your approval, these measures will be made public knowledge so the commoners will understand that harming His Majesty will not result in a fortunate outcome."

"Continue," the king said. His eyes were narrow from the pain he still suffered.

"Previously, the Plate was easily recognizable by sight," said Dagan. "As of now, it has been disguised and hidden in the cave with many other bronze plates. Anyone looking for it will not know for certain which one is the Plate of Destiny. Only a person wearing all four pieces of Armor Jewelry will notice the sheen upon the correct Plate. It will sparkle like the sun on the Baltic Sea.

"In addition, the wisdom written on the Plate has been hidden in the Realm of All Time. Since we live in a world with fixed linear time, no human eyes shall ever be able to read the Plate, even if they figure out which one is the Plate of Destiny.

"I have also taken care to construct another amulet for His Majesty to wear in case of threat to his person. My most humble apologies that I did not have one ready when the first wore out."

"Good work, Dagan!" the king praised. "Although I should like to know more about where the wisdom from the Plate resides, if not on the Plate itself. What is this 'Realm of All Time' you speak of?"

"Certainly," replied Dagan. "The wisdom is still written on the Plate," he explained. "However, it can only be read by the gods, as they live eternally with no time and all time. Allow me to show you a demonstration." He took out a small, flat piece of bronze and a chisel. Working quickly, he carved some writing in the metal. "Here you can see my writing." Closing his eyes, he took a deep breath. The occupants of the room gasped as the writing disappeared. "Now the writing is hidden in the Realm of All Time. No human eyes shall ever see it again."

"Amazing!" he heard the healer say.

The healer reached out and touched a finger to the bronze piece Dagan held. "Your stunt fails to impress me, Dagan," she spoke up. "I can still see your writing clear as day."

"What? Impossible!" said Dagan.

"Very possible," argued the seer.

"No!" protested Dagan. "I've met seers who have vision into minds, hearts, or several cities away, but never a seer who can peer into the Realm of All Time! It is where the gods reside!"

"Explain yourself, seer," the king said.

"Different seers have different abilities," she began. "I have been blessed with the very rare ability to see within the Realm of All Time. I can see the present fully, no matter where it may be happening. Other seers like me may either see the past or future, but all of us can see into only one segment of time. Regardless, as soon as I touched the piece of bronze, your writing appeared well within my view, Dagan."

"I cannot believe that!" argued Dagan. He quickly made another carving in the metal, showed it only to the king, and then made it disappear. "What did I write?" Dagan demanded of the seer, showing her the seemingly blank piece of bronze.

She touched a finger to it. "You wrote that I'm a liar. That's obviously false, Dagan," she replied.

The seer was correct. Frondok watched his father's eyes close as he accepted his fate. One didn't have to be a seer to know what was in store for Dagan.

"There is no room for mistakes from the royal Jewelry engineer," the king said to Dagan with regret in his voice. "I want you to know, Dagan, that you have always been an excellent engineer. However, perhaps you are getting too old. Mistakes could lead to my death or the loss of the Plate of Destiny. I cannot take any more chances, not when the gods are depending on me." He closed his eyes for a brief moment. "Privately and with dignity," he added, directing his last comment to his guards.

"Good-bye, son," Dagan said as he was ushered out of the chambers, a look equal parts fear, shame, and acceptance on his face. "I know you'll make your family proud."

Frondok tried to protest in horror, but only a squeak came out. Before he could compose himself, the king spoke to him.

"Frondok, as Dagan's only assistant, I hereby appoint you to the position of my new royal Jewelry engineer. You have one week to fix your father's mistakes. Now leave me." He lay back and accepted the medicinal tea the healer had prepared for him.

"Yes, Your Majesty," Frondok replied, still in shock. His breath was heavy as he made his way back to the royal engineering lab.

LITHINY WALKED CAREFULLY TO NOT SPILL the tea she made for her husband Frondok that morning. She had been a gift from a far-away land to the king. Since the king had no unmarried sons, he had gifted Lithiny to Dagan's son as an honor. Her red hair flowed gently in the breeze, and she was aware of the stares she received from the people she passed. She was from another land, and her exotic looks brought her more attention than she cared to receive. Lithiny did her best to ignore the unwanted looks and spent all her time with her husband or learning the language of her new people. She was grateful that her intelligence had allowed her to pick it up very quickly. "Frondok?" she called upon reaching the lab. "Are you back yet?"

She heard a low mumble. "Yes."

He sat on a chair with his head in his hands. With hurried steps, she reached her husband, placed the tea on the table in front of him, and put a hand on his shoulder. "What's wrong?"

"They made me royal Jewelry engineer," he replied through his hands.

"That's a great honor!" she stated and then realized what might be amiss. "But wait, where's Dagan?"

"They killed him," he spat, raising his head, his eyes full of fury.

Lithiny was already crying for him. Dagan had been such a good, kind man. "What happened?"

Frondok told her the whole story. "I swear I will avenge his death!" he concluded.

Lithiny sat beside him, her face scrunched in worry. "If you attempt to bring harm to the king, you will be killed as well. Do you have a plan?"

"Don't worry," he told her as he took her hand. "I won't kill him myself. I know what my fate would be if I did, and I promise I'll never leave you."

"So what will you do?"

"The commoners are already after the king's blood in order to make the cuff work correctly, in hopes of controlling the army and being unstoppable in finding the Plate of Destiny for themselves. I plan to use their greed as the means of indirectly killing the king."

"How so?"

"I plan on using the magic Dagan taught me that the gods had given to him through his visions. The writing on the Plate of Destiny will still be hidden in several different remote pockets of the Realm of All Time, in the past, present, and future, but *also outside of time* so no one seer can see it all, only small bits and pieces that will not make any sense to them. Only the gods will be able to see it fully. Also, from now on, king's blood will need to be spilled on the Plate in order for human eyes to see it reappear. The king will not be told this information, but I will make sure the commoners hear a rumor of this. The king's life and the lives of all his descendants will forever be in danger for the rest of all time."

"Why make the writing visible to human eyes at all?" asked Lithiny. "Why not just start the rumor? It need not be true. We do not want to upset the gods."

"There must be a way for humans to see it!" cried Frondok. "I want access to the knowledge of the Plate. With the power of the gods, I may be able to bring Dagan back from the dead!"

"But if the blood is spilled, will you and all other people be able to see the writing on the Plate or just seers?"

"No one will be able to see the writing completely. Most people will see nothing. Some seers may see small pieces, depending on which part of the Realm is visible to them, but it will not be enough to make any sense to them."

"Then how will *you* be able to read the Plate?" Lithiny asked.

"I have a plan," Frondok explained. "I've just finished creating another jewel that will allow me to bestow upon someone the powers of a very special seer. This seer will be able to peer into the Realm or anywhere and see things as they really are. This includes seeing the knowledge on the Plate as the gods have written it."

"Who will be this new seer? You?"

"Of course not. All seers are women." He took his wife's hands. "That's where you come in."

"Me?" she asked nervously.

"Yes. I have just now finished creating a seer's jewel out of this obsidian," Frondok told her, holding up a shiny black stone in a setting of an alloy of gold, silver, and copper. It was attached to a long, straight handle of the same metal. "There will be a brave commoner willing to risk his life for a chance at the Plate's knowledge. When searching for the Plate, in order to recognize the special sheen Dagan put on it, he would need access to the four pieces of Jewelry. I will do what needs to be done to help this commoner obtain the Armor Jewelry so he will be able to find the Plate, bring it to the kingdom, kill the king, and spill his blood on the Plate."

Lithiny looked down in thought. "I thought you told me the king's blood had to be willing blood."

"For the *cuff* to work properly, yes," Frondok replied. "The blood spilled on the *Plate* need only be from the king or his descendants, it need not be willing."

"So once the blood is spilled, then what?"

"I have no doubt I'll be notified immediately, as they will want someone to blame for the king's death, just as they blamed Dagan for the assassination attempts. This is a good thing, as the blood that is spilled on the Plate will only work while the blood is still fresh. You and I will make our way to the dead king and the Plate. The commoner will be killed. The king's seer will admit she cannot read the Plate and no one will have any proof that I have done anything wrong. In fact, the seer will be blamed for the entire event."

"How is that?" asked Lithiny, wondering how that could possibly be.

"She sees the present. She should have seen the commoner coming to kill the king and warned him. Since she will not do that, they will believe she was part of the plan."

"Why will she not warn the king?"

"Because I have invoked a curse on the seer. If she tries to warn the king or any of his descendants that a royal must be killed for their blood in order to view the Plate's knowledge, she shall perish immediately, before her words of warning can move past her lips. It even matters not if the seer is using her powers to listen to our conversation right now. If she attempts to warn the king, she will die before he can hear her out. You will be able to read the Plate, and together we can bring back Dagan. And who knows what else we will be able to do with the knowledge you discover? The possibilities are endless!"

"A curse?" muttered Lithiny, a little fearful. "Surely the gods did not give Dagan the knowledge of curses?"

"I do not know all of Dagan's visions, but I have had my own, and I know the magic of curses."

Lithiny frowned, not sure of this reckless plan. "But so many things could go wrong! What if the king is killed by the commoner and we are not able to get to him in time to collect his fresh blood? Or what if you gain control of the army but several of the king's blood relatives are able to use the cuffs and overtake us?"

"Worry not. I have a plan for that as well. I cursed the king and his family. There must always be one royal with king's blood alive at all times. If we are not able to get to the king's fresh blood in time, we will always have another chance. All other relatives shall die an early death so there will not be enough to overtake us. The king's female relatives will all die in tragic accidents. The male relatives will simply sleep longer and longer until they wake no more."

"Another curse? Oh, Frondok!"

"I had to! Now stay still. I need you to create a connection with the seer's jewel. Hold it to your heart for several moments, then to your forehead for the same length of time."

"But Frondok," Lithiny said, "what if someone else should get a hold of this seer's jewel? Will they be able to become a seer as well and be able to read the Plate?"

"No," he replied, handing her the wand with the obsidian on it, "because I made this especially for you. Only a beautiful woman with hair of flame can use this seer's jewel, and you are the only woman I have ever seen that fits that description. Now, hold it to your heart and forehead as I have instructed."

Lithiny did as he asked and then saw a quick flash of red in the obsidian. "Am I now able to see things as they really are?" she asked.

"Almost. I will need to have the king use the powers of the cuff along with the rest of the Armor Jewelry on you. This will awaken your seer's abilities."

"How will we get the king to do that without telling him about it?"

"The king does not need to know why he is using the cuff. He simply needs to do it in order to awaken your abilities. He will not refuse to help us in an emergency situation, so we will fool him by begging him to use the cuff to heal your injury."

"What injury?" she asked him, feeling her body tense up.

"This one," he replied, as he picked up his dagger and sliced her arm nearly in two.

Chapter 30

Present day

Saturday, October 3, 2015

"I don't understand," Morty bewailed to the prison official as he sat on the visitor's side of the official's desk. "How did you get my name?" The headache and stomachache that plagued him wasn't just from the news he'd received the day before, but also from a case of insomnia the news had inflicted upon him.

"Your name was on some writing she had in her cell. We thought you might be a distant relative or a friend."

"So why call *me*? She has a son and a grandson."

"Her son is in prison. We left her grandson some voice messages, but he didn't respond. Probably isn't interested in picking up her personal items. Honestly, I can't blame him; there isn't much. She had some clothes and a watch. Her medication went to the coroner's office for further investigation." The official pushed the bag that contained the items over the desk to Morty.

"What happened?" Morty asked, fighting the sick

churning in his stomach.

"It was a suicide," the official replied, a somber look on his face. "I'm very sorry for your loss."

Morty narrowed his eyebrows. Grace would never commit suicide. Something wasn't right. "I want to see her. Where is she?"

The official wrote down an address and phone number for Morty on a small piece of paper. "This is the county coroner's contact information. But you better hurry. The autopsy is scheduled for later this afternoon."

* * *

"I'D LIKE TO SEE HER," MORTY said to the pathologist.

The pathologist cocked his head. "I'm sorry, the autopsy has already been performed."

Morty glared at him. "What do you mean? I was told that she'd be available for me to see until late this afternoon!"

"Her autopsy was moved up."

"Is it complete?"

The pathologist gave Morty a strange look. "...Yes. Why?"

"I'd still like to see her!" Morty demanded. "Where is she now?"

"She's being cremated as we speak."

Morty let out a deep, loud sob and sat down in the nearest chair. He pressed a handkerchief to his eyes. So that was it. Grace was gone. *I failed her.* Everything horrible and unforgivable he had done—the brainwashing of his associates, lying to Jonathan and Anise, and of course what had happened to Anise's parents and Lorelei—had all been for naught.

"I'm very sorry for your loss, sir," the pathologist comforted.

"What were the results of the autopsy?" Morty

demanded, standing up again.

"All the information you'd want to know will be in the autopsy report."

"I want a copy! Where can I get one?"

"Sir, I haven't finished writing it yet."

"Listen to me," Morty fumed. "Grace was a lifelong friend. Please save me the hassle and just tell me how she died."

"I can only disclose the results through the official autopsy report."

Morty had just about enough. He slammed his palm on the pathologist's desk. "Where is the crematorium? Who is claiming her remains?"

"Well, sir, there are several crematoriums in town and...uh...I'm not sure which one she went to."

Morty rose and took a step closer to him. The pathologist was trembling. "Something isn't right here. I want to know what happened to Grace," Morty hissed. "And I'm going to find out." He turned and left.

***

MORTY WATCHED FROM THE SHRUBBERY. AFTER a few hours of scratchy thorns and branches protesting his presence, he finally saw what he was waiting for. The pathologist's tires screeched as he pulled full speed into his driveway and then slammed on the breaks. He jumped out and started running at top speed toward his front door. Morty jumped from the bushes with one hand grabbing him as the other covered his mouth.

The pathologist squirmed and let out muffled shouts. "What do you want?" he mumbled through Morty's gloved hand.

"All I want are the results of the autopsy," Morty hissed in the pathologist's ear, as he dragged him behind a tall shrub in the yard and pointed a gun in his face.

"There's a copy of the report in my bag!" The pathologist reached into his bag with a shaky hand and pulled out a form to hand to Morty.

Morty took the form and released the pathologist. "Not a word about this," he warned.

The pathologist shook his head rapidly in agreement, then ran inside his house. "Is everyone okay?" Morty could hear him shouting. "Is everyone back home? Is everyone okay? What happened to you?"

Curious. What was that about?

Shrugging it off, Morty walked the half block to his rental car, got inside, and sobbed. He tried to compose himself as he read the report. "Oh, Grace," he kept repeating, hanging his head. After reading the report three times, he set it down on the passenger's seat and stared out the window as he thought about the pathologist's exaggerated worrying about the safety of his family. His eyes narrowed as his brain tried to make sense of the situation. But nothing made sense. His grief was so painful he wanted nothing more to do with the Armor Jewelry or the Plate of Destiny. Although, if he quit helping Dromly search for them, would he end up gunned down like Thomas? He pulled his new smartphone out of his pocket and turned it on, trying to remember the lessons Jonathan had given him in how to use it. He'd never wanted one, not understanding how this fancy phone was any better than the ones with actual buttons. Squinting through his glasses, he dialed George's number. "Get everyone ready," Morty commanded. "We act on the plan as soon as I get back!"

Monday, October 5, 2015

EXHAUSTED FROM HIS TRIP, MORTY SLOWLY trudged

through the hallway at the museum just after closing time. His umbrella left a trail of drops in the hallway. "Hello, George," he said, poking his head in his colleague's office. "Is everyone ready to go?"

"Yes, boss," George answered. "We're ready as soon as you are."

"Good. Thank you." Morty wondered what the museum director would do when he and all of his colleagues left for a "vacation" at the same time. The idea made him chuckle. No matter. Once he had the Plate of Destiny, maybe he'd consider retirement.

"You have a visitor in your office," George told him as Morty turned to leave. "She's been waiting there for the last hour."

What now? Morty wasn't up to dealing with anyone at the moment. He balked when he stepped into his office. "Anise? I certainly didn't expect you here." Her hair was damp from the inclement weather, and she'd pulled it back into a braid that'd left a wet mark on the back of her jacket.

"After what happened last time, I didn't think I'd ever come back here, either," she replied.

"Well, what do you want?" he asked curtly as he sat at his desk. He eyed the amulet around her neck. It would be so easy to put on the other Jewelry and take it from her. However, then he'd never get her willing blood. Not unless he blackmailed her. Jonathan was supposed to come up with that plan, as he knew Anise best, but it seemed he'd been putting it off. Morty made a mental note to discuss that with him.

"I actually wanted to see Jonathan and apologize to him," Anise began. "But he's not here, so I thought I'd start with you."

"Jonathan's not here?" asked Morty. "He should be." He wondered if Jonathan was still at home packing for their upcoming trip.

"No, he's not," she replied. "Anyway, I wanted to

apologize for how dismissive I was about your utopian vision. At first, I thought it was a joke that got out of hand, so I didn't take it seriously. But the last time I was here, Jonathan told me that you really do have a way to bring it to fruition and that it was up to you whether or not you'd share it with us."

"What's your point?" Morty asked, unable to hide his irritation, still thinking about everything that needed to be done.

"My point is that he was right," she continued. "Dr. Smithton, you're one of the smartest people I've ever met. If you truly think that you have a way to make our world a utopia, then I believe you. I mean, it's not like I haven't seen stranger things," she said with a smile as she touched her amulet.

He stared at her, trying to decide what her motive was for telling him this. Did she mean what she was saying? Or was she trying to pull the wool over his eyes for some reason? Had the young Brevain put her up to something?

"Anyway," Anise continued, "Jonathan really believes in you and your utopia plan. I want to support him because he's always been supportive of me. And even though he doesn't want to be in a relationship with me anymore, I'll always consider him to be a good friend. Good friends believe in each other, help each other, and trust each other. So, that's what I'm trying to do today. I owe him that much. And I owe you, too, since you helped me when Grace was trying to take my amulet. I just ask that you don't try to keep me captive and brainwash me like the last time I was here. That was really frightening, and I want to be able to trust you."

Morty wanted to believe her. And he would have in a heartbeat if she hadn't gotten mixed up with Grace's grandson. She'd have to prove herself to him. "To be quite frank, I don't think Jonathan is interested in hearing apologies," he informed her. "And neither am I."

"I realize an apology is not enough," Anise agreed. "Which is why I wanted to make it up to you by donating my blood. I know that's something you've been asking for, and I'm almost ready to do so."

Morty couldn't believe his ears and sat up straight in his chair. Anise was going to give him willing blood? "I would appreciate that greatly," he told her. "But what do you mean you're *almost* ready?"

"Well, you have to admit, an idea for a utopia is a really difficult concept to accept for the average person," she began. "I'm trying, but if you don't explain your plan to me, I don't know that I'll be able to get fully on board with it. Think of me as an investor—someone who wouldn't front any money without truly understanding the business venture they're considering to help finance."

"That's fair," Morty said. "I certainly want you to be completely on board."

"I'm sure you have a very good reason for everything that you've done," Anise said. "Explain it to me, and I'll donate some blood."

If she was telling him the truth, this was his chance to get her blood—her willing blood. "What exactly do you want to know, my dear?" he asked, hoping he could get away with revealing only bits and pieces of his master plan.

"I want to know why you need my blood. And why are you using the cuff to brainwash Jonathan?"

"The cuff wasn't meant for brainwashing," explained Morty. "It was originally used by the Mallandian army to get all the soldiers on the same page. You see, some soldiers led a revolt because battle conditions were especially harsh back then, and the soldiers didn't always agree with what they were commanded to do, to put it mildly. The king and his officials lived in constant fear of mutiny. The cuff was created for that purpose. Once it was used to get everyone on the same page, the officials had nothing to fear from their army. My intentions in using the cuff are the same as the Mallandian king. I merely want to get all of my team on the same page when it comes to creating this utopia."

"How is that not brainwashing?" she asked.

"I have no doubt everyone on my team would be in agreement with my actions, if they understood my plan fully," Morty asserted.

"So why not just explain it to them?" Anise asked.

"Because I imagine they'd react the same way you did when Jonathan introduced it to you—with extreme skepticism or disbelief. In addition, I'd first have to convince them of the authenticity of the Armor Jewelry, something that's best left to a limited few, don't you agree?"

"I suppose, yes, given all the trouble it's already caused for us."

"Using the cuff is a much faster way of getting to where everyone would be anyway. I'm simply taking the easier, quicker route."

"Okay, well, why do you need my blood?" she asked again. "I don't believe that it's for reserves in case of battle."

"You're right," Morty agreed. "It's to cure my team of the negative effects the cuff has had on them. I know you've noticed the change in Jonathan's behavior lately. These side effects were something I was unaware of until they began happening. I of course don't want to leave my team to suffer these consequences forever, so I need your blood to cure them."

"How will my blood cure them?" Anise asked.

"You always wanted to know which piece of Armor Jewelry was used for healing. Now you know – it's the cuff coupled with king's blood." Morty explained to her about the necessity of the wearer of the cuff having king's blood for the cuff to work instantaneously.

"I'm a descendant of Mallandian royalty?" she asked with wide eyes.

"You are."

"Wow. Dr. Smithton, I'm sure you realize this is a lot to take in, and given that you were untruthful to me before, I'm sure you also understand that I have some reservations about simply taking your word for it."

He frowned at her. She got the explanation she asked for. What could she want now?

She continued. "Before I give you some of my blood, I'd like some proof that the cuff works the way you say it does. I'd like to put on all four pieces of Armor Jewelry and try to cure Jonathan of the cuff's side effects. If it works, I'll donate my blood immediately."

"Absolutely not!" huffed Morty, getting up and opening his office door for Anise. What a waste of time. "Get out," he commanded, trying to control his anger. Once Jonathan came back to the office, they'd need to immediately sit down and come up with a way to force her willingness to donate her blood.

"Wrong answer, Morty," said a voice coming through the doorway. "Where's the Jewelry?"

Morty turned his head and found that the voice was coming from his old friend who had just stepped into his office. "Kent?" Morty choked out in disbelief. "What's going on?"

Kent's expression showed mixed emotions as he closed and locked the office door and pointed a gun at Morty. "I know your plan, and it's never going to work. Just hand over the Jewelry, Morty."

"Where's Nate?" Anise mumbled to Kent. "He's supposed to be here, too."

Morty felt his heart start racing, and he wanted to run away, but a hasty retreat would be impossible with the locked door and Kent and the young lady blocking his path. He could hear Grace's voice in his head calling him a candy-ass. Attempting to look composed and unafraid, Morty laughed. "The museum offices are full of people. You'd never get away with shooting me."

"Do you know where Jonathan Casley is right now?"

Kent asked him.

ANISE FELT HER STOMACH CHURN. WHY was Kent bringing up Jonathan? And where *was* he anyway? Not to mention Nate? This wasn't part of the plan they had come up with the night before. She watched as Dr. Smithton's nostrils flared and his eyes narrowed. He had a lot of unforgivable faults, but it was obvious he really cared about Jonathan.

"What do you know about it?" Dr. Smithton demanded. He glared Kent and Anise.

Kent took out his phone and showed Dr. Smithton the screen. Anise peeked at the phone as well. They could see that Kent had the video chat application open and that Nate was on the line.

"Have you been wondering where Casley is, Smithton?" Nate asked him.

"What have you done with him?" cried Dr. Smithton.

Nate turned his phone so Dr. Smithton could see Jonathan in his own apartment, tied to a chair with his mouth duct taped shut. The fear in Jonathan's eyes was undeniable. "*Kent* may not be able to shoot *you*," Nate smirked, "but I'd have no problem blowing Boy Scout's brains out right now."

Anise and Dr. Smithton both let out a cry of horror.

"No!" cried out Anise with a wavering voice. "Nate, what are you doing? This wasn't part of the plan!" Tears began to roll down her cheeks. "Let him go!"

"Sorry, honey. Plans change," Nate said coldly. "Smithton, give them the Jewelry."

Dr. Smithton took a deep, shaky breath. He grabbed a key from his desk drawer and then took an unabridged dictionary from his bookshelf and put it on his desk. The book made a loud, metallic sound on the wooden desktop.

Anise realized the dictionary was a safe in disguise at the same time she felt a panic attack coming on. Her breathing quickened and her arms began going numb. She hadn't noticed Nate and Kent adding to their plan without her. Why didn't they include her? The purpose of this whole venture was to get the Jewelry in her possession. She wasn't sure if she should trust either of them now. Nate was being a completely different person than he was yesterday.

She watched Kent walk up to Dr. Smithton to be closer to the safe as they had planned. That way, Kent could grab it once the dictionary-safe was opened, and Dr. Smithton wouldn't be able to quickly put on the Jewelry and fight back. At that moment, Anise decided that if the Jewelry was her birthright, she should be the one to grab it from the safe, especially now that she knew Nate and Kent had gone behind her back. If they could change the plan at the last minute, so could she.

She walked up to Dr. Smithton and ducked in front of him the moment the safe was opened. She reached in and grabbed the earrings at the same time the two men reached in as well. Dr. Smithton grabbed the ring while Kent snatched the cuff. Hurrying, the three of them put on the Jewelry.

Morty grabbed Kent's wrist. To Anise's surprise, the older man was surprisingly strong and was able to wrestle the gun from Kent.

Dr. Smithton pointed the gun at Kent. "Hand over the cuff!" he demanded. "And let Jonathan go!"

"I'm on my way," Anise heard Nate say through Kent's phone.

Since Anise had two pieces—the earrings and the amulet, she knew the situation was in her control. She lightly pushed Dr. Smithton, and the tremendous force caused him to lift into the air and slam against the wall behind him near the ceiling. He fell to the ground and winced, grabbing his arm and hip. Anise's guilt caused her to look away.

Dr. Smithton pointed the gun at Kent again from where he sat on the floor. "Come near me again and he dies," Dr. Smithton told Anise.

"No one's shooting anyone," said Anise in a firm voice as she stepped between them. "Now give me the ring, Dr. Smithton."

There was a hard *knock-knock* at the door. "Morty, I thought I heard something fall," called a male voice from outside Dr. Smithton's door. The handle rattled. "Morty? Are you okay?"

"George!" Dr. Smithton shouted. "Help!"

Anise heard a key being inserted into the lock and the door opening.

"What's going on here?" cried George, looking at his colleague on the floor with a gun and the two strangers with pieces of the Armor Jewelry. He awkwardly entered the room on his crutches that he still needed because of the car accident.

"Alert everyone," Dr. Smithton told him. "We have a situation."

"Yes, Morty," agreed George, his eyes glazing over.

"George, stay right where you are," said Kent, grabbing George and pushing him into a chair. Anise noticed that George's eyes immediately became clear again at the sound of Kent's voice.

"George, get up!" commanded Dr. Smithton.

George's eyes glazed over again, and he attempted to rise from the chair.

"Stay seated!" said Kent. George's eyes cleared.

"What's happening?" cried George, pulling on his hair.

"I'd like to know that too," Anise said to Kent.

"I read about this in my father's trip journals," Kent explained to Anise. He turned to George. "George, even though Morty isn't wearing the cuff right now, you're loyal to him because of the ideas he's already implanted in your head. But once *I* try to use the cuff on you, you're receiving new ideas from me. Since I don't have king's blood, it's like the brainwashing is starting over, so your mind has to be clear to be able to receive the messages."

"Brainwashing?" George repeated, a confused look on his face.

"Yes. It's futile for me to try to control your mind though, as it would take months to years for me to be able to do so. However, there's someone here that does have king's blood." Kent looked at Anise, and she could tell he was about to throw her the cuff.

In one swift motion, George used a crutch to assault Kent's shin bone as hard as he could. Kent let out a cry of pain as he doubled over to grab his leg. George smashed his crutch against Kent's face as he was bent over, sending him straight to the ground by George's feet. George bent forward and ripped the cuff off Kent's wrist. Kent and Anise both lunged at George but were unable to touch the cuff before he threw it to Dr. Smithton, who fastened it onto his wrist. Anise took in a deep breath and started backing away. Now that she and Dr. Smithton both had two pieces of Jewelry, they were equally matched. If either attempted to use the Jewelry's powers on the other, they would find themselves at a stalemate. And when the Jewelry's powers cancelled each other out by being used against each other, Anise would be vulnerable to being harmed at that time. Frustrated at Kent for losing a piece of the Jewelry, she shouted at him, "Now it's time to go! Before you lose another piece of Jewelry!"

"You're not going anywhere," said Dr. Smithton, finally able to stand up. "TEAM!" he shouted. "My office!"

Within seconds, several of Dr. Smithton's glazed-eyed colleagues began filing into the room. At least twenty men and women of varying ages were surrounding Anise and Kent.

"This young lady has two pieces of Jewelry that belong to me," Smithton told his brainwashed army. "Get them back."

Chapter 31

Two years ago

Wednesday, January 9, 2013

W hat do you mean, you didn't get it?" Morty boomed at George.

"I'm sorry, Morty, she didn't want to participate in the blood drive. Said blood donation always makes her faint."

"Damn it!" Morty plopped in his office chair and took a moment to sulk. All that time setting up the fake blood drive wasted. Deborah Viston had also escaped the fake mugging and the fake carjacking George had attempted with the intention of using a knife and a vial. They had followed her into every public restroom she used for a month, waiting to steal a used feminine product, but discovered that she must've already gone through menopause as she no longer menstruated. *Now what?* Morty was getting frustrated. "Follow her, and see what she does and where she goes," Morty demanded. "Report everything back to me. In the meantime, I'll try to come up with another plan. We *must* get her blood."

✶ ✶ ✶

"GET UP," BEN VISTON ORDERED HIS wife.

"Leave me alone. I'm not going." Deborah Viston rolled over in bed and squinted up at him as he loomed over her. *Asshole.* "You've gotten old."

"If I have to go, so do you." He yanked the covers off of her and pulled her to her feet.

"Have you seen an older man lurking around the neighborhood?" she asked after she pushed him away from her.

"Nope," he answered, probably not even listening as he straightened his tie in the mirror.

"There was a blood drive at work today," Deborah continued, sitting back on the bed. "I could've sworn I saw the man who was running it walking by the house when I got home."

"You haven't gotten fired yet with all the days you've missed?"

"What would you know about that?" she snarled.

"Anise told me you stay in bed all day. You miss at least one day of work every week."

Deborah snorted. "Our daughter lies. She takes after her father."

She knew what he was seeing as Ben looked around the room. The hamper overflowed with dirty clothes. Crumbs had taken over the bedsheets and the floor. Dust bunnies had gathered in every corner. "I'm inclined to believe her," he said.

"Oh, what would you know?" Deborah spat, pulling a dress out of the hamper and spraying it with perfume. "You haven't been here in years. Why are you here anyway? You missed her graduation, but you're here for a dinner with her friends?"

"I happened to be passing through," he said. "It worked out."

"Do you even know what she's celebrating?" She slipped the wrinkled dress over her head.

"Of course I do," Ben replied. He looked at her and walked out of the room.

"It's her birthday," Deborah called out after him.

"I know!" came the annoyed voice from in the hall.

"She was also promoted to a manager last week," Deborah added.

His head popped back in the doorway. "Really? That's a great accomplishment."

Deborah rolled her eyes. "Oh, please. She works at the mall. I'm embarrassed for her."

Ben shook his head at her. "You need help. Go to the doctor. Get some drugs. Or therapy."

"You left. Don't pretend you care about me now." She looked in the mirror. Her hair was frizzy. Her eyes were droopy. Her mouth frowned. "Disgusting," she muttered to herself as she turned away.

"I've cared about you practically my entire life. I've cared *for* you practically my entire life."

"What the hell is that supposed to mean?" She found some old black boots with scuff marks on the floor of the closet and pulled them on.

"It means ever since we gave our son up for adoption, you've been acting like this. I tried everything I could to make you happy. I married you as soon as we turned eighteen."

"Out of guilt."

"I worked hard to support us."

"If by working hard you mean taking lavish vacations with each floozie du jour, then yes, you sure did."

"I know you miss our son. So do I. I think about Les a lot."

Deborah snorted. "Who names their child 'Lester?' That's an old man's name, even for back then. I would've named him Alistair.”

Ben rubbed the bridge of his nose. “They're practically the same name.”

“Oh, what do you know?” she scoffed.

“I even gave you another child. Why didn't having Anise make you happy?”

Deborah narrowed her eyebrows at him. “That's a lot of responsibility to put on the shoulders of a child that neither one of us wanted in the first place.”

Ben closed his eyes and sighed slowly. “I'm trying really hard to maintain my composure here. Can we *please* just get along for tonight?”

“Fine. And then when we get back home, we'll get to why you're really here. I have the papers. I'll sign them. Then you can leave again like you always do. But this time you won't ever have to come back.”

“Sounds good to me.”

✳ ✳ ✳

“DEBORAH AND BEN VISTON JUST LEFT in the car, Morty,” came George's voice through the phone. “I'm following them now.”

“Good, let me know where they go,” Morty replied. He felt his heart beat quicker. *I'm going to have king's blood! Tonight!*

“Do you want me to use the ring?” George asked. “It's clean and quick.”

“For heaven's sake, no! I don't want to kill them! Besides, there can't be any poison in the blood.”

“I have my gun with me. That's quick, too,” offered George.

“Open your ears, George, I said I don't want to kill them,” Morty replied. “No one needs to die. I just need a little bit of Deborah's blood.”

“That's going to be difficult to set up, Morty.”

"Difficult, but not impossible, George. Follow them. Tell me where they go, and we'll figure out how to do it depending on the route they take."

"Will do, boss."

Morty waited for George's phone call by pacing his office. He could think of nothing else. Half an hour later, the phone rang. "George?" he asked.

"Yeah, it's me. They drove out over the pass to go to dinner with a big group. Looks like they just sat down."

"We'll have to abort the mission for tonight. She's with too many people."

"No, Morty, she's a smoker. At some point she's sure to step outside by herself and that's when we'll do it. Get over here as fast as possible."

MORTY GOT OUT OF HIS CAR and met George in front of the restaurant where Anise, her friends, and her parents were having dinner. "I never knew this place was here." He'd almost driven right by the dirt road turn off. The small, family-owned restaurant was situated in a tiny mountain town at the end of the hidden road. Morty looked around and saw no other buildings in sight, only pine trees and a weak light that attempted to illuminate the parking lot.

"This is perfect," George told him. "No cameras on the building or in the parking lot. No other businesses where there might be cameras."

"Yes, agreed," said Morty. "Did you bring everything?"

George opened a tote bag that sat on his shoulder so Morty could see inside. There was a knife, a vial, gloves, rags, and chloroform.

"Excellent, thank you."

They waited in silence for several minutes and turned their heads when they heard the door swing open. Deborah Viston stepped outside and lit up a cigarette. "Good evening," she said, greeting the two men with a nod but barely glancing at them.

"Good evening, madam," Morty replied. "If you don't mind, the smoking area is around the side of the building."

"Oh, sorry," Deborah mumbled. She took another puff and turned around the corner of the restaurant.

"Now!" Morty whispered to George.

They put on their gloves. The two men quietly walked up behind Deborah, and George held a chloroform soaked rag over Deborah's face until the struggling stopped and she passed out. He cut her palm with the knife, and Morty caught her blood in the vial. They packed up their gear, left her on the ground, and made a hasty retreat back to town.

Thursday, January 10, 2013

THE NEXT DAY, GEORGE POKED HIS head into Morty's office. "Here," he said, putting a newspaper on Morty's desk. "You should read this."

Morty looked at the paper, and he felt his head start to spin. "Wait a minute! Deborah and Ben Viston are dead? How did this happen?"

"An accident. Looks like their daughter saw the whole thing. Paper says they were speeding because they were on their way to the hospital after Deborah was found passed out and bleeding. They swerved to avoid hitting a deer and were hit and pushed off the side of the road by an oncoming vehicle. Rolled down a cliff and were killed instantly."

Morty's stomach lurched with horror. This was all going terribly wrong. Putting his head in his hands, he almost screamed from the guilt. Even though he hadn't directly killed them, their deaths wouldn't have happened if it hadn't been for his actions. After a few minutes, he somewhat regained his composure and let out a shaky sigh. He hated himself but couldn't be angry with his colleague. George had been the easiest to brainwash and happily went along with everything Morty commanded him to do. "George, thank you. For everything you've done for me. At least we got what we needed. Because of the Viston's, we're one step closer to a utopia."

George gave him a quick nod and left the room.

Morty locked the door behind him and wept, wondering if all of this was worth it. He thought about Grace. "I can't stop now," he told himself. "I can't fail her." Morty took the vial he'd filled with Deborah Viston's blood the night before out of his desk drawer. He wiped his upper arm with a cotton ball he'd dipped in rubbing alcohol and removed the cap off the needle. Once some of the blood was inside the barrel of the syringe, he injected the blood into his arm and removed the needle. With anticipation, he put on the cuff and walked outside the museum to put his theory to the test.

"Hello," Morty said to a woman walking by. "Come in and check out the museum. We have a new exhibition."

"Some other time," the woman mumbled as she quickened her pace.

Morty frowned. When someone with king's blood used the cuff to brainwash another, the brainwashing effects were supposed to be instant. He now had Deborah's blood—king's blood—pumping through his veins. Why wasn't it working? He tried again. "Run and get me a coffee," he said to a man on a bench at the bus stop as he motioned toward the coffee shop across the street.

"Get your own fucking coffee," the man answered with a glare.

It's not working.

With his mind reeling from devastation and confusion, Morty returned to his office and opened the book of legends he'd taken from Lorelei Brevain. He'd read and reread the passage about the king's blood and the cuff several times, but this time he considered it more carefully. It said: "Any thought of the king's that he wishes to share shall become the thought of the target. The wishes and desires of the king will be fulfilled immediately by the target. The same power shall be held by anyone who possesses king's blood. Whatever their heart wills shall be done. Any thoughts the cuff's wearer does not will to be passed on shall not pass to the head and heart of the target. Transferrable thoughts and wishes, no matter with whom they originate, must come from the owner of willing blood, and willing blood must come from a willing heart."

"Wait a minute," Morty said out loud as he began to make the connection. Up until now, he'd thought that passage had meant whoever owns king's blood would be able to control the minds of others by will alone—with the cuff, of course. However, he misinterpreted it. It wasn't enough that he had king's blood and that he was willing to brainwash others. The blood itself had to be willing and had to originate from a heart that was willing to either transfer thoughts or donate blood. Deborah Viston's blood had been stolen. There was nothing willing about that.

Damn it!

Nausea threatened him, and he put his head on his desk as tears fell out of his eyes once more. The guilt he felt for the death of two innocent people was overwhelming. He also considered how he had negatively altered Anise's life forever. Anise, one of the kindest, most innocent of all people he had ever met, and the girl Jonathan couldn't stop talking about. He heard Grace's voice in his head telling him to stop being such a candy-ass. Still reeling from the guilt and shame, but somewhat comforted by the thought of his old friend, he wiped his tears

POISONING OF MINDS 439

and disposed of the blood in the restroom. He wondered how Grace was faring in prison.

Realizing that Anise was now his only chance at getting willing king's blood, he returned to his desk and put his head in his hands again. It was too heavy to stay up on its own, especially with all the thoughts swirling around inside it. The cuff worked without him having king's blood, but the effects took months to years and caused side effects in his targets. With king's blood, he would be able to use the cuff instantaneously without side effects, even if it didn't originate in his own body. However, the person from whom the blood was donated had to willingly relinquish control of their blood. So how was he going to get Anise to willingly give him her blood without telling her why? The fact that her blood was so valuable *could not* get back to Grace. Perhaps she already knew? Morty hoped that wasn't the case.

He looked at the cuff around his wrist as a plan formed in his mind. Ever since Jonathan began working for him, he had felt a great connection to the young man and considered him to be like the son he never had. Morty had promised himself he'd never use the cuff on Jonathan. He couldn't bear to see Jonathan suffer the side effects that the others had. However, brainwashing his young protégé may be the only answer to his current dilemma. Jonathan was very close to Anise and she listened to him. If he made Jonathan believe in the utopia, perhaps Jonathan, in turn, could convince Anise of its significance, and she'd be willing to give up her blood. Or at the very least, Jonathan could bring Anise to the museum often so she could be brainwashed directly.

He pulled his sleeve over the cuff and picked up his office phone. "Jonathan," he said, "could you come into my office, please?" He hung up the phone and took several antacids to settle his stomach as he thought about what he had to do. "You want to obey every order I give," he began, as he had with his other colleagues, once Jonathan entered the room.

ONCE HIS CONVERSATION WITH JONATHAN WAS over, Morty chewed another handful of antacids and kept the waste basket nearby, just in case the nausea he was fighting won the battle. He put his head on his desk and sobbed into his arms. When he noticed that his tears were soaking the old book, he sat up quickly and dabbed the pages with his handkerchief. He realized two of the pages had been stuck together and that the soggy sentences had more about the cuff to reveal to him. He read them carefully.

"Dromly and I were wrong. The *cuff* is what's used for healing, not the other pieces of Armor Jewelry, and not the Plate of Destiny," he muttered to himself. "Fascinating. The cuff both harms and heals." Sitting back in his chair, he wondered what else he might still not know about the Armor Jewelry. Regardless, if he could learn the healing workings of the cuff, he'd be able to reverse any headaches or hallucinations Jonathan may begin to have. Putting the receiver to his ear, he dialed a number. "Professor Dromly, do you have a moment? There's much I've discovered."

Chapter 32

Present day

Monday, October 5, 2015

A nise's eyes scanned Dr. Smithton's office as she looked around for an escape. A few of Dr. Smithton's colleagues grabbed Kent and held him in place, awaiting further instructions from their commander. He struggled but couldn't break free of their grip.

Anise could just barely hear Dr. Smithton's colleagues whispering to each other about what to do over the sound of the pounding rain on the windows. When the whispering stopped, two dark-haired women and one blonde woman started toward Anise. Reminding herself that she was wearing both the amulet and the earrings, she was able to put her fear aside and ready herself for the inevitable fight. The amulet would protect her from anything these women had to dish out and the earrings made her stronger than the three of them put together. The two brunettes grabbed Anise's arms while the blonde reached for the amulet. Suddenly, the blonde woman screamed in pain and grabbed her arm. Anise watched with confidence as the woman again tried to grab the amulet and once more suffered the same stabbing pain as before.

Taking a deep breath, Anise knew she needed to start fighting but hated what she was about to do. Violence was something she detested with her whole being. Unfortunately, there was no other option. She whipped her arms in an upward motion. The two brunettes holding her arms were thrown into the air with exceptional force. Their bodies slammed through the ceiling. One crashed into the ceiling fan, causing the blades and broken light fixture to rain down on the people below. The women landed on the floor with almost as much force as their ascent, taking out a couple of their co-workers each on their way down.

Anise looked at them as they lay unconscious on the floor and could tell some of their limbs were broken. She felt her eyes try to well up from guilt, but she didn't allow it. Now was not the time for tears. She noticed the blonde woman trying to sneak around behind her. Needing to put a stop to whatever the woman had planned, Anise stepped toward the blonde woman, wrapped five fingers around her throat, and picked her up by the neck, holding her at arm's length. The entire room gasped as they watched the woman clawing at Anise's hand and her feet kicking in the air. Before anyone else had the time to react, she threw the woman toward the wall behind Kent. The woman flew over the heads of her co-workers and crashed straight through the drywall and studs, landing on George's desk next door. She groaned before passing out. "Who's next?" Anise yelled over the thunder outside, hoping there wouldn't be any takers.

Dr. Smithton's gray eyes flashed in anger as his colleagues scrambled for the door in an attempt to escape Anise. "I need you to believe what I'm about to tell you," said Dr. Smithton to his colleagues. Anise watched in horror as all of their eyes instantly glazed over and they froze in place. "Right now, this girl has ten times her strength! More than ten of you need to attack her at the same time to overcome her power!"

"Yes, Dr. Smithton," all his colleagues responded in unison. With the exception of the two that were holding Kent, they all started toward Anise.

"Remember, you have more than just strength—the amulet will help protect you!" Kent yelled to Anise.

"The amulet wasn't made for a fight of one versus twenty!" snarled Dr. Smithton. "Even *it* has its limits. She'll never win!"

Anise felt like a fist was squeezing her stomach and her windpipe at the same time. Her arms started going numb as she watched Dr. Smithton's army of brainwashed co-workers step toward her.

"Just concentrate on two at a time," Kent yelled to her. "You can fight them off!"

Anise braced herself for the attack. Some of Dr. Smithton's army jumped toward her as if to tackle her, and it was almost funny how they all landed on the floor in a pile next to her. She was grateful for how the earrings were increasing the strength of the amulet. It had been glowing ever since Dr. Smithton had called in his army, but once they all started attacking, the amulet started flashing—something Anise had never seen before. It lit up the room as much as the lightning outside the window. "What the hell?"

"That flashing means the amulet is reaching its limit in how much it can help you," Dr. Smithton told her. "You are not invincible, Anise. It can't protect you if the threat is too strong. Give up now and you won't get hurt."

"Forget it!" Anise snapped at him.

The attackers scrambled to their feet to try again.

"Hold her in place!" someone shouted. Two of the strongest men held her arms while others tried the tackle again. Once more, they landed to every side of her.

Anise flung her arms forward to shake off the two men who had a hold of her. The men flew into the chests of their co-workers, knocking them over. It reminded Anise of the last time she and Jonathan had gone bowling. The two men, along with those that had broken their fall, began groaning and struggling to get up.

Once on their feet, they came at her again. Anise followed Kent's advice and grabbed two of them at a time, noticing that the amulet was only glowing now, not flashing. Kent's advice was going to work! The first two were knocked out when she clocked their heads together. The next two she pushed backward and watched them tumble head over feet through the crowd, taking others along with them. The next two she picked up and threw on top of Dr. Smithton.

"Stop!" commanded Dr. Smithton, gasping for breath as he pushed his co-workers off of him and stood up. "You're going about it all wrong!" He made his way toward Anise. "On my command, attack again!" he yelled. He made sure the cuff was firmly attached to his wrist, and then he twisted the top of the ring 90 degrees so the stone flipped over to reveal the poisonous side that contained the cinnabar and orpiment.

Anise knew his plan. He was going to cancel out the power of the two pieces of Jewelry she wore by attacking her with his two pieces. At that point, neither of them would have any powers. Kent was still being held back by two of Smithton's colleagues, so he wouldn't be available to help her. As soon as she was powerless, one of Smithton's glazed-eyed followers could remove the Jewelry from her neck, and who knows what they'd do with her and Kent afterward? She couldn't allow that to happen. She swore under her breath as she realized her mistake. She could've already taken out Smithton's entire army if she'd decided to attack instead of just defending herself. As much as she hated it, she'd have to go on the offensive. She stooped over and picked up Dr. Smithton's large mahogany desk. Looking him straight in the eye, she held his desk over her head and took aim.

"Protect me!" Dr. Smithton yelled, and several of his army members jumped in front of him.

Anise threw the desk, aiming for slightly above Dr. Smithton's head. To her relief, the desk missed him and dove into the corner and halfway through the wall, the noise of its landing drowning out some of the screams.

Dr. Smithton yelled out over the sound of thunder, "Attack her again—now! Keep her busy so I can get to her!"

Anise began fighting them off again. They came at her in droves, and by the time she had shoved the last of them away, the first attackers had recovered and came at her again. She felt her breath catch when the office door opened and in marched at least 20 more glazed-eyed followers. Anise hadn't realized Dr. Smithton had taken the time to brainwash so many people. With over 40 people in Smithton's office, and almost all of them trying to attack her at once, Anise found herself fighting back as hard as she could. She noticed the amulet was flashing again. Was she going to lose? Her head started spinning.

In her peripheral vision, Anise could see that Kent was trying his best to free himself from his captors. He kicked them in their shins and jumped up, lifting his feet as if to land on his knees. His full weight being pulled down made his captors drop him, and he scrambled to his feet, heading for Anise. With all the people in the room, however, he was grabbed again by others in the army far before he got to her.

Anise knew that if this entire army attacked her at once, the amulet wouldn't be strong enough to help her. She'd have to take them on in groups again, but there was no time to do it two at a time anymore. She'd have to shoot for eight or nine. Her stomach ached, and she wished she had a better plan.

The army started coming at her and she shoved,

pushed, and kicked as hard and as fast as she could. The amulet flashed its warning as the crowd kept attacking. Her defensive moves weren't holding them off well enough, and more and more kept attacking at one time. She picked someone up and threw him into the crowd, knocking several of them to the ground. However, the time it took for her to do that allowed her to be attacked from behind. At least 15 men tackled her, and she landed face first on Dr. Smithton's Berber carpeting. Hands and knees forced her head down, and she felt her nose and cheek getting a carpet burn as she struggled to free herself.

Dr. Smithton walked up to her. "Just relax, Anise," he said in a soothing tone, as the lapis lazuli stones in the cuff sparkled. "Stay quiet," he continued, to keep using the cuff against her. He twisted the ring again to expose the poisonous side.

She shrieked into the carpet, knowing what was coming. She was still strong and the 15 men were using all their strength to hold her down. They were sweating, growing tired, and she had a chance to fight back still. However, as soon as Dr. Smithton used both the cuff and ring against her, the powers of all the Jewelry would be cancelled out, and they could take her amulet and the earrings away from her with no problem whatsoever.

"As soon as this ring touches her skin, take her Jewelry," Dr. Smithton commanded his army.

Anise startled when a loud noise rang through her ears. But this wasn't thunder. It was a gun shot. The entire room screamed and dropped to the floor. Anise looked up. In the commotion, no one had noticed the window being opened from the outside by a man on the fire escape. Anise saw Dr. Smithton lying unconscious on the ground and Nate holding his gun in one hand and Kent's gun that Dr. Smithton had been holding onto in the other. He pointed both guns at the crowd as the rain and wind rudely invited themselves inside behind him.

"Get off of her!" he shouted at the pile of men holding Anise down. "And let him go!" he added to the men who held back Kent. They complied immediately. "Grab the rest of the Jewelry honey, and let's get the hell out of here," he said to Anise in a softer voice as he stepped on Dr. Smithton's arm, just in case he should wake up.

Anise removed the cuff from Dr. Smithton's wrist and the ring from his finger. She saw no blood coming from his body, and he was still breathing. She noticed a lump forming on his head. Relieved, she realized that Nate must've only hit Dr. Smithton on his head, and the shot he had fired was only to get everyone's attention. She and Kent headed out the window and down the fire escape with Nate following. They ran through the ever-growing puddles in the alley and jumped into a brand new black Camaro ZL1. Nate started the engine and took off. Anise, riding shotgun, looked in the side mirror to see some of the army had been running after them and were now fading into the distance.

"Thank you," she said while trying to catch her breath, watching the windshield wipers dance to their own rhythm, forgetting for a moment that she was mad at him.

Nate said nothing but took her hand as he sped down the highway.

"Great timing, Nate!" praised Kent from the backseat. "Let's head back to the house I rented in town."

"Was the house really necessary?" Nate asked. "My mother could've stayed at my condo with me."

"Like I said," Kent reminded him, "Lorelei needs a medical professional looking after her. And there's a lot of equipment that goes into that care. A one bedroom condo isn't going to be big enough for three adults and lots of medical equipment."

Nate reluctantly nodded his agreement.

"Lorelei has been in stable condition—moving her here from Springfield didn't seem to be harmful to her in any way," Kent continued. "Now that Anise has all the

Jewelry, we can help your mother."

"Finally," Nate sighed. He looked at Kent in the rear-view mirror. "Thank you, Kent, for keeping your promise to me."

"I'm just glad she's going to be okay," Kent replied. "When we have Lorelei healed and settled, we'll need to head back to the airport right away. Once Smithton wakes up, he'll figure out that we'll be on our way to find the Plate of Destiny so Anise can protect it. We have to find it before he and his army find us."

Anise cringed at the thought of having to travel again when all she wanted was to crawl in bed and sleep. Her nervous system was screaming at her for all the fear and violence she'd had to endure. "I don't want the Plate of Destiny," she told Kent. "I don't particularly want the Armor Jewelry, either. I just want to heal Lorelei and Jonathan. There's someone else I need to heal as well." She felt Nate squeeze her hand and knew that he understood she was thinking about Les. "Then I really don't care who has the Jewelry." She closed her eyes and settled in her seat, listening to the comforting sound of the rain and letting the gentle motion of the car lull her into a less tense state.

"I understand you've been through a lot," Kent sympathized, "but it's not that simple, Anise."

"She said *no!*" Nate snapped.

Kent continued. "Morty Smithton will keep coming after you. So will my father."

"Then as soon as everyone I want to heal is fine, I'll give the Jewelry to you, Kent. You can go and protect the Plate of Destiny and get chased by Dr. Smithton all you want."

"It doesn't matter. They won't stop coming after *you*, Anise," Kent insisted. "If you do have king's blood like we suspect, they'll *never* stop coming after you."

"If I have king's blood, then I can use the cuff to brainwash them into not wanting my blood, right?"

"I'm not sure it works like that," Kent argued. "According to my father's trip journals—"

Anise's chest was tight, and it felt harder to breathe. She'd had enough stress for now. "I will not talk about this anymore!" she interrupted Kent.

An awkward silence filled the air, and Anise was grateful when Nate changed the subject.

"How do you like the car?" he asked her.

"It's really nice. I love it," she said. As much as she wanted to relax, her mind traveled back to Dr. Smithton's office and the events that had just happened there. Her eyes narrowed as she remembered how angry she was with Nate.

"I'm glad you like it. I bought it this morning. Now you don't have to be cold when we go out anymore." Nate looked at her face when she ripped her hand away from his. "Is something wrong?"

She looked at Nate, then over her shoulder at Kent, then back at Nate again. "I'm really angry at both of you!" she exploded. "Taking Jonathan hostage was not part of our plan!"

Both Nate's and Kent's eyes grew large.

"I knew you'd never agree to it, honey," Nate explained. "So I convinced Kent not to tell you. But we needed some kind of leverage over Smithton. He would never have opened his safe otherwise." Nate continued when Anise's only response was a glare. "I'm sorry I had to blindside you. But I promise I didn't hurt Boy Scout, and I wouldn't have under any circumstances. He's safe at home, and I'm sure Smithton will head over there to untie him." He glanced at her before looking back at the road. "Besides, Smithton would have never bought that you went along with capturing Jonathan. The look of shock on your face made it all the more real for him."

"I'm sorry too, Anise," added Kent. "But I have to agree with Nate. We needed something to make Smithton show us where he was hiding the Jewelry. And the way you reacted made him fear for Jonathan's safety. Without that, we probably would be leaving the museum right now empty-handed."

"You were able to find the Jewelry in his office before," Anise snapped at Nate. "I don't see why you couldn't have done it again."

"I did my research. I know Smithton has an alarm and a camera in his office now," Nate explained. "He had one guard hired just to sit outside his office all night. The police have been driving by the museum during their rounds every night. Plus with all the added guards and extra security the museum installed since our last break in...as good as I am at getting around shit like that...it's too much. We wouldn't have gotten away with it."

She thought about what they were telling her, and she begrudgingly saw their point. "Fine," she mumbled, still miffed. "But I *hate* that you used Jonathan like that. He must have been so afraid. I certainly was. You scared the shit out of me when I saw you hold that gun to his head! He's a good man and doesn't deserve to be treated that way!"

"You're right," agreed Nate. "He doesn't. And if I could've thought of another way, I would have. But I don't know what else would have gotten to Smithton as much as seeing Boy Scout in danger. And I promise you, he was never in any *real* danger."

Anise sighed. "I know that you wouldn't kill him. But you made me doubt you for a moment there. And I'm still upset that you kept this from me. I thought we talked about this already when you didn't let me in on your fire escape plan at the museum that night we were there. I know you want me to trust you, and this is the second time I've had to tell you that I can't if you continue to keep things from me."

"I *do* want you to trust me. I want you to feel safe with me." Nate looked over at her. "I want us to be together," he added.

"I want to trust you, too," she said, shaking her head. "I'm trying. But you're not making it easy. And for the record, I *do* feel safe with you. I feel safer with you than with anyone. I know that you'd protect me with everything you have and that if anyone has a chance at keeping me safe through all this, it's you. I trust you completely when it comes to my *physical* safety. I really want to trust you with my heart, too, but I just don't know if I can."

Nate pulled into Kent's driveway, and Kent jumped out of the car, running through the heavy rain and away from the private conversation.

Nate looked at Anise with his intense gaze right before he kissed her. "I promise you, I'll do everything I can to change that. I want to talk more about this later, okay? And when we do, I have something else I need to tell you, too."

"Okay," Anise agreed. She wasn't completely over her anger, but that look he gave her still made her heart beat faster. Sighing, she wished she could talk to her friends about the strong, confusing feelings she was experiencing. Although she still loved Jonathan, she had to admit to herself that she was falling for Nate—and had been for some time now. It was so overwhelming in the best way possible. It was the awe she felt for his uncanny ability to do anything he set his mind to do. It was the way he made her dream about him when he was away. It was how he had a completely different side of his personality that he reserved only for her. It was the way he made her feel so alive in a way she couldn't explain to even herself. How he did it, she didn't know, but she loved every second of it.

KENT WAITED FOR NATE AND ANISE inside the house. Sitting on a soft chair, he put his head in his hands. He was disappointed that Anise and Nate didn't want to search for the Plate of Destiny, but that wouldn't stop him from looking for it. He couldn't not go. Anise didn't realize the danger she was in. He hadn't been able to help the little boy that Nate had been. He hadn't done enough to try to get him away from his abusive caretakers. He hadn't been able to save Lorelei. He hadn't told Nate immediately that he'd found her. The least he could do now is try to help save Nate's girlfriend. There was too much guilt that needed to be assuaged.

Kent took a deep breath in and let it out slowly. And then there was Fred. As angry as he was that Frederick Dromly hadn't tried harder to be a father to him, Fred wasn't the only one to blame for their estrangement. When Fred had reached out, Kent had pushed him away with cruel words. Even then, Fred sent him a trip journal every time he filled one up with a personal letter asking him to please write back. Kent never had. He'd flipped through the journals, reading a few entries here and there, but mostly throwing them in a box in his garage because the sight of them filled him with a hate he'd rather forget. It was time for him to see Fred, and one way or another, put the unresolved anger to bed.

NATE HELD HIS JACKET OVER THEIR heads as he and Anise made a mad dash through the storm for Kent's front door. He'd made up his mind to tell her that he visited Grace. There was no other woman that he could imagine ever being with, and he wanted to do everything he could to make it work this time. He only hoped he hadn't already lost her.

Nate and Anise followed Kent as he led them to Lorelei's room. Even though Nate had been in there before, his breath still caught. Seeing his mother attached to so many machines, tubes, wires...he turned away and watched Anise instead.

Anise walked up to Lorelei and then looked up at Kent. "What do I do?" she asked. "How do I heal her?"

"I'm not sure exactly, but according to my father's journals, the cuff is about intention," Kent told her. "Do what feels right to you."

"I'm not sure what feels right to me. But I'll try my best." Anise picked up Lorelei's hand with one of her own and held it. With her other hand, she stroked her hair with her fingertips while looking at her face. She then put her hand over the place where Lorelei had been shot. "Please heal. Even though you're in a coma, I can feel that you have such a lovely presence, and your only son needs you. Lorelei, wake up," Anise whispered to her while the cuff sparkled.

Lorelei's eyes fluttered.

Nate's heart raced. This was the moment he'd wanted for decades now. *Will this really work? And what if it doesn't?* His vision darkened while every hopeful emotion fled his mind, leaving him feeling numb.

Lorelei's brown eyes opened as if she'd awakened from a refreshing nap. They blinked and turned toward Anise.

"Holy...," Nate whispered. He heard Anise take in a deep breath. Nate felt a new, uncomfortable feeling. In his head, he ran through the list of emotions the prison shrink had given him. Was it possibly apprehension? He hadn't seen his mother in 26 years. What would she think of him once she found out how his life had turned out?

Lorelei turned her head in the direction of his voice. Her eyes focused on his face. "Nathan?" she said in a quiet, strained tone.

Anise and Kent stepped out of the way as Nate sat on her bed to hug her. "Mom?" It was hard to breathe. "Are you okay? How are you feeling?"

"I'm feeling great!" she responded as she sat up and

held Nate's face in her hands. "Oh, look at you! My little prince isn't little anymore." Tears ran down her face, and she embraced him. He felt...he wasn't sure. He just felt.

After a moment, he pulled back to look at her. He opened his mouth to speak but closed it again. There was a lifetime of things to tell her, and he couldn't think of anything to say. He saw his mother's eyes look over his shoulder.

"And who is this?" Lorelei asked Nate as she looked at Anise.

They hadn't yet officially defined their relationship, and Anise looked to Nate to introduce her.

"This is Anise Viston," was all he said. "She's the incredible woman who saved your life."

Lorelei smiled at her. "You have the Armor Jewelry. I'm so glad." She reached out her hand. "It's such a pleasure to meet you, Anise. Thank you for all you've done for me."

"The pleasure is all mine," Anise replied, taking Lorelei's hand and sitting next to her and Nate on the bed. "I'm so happy I could help."

Lorelei lay back down. "I just woke up, and I'm so drowsy," she said with a little laugh.

"That's the medication in your IV," Kent told her. "I'm sure you're anxious to get up, but you need to take it slowly."

"Kent Dromly?" she asked, squinting at him. "Is that you?"

"Yes," he confirmed, and grinned at her. "It's great to have you back."

"How...what happened?" she asked him.

"I'll fill you in on all the details while I get ready for my trip."

"Where are you going?"

"To find the Plate of Destiny." He turned to Nate and Anise. "I know you'd like more time with your mother, but I really need to leave. I'm going to need to take all the

Armor Jewelry with me, and I know you have someone else you wanted to heal. Go and heal whoever it is," he told them both. "Then please bring back the Jewelry."

"No way, Dromly," Nate protested, standing up to look Kent in the eyes. "She just woke up. I'm not leaving her now."

"Then stay here. But I need to take the Jewelry."

"The person I want to heal is in Philadelphia. I need to fly there now," Anise explained to Kent.

"Okay, then I'll fly there with you," Kent agreed. "As soon as your friend is well, I'll take the Jewelry and head to Florida."

"What's the hurry?" Lorelei wanted to know.

"Anise is in danger," Kent began.

"Because she has king's blood," agreed Lorelei.

"Yes."

"Then you do need to hurry."

"Wait," Nate interrupted. "Anise, if you're in that much danger, I don't want you to go alone."

"I'll be fine," Anise asserted.

"Go with her," Lorelei insisted to Nate, grabbing his arm.

"You just woke up; I'm not leaving you now!" Nate felt himself getting upset.

"I'll come with you to Philadelphia," Lorelei offered. She tried to get up but put a hand to her head and settled back in bed. "Or not. I'm a little dizzy."

"That's the medication in your IV," Kent reminded her. He unhooked it. "You don't need it anymore, but it'll be a little while before you'll be strong enough to get up."

"There's a simple solution," Anise said. "Please Kent, give Nate and Lorelei just a little more time. Then we can all fly to Philadelphia together."

After a short debate, they all agreed upon another half hour. Kent and Anise left the room to give Nate and his mother their privacy.

Nate fluffed and propped up her pillows so she could

sit upright in comfort.

"Anise and I went to Nevada to look for you," Nate said. "Did your captors shoot you?"

"It was an accident. They were trying to shoot someone else. But I don't want to talk about that. Tell me about you!" She patted the bed.

He sat next to her. "Sure. What do you want to know?"

"Everything! Do you have a family? A job? Things that make your heart happy?"

He shook his head. "No family. Well, I take that back. I have you now."

"Yes you do." She beamed at him. "What about a girl-friend?"

"No. But I hope to change that soon."

"Anise?" she asked with a knowing smile.

A quiet laugh escaped his lips. "How did you know?"

"She couldn't take her eyes off you." She smiled again. "And now I want to ask you everything I was dying to know while I was held captive."

Answering her questions, Nate saw a horrified expression on her face as he explained what Motocross was and an interested look when he explained what his former job had been.

"Were you in prison?" she asked softly, as if she were afraid to hear the answer.

He looked at the ground, and his heart ached from an emotion he'd never had before. "Yeah. But how I got there is a long story. I'll explain when we have more time." He felt a burning sensation in his cheeks. *Weird.* That'd never happened before. Wondering what the hell was going on with him, he ran through the list of emotions in his head. *It's shame,* he decided. He felt her hands on his warm face.

"My baby," she said. "I love you no matter what." Her arms wrapped around him and she pulled him closer in her embrace.

Her last statement made him feel another emotion

that took his heartache away. This one wasn't on the list, but maybe just this once, it was okay to skip the analysis and just bask in it.

AFTER THE HALF HOUR HAD ENDED, Anise followed Kent into Lorelei's room and wondered how Nate's visit with his mom went. Her heart was bursting just thinking about how happy he must be.

Kent busied himself with packing a bag for Lorelei and one for himself. "Take one of the umbrellas by the front door," Kent offered Anise and Nate. "Go home and pack a bag. We'll meet you at the airport in two hours." They said their goodbyes to Lorelei with a promise to see her soon, left the room, and headed to the front door of the house.

As Anise reached for the front door's knob, Nate wrapped his arms around her tightly. "You're amazing. Thank you," he whispered in her ear.

"No thanks necessary," she told him, hugging him back. "I'm just glad she's okay."

"I'm so happy to have her back."

Anise took his hand. "I can't even imagine how you must feel right now."

"Me either," Nate shrugged. "I'm kind of numb. It's surreal."

Under Kent's large, black golf umbrella, they walked hand-in-hand to Nate's car, and he opened the passenger door for her.

"About earlier," Anise began, still standing by the car door. "I don't like what you did to Jonathan, but I know you acted in everyone's best interest. And your plan worked. If you hadn't done what you did, Lorelei wouldn't be awake."

"Thank you," he said, his expression looking hopeful.

"So, I forgive you. And I want us to be together, too."
She meant every word she'd said but hoped she wasn't
making a mistake. What if he continued to keep things
from her?

His elation at her words showed in his smile. He
swept her up in an excited embrace and spun her around.
Water shot off the umbrella in circles around them like a
choreographed fountain. She laughed and held on until
he set her down. Holding her tightly, he nuzzled her hair.
"God, I love you." He then immediately let her go and
stood up straight; stiff as a petrified tree. "I'm sorry. I
shouldn't have said that."

"So you don't love me?"

He looked down at the ground. "I do. It's just...too
early, and..."

Anise almost teared up when she looked up at his
face and saw his wide, nervous eyes. She'd never seen
him look more honest and more scared at the same time
before. The openness and vulnerability he'd let himself
feel for that brief moment was beautiful. She beamed
at him and took his hand. She couldn't tell if the slight
trembling she felt was him or herself. "It is early, but it's
also not. I feel like we got to know each other really well
over the phone these last three years, and if I'm being
completely honest, a part of me has been yours since the
day we met. Anyway, what I'm trying to say is...I love you,
too."

With the open umbrella resting on the top of his
head, he took her face in his hands and gave her a kiss
that made the rest of the world disappear. Completely
engulfed by the effect his lips and tongue had on her, she
stood mesmerized for a moment after he pulled away.
They stared at each other, not needing to say anything. It
made her forget what she'd wanted to add. Ecstatic and
dazed, she turned and sat in the car when she remembered.

Oh, right.

She got back out of the car. "I need to tell you that I'm not over Jonathan yet. We broke up so recently; I still have feelings for him. Although I want to be with you, we should wait a while, or at least take things really slowly. I don't want you to ever think that you're just a rebound guy to me or like I'm not completely committed to you."

"I don't think that," he told her. "But honey, if you think you'd rather be with Boy Scout, please tell me now."

"No," she said, shaking her head. "I know I want to be with you. I've *always* wanted *you*."

He took a step closer to her, his face serious. "And I know I don't want to wait to be together. I'll do everything I can to make you forget him," Nate promised.

"I have no doubt," she agreed when he took her in his arms again. "I just want to do this right."

"I understand. We'll take it as slowly as you want."

"You're okay with that?"

"Yeah, there's no hurry. We have the rest of our lives."

Something about the honesty in his words and the thought of eternity made all her doubt disappear. "I think I love you even more now." Giddiness exploded in her chest. She grabbed the zippered edges of his open leather jacket and pulled him in for another kiss. "Dance with me?" she heard herself say and immediately regretted it, feeling stupid at making such a ridiculous request out of a moment of unchecked, childlike excitement. But he just grinned at her, dropped the umbrella on the driveway, and twirled her around Kent's front yard to the rhythm of the raindrops that soaked their hair and ran down their joyful faces.

Chapter 33

Present day

Monday, October 5, 2015

After they'd each packed a bag, Nate and Anise got in his Camaro, and they headed toward the airport. She couldn't wait to see Les again now that she knew she could finally help him.

"Listen to this," Nate said, getting out his phone.

"I can't believe that Grace is dead," Anise mumbled after Nate played the voicemail for her. "I don't know what to say."

"I think congratulations would be appropriate."

Anise felt a huge sense of relief while wondering if there was anyone who'd actually miss Grace. The thought made her a little sad.

"Honey, there's still something I need to talk to you about," Nate added.

"That wasn't what you wanted to tell me?"

"No, there's something else. Something more important."

"Okay," she agreed, "but we need to make one stop first. We're almost there, and I don't want our conversation to be interrupted."

"Where to?"

"Jonathan's apartment."

"No way in hell." Nate looked at her with disbelief. "Smithton could be there. Who knows what tricks he has up his sleeve? We don't want a repeat of what just happened in his office."

Anise felt herself growing angry. "Nate, I finally have all four pieces of Armor Jewelry. You know I want to cure Jonathan from the headaches and hallucinations he's been having! I can't go anywhere without helping him first!"

"Okay," Nate surrendered. His eyes darted back and forth between the windshield and the rear view mirror. "What kind of car does Smithton drive?"

"A Lexus I think. Why?"

"There's a car that I thought was following us for a while. But it's gone now, and it wasn't a Lexus."

Once they arrived at Jonathan's place, they walked in the door to find that he was still tied up. Max wagged his tail at them and went back to sleep. He'd never been much of a watchdog.

"Oh my god! Dr. Smithton hasn't come for him! Who knows how long he'd have stayed like this?" Anise cried as she hurried over to untie him.

"I think you should heal him before you untie him," Nate suggested. "Remember he's brainwashed right now. Who know what he'll do if you untie him first."

"Good point," Anise agreed. "I'll just remove the duct tape from his mouth." She yanked off the tape as quickly as possible so as to not hurt him. "Are you okay?"

"What do you think?" Jonathan spat. His eyes narrowed when he looked at Nate. "Why the hell is *he* here with you?"

"Don't start that again," Anise told him gently. "We're

both here to help you."

Jonathan stared her down with his glazed eyes. "He's a psychopath! He tied me up and held a gun to my head!"

"That was just for show, Jonathan. Otherwise, we wouldn't have been able to get all four pieces of Armor Jewelry. Look!" She showed him that she was wearing the cuff, earrings, ring, and amulet.

"Great. You stole the Jewelry. You're a delinquent like him. Good for you," Jonathan snarled.

"Shut up," Nate scolded. "She's trying to help you."

Anise ignored Jonathan's sarcasm. "Since I have all the Jewelry, I can cure you of the headaches and hallucinations you've been having. They were caused by Dr. Smithton brainwashing you with the cuff."

"I'm not brainwashed," insisted Jonathan. "You are—by Nate. I can't believe you trust this criminal."

"Just ignore what he's saying and cure him," Nate told her impatiently. "We need to go."

"You're right." She dragged a chair over to Jonathan and sat in front of him, putting her hands on his knees. As strongly as she could, she wished for the brainwashing effects to disappear. Several minutes later, Jonathan still had the glazed look in his eyes and a scowl on his face.

"It's not working," Anise fretted, as she walked over to Nate. "What am I doing wrong?"

"Nothing." He comforted her with a hug. "You used the Jewelry a lot today in the fight and then you cured my mother. That probably used a lot of energy. Maybe it just needs to be recharged."

"Of course!" she exclaimed, quickly stepping over to Jonathan's kitchen sink. "I charged the amulet earlier today, but it could probably stand another charge. And who knows when the earrings and ring were last charged." She removed the Jewelry except for the amulet, washed it under the running faucet, and placed it by the window where the sun was shining in. "I'm about to take off the amulet," she told Nate. "Please don't leave the room."

"I'll be right here," he promised. "How long do we have to wait? We really need to leave."

"About half an hour," she estimated. "An hour would be better though."

"We don't have that long." Nate argued.

"I won't leave him like this!"

"Just untie me and go!" Jonathan sneered. "I don't want either of you here!" He glared at both of them.

"I'll call Kent and ask him to hold the plane," Nate said, grabbing his phone.

While Nate was on the phone, Jonathan asked Anise, "Are you two together now?"

"Yes. We are. I'm surprised you care," she answered, noticing that the glaze in his light green eyes was waning.

"I'll always care about you. I don't want to see you get involved with a criminal. I don't trust him to keep you safe. You getting hurt is my biggest fear."

"Thank you for your concern," Anise replied. "And I care about you, too. But don't worry. He does a great job of keeping me safe."

Jonathan's eyes flickered and glazed over again. Anise's heart beat faster as she wondered what was going on. His eyes usually glazed over when he talked about Dr. Smithton. Hearing a creak in the floorboards, she turned to look and gasped when she saw Dr. Smithton, who had snuck in the door and was headed toward the Jewelry. Nate, Dr. Smithton, and Anise raced to the window. Dr. Smithton grabbed and put on the cuff and amulet. Anise managed to claim the earrings and put them in her ear piercings as quickly as possible. Nate slipped the ring on her finger.

She'd never been in a confrontation without the amulet before. What was she going to do? Her arms started to go numb. Nausea gripped her stomach.

"Give up the Jewelry, Smithton," Nate commanded, holding a gun to Jonathan's head.

Dr. Smithton's eyes opened wide. He looked at Jonathan and then at Anise. "Anise doesn't seem quite as frightened as she did the last time you threatened to hurt Jonathan," Dr. Smithton said, coming over to Nate. "You're bluffing."

"You don't know me very well," Nate told him with an arrogant grin. "Are you willing to take a chance?"

Dr. Smithton scowled and stopped walking. He stooped to pick something up. "What do we have here?" He lifted the object to his ear.

Anise gasped as she touched her lobes and realized one of the chalcedony hoops had fallen out of her piercing. "How do the earrings work when they're separated?" she asked Dr. Smithton with a shaky voice. It was something she'd always wondered, but she certainly didn't want to find out this way.

"They each work as half a piece. The problem for you is that I now have two-and-a-half pieces of the Jewelry, where you only have one-and-a-half pieces. I've always liked you, Anise, so I'm going to offer you a deal. Give me the rest of the Jewelry and a few drops of your blood, and I'll allow you and your hoodlum friend to walk out of here unharmed."

"No way in hell, Smithton!" snarled Nate.

With immense speed from the strength he was granted by the earring, Dr. Smithton bounded over to Nate, easily removed the gun from his hand, and clocked him over the head with it. Nate blacked out and fell to the ground behind Jonathan's chair.

"No, no, no!" Anise hurried over to Nate and tried to wake him up. Her heart pounded and sweat drenched her shirt. Dizziness took over her head, and her arms went numb. The nausea worsened.

Dr. Smithton untied Jonathan.

"Thanks, Dr. S." Jonathan gingerly touched the rope burns he had on his wrists. He took the gun from Dr. Smithton's hand and aimed the gun at Nate who was still passed out on the floor.

"Jonathan, you wouldn't!" Anise cried. She stood and positioned her body in between the gun and Nate.

"I can't believe you're protecting him!" Jonathan exclaimed. "Did you forget you're not wearing the amulet?"

"I didn't forget." The panic attack wouldn't let her forget. Doing her best to ignore her panicked state, she leapt to action. In one swift motion, she grabbed the gun and easily removed it from Jonathan's hand. "Did you forget I'm still wearing an earring?"

"And I still have more Jewelry than you," Dr. Smithton reminded her as he wrestled the gun from her hand. "You never gave me your answer. Are you willing to hand over the Jewelry and a few drops of blood for your life and Nate's?"

"No," she said, glaring at him. She tried to come up with a plan, but nothing came to mind. Dr. Smithton and Jonathan stepped closer to her.

Before she could dodge him, Dr. Smithton grabbed her and held her so she couldn't move. "Jonathan, remove her Jewelry."

Jonathan looked at her with glazed eyes and removed the ring from her hand and the earring from her ear. Dr. Smithton put the Jewelry on.

"I'm still willing to make that deal," Dr. Smithton offered. "Just give me a few drops of blood."

"No deal." Anise knew that Dr. Smithton would never kill her as long as he didn't have her willing blood. Once she gave it to him however, who knows what he'd do?

"Jonathan," Dr. Smithton began, handing him the gun. "It's time to do what we discussed. Make Anise willing to donate her blood. Kill the young Brevain."

"No!" Anise shouted, as she stepped in between Jonathan and Nate again.

"Get out of the way! I don't want you to get hurt!" Jonathan warned.

"I don't want you to get hurt either, Jonathan. But I

won't let you kill him!"

"Move, Anise!" He pushed her away and took aim at Nate's head.

"No!" She lunged at Jonathan, pushing her thumbs under his glasses and into his eyes. He pulled back, and she stepped forward, driving her knee into his groin. He doubled over, dropped the gun, and she slammed her forearm into the back of his neck. He fell to the ground, groaning.

Anise spun around to see that Dr. Smithton had picked up the gun and was pointing it at Nate.

Anise threw her body on top of Nate's, making sure to block his head and torso. "You hurt him and you'll never get my willing blood!" she screamed. "Ever!"

She felt Jonathan grab her by her arm and her hair and pull her to her feet. She screamed and kicked him in the shins as he reached up and put his hands around her neck. He pulled his hands back down suddenly, and she saw the glaze in his eyes waning. The rage came back just as quickly, and his hands were reaching for her neck again. She took a step back, readying herself for another round with him. He dropped his hands by his sides while wearing a horrified expression. "What's happening?" he cried as he put his face in his hands. He reached for her neck once more. "No!" He grabbed his head and moaned loudly in agony from the pain while he pulled on his hair.

"Look what you've done to him!" Anise shouted to Dr. Smithton.

Jonathan started screaming over and over again while swatting the air in front of Anise. "The bullets! They just keep coming!" he cried, waving his arms frantically. He looked at his hands as if he could see through them. "I've been hit!" He fell to his knees.

Dr. Smithton grabbed Jonathan in an attempt to calm him down. "It's okay, son. It's just a hallucination!"

"No!" Jonathan screamed. "Let me go! Let me go or she'll die!" He pulled on his hair.

Dr. Smithton knelt on the ground with Jonathan struggling in his grasp. He squeezed his eyes shut as he gripped Jonathan tightly. "I'm so sorry, son. But hold on. We're so close now."

Anise noticed Nate waking up. He held a hand to the bump on his head and groaned. She saw that the cuff had fallen and rolled next to Nate.

What?!

She pointed at it, and Nate grabbed it and threw it to her. How had it come off of Dr. Smithton's wrist? Anise realized that because Jonathan hadn't had any ill intentions toward Dr. Smithton, the amulet hadn't needed to protect him, and Jonathan was able to accidentally knock off the cuff. Slipping it on, she gathered her courage. She wasn't exactly sure how it worked but knew from the legends that she should be able to transfer her thoughts to anyone immediately because of her king's blood. Well, almost anyone. Dr. Smithton was wearing more pieces of the Armor Jewelry than she was, so she wouldn't be able to transfer thoughts to him. An idea popped into her head. She went over to Nate who was still sitting on the floor, trying to get his bearings. "Babe, can you cause a distraction with Dr. Smithton?" she whispered.

He grinned at her. "Absolutely, honey." Looking around him, he picked up the gun that Jonathan had dropped. Getting up and heading toward the door, he announced loudly, "I'm gonna go find Smithton's army and pick them off, one by one!" He waved the gun dramatically in the air. "We'll see how tough you are, Smithton, without your brainwashed cult to hide behind!" He dashed out the door.

Dr. Smithton got up and ran after Nate.

While they were gone, Anise looked at the cuff on her wrist. "Jonathan, you need to get the rest of the Jewelry from Dr. Smithton and give it to me." She watched the stones of the cuff sparkle.

Jonathan stopped screaming to listen to her words.

"Yes, Anise," he agreed, his eyes glazing over.

Dr. Smithton walked back inside the apartment alone with bruises beginning to form on his face and blood running out of his nose. Anise grew worried. "What did you do to Nate?" she asked, heading toward the door. She opened it and found Nate on his hands and knees in the hallway, a bloody mess. "Oh, god!" she exclaimed. "I'm so sorry!"

"Nothing I can't handle," he replied, getting to his feet. She helped him inside and had him sit on the couch.

"Come on, son. We have to finish our mission here," Dr. Smithton said to Jonathan.

Anise began cleaning Nate's wounds. Out of the corner of her eye, she watched to see if Jonathan would do as she'd asked.

"Hold on Dr. S," Jonathan said, "I've noticed the earrings are getting weak. I could hear you in the hallway, and you had a lot of trouble overpowering Nate. Anise had it in the window to recharge before you came in. I think you should do the same. Hold them off with the gun, and I'll put the Jewelry in the window."

"I noticed the same thing," Dr. Smithton agreed. He wiped the blood from his nose. "The young Brevain was ruthless in fighting back, and I believe I used the last of the Armor Jewelry's energy in our scuffle...Or I can simply shoot Brevain and make Anise willing to give me her blood in exchange for his life."

"Would you actually shoot someone?" asked Jonathan with doubt in his eyes.

"You know me well," Dr. Smithton said with a sigh. He handed the amulet and earrings to Jonathan. Dr. Smithton's eyes then narrowed in confusion as he looked at his hand to remove the ring. "Wait, where's the cuff?"

Jonathan was bounding toward Anise. "No!" demanded Dr. Smithton, as he followed. He lunged at her but was held off by Nate. The amulet was already around her neck.

She took the earrings from Jonathan and put them in her ear piercings more carefully this time. "Give me the ring," she demanded of Dr. Smithton. His eyes glazed over as the lapis lazuli stones on the cuff sparkled. He removed the ring and gave it to her. "Thank you," she said, as she placed it on her finger. She stood in front of the window and let the sun shine on the Jewelry.

Dr. Smithton's and Jonathan's eyes returned to normal.

Jonathan turned to look at Dr. Smithton. "For the first time in a long while, my mind feels clear. You tried to use me to get Anise's blood," he recalled, with a look of disgust on his face. "You told me that your utopia plan was just a cover. What the hell do you really want?"

Nate chimed in, "Anise's parents were found killed in a car crash. Was it really an accident, Smithton? Or was that you who killed them for their king's blood?"

Anise's head was reeling from Nate's accusation. She hadn't thought about that before. "Tell the truth!" Anise commanded Dr. Smithton with the cuff.

His eyes glazed over. "George and I cut Mrs. Viston's hand for her king's blood. But their deaths were truly an accident! I did not cause their car to crash!" As quickly as it started, the glaze disappeared.

"But if you hadn't cut her hand and caused her to pass out, they wouldn't have been racing to the hospital," Anise cried. "You may not have meant to kill them, but their deaths are still your fault!" She put her tearful face on Nate's shoulder for a moment.

"You're sick!" Jonathan exclaimed. His hands clenched into fists, and he started toward Dr. Smithton but stopped suddenly. His fists grabbed his hair, and he groaned while dropping to his knees. His body began writhing around from the pain.

"What the hell is happening in here?" A neighbor was poking his head in the door. "I've been hearing screams and yelling..." He looked at Jonathan moaning on the floor. "What the hell have you done to Jonathan? I'm calling the police!"

"Forget all of this and go home!" Anise commanded him. The cuff sparkled.

The neighbor's eyes glazed over. "Okay." He turned and left.

Jonathan was still writhing around in pain. "I need to heal him—now!" Anise told Nate, as she pulled herself together. "I've been standing in the sun for these last few minutes, so hopefully the cuff already has enough of a charge. Can you please hold him still?" She hoped she wasn't using the cuff on Nate, as she hadn't meant to. She was just asking for a favor. The stones weren't sparkling, and Nate's eyes weren't glazed over. She was impressed. The cuff really was run by intention.

"Absolutely." Nate held Jonathan in place.

Anise grabbed Jonathan's hand and willed it with her whole being for him to be free of all the effects of the cuff. After several seconds, Jonathan stopped his moaning and opened his eyes.

"The headache's gone," he marveled. "It never goes away that fast."

"Anise just cured you of the side effects from the cuff," Nate told him. "Give her the credit she deserves." He dropped his grip on Jonathan's arms and looked around. "Shit! Smithton's gone!"

"It's okay," Anise said. "We know where he's going, and we'll warn Kent about it."

"Where is he going?" asked Jonathan.

"Florida. To find the Plate of Destiny."

"Dr. S. mentioned that to me once," Jonathan recalled, "but he didn't go into much detail about what it is."

"We're headed to Philadelphia. Come with us," Anise offered, "and I'll explain everything along the way."

"I will," Jonathan said. "I'll tell you anything I can remember that might be of help. And thank you."

"I'm glad you're back!" she cried, throwing her arms

around Jonathan. "I've missed you so much!"

"I've missed you, too," he replied, returning her hug. "I'm so sorry. I said and did horrible things. I'm so sorry!"

"It wasn't your fault."

"I'm so sorry!"

"You're forgiven."

They held on to each other, and Anise didn't want to let go. She squeezed him tighter. Jonathan's familiar embrace felt so comforting.

Nate touched her on the arm. "We should get going."

"I know," she agreed, "but let's wait just twenty more minutes. I want to splash some cold water on my face and let the Jewelry charge in the sun a little more. Kent will need it fully charged."

"Sure," said Nate. "Whatever you need. I'll text Kent that we'll be on our way soon. But first, I really need to tell you something. It's important."

She nodded, "I know you do, and I want to hear it. But can it please wait just a few more minutes? Today has been exhausting, I'm kind of nauseated from the panic attacks I've had, and I don't think I'm in a good frame of mind to really listen like I want to."

"Are you okay?"

"Yeah, it's just the stress getting to me."

"I can get you a soda."

"Maybe later. I just need a few minutes to myself to decompress, and then we'll talk, okay?"

She squeezed his hand. "We'll go out in the hallway for some privacy," she added in a quieter tone, noticing that Jonathan was listening to everything they were saying.

Nate frowned, but he nodded his agreement.

"Thank you." She gave him a kiss and saw the troubled look on his face. "Don't worry. I'll be right back. And whatever it is, we'll deal with it. I love you."

"I love you, too," Nate said.

∗∗∗

ANISE HEADED TO JONATHAN'S BATHROOM, AND Nate sat in the chair next to Boy Scout's couch to send his text to Kent. He hoped Anise wouldn't take too long in the bathroom. He didn't want to wait any longer to tell her about his visit with Grace. He wanted her to be able to trust him and not have any doubt that he was the one she should be with, especially now that Boy Scout was back to normal. He glanced at Jonathan out of the corner of his eye. He wasn't in the mood for small talk and hoped Boy Scout would stay quiet but could tell from his constant movements that the silence was bothering him. That, and the fact that his dog was curled up by Nate's feet.

Jonathan asked, "Is she okay?"

"Yeah."

"I have soda in my fridge."

"She didn't want any."

Boy Scout shut his mouth, and Nate hoped that would be the end of their conversation.

Jonathan rose and grabbed a couple of ratty dish-towels out of a tiny kitchen drawer that stuck when he pulled on it. He dampened them both under the faucet and tossed one to Nate. "Clean your face," he said, lifting up his pant leg and wiping off the blood from his shin where Anise had kicked him.

"Thanks." Nate ran the towel over his wounds until there wasn't a clean spot left on it. The Jewelry had had just enough juice to let Smithton get in some good hits.

"So..." Boy Scout began.

Here comes the small talk.

"...you and Anise?"

"Yes."

Jonathan frowned. "Don't get used to it."

Insecurity was the emotion Nate had identified when

Anise had given Boy Scout the big hug, and earlier when she said she still had feelings for him. He thought about the affirmation card Anise had given him on their first date. The one that said something like, 'Who do I want to be in this situation?' It really could bring you back to the right frame of mind. With her especially, he wanted to be confident and trust in what she'd told him: 'I know I want to be with you. I *always* wanted *you*.' Nate chose not to respond to Jonathan's pathetic threat. Boy Scout could have the last word. That was all he'd be getting.

ANISE TOOK SOME DEEP BREATHS IN an attempt to relax after the overwhelming stress of the day. Trying not to think about how she'd handle her panic attacks once she gave the Jewelry to Kent and how upset her boss would be when she called in sick *again* tomorrow, she instead thought about what it might be that Nate wanted to tell her. Thinking about him made her smile.

She splashed some cold water on her face which lessened her mild nausea that was still lingering after the panic attack. She took off the ring, cuff, and earrings and placed them on the window sill where the light was coming in through the open blinds. She cursed under her breath when she realized there wasn't enough sun in the room to keep the amulet on and let it charge around her neck. Removing the amulet to put it with the other Jewelry made her anxiety flare up in a surge throughout her entire body, but she reminded herself that Nate was in the next room. She tried to relax so her stomach would settle, but that was difficult when her anxiety about not wearing the amulet kept nipping at her. Maybe if she asked Nate to come into the bathroom to sit with her... no. That would be embarrassing. She was an adult and should act like one.

Not being able to take her eyes off the amulet was making her crazy. She paced the small bathroom which was more like spinning in a circle. The constant turning made her nausea worsen. She sat on the closed toilet lid and her hands fidgeted, spinning the garnet ring around her finger. She wished she had her sketchbook to distract her.

The nausea grew worse again, her head spun, and her arms began going numb. She had a humiliating urge to run out of Jonathan's apartment screaming all the way home. This was getting ridiculous. She'd ask Nate to come in and sit with her. She opened the bathroom door to call for him but heard him and Jonathan arguing over stupid shit they should let go of. She closed the door again. Hearing them bicker was not what she needed right now, and her annoyance at the both of them stressed her out more. She didn't want to see either of them now, but this panic attack was getting bad. Her hyperventilation wouldn't allow her to take slow, deep breaths, and she felt close to passing out. What could she do to stop it?

Anise realized all she wanted right now was her friends. Dealing with the Jewelry and the murder attempts and the supernatural fighting, not to mention the panic attacks and the stupid arguments the guys were having, was all too much. It felt lonely. She could call her friends now and have them come over and tell them everything. Maybe she should've already done so even though she'd promised Jonathan she'd keep the Armor Jewelry secret for their safety as well as the safety of the Jewelry. But these were her *friends*. She could trust them.

On the other hand, would they believe her? The Jewelry was magical. Who in their right mind would believe that? Vanessa had a very logical brain and would probably worry about her sanity. No thank you. Joy would at least humor her, but she couldn't keep a secret to save her life. Would she tell others about the legends, possibly putting her in danger if it reached someone else who wanted to take the Jewelry from her? Honestly, she probably would. But Erin...she already believed in the power of gemstones. She wore them and carried them with her daily, fully believing in their metaphysical powers. If anyone would believe her, it would be Erin.

Anise grabbed her phone. "Erin, hi, it's me." She could hear the shakiness in her own voice.

"What's going on? You don't sound okay."

"I'm not. I'm having a panic attack."

"Oh no! Where are you?"

"In Jonathan's bathroom. He and Nate are both in the living room, but they're arguing and pissing me off, and I could really use a friend right now. I have something important to tell you, too, but I need you to have a very open mind about it. Can you come over here?"

"Yeah, of course. I'm leaving now."

"Thank you," Anise said gratefully. She couldn't stop trembling. "And please hurry."

It would take Erin at least ten or fifteen minutes to get there, and Anise didn't know if she could stand to deal with her panic attack for that much longer. The amulet was right there, but it couldn't help her unless it was around her neck. But with a low charge it couldn't help her even if it was around her neck. It had to stay in the window for now. But what if something happened and she couldn't get to it in time?

That's ridiculous. What could happen in this tiny bathroom?

She closed her eyes and took a deep breath, letting it out slowly. But her eyes wouldn't stay closed. They insisted on being locked on the amulet. She turned on the faucet again and splashed more water on her face. Raising the blinds, she checked to make sure the window was locked.

What the hell?

She took a closer look at the perfectly round hole in the glass by the lock. She heard the shower curtain being rapidly pulled aside, and before she could turn around, everything went black.

NATE WONDERED WHY ANISE WAS TAKING so long. He was about to get up to check on her when Boy Scout started flapping his trap again.

"Why did you have to involve me in your fucked up plan?" Jonathan demanded. He glared with a clenched jaw.

Nate resisted the urge to roll his eyes. "What?"

"You broke in here, tied me up, and threatened my life, jackass! What the hell was the point of that?"

"I was never going to hurt you, so stop whining. We needed to give Smithton a good reason to hand over the Jewelry. And because of my 'fucked up' plan, Anise has the entire set of Armor Jewelry, and you're cured from the brainwashing. You're welcome, by the way."

Jonathan scoffed. "Okay, if you're so brilliant at coming up with plans, tell me, what's next? Why are we all going to Philadelphia?"

"If Anise hasn't already told you, it's not my place to say."

Jonathan frowned. "Well, who is that Kent guy that Anise mentioned? And why does he and Dr. S. want the Plate of Destiny?"

Nate explained who Kent was and how they'd met. "He thinks the Plate is near the Emerald Coast of Florida, so that's where he's headed. We assume Smithton's headed there too."

"And Kent thinks Anise should have the Plate because it's her family's duty to protect it?"

"That's what he said."

"And Anise doesn't want it? Why not?"

"Because she's tired, Boy Scout. If you had Grace trying to kill you and Smithton trying to take your blood, you'd be sick of it too."

Jonathan frowned again. "Did you figure out why Dr. S. wants her blood?"

Nate nodded. "Smithton is after her king's blood. It's what makes her be able to use the cuff for brainwashing instantly instead of it taking years."

"But that's the cuff. What does that have to do with the Plate of Destiny?"

"Good question. I don't know."

Jonathan crossed his arms. "I don't like any of this. It sounds like we need to figure all of this out or else Anise is still in danger from Dr. S. I think we should all go to Florida and help Kent find the Plate for Anise's sake. If Dr. S. wants it so badly, it must have powers, too. Maybe if we find it first, we can keep Anise safe."

"I don't disagree with you," Nate said. "But I'm not going to force her to do anything she doesn't want to and neither are you."

"If we can convince her to go, where do you think we should start?"

Nate sat back and sighed. "Unless Kent has a better idea, I think the best plan of action would be to find Smithton once we're there and follow him."

"He *does* know something we don't." Jonathan agreed. "I just don't know what. He confessed to me that his utopia goal was just a cover for his actual plan, but he never told me what the actual plan is."

"I can't believe you ever bought that utopia shit," Nate said with contempt dripping from his words.

"I was brainwashed!" protested Jonathan.

"Only the weak allow themselves to be controlled by the cuff," Nate retorted.

"Fuck you. You're making that up."

"Think about it. Smithton tried to brainwash Grace, same as you, only much longer. She never took orders from Smithton or anyone. She's a fucking villainous bitch, but you can't deny her strength and resolve. But you, you're just weak and..."

Where the hell did that come from?

Nate stopped when he became aware that he was about to say 'worthless.' If he had, he'd have just been repeating something hateful Grace had said to him practically every day of his life up until he left home. He loathed the woman and wanted to be nothing like her. He thought he'd made big strides in becoming a better man, but obviously he still had a long way to go. This realization disturbed him so much that he mumbled a quick apology in Jonathan's direction.

Jonathan shrugged. "We're all stressed."

Still troubled over what he'd almost said, Nate wondered what it was about Boy Scout that had brought out the worst in him. He felt some kind of negative emotion toward Jonathan, but what was it? Nate thought about his mental health sessions with the prison shrink. In his head, he ran through the list of emotions she'd given him. None really seemed to fit except maybe...jealousy? The only thing Nate truly disliked about Boy Scout was that Anise loved him. That, and the fact that he'd forgiven him so quickly for calling him weak. Boy Scout's incredible decency was irritating.

Not wanting to think about it anymore, Nate checked his watch and walked over to the closed bathroom door. "Anise? Are you okay in there? It's been 15 minutes." He knocked. "Anise?" She didn't answer. He opened the door. "Shit!"

Jonathan rushed over. "What's wrong?" He shoved past Nate into the bathroom.

Anise's pencil was on the floor. The faucet was still running, the window was open, and Anise was gone. The screen had been removed from the first story window, and a piece of her blouse that had caught on a splinter on the other side of the sill was flapping in the wind.

"Smithton took her," Nate answered, his chest filling

with burning rage. "She must've taken the Jewelry off to put it by the window."

"She told me she trusted you to protect her!" Jonathan yelled. His eyes were furious. "Great job, psychopath!"

"You're the one who knew about the window in the bathroom! I can't believe you let her come in here!" Nate fired back, noticing the hole in the glass that had been cut just large enough to reach a finger through to open the lock. He inspected the cut and was both impressed and puzzled by how Smithton had been able to do it so quickly and precisely. What would Smithton know about that? Did he learn that from Grace somehow?

"Anise came into the bathroom to charge the Jewelry," said Jonathan as he turned the faucet off. "Did you really not know there was a window in here? What did you think she was going to do, asshole? Hold it up to the goddamn lightbulb?"

Nate stood up straight and narrowed his eyes. "Do you wanna fucking throw down right now, Boy Scout, or go find Smithton?" Still glaring at Jonathan, he pulled out his phone from his pocket and called Kent to tell him of the situation. Jonathan dropped Max off at a neighbor's apartment and followed Nate out to the parking lot.

"Hey, my car is this way," Jonathan called, as Nate started in the other direction.

"We might not make it there alive in that piece of shit," Nate replied. "We're taking *my* car."

Jonathan followed Nate. "Fine, have it your way. But only because finding Anise is the most important thing right now, and I don't want to waste precious moments arguing. You need to get your priorities straight."

Nate had already tuned him out. Getting to Smithton's house as fast as possible was the only thing on his mind.

✳✳✳

MORTY THREW THINGS IN THE TRAVEL bag he'd placed on his bed. Remembering his medication, he spun around to get it and gasped. "Who are you?" Two very large men were watching from Morty's bedroom door.

"Boss hasn't heard from you in a long while," the one with the crooked nose replied. "He wanted to make sure there weren't any problems."

"I've got everything under control," Morty replied.

"Glad to hear that. So you have the Jewelry? And everyone he needs?"

Morty swallowed nervously. "Anise has the Jewelry. But I'm sure she'll be on her way to Florida soon!"

"You lost the Jewelry? *And* the girl?" The one with the big ears stepped forward. "Boss isn't gonna like that."

"I'm sorry," Morty said, nervously eyeing the large men. "It just happened earlier today. But like I said, I'm sure she's headed to Florida. I'm on my way there right now to reclaim the Jewelry from her when she arrives."

"How can you be sure she's on her way there?" Crooked Nose asked.

Morty let out a nervous laugh. He wasn't sure. At all. But he could worry about that later. One thing at a time. "Because I know her. Trust me."

The two large men shook their heads, unconvinced.

"And what about Grace?" Big Ears asked.

Morty swallowed. "That's the other problem. She passed away."

Big Ears sighed. "Boss is gonna be pissed."

"There's nothing I can do about that!" Morty snapped back. "But I have all of my co-workers under my command just like he wanted. They'll be joining us."

"Good. You and your associates will be at the airport in one hour," Crooked Nose commanded.

"Of course," Morty said. "But there's something else you should know. I overheard Anise talking and...she isn't doing this alone. She has friends helping her—one of them being Kent Dromly."

"Kent?" said Big Ears. The two large men glanced at each other. "Boss isn't gonna like that either."

NATE PULLED UP IN FRONT OF Morty's house, and he and Jonathan got out of the car. Kent and Lorelei pulled up behind them. Kent insisted Lorelei stay in the car as she was still a little weak from the medication. Reluctantly, she agreed. Within seconds, Nate picked the lock on Morty's door, and the three men barged inside, opening doors and calling for Anise.

"What is the meaning of this?" demanded Smithton as he came out of his bedroom with his packed bag.

Nate pushed him up against the nearest wall. "Where's Anise?"

"She's not with you?"

"Don't act so surprised. We know you have her and the Jewelry!"

"I don't!" wailed Smithton, looking panicked. "How could you have lost her? And the Armor Jewelry too?!"

Nate, Jonathan, and Kent searched every nook and cranny of the house but found nothing. Kent went through Smithton's packed bag. "There's no Armor Jewelry here."

"If you don't have her, where is she?" Jonathan asked.

Smithton narrowed his brow in thought, and suddenly he laughed out of what appeared to be both amusement and fear. "I assume someone else took her," Smithton said, a weird smile spreading over his face.

"One of your cult followers?" asked Nate.

"I wish," said Smithton. "But, no."

"Then who?"

***

ANISE GROANED AS SHE OPENED HER eyes. She felt dizzy and disoriented. Shivering, she pulled the blankets up over her shoulders. Her bed felt like it was moving, and her vision was blurry. Her ears sensed a loud white noise. She noticed someone walking around a room with a lot of small windows all in a row. Wait, was she on a plane? Her muscles tightened. "Where am I?" Anise asked. "What happened? Who are you?"

The stranger stood over her bed. As her vision cleared, Anise noticed that the stranger was a woman who was wearing all of the Armor Jewelry. Her eyes focused on the woman's face.

"Hello, Anise."

"No." Anise struggled to sit up. She didn't trust what she was seeing and squeezed her eyes shut in an attempt to stop the increasing vertigo.

No. It can't be. That's impossible!

Anise opened her eyes again and inhaled sharply in horror as her stomach started churning. "Grace?"